Also by Carolyn Brown

Lucky Cowboys
Lucky in Love
One Lucky Cowboy
Getting Lucky
Talk Cowboy to Me

Honky Tonk
I Love This Bar
Hell, Yeah
My Give a Damn's Busted
Honky Tonk Christmas

Spikes & Spurs
Love Drunk Cowboy
Red's Hot Cowboy
Darn Good Cowboy
Christmas
One Hot Cowboy Wedding
Mistletoe Cowboy
Just a Cowboy and His Baby
Cowboy Seeks Bride

Cowboys & Brides
Billion Dollar Cowboy
The Cowboy's
Christmas Baby
The Cowboy's Mail
Order Bride
How to Marry a Cowboy

Burnt Boot, Texas
Cowboy Boots for Christmas
The Trouble with
Texas Cowboys
One Texas Cowboy Too Many
A Cowboy Christmas Miracle

What Happens in Texas
A Heap of Texas Trouble

HELL, YEAH

CAROLYN BROWN

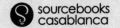

sourcebooks
casablanca

Published by Sourcebooks Casablanca, an imprint of Sourcebooks
P.O. Box 4410, Naperville, Illinois 60567-4410
(630) 961-3900
sourcebooks.com

Originally published as *Hell, Yeah* in 2010 in the United States of
America by Sourcebooks Casablanca, an imprint of Sourcebooks.

Printed and bound in the United States of America.
OPM 10 9 8 7 6 5 4 3 2 1

This book is for Joe and Ken Gray with much love!

CHAPTER 1

"Ten, hell yeah!"

The women yelled with Gretchen Wilson as she sang "Redneck Woman" and asked the redneck girls to give her a big "hell yeah" as the New Year's countdown began.

"Nine, hell yeah."

"Eight, hell yeah."

Everyone held up their plastic flutes of champagne.

"Seven, hell yeah!"

The men in the Honky Tonk beer joint joined in with the women.

"Six, hell yeah!"

"Five, hell yeah!"

Cathy O'Dell was halfway across the dance floor headed for the bar when she stopped to look at everyone who'd be kissing someone in four more seconds. She remembered the previous year when she'd had someone to kiss. Even if he did turn out to be a first-rate son-of-a-bitch, she missed the excitement of bringing in a brand-new year with a kiss.

"Four, hell yeah!"

She looked up to see a cowboy coming right at her. She blinked several times. It wasn't possible. Her imagination was playing tricks like it had for twelve years.

"Three, hell yeah!"

Watching him cross the floor in those long strides made goose bumps the size of mountains rise up on her arms.

"Two, hell yeah!"

Was he deranged or just drunk? If he didn't stop soon he would plow right into her.

"One! Hell yeah!" The noise shook the rafters.

He stopped with the toes of his scuffed-up boots barely an inch from her feet and wrapped his strong arms around her, tilted her chin with the flat part of his fist, and kissed her hard and passionately.

"Hell yeah!" the whole crowd roared when their kisses ended.

"Hell no!" Cathy mumbled. She wiped the back of her hand across her mouth, but it didn't take the red-hot sting from her lips.

He was exactly what she liked in a man. Tight jeans, denim jacket over a knit shirt, blond hair, and dear lord, were those blue eyes? He looked so much like a grown-up version of her first love that, after the kiss and when time and noise at last stood still, she wondered why he didn't wear contact lenses. Eyes the color of a Texas summer sky stared down into hers from behind wire-rimmed glasses. A wide grin split his face, showing off perfectly even and white teeth. No one had teeth that perfect. No one except Bobby Cole, and that was water under a bridge that had been burned years and years ago. Evidently a million-dollar smile hadn't left much for haircuts, though, because blond curls touched his shirt collar.

"Happy New Year." He was surprised that he could speak a coherent sentence. He only meant to kiss the woman for New Year's. He didn't mean for it to glue his boots to the hardwood dance floor and put a shit-eating grin on his face. If he'd had to wipe the smile from his face or eat dirt, he'd have had to open up his mouth and shovel in a spoonful.

Hot damn, but that woman had the softest, sexiest lips he'd ever kissed.

"Who the hell are you?" Cathy asked.

"I'm Travis Henry. I'm supposed to meet Merle and Angel Avery here. I am at the Honky Tonk, aren't I?"

Cathy pointed to the pool tables. His name was Travis Henry but he damn sure reminded her of Bobby Cole with those pretty blue eyes. On second look, Travis had darker blond hair and wore it a lot longer than Bobby's crew cut. After a third look, she decided Travis Henry was a hell of a lot sexier.

"Angel, darlin'," Travis yelled and left Cathy standing there with a bar rag thrown over her shoulder, a tray in her hand, a burning mouth, and a gushy warm feeling down deep in her gut.

She got out a dozen Mason jars for the next rush to the bar for beer. Her crowd might toast with champagne, but it wouldn't be long until they'd be lined up wanting something to take that sweet taste out of their mouths. Besides, she needed something to focus on other than the tall cowboy who reminded her of the boy who'd set her hormones into overdrive when she was sixteen. He'd been so damn pretty and was the star of the football team. He'd been the one to kiss her the first time and then the next day he asked Alice James to the prom. He and Alice married right out of high school and he ran a service station in Mena, Arkansas. Alice worked as a teller at the bank and they had two kids in grade school.

"Who kissed you? You been holdin' out on me. That is one fine-lookin' cowboy. If I was twenty years younger he'd be goin' to bed with me tonight. Give me a Miller, darlin'.

Gawd Almighty, but that champagne shit is horrible," Jezzy said as she set her empty champagne flute on the bar and slid onto a stool.

"He just plowed through the door, came across the floor, and kissed me when the countdown hit one," Cathy said.

"Looks like he's big buds with Angel Avery. Guess he didn't kiss her because Garrett had a lip-lock on her. Wonder if Garrett's kiss is powerful enough to throw her off her pool game. Handsome as that Garrett McElroy is, it would damn sure make me think about something other than racking up wooden balls if I was thirty years younger."

Cathy drew up a quart of Miller and set it in front of Jezzy. "Who were *you* kissin'?"

"See that big old biker back there with the Celtic cross tat on his arm?"

Cathy looked across the room at a middle-aged biker with a Mohawk haircut, a braided goatee, and a leather vest with enough chains to rope in a forty-acre farm. She quickly scanned the rest of the room and didn't see another tattooed cross.

She couldn't take her eyes from the biker. "Are you serious?"

"Not him. That cute little feller next to him in the red sweater. Couldn't you just take him home and eat him up for a midnight snack?" Jezzy fanned her face with her hands.

Cathy sized up the man. Tall, lanky, middle-aged with a few wrinkles. Definitely not sexy and absolutely not Jezzy's type.

Jezzy laughed so hard that she lost her breath. When she finally got control, she wiped her eyes with a paper napkin then held up her finger and thumb like a gun. "Bang. You've been had. I really did have you goin', didn't I? I kissed the biker, Cathy. That man next to him is married. His wife is in the bathroom. Can't you see the cottontail expression on his face?"

"I'll get even," Cathy said. "And what is a cottontail expression?"

"Little wifey is in the bathroom. He's imagining that all the cute little things with perky boobs and barely enough on top to cover them are honing in their sights on him. He's gettin' ready to run faster than a cottontail with a coyote hot after his cute little white tail."

"Why?"

"Because if the wife comes out of the bathroom, she'll think he encouraged the women to make a play for him and he won't get anything but a cold shoulder tonight. And he only gets *laid* once a year on New Year's when she's about half plastered," Jezzy explained.

"You should write a book," Cathy said.

"Not me. I'm no writer. I'm a plain old beer-drinkin', good-timin' woman who's going to learn the difference in bull balls and cow udders if it kills me. Don't be oversleepin' tomorrow mornin'. Dinner is at noon. Come late and you might find yourself goin' hungry." Jezzy picked up her beer, slid off the stool, and carried it over to the table where her friends, Leroy and his daughter, Sally, waited.

Cathy made her way down the bar, refilling pint and quart Mason jars of beer, making an occasional mixed drink, and wiping the spills. When she reached the end toward the pool tables, Travis waited with a bill in his hand.

"One of them big jars of Coors and not that damned light stuff, either. And Angel wants a margarita," he said.

She reached for the bill and he dropped it. They both grabbed at the same time and their hands touched, sending sparks flashing around them like a meteorite shower. It didn't surprise him, since he'd always been drawn to tall blond girls. Besides, she was downright hot. Cheap whiskey hitting an empty stomach wouldn't be a bit hotter than that kiss. He got a sudden visual of those long legs stretched out beside him on a bed with her hair spread out on a pillow right beside him. It put another idiot grin on his face.

"Patrón or Jose?" she asked.

"Patrón. Only the best for the Angel." He liked the bartender's voice. Just enough husky to go with that deep southern accent.

"You from Alabama or Georgia?" he asked.

"Neither. I'm from Arkansas." She filled the beer first and slid it toward him.

He reached out, stopped the motion, and brought it to his mouth for a long draw. He'd grown up in Fort Smith and he didn't have that much of a Southern accent. She must be from way down south toward Louisiana.

Anger rose from Cathy's boots all the way to the top of her blond hair. Travis had kissed her and minutes later ordered an expensive drink for another woman. Something damn sure wasn't right with that picture other than it was a hell of a way to start the New Year!

Someone plugged coins into the jukebox and Gretchen's voice singing "Redneck Woman" once again had dancers on the floor with the women yelling "hell yeah" every time Gretchen asked for it.

Travis scanned the crowd, but there was no way to know which woman owned the place. With a name like Cathy, he'd imagined her to be about fifty. She could be that redhead over there sitting with the dark-haired man and younger girl. Or perhaps she was the gray-haired woman sitting in the back corner with a table of other middle-aged women. He'd ask Merle or Angel to point her out before they left. He sure didn't want to get on her bad side. Not when he'd be living right there in Mingus.

Gretchen sang that folks might think she was trashy and a little too hard-core but that she was a redneck woman and not a high-class broad. Travis eyed the bartender up and down and decided that she was the poster child for the song. She might look the part of the Barbie doll with all that height, a blond ponytail, and a flawless complexion, but she was a redneck woman for sure. Her jeans stretched tight across her rounded bottom and cinched into her small waist with a tooled leather belt laced on the edges with silver. A bright blue T-shirt, tight enough to hug every curve, was tucked into the jeans. Heavy lashes framed her steely blue eyes. Her face was angular but soft, and those full ripe lips begged to be kissed again. She definitely brought in the customers and was damned efficient behind the bar. Other than the bouncer sitting beside the door making the Terminator look like a pansy, she was alone and nothing appeared to rile her.

He touched his lips where her kiss was still warm. He'd never done anything so impulsive in his life, but when he walked in the Honky Tonk door and the countdown had begun, well, he wanted to bring in the New Year with a kiss. And there she was in the middle of the floor looking around like she was lost. He hadn't realized she was the bartender until after a jolt of desire shook up his insides and had his heart pumping like a field mouse with a buzzard zeroed in on him.

"Too bad," he muttered.

Leroy perched on the stool next to him. "What's too bad?"

"Nothing," Travis said. "Hey, what part of Arkansas are you from?" he yelled at Cathy above the noise of a full house and the music from the jukebox.

"Why?" Cathy said.

"Ever been to Fort Smith? That's where I grew up," he said.

"I know where it is," Cathy said. She touched her lips. They hadn't burned completely off her face but they were still pretty damn warm.

Leroy signaled for another beer. He was Jezzy's best friend and lived with her out on the ranch. A heavy sprinkling of gray salted his dark hair. His face was a study in angles and planes and his eyes didn't miss a thing, including the puzzled look on Travis's face. His green eyes were set in a face that had more secrets than the government. He'd spent twenty-five years in the marines and had seen four stints in two separate wars.

"I'm Leroy Folsom, and you are…?" He bumped Travis on the shoulder.

Travis peeled his eyes off Cathy. "I'm Travis Henry. Pleased to meet you. Is that lady you are sitting with the owner of this place?"

"Hell no! Jezzy owns a spread between here and Gordon. She don't know jack shit about cows or ranching. I came down to these parts to teach her. Haven't seen you around before. What are you doing in Mingus?"

"Then who's the owner?"

"That'd be…"

"Here's your beer, margarita, and change. Angel likes them stout with a double shot of Patrón, if you're wondering why it's so expensive. What can I get you, Leroy? Something to get that champagne out of your mouth?" Cathy asked.

Leroy nodded. "I need an icy cold Coors. Damn champagne tastes like warm piss."

"How would you know what warm piss tastes like?" Cathy asked.

Leroy leaned across the bar. "I'd tell you but then I'd have to kill you."

"That line is so old it's threadbare." Cathy handed him the beer, took his money, and headed down the bar where someone waved to get her attention.

"You know Cathy?" Leroy asked.

"Nope," Travis answered.

"Then why'd you kiss her?"

"It was just a New Year's Eve kiss," Travis said.

"You stole my kiss," Leroy told him.

Cathy had worked her way back down the bar and got in on the end of the conversation. She shook her finger at Leroy. "He didn't steal your kiss. You were locking lips with that cute little brunette out there on the dance floor, and I wouldn't have kissed you anyway, Leroy. You are old enough to be my father."

"Hey, I'm only eighteen years older than you. That's not even enough for a May-December!"

"My father was only eighteen when I was born."

Leroy sighed. "When I was wearing a uniform women didn't hurt my feelings like that."

"You are out of uniform now and you're too damn tough for your feelings to be hurt," Cathy said.

Leroy chuckled, picked up his beer, and carried it back to the table where he and Jezzy put their heads together.

Cathy shook her head. "That was an obvious fishin' expedition."

"What?" Travis asked.

"Nothing. You'd better get that drink over to Angel before it gets warm."

"Guess so." Travis carried his beer and Angel's margarita back to the tables.

Cathy had pegged Angel Avery and Garrett McElroy for a couple, but maybe she'd been wrong. They'd gotten on like wildfire from the moment they were introduced. They both loved eight ball and they looked so danged cute together; Angel with her kinky red hair and feisty attitude and Garrett with his dark brooding looks. Cathy could see their relationship going into one of those things that lasted right on past life and into eternity. At least until Travis Henry arrived. If he was the thing that kept them apart, she'd never forgive him.

Garrett had come to the area the previous fall to run the Double M Ranch between Huckabay and Morgan Mill. At the time he'd had a serious girlfriend, but she hadn't been able to withstand a long-distance relationship. The first time he and Angel met across the pool table in the Honky Tonk, Cathy knew they'd found their soul mates, and now fate had thrown Travis into the mix. Was it going to be one of those horrid love triangles?

Merle leaned on her custom-made cue stick and watched from the sidelines for a while, then put the stick in a hard case that looked like a gangster's rifle case and headed for the bar. Merle and Ruby Lee had moved to Mingus together back in the sixties. Ruby built the Honky Tonk beer joint and Merle designed fancy Western shirts that sold like hotcakes in Japan and other foreign countries. Both of them were rich enough to buy Palo Pinto County and plow it under when Ruby died.

The only thing blacker than Merle's hair was road tar, and the only thing with more rats in it was the slums in a third-world country. It was teased and sprayed into submission and stacked high on her head. She wore tight jeans and a purple Western shirt with a multicolored butterfly appliquéd on the back yoke. To reach five feet she had to rely on cowboy boots with a heel. That night they were yellow and matched a Western belt that closed with a big rhinestone buckle in the shape of a horseshoe.

"So Travis kissed you?" She hopped up on an empty barstool.

"Why in the devil is everyone so intrigued with the fact that a cowboy kissed me? It's New Year's, for God's sake. It was a kiss. I didn't have sex with him on the dance floor."

"Why?"

"Why what?" Cathy asked.

"Why didn't you have sex with him on the dance floor? Might've done you some good. All you do is run this beer joint. You're as big of a hermit as Daisy used to be."

Cathy shrugged. "Anything wrong with that?"

Merle set the beer bottle down after a long drink. "You're going to grow up to be just like me. Seventy years old. Enough money to buy Texas and couldn't care less. Time to retire, but what the hell would you do if you did?"

"So?" Cathy asked.

Merle laughed. "Just remember I told you so. I'll bring around all those tax papers in the next couple of days. I like to get that done early on so the good old government can have my money to buy fancy jets."

"Bring it by anytime next week after noon. I'm a bear in the mornings."

"So is Angel, but she has to get up and get to work come Monday morning." Merle looked out over the Honky Tonk. "I miss the old crowd."

"Me too," Cathy said.

"I've seen 'em come and go for years, but that last one was sure a lot of fun. Who'd have thought Chigger's momma would have really got old Joe Bob and Billy Bob Walker both married off in three months' time?"

Cathy shivered. "You see that woman comin', you yell right loud and I'll light a shuck for higher country. I swear if she wasn't religious she'd be sellin' voodoo out of her back door. She might be anyway. The religion thing might just be a cover to keep them from stringin' her up."

"They don't hang witches. They burn them at the stake." Merle laughed. "Why are you so afraid of the woman?"

"You remember back when Chigger and Jim Bob got married and Daisy and I went to her backyard dinner reception thing?"

Merle nodded.

"Well, Chigger's momma said that she was findin' a wife for Joe Bob and Billy Bob and a husband for me. I'm hopin' she forgot about me, but she might sneak up on my blind side."

"I'll keep an eye out for you. I see her comin' around

with one of them little dolls that's got pins stuck in it, we'll both head for the hills." Merle carried her beer back to the pool tables. Angel was bent over the table and Garrett was looking at her like he could carry her back to his ranch and never let her out of his sight again.

It was love at first sight and those kinds of miracles were what made all women believe there was a knight in shining armor out there waiting for them. It was the pot of happy-ever-after gold at the end of the rainbow. Cathy swore she'd shoot Travis Henry between the eyes if he messed it up. Who was he anyway and what evil wind blew him into the Honky Tonk?

Travis had a hip propped on the side of the other pool table. Merle said something to him and he smiled. Heat vibrations started in the depth of Cathy's heart and warmed her from the inside out. Between customers she stole glances that way and looked her fill of him. He was at least six feet three inches because he was slightly taller than she was. He had dishwater blond hair with that just-crawled-out-of-bed look. Light brown, thick lashes and brows. Nice wide chest that narrowed to a tight, firm rear end. The whole picture set her hormones to singing one of Dolly's old country tunes, "Why'd You Come in Here Lookin' Like That?"

By closing time the beer joint had thinned out to only a few pool players. "Five minutes and the party is over," Tinker called out as he carried a cooler filled with empty Dr Pepper cans to the bar like he did every night. New Year's Eve wasn't one bit different from Wednesday night in the middle of the summer. Closing time was closing time and he always told the hangers-on that it was time to go at five minutes until the hour.

He was the size of a double-door refrigerator, shaved his big round head, and had eyes that could stop an armor piercing bullet with one glance. Folks might have the balls to start a fight in the Honky Tonk, but they didn't keep them long enough to finish it. And no one argued with Tinker when he said the Honky Tonk was shutting the doors in five minutes.

"I'll get that money back next week," Garrett told Angel as he slung an arm around her shoulder and walked out with her.

"Don't hold your breath until you do," Angel said.

"And don't bet the ranch on it," Merle said. "You'd do well to buy a table and do some practicin' at home, boy."

"Been thinkin' on that very thing," he said.

"Thanks for the kiss," Travis threw over his shoulder at Cathy as he followed them out.

"You are surely *not* welcome," Cathy hollered at him.

He stopped so fast that he almost pitched forward before he caught his balance. "What did you say?"

"I said you are *not* welcome. If you ever do that again, I intend to whip your sorry ass," she said.

"Better bring your lunch and your best friend. It'll be an all-day affair," he smarted off.

Tinker took a step.

Cathy caught his eye and shook her head. "I can take care of this."

Tinker sat down on a barstool, folded his massive arms across his chest, and said, "You don't want to tangle with her, mister. Ever heard of an equalizer? Well, I'm her equalizer. She can't take care of you then she nods at me, and believe me, I can. If the lady says she don't want another kiss from you, I reckon you'd damn sure better not kiss her again."

Cathy was shocked. She had never heard that many words from Tinker all combined, much less at one time.

Travis shot her a dirty look and stormed out of the joint. He hadn't gone into the beer joint with intentions of making anyone angry. He'd thought the kiss was a damn fine one. Why was she so angry? Was the good-lookin' redneck woman married? Shit, was she married to that bouncer? What in the hell had he done?

Cathy kicked off her sneakers and propped her feet on a table as she tilted up a longneck bottle of Coors and downed a fourth of it before coming up for air with a big healthy burp.

"And that is proof positive that I'm a redneck woman. Happy New Year's to me." She raised her bottle high and looked around at the mess. It would take most of the next morning to clean it, but that was the life of a bar owner. Daisy had taught her that in the beginning. Have a beer to relax and go to bed after closing. Get up the next morning to sweep up the mess and mop the floors, restock, and prepare for that night's business.

The Honky Tonk phone sitting on the bar rang and she ran to answer it. Caller ID let her know it was Daisy calling from northern Oklahoma.

"Daisy, I survived," she shouted excitedly into the phone. "I made it through the first big holiday and everything went good all except for one incident. Tinker only had to break up one fight and that was between two women who bared their claws over an old boyfriend. Tinker put them on the porch to cool off and they'd come back inside a few minutes later giggling like schoolgirls with their arms around each other."

"I knew you'd do fine," Daisy said.

"What are you doing still up?" Cathy asked.

"Party ain't over yet here," Daisy said. "I just wanted to tell you Happy New Year."

Cathy sighed. "I miss you."

"Me too. Now what about the incident?"

"I'd love to see your face when I tell it but here goes." Cathy told her the story of being kissed on the dance floor by Travis Henry.

"Did you deck him?" Daisy asked.

"No, I didn't. I was too damned shocked. Remember when we were sixteen and you loaned me that old junker to go to the football game so I could watch Bobby Cole play? Remember he was the quarterback and I had a horrible crush on him?"

Daisy giggled. "I remember that you totaled my car. Seems like I do remember you were going to a football game."

"Well, Travis Henry reminded me of that quarterback. I swear the devil sent him here to tempt me. He's evidently a friend of Angel's and just passing through. The way his kiss made me go all gushy it'd be better if he wasn't around. The temptation might send me right into another messy relationship. My lips are still burning like hell from the kiss and that was more than two hours ago."

"Think Chigger's momma has been praying to God to knock you off the wagon?" Daisy asked.

"What wagon? I'm not an alcoholic," Cathy said.

"The WPSA wagon. You know, the Wild Passionate Sex Anonymous wagon," Daisy teased.

"I hadn't thought of that. I figured she'd be trying to fix me up through Chigger, not praying for me. But one kiss isn't going to make me fall off my wagon, yet."

"Got to go. Jarod is kissing my neck and, honey, I'm not on the wagon." Daisy giggled again and the line went dead.

Cathy slumped down on the nearest barstool.

Everything changes; everything stays the same. The Honky Tonk hadn't changed a bit since she'd inherited it. The building was the same old weathered wood saloon it had been for more than forty years. The two jukeboxes still stood on the south wall with the pool tables. The bar still stretched out across the length of the back of the big rectangular room. The neon sign still flashed HONKY TONK from eight o'clock until two.

But the customers had changed, and yet they stayed the same, if that was possible. Human nature didn't change with time, blood, or tears. Folks who liked to party and shoot pool stayed the same from one year to the next. Only their faces changed. A picture of Chigger back in her glory days flashed in Cathy's mind along with her mother and the curse she'd put on the unmarried folks at the reception.

Cathy moaned out loud. "I do not want a husband. A nice long affair might be nice, though. Say about six months' worth of romping around with Travis Henry in a big king-sized bed or a fancy motel with a Jacuzzi."

She fanned her face with the back of her hand. *Get thee behind me, Satan. I've sworn off men, and besides, the way he kept looking at me says he damn sure wouldn't be interested in a bartender for anything more than a quick one-night stand.*

She tipped the bottle back again. She missed Daisy even if she did enjoy having a bed and not having to pull out the sofa bed every night like she did when she and Daisy shared the apartment. She couldn't wish that things would go back to the way they were because Daisy was so happy. But sitting there in the deafening quietness, she wished she had someone to share the rest of the night with.

She looked across the dance floor at the door into her apartment. She didn't even have to go outside and drive to her home, but the distance from the table to the door looked to be about twenty miles to her sore, tired feet. Back eight years ago when Daisy inherited the apartment with the job, it came with one rule. No men in the apartment. Ruby had told Daisy that she didn't care if she got laid but to do it in a hayloft or a motel. Somewhere away from the Honky Tonk so she'd have time to think before she acted.

Daisy had abided by it and told Cathy that it would save her a ton of heartache if she did the same. The question of whether she would or not had never come up until that moment. Would she let Travis into her apartment if he showed up?

A cold breeze waved over Cathy and made her shiver.

Does Ruby's spirit still live in the Tonk? she wondered as she forced her tired legs to stand up and turned off the Honky Tonk lights.

Yep, I think it does. It has to be the spirit of the Honky Tonk or else I'd done have that cowboy's jeans down around his ankles and he'd be on his back in my bed. I'm a grown woman. I don't pine after what I can't have. I go after it or I let it go. I'll decide later which one I intend to do. Probably won't have to decide, though, because he won't ever come back here again.

The living room still had the same leather sofa Daisy had left behind and the entertainment unit that housed a television and a CD player. Cathy had added a rocking chair with bright yellow cushions and a grouping of pictures of her family on the wall behind the sofa. Scented candles were scattered everywhere, aromas blending to give the whole apartment the smell of a candle shop.

Cathy looked at the picture of her mother and father on their wedding day. They'd both been gone for several years now, but time hadn't erased a longing to talk to them. There was an old black-and-white photo of her grandparents and several of her and Daisy when they were kids: when they went fishing in Grandpa O'Dell's pond; making cookies with Granny O'Dell; camping out at the foot of the mountain with the whole family.

Perched on the television and the end tables were photos of the happy times in Mingus: Cathy and Daisy at Daisy's wedding the previous fall; one of Cathy just seconds after she caught the bride's bouquet. Evidently that old wives' tale about the girl who caught the bouquet being the next bride was an urban myth. Joe Bob and Billy Bob had both beat her to the altar and stopped coming into the Honky Tonk when they did.

Nothing—be it man, woman, or an angel with a golden halo walking a tightrope bearing roses and singing "Redneck Woman"—would keep her from the Honky Tonk. That was the pure guaran-damned-teed gospel and could be written in stone and propped up beside the neon Honky Tonk sign.

"I'm glad I came to Mingus and I'm so tired that if I don't get a shower, I'm going to fall down on this floor and wake up tomorrow morning smelling like the bottom of a two-day-old ashtray," she mumbled.

She tossed her jeans and T-shirt in the general direction of the hamper at the end of the hallway and headed for the bathroom where she let the water warm up before she stepped inside. She lathered up her hair and then let the hot spray beat down on her tired shoulders.

When she finished she wrapped up in a towel, padded back to her bedroom, and put on her favorite pair of faded red flannel pajamas before slipping into the big king-sized bed.

"I might not have put the fear of God into Travis, but that look he shot me as he left said he'd never set foot in the Tonk again. I wonder what he does for a living. Is he a rancher like Jarod or is he a professional football player for the Dallas Cowboys? Whatever he is or does, he's one fine-looking cowboy and his kisses are delicious."

She fell asleep quickly and dreamed about Travis. They were arguing on the porch of the Honky Tonk about whether or not she was going to sell it.

Normally, Cathy slept until ten or eleven o'clock, but the next morning she sat straight up in bed, glanced at the clock to see that it was only eight thirty, and grabbed her head in an attempt to erase the crazy dream as well as all the racket. She'd never heard so much noise in her life. Not even when the countdown had all the women yelling "hell yeah" the night before. It sounded like Armageddon had arrived in the middle of a hurricane and tornado combined.

She threw back the covers and jumped out of bed, already getting a speech ready for whoever or whatever was making so much racket. She pulled up the mini-blinds to discover a backhoe digging a trench right down beside her property line to the road. Men were hanging on the electric poles like monkeys in palm trees. Chainsaws were tearing up the forest where the deer and wild possum lived. A plumber's truck pulled in and two men threw open the back door and commenced to hauling out vicious looking black tubing. And everywhere the men were yelling above the machinery.

She jerked a fleece-lined leather jacket on over her faded flannel pajamas and stomped across the bedroom and living room cussing all the way. She slung open the front door expecting her very presence and drop-dead looks would quiet the noise and put her world to rights.

It didn't.

Cold wind rushed across her bare feet and shivers danced up her spine. She slammed the door shut and shoved her feet down into a worn pair of brown cowboy boots. Frozen grass crunched under her feet with every step. Her anger was fueled to the overfull level by the time she reached the edge of the wooded area.

Leave it to a bunch of idiot men to make a mistake and start tearing up the wrong property. When she got through with them, they'd all have their little tails tucked between their legs and be glad to go home to watch the New Year's Day parade on their television sets. Why in the hell were they working on New Year's Day? Didn't they know it was a holiday?

Someone had made a major mistake. That land belonged to Amos and he was going to be madder than a rabid coyote when she called him. She felt around in her coat pocket but her cell phone was in the apartment. Besides, she couldn't hear jack shit with all that noise going on anyway.

An enormous tree fell and landed so close to her back-side that the dead branches tangled up in her hair. She grabbed her head and ducked.

"Lady, what in the hell are you doing out here?" the tree trimmer yelled.

"What in the hell are you doing out here?"

"Getting ready for a trailer to be brought in on Monday," he said.

She gritted her teeth until her jaws ached. She was truly living a nightmare; maybe not one where that sexy hunk of a cowboy was arguing with her, but a bad, bad dream still. What was she going to do with neighbors? And why in the devil would they want to live right behind a noisy beer joint?

A familiar voice yelled behind her. "Hey, Cathy!"

She whirled to see Amos only a few feet from her. "What are you doing here?"

"I didn't think about all this noise and confusion interrupting your beauty sleep, but it won't last but a couple of days. We'll have the trailer in by Monday and then it'll be quiet around here again."

"Trailer? Nobody asked me if I wanted a trailer on my land," she hollered, even though he was right behind her.

"It's not on your land. The Honky Tonk land ends one foot behind your garage. Think about where you mow the backyard, Cathy. All the acres behind it belong to me," Amos said.

"Oh." All the air left her lungs.

Amos took her arm and led her back to the Honky Tonk. "Come on inside. I'll explain."

When they were inside the apartment she shook off his hand and threw her coat on the couch.

"It's not a nightmare, is it?" she moaned.

"No, it's not a dream. I'm really putting a business back there, at least a temporary one. It'll be there at least two months, maybe longer." Amos pulled out a chair at the small kitchen table and hung his coat over the back before sitting. "You going to make coffee or you want me to do it?"

"I'll make coffee. You explain," she said.

Amos chuckled. Cathy reminded him more of Ruby than Daisy ever did. Slow to wake. Grumbling when she did. Neither of the O'Dell women looked like Ruby and Daisy didn't even act like her. But if he shut his eyes and didn't look at Cathy, she could be Ruby's daughter.

"I'd thought to put my business trailer over on my property next to Tinker's rent house, but there will be times there'll be equipment parked around and kids live there. So I changed my mind at the last minute. Meant to come by and tell you but got all involved with the holiday parties at work and just forgot. Merle's niece, Angel, is going to work for me but you already know that. She's been in the Honky Tonk pretty often. The rig crew will be in and out of it in the daytime. The trailer I'm putting back there will be mainly an office and will shield the sight of the smaller travel trailers the rig crew will live in. So there shouldn't be a conflict of interest here. If we hit oil in this area I may put up a more permanent office building. If not, well, we'll cross that bridge when it gets here. Sorry I didn't tell you before."

"You promise all the noise will stop by Monday?"

"Cross my heart. Had to pay out the nose to get these men out here on New Year's Day, but I want this place up and running coming Monday morning." He went to the kitchen and poured two cups of coffee.

Cathy eyed him. He didn't look seventy and he damn sure didn't look like he dressed up in leather and rode motorcycles with a gang out of Dallas on weekends, either.

That morning he looked the part of a businessman in his khakis and starched blue shirt. Gray hair rimmed his otherwise bald head and his lean face was etched in deep wrinkles.

He handed her a cup of coffee and sat back down.

"No men in the apartment," she said.

Amos's eyes twinkled. "I was part of the reason Ruby made that rule. I don't expect at my age there's a chance I'm going to get lucky with you, is there?"

Cathy grinned and sipped the hot coffee. "Not today."

"Okay, then, I'm going back out to supervise the work. I'll bring the cup back before I leave. Oh, besides the trailer they'll use for the office, they're bringing in gravel this weekend. There'll be twenty travel trailer spaces back there for the oil crew. It's probably only for a couple of months and then it'll all be gone," he said.

She swallowed quickly to keep from spewing coffee onto the carpet.

"I'll get back out there and make sure it's all coming along. By Monday you can sleep until noon again." He opened the door and said, "Come right in out of the cold."

Cathy looked up to see who he was inviting into her apartment. Surely that wasn't... But it was!

Amos threw an arm around Angel's shoulder. "Cathy, I don't know if you've met my new team. This is Angel Avery, Merle's niece. And this is the best damn petroleum engineer in the whole state of Texas, Travis Henry. He's been working for me several years. The trailer's living room will house our office and one bedroom will serve as a filing room. The other one is where Travis will be living the next couple of months. Meet your temporary new neighbor. Travis, this is Cathy O'Dell. She owns the Honky Tonk."

Cathy mumbled something.

Travis muttered a "hello."

Angel patted Amos's arm. "We were at the Honky Tonk last night for the New Year's Eve party. I whipped Garrett McElroy's ass in pool but just barely. Just looking at that cowboy almost puts me off my game. And Travis kissed Cathy."

"I didn't know she owned the place," Travis said with clenched teeth. What in the hell had he done? At least he didn't see that enormous bouncer anywhere in the small apartment, so maybe he wasn't on a hit list. Not yet, anyway.

"Damn, Travis, I swear you have no tact. Forgive him, Cathy. He's outside material. I'll try to get him housebroken so he won't be a horrible neighbor," Angel teased.

"You kissed Cathy?" Amos asked.

"New Year's kiss. You can bet it won't ever happen again," Travis said.

"That's right," Cathy smarted off.

"Well, it looks like you two got things worked out between you. Let's get out of here and let Cathy go back to sleep. She's unbearable when she first wakes up. We don't want to get bit." Amos chuckled and ushered them out to the porch.

Cathy rolled up into a ball and moaned. He would be living within spitting distance of her back door—so much for not having to deal with him ever again.

"Why in the devil didn't you tell me the bartender was the owner?" Travis sputtered when they were outside.

Angel ignored the question and explained to Amos, "Travis kissed her at the stroke of midnight without asking."

Amos threw back his head and roared. "Never a dull moment at the Honky Tonk, is there? I can't wait to tell…" he stopped.

"Who?" Angel asked.

"No one. Just a slip of the tongue. So you kissed Cathy without her permission and you are alive? Count your blessings, Travis," Amos said.

"Why?"

"You figure it out."

"Well, I thought the owner was some old broad and that the bartender was just hired help," he groaned. He'd never tell Amos and Angel that the kiss had stayed hot on his lips for hours and that the barmaid, Cathy, had been in his dreams all night.

Angel poked him in the ribs. "That's what happens when you think about anything other than finding oil."

"For the next eight weeks, I'm staying in the field and thinking of nothing but oil," he declared.

Amos chuckled. "Don't lie to me, son. If you can kiss something that looks like Cathy and not ever think about it again, there's something terrible gone wrong with that brilliant brain that's been working for me all these years."

CHAPTER 2

BLESSED QUIETNESS FILLED THE CAR. A FEW SNOWFLAKES fell from the gray skies but nothing that would accumulate according to the weatherman. Cathy reached out to turn on the radio but pulled her hand back. The silence was wonderful, especially after waking up to noisy machinery and yelling men.

The bright red Cadillac was a joy to drive and Cathy still couldn't believe the car was hers, or the Honky Tonk, or the Harley cycle. She pinched herself at least once a day to make sure it was real. Daisy had always said that Toby Keith's "I Love This Bar" was her theme song, and the only way she'd ever leave it was when they carried her cold dead body out the front door, and she'd die with her fingers wrapped around a longneck bottle of Coors beer. It hadn't happened that way, but Cathy made the same boast after Daisy had married Jarod and moved to Oklahoma. Jarod was one of those special men that God only made one of and then broke the mold, so Cathy had no misbegotten illusions that she'd get the same miracle in her life that her cousin had gotten.

Besides, after Brad Alton, Cathy didn't trust her own judgment anymore. She'd loved Brad, accepted an engagement ring from him, and let him move into her apartment. For all that she'd gotten to fall on the floor and be whipped with a belt while he screamed obscenities at her. Travis might be a wonderful man as well as a sexy one, but Cathy couldn't take a chance. Another mistake like Brad would wipe out every last thread of her self-confidence.

She passed two pickup trucks before she made a right-hand turn toward Gordon. A couple of deer grazed in the ditch beside the road. They raised their heads but didn't bolt and run when she passed them. A little farther down the road a momma skunk with a couple of half-grown babies behind her scooted across the road.

Anger replaced the peace in her heart. Progress came at a great price, but why did it have to come out of her yard? Most weeks she saw at least a dozen deer from her kitchen window. And poor old Rascal, the possum she fed dry cat food to on the porch, would never wander through that maze of trailers. Come Monday the only view would be a tin can trailer house, pickup trucks, and travel trailers. The only wildlife she'd see would be thirsty oilmen and the lusty women and men in the Honky Tonk.

She was still aggravated about the change when she made a right-hand turn onto Jezzy's ranch. Three hundred acres of rolling hills covered up in mesquite and rocks with a few head of Angus roaming about here and there. Two extra trucks in the driveway said that she wasn't the only dinner guest that day.

"Well, shit," she fussed. She'd looked forward to a long, lazy afternoon with Jezzy, Leroy, and Sally without anyone else around. Call it downright selfish, but Cathy figured she deserved it after the way the day had started. Sharing another bit of her life with strangers didn't seem a damn bit fair.

She crossed the yard slowly, wiped her boots on the doormat, and knocked. The house was a small three-bedroom white frame with a tiny porch flanked on either side by dormant rose bushes. According to Jezzy, the roses were in a live-or-die situation. They could live or they could die, but she wasn't telling them bedtime stories and hand-picking aphids from them the way her grandmother had. That almost put a smile on Cathy's face…but not quite.

"Come on in," Jezzy called out.

Cathy stepped inside and slung her coat on the rack behind the door.

Jezzy called out from the sofa in the living room. "Happy New Year's Day. We're at the end of the parade. Everyone, this is Cathy O'Dell, who I'm sure you've already met. She owns the Honky Tonk." Jezzy had naturally red hair and freckles across her nose. Red was not her best color, but she wore a Crayola red sweater that day with her jeans.

Cathy looked around the room and came close to grabbing her coat and lighting a shuck right back to the safety of the Honky Tonk. Jezzy, Merle, and Leroy sat on the sofa. Sally and Travis Henry were on one love seat, and Angel was on the other.

"Hi, Cathy. I didn't know you were having dinner here today," Angel said.

Jezzy patted the sofa between her and Leroy. "Sit, girl. After all that standing last night your feet have to still be tired."

Merle piped up from the corner, "Did you know that Travis kissed her?"

Cathy wished she could dig a hole, fall into it, and pull the dirt in with her.

"It was New Year's Eve," Cathy said.

"If I'd known what a stir it was going to kick up, I wouldn't have done it," Travis said.

Jezzy laughed. "You are an idiot. I don't know a man alive who wouldn't give his left ball to kiss Cathy or one that would apologize for it."

Travis intended to shoot Jezzy a dirty look even if he was a guest in her house, but when she winked he chuckled. "In my defense I had no idea she was the owner. I figured someone with a name like Cathy was at least sixty years old. Besides, what's a pretty young lady like you doing in a place like that anyway?"

Sally slapped his arm playfully. "That line is older than me and it wasn't a good one when it was new."

Sally was Leroy's twenty-three-year-old daughter who'd graduated college and gotten a midterm position in Gordon as a kindergarten teacher. She'd moved in with Leroy and Jezzy a couple of weeks before. Her mother was Asian and Sally had inherited her barely toasted skin, almond eyes, and complexion that a modeling agency would pay big bucks for.

Cathy looked across the room at Travis. "The line really is old. And what I'm doing at the Tonk is running a beer joint. I like my job. I love the Honky Tonk. So don't bad-mouth it."

Travis was her dream man. Blond hair. Blue eyes. The glasses had never been part of the dream, but even they were a little sexy. Jeans that fit just right. Boots. So why in the devil was she angry and not flirting? Other than kissing her, dancing through her mind all night, and showing up in her morning, he hadn't done anything wrong.

Travis held up his palms in defense. "I quit. I'll talk about oil wells and soil samples the whole time I'm in Texas. At least I won't have to eat my shoes that way."

Angel patted him on the arm. She was short and had naturally red hair that lay in ringlets around her face and green eyes. She wore a flared denim skirt and an army green sweater the same color as her eyes. "It's all right, darlin'. You're a geology geek. They aren't supposed to be able to sweet-talk the women. Folks understand when you put your big old size twelve boot in your mouth."

Travis blushed as red as the flannel shirt he wore with faded jeans. Angel's jokes about him had been funny before. Now they weren't. Cathy would think he was a country bumpkin who picked his nose and didn't know how to use a fork.

"Ah, y'all give him a chance," Jezzy piped up. "If Leroy Folsom can be tamed, Travis can, too. Why, I've even taught Leroy where the bathroom is and he's even quit pissin' off the back porch."

"Only when she's lookin'," Leroy teased back. "We didn't have fancy toilets in the desert."

Cathy smiled.

"Ah, a grin. She's going to forgive old Travis," Angel said.

"I wouldn't get that enthusiastic," Cathy said. "Are the peas about ready, Jezzy? I went to sleep listenin' to the sounds of a few lonesome old cold crickets and the wailing of a coyote. I got rudely awakened by a scene from that old movie *Red Dawn*. It sounded like terrorists were surrounding the Honky Tonk with armored tanks. I thought I heard machine guns and a cannon, but it was just every kind of construction machine in the world out there tearing up my peaceful backyard. I was so mad I went straight into the Tonk and cleaned up last night's mess. I didn't eat breakfast and I'm starving."

"Soon as the parade is over we can eat. Cathy, you and Sally come on and help dish it up and put it on the table. Sally made a banana nut cake for dessert," Jezzy said.

"What about me?" Angel asked.

"You and Travis need to talk to Leroy some more about this oil idea. We can take care of the dinner," Jezzy said.

"It's your property," Leroy said. "I'm just the hired help."

"You know more about that end of the business than I do. That's why you are the hired help. Listen to what they got to say. If you think it's a good idea, they can put one of them black pumpin' devils in the middle of my kitchen floor. I can just see Elijah and Paul's faces. Those self-righteous sumbitches would pass little green apples if this old rocky ground makes me rich. And that would make me very happy," Jezzy said.

"Rich?" Sally laughed. "You already own ninety percent of the stock in Fort Knox."

"Well, maybe I want to buy out the other ten percent, and this oil well will let me do it." Jezzy headed for the kitchen through an archway to the left of the living room. The room was oversized with cabinets on one side; a refrigerator, stove, and sink on the other; and a round table with eight chairs circling in the middle of the floor.

"Eli and Paul will just pray harder for your wild and wanton ways," Sally teased.

"All goes to prove their prayers don't go no higher than the ceiling. I got a feeling that my brother prayed for the same thing and it didn't do any good." Jezzy pulled a pan of ham from the oven. "Cooked it last night and carved it this morning so I wouldn't be so rushed. That's enough talk of money and oil. Cathy, you tell me why are you being mean to that sexy cowboy? If you don't want him then don't be selfish, kick him over the fence to Sally."

Sally whipped around and shook a hot pad at Jezzy. "I don't want him. I've got a boyfriend."

"Damn, Sally. You're supposed to play along with me. I was trying to make her jealous," Jezzy whispered.

"Jealous of who? What'd I miss?" Merle pulled out a kitchen chair and sat down. "I couldn't hear a damn word with y'all whisperin'. It's got to be good or you'd be talkin' louder. For a minute there I thought I was losin' my hearin'. Wouldn't surprise me none what with all the wooden balls I've knocked around in my lifetime."

"They were talking about Travis kissing Cathy," Sally said.

"I'm surprised she didn't kill him," Merle said.

"It's not too damn late. Hell, he's done disgraced my honor by kissing me in the Honky Tonk so he deserves to die. God knows it's an unforgivable sin to be kissed right smack on the lips in a beer joint. That's supposed to go on in the back seat of a car in the church parkin' lot after a prayer meetin'. Load up Granny Green's old blunderbuss over the fireplace and I'll avenge my honor. I'll gut shoot him and he can die a long and painful death. Teach him to go around kissing women on New Year's that he don't know," Cathy whispered.

Jezzy giggled. "Take him outside first. I don't want blood on my new carpet."

"Give me ten minutes and you and Sally bring the shovels. We'll bury him down by the pond," Cathy said.

Sally threw up her hands. "Don't bring me into this. I'm not digging in the cold, hard dirt. I'd break a fingernail. I'll talk to the cops and give you an alibi, but I'm not touching a shovel."

Cathy smiled. "There's nothing to worry about. He's not my type. I like bad boys and he's too pretty to be a bad boy. He's not much good for anything other than oil wells."

Jezzy began stacking ham slices on an oversized platter. "Maybe he's good in bed. Ever think of that? With all those muscles to wrap your legs around and those blond curls to hang onto, I bet that cowboy would give you a damn fine ride."

"Remember that old song that said not to call him a cowboy 'til you've seen him ride?" Cathy asked.

"You gonna see if he's a cowboy when he shucks out of them boots and that belt buckle? Did you notice that it had a bull rider on it?" Jezzy asked.

"Hell no! And you shouldn't be looking at that area of his anatomy, either." Cathy blushed.

"Why not? If he's wearing a big silver buckle with a bull rider on it, then it's beggin' to be looked at and a woman's eyes can't help but fall a few inches further down to check things out. You're not that innocent, Cathy," Sally said.

"Honey, I was the inspiration for Gretchen Wilson's 'Redneck Woman' and I'll look at any belt buckle I want to," Cathy declared.

Leroy called from the living room, "Dinner about ready in there?"

"Herd 'em in," Jezzy said. "I'm puttin' the peas in the bowl now."

Jezzy sat at the head of the table with Leroy to her right. Angel sat to her right and Sally next to her with Merle at the other end. Cathy sat to her right with Travis beside her. It wasn't the best-case scenario, but it wasn't too bad. If she'd been on the other side of the table then she would have had to look straight into his crystal clear blue eyes. Just knowing he was sitting beside her almost gave her an acute case of hives. If someone had told her a week ago that she'd be having dinner with someone who took her breath away on New Year's, she would have sent for a straightjacket and had the person committed.

Cathy's hands shook when she picked up the tea pitcher, filled her glass, and passed it on to Travis. His big hand closed over hers in the transfer and she clamped her jaw shut to keep from gasping at the scarlet blush rising up on her neck. Any minute now she'd be blushing like a pre-pubescent teenager with a crush on the next big name in Hollywood.

"Is this sweet tea?" he asked.

"You diabetic? Only thing we drink in Texas is sweet tea. And besides, Sally made banana nut cake."

"No, I'm not diabetic. I drink sweet tea. Hate that stuff they sell in stores that takes two cups of sugar that never dissolves. Glad you told me about the cake. I'll have to save room," he said.

Angel groaned. "Travis?"

"Get ready for it, Angel. I'm going to embarrass you. You been tellin' everyone I ain't housebroke. Well, if you're goin' to give me the name, then by damn, I'll have the game. This reminds me of home and I'm not going to be bashful," Travis said.

Leroy handed him the platter of corn bread. "Man works all day in the hot sun or the freezing cold, he ought to be able to enjoy his vittles without worrying about etiquette.

You want seconds or thirds you better eat fast, though. New Year's dinner is my favorite one of the year. So you best load your plate up real good. We might even fight over the last chunk of corn bread."

"I love this kind of food and I would be willin' to arm wrestle you if it comes down to that last piece of bread," Travis said.

He was glad to have a table full of folks around him on the holiday. He'd like it even better if one of his sisters was sitting beside him instead of that bartender who thought she was mean enough to take him on in a fistfight. He wasn't a fighter by nature but a lover and he damn sure didn't want to fight something that pretty. He'd much rather brush that errant strand of blond hair back and kiss the soft spot on her neck. Or maybe taste those luscious lips one more time. The fire that idea produced made him remember what Leroy said about working all day out in the weather. Maybe if he changed the subject, he wouldn't think of Cathy with every single breath.

He looked at Leroy. "Gets hot down here in the summertime, does it?"

Angel answered, "Ah, honey, come July the lizards will be carrying a canteen slung over one shoulder and a sawed-off shotgun slung over the other one. I used to visit Aunt Merle in the summer and thought I'd die."

"Why a shotgun?"

"To shoot anyone who tries to take their canteen," Cathy said.

Travis laughed with everyone else. "Well, then I've been warned. Summer will be hot. Except I expect I won't be in this area when it gets that hot. We got two months to bring in this well if Jezzy's land looks good. The day it comes in I'll be long gone. This ham is delicious, and what's your secret in these peas? They taste smoky."

Jezzy smiled. "Granny Green taught me to cook and she used lots of bacon drippings for seasoning. That's what's in the peas. She said a woman like me had best learn to cook because that's the only way I'd ever get a man."

"Why'd she say something like that? A woman like you? What's wrong with you?" Angel asked.

"I'll tell you the short form. Granny Green had a son, Joshua Noah, who was born with a perfect halo that floated exactly six inches above his head at all times. Not once from womb to tomb did that thing ever get off-kilter. He grew up to be a fine preacher man and had two godly sons of his own. Named them Elijah and Paul right out of the Bible like he and his wife, Deborah, had been. My mother was two years younger than my uncle and she'd been named Rachel Ruth. She had the holy name but somehow she must've been hidin' behind the door when they gave out the baby halos in the nursery. But when they were givin' out hellion horns she did get a set of those. She got a degree in business and went to work in Dallas. She was in her late twenties when she got pregnant and she did not get married. Granny threw a fit and that's putting it mildly. She told Granny not to fret. She would name her child a name right out of the Bible just like David and Samuel. She named me Jezzy Belle. Granny thought I was the devil reincarnated into a red-haired kid's body. Anyway, that's the reason Granny thought I needed to cook. Tainted as I was, not many men would even look at me."

"You ever get married?" Angel asked.

"Hell no! Leroy did three times and proved it wasn't for either one of us, didn't you?" She looked at him for confirmation.

"She's right. I should've listened to her. We was best friends from the time we both crawled on the school bus out of Bugtussle, Oklahoma, on our way to kindergarten. And all three times the day of my weddings she said I was makin' a big mistake, but I didn't listen. Got Sally out of the first deal so I can't gripe. The next two didn't last long enough to produce anything other than bad feelings," Leroy said.

"How about you, Cathy?" Angel asked. "You ever been or expectin' to get married anytime soon?"

"That wouldn't be a no, but a hell no. I have not been. Do not intend to be. When I die I will have never been. They're going to take me out of the Honky Tonk with my cold dead fingers wrapped around a bottle of Coors after I've worked all week. Now it's your turn. You been married, Angel?"

"I'm only twenty-three. I've been in school my whole life, but that could change if the right cowboy came along and asked me at this point in my life. I think I'm ready to fall in love," Angel said.

Cathy wanted to ask Travis about his love life but the words wouldn't go from her brain to her mouth. Instead she looked across the table and said, "What is it that you and Travis do, anyway, with this oil business?"

"Travis and I are petroleum engineers. We go in first and determine if there's a possibility of oil. And he's right about the two months. Once we start drilling Amos says we've got that long to bring it in or move on. That's why the operation behind the Honky Tonk is temporary," Angel said.

"We'll bring one in. Angel can smell it. I swear her nose

is as good as an old divining rod. It twitches if you look real close," Travis said.

Angel pointed at the bowl of potatoes. "Pass those please. And you're just payin' me compliments so I won't say anything else embarrassin' about you, darlin.'"

If he is really her darlin', why didn't he kiss her on New Year's Eve? There's too much age difference for them to have gone to school together. So what are they to each other? Cathy wondered.

Travis sent the potatoes around to her. "Yes, I do love you, sweetheart. I've always loved you. You shoulda been my fifth sister instead of my bratty cousin."

Something akin to a helium balloon arose in Cathy's spirits. He hadn't kissed her and then thrown her over for another woman within minutes. Angel was his cousin.

Angel dipped heavily into the bowl. "Real potatoes. I can tell the difference in them and the instant kind. Instant potatoes stink."

"I agree. No amount of butter and sweet cream will hide that smell," Cathy said.

"I hate to cook so I don't get meals like this very often. If we hit oil I'm going to tell Amos to give you a bigger cut than normal with the stipulation that I get to come to dinner every week," Angel said.

"Now that sounds like a deal," Jezzy said.

"Is that a true story about your name and your mother?" Cathy asked Jezzy.

"It is," Leroy answered for her.

"I thought Jezzy was a nickname for Jessica," Cathy said.

"Nope, it's really Jezzy. Got the name and the reputation." Jezzy laughed.

"Ah, come on now. I can't believe…"

"That I'm a Chigger?" Jezzy's eyes twinkled.

"Who's Chigger?" Travis asked.

"Chigger would've been a hooker but never could charge for her services. Said it would be a sin to charge for something so much damn fun as sex."

"Then I must be a Chigger," Jezzy said.

Cathy noticed that Travis's tea glass was empty and handed him the pitcher. "You might meet her sometime. She and my cousin, Daisy, were best friends. She and Jim Bob still come to the Honky Tonk every so often. Used to be every weekend but she's seven months pregnant now. She can't drink and says she's too fat to dance. Plus Jim Bob says the smoke isn't good for the baby. I miss them all, even Billy Bob, who was constantly trying to get me to marry him."

"Why?" Travis asked. Jealousy slapped him in the face and he couldn't understand why. He'd only met Cathy the night before so he shouldn't care if another man was in love with her.

"You think no one would want to marry a bartender?" Cathy asked.

"No, I just wondered why he quit coming to the beer joint if he wants to marry you. Doesn't he love you anymore?" Travis stammered.

Lord but the woman was prickly. It was almost as if he'd pissed her off in another life.

"Billy Bob Walker was in love with the Honky Tonk more than the owners. He'd marry Marie Laveau if she owned the joint," Merle said.

"Who's that? Where does she live?" Travis asked.

Jezzy swallowed quickly to keep from spewing tea. "You ain't never heard of Marie Laveau?"

Travis shook his head. "She from around here?"

"It's the woman in an old Bobby Bare song. She's a witch. It's on the old jukebox. Don't you listen to country music?" Cathy asked.

"Of course I listen to the old country music. I'd forgotten about that song. Why was Billy Bob in love with the Honky Tonk?" Travis asked.

"He's always wanted a beer joint. Since he was a kid, it'd been his dream," Cathy answered.

"Then why didn't he just build one?" Travis's curiosity was piqued and he wanted to know more about this Billy Bob character who loved Cathy for all the wrong reasons.

"Because there's already two others in Mingus. The Trio Club and The Boar's Nest. But owning a beer joint was only half his dream. The other half was marrying a barmaid."

Travis gave her his undivided attention. "Did he finally marry one?"

"No, he married a Sunday school teacher. All goes to show that sometimes love don't take you where you want to go," Cathy said.

He carefully let out his breath. Heaven help him if Angel heard a whoosh of air that said he'd been holding a lungful of air. "Ain't that the truth. My sister Rose wouldn't even date someone outside the law department in college and she wound up married to a hospital administrator."

"So your sister is a lawyer?" Cathy asked.

"Rose and Grace are lawyers at Henry Law Offices in Fort Smith with my dad. Gwen is a pediatric doctor. Emma is a kindergarten teacher. All in Fort Smith. I'm the wandering child."

"How about you, Angel? You got brothers and sisters?" Cathy asked.

"One of each. Gabriella is ten years older than me. We call her Gabby. She teaches on the college level at the University of Tulsa. Nathanael is eight years older than me and he's a business executive with my father's import/export business. We call him Nate. Momma loves angels. That's where they got their names. When I was born Daddy told her to forget all the research into finding what angel to name me after and to just name me Angel, so she did. Of course, she tempered it with Merlene. That's to keep one foot on the ground when my head is floating in the clouds."

"After Merle?" Cathy asked.

Angel handed Travis the platter of ham to send around the table again. "That's right, but I think it backfired because Aunt Merle don't keep her feet grounded all the time, either."

"Here, here, don't be airin' dirty laundry at Jezzy's New Year's dinner party." Merle laughed.

Travis passed it on without taking a second helping. Suddenly his stomach was filled with quivering knots. He hoped he wasn't getting sick.

Cathy elbowed him and was glad everyone else was teasing Merle about her wild days and didn't see all the blazes dancing around the table. "Thought you were going to embarrass Angel. You didn't even take a second helping. It'd take at least three helpings to embarrass Angel, wouldn't it? She was yellin' 'hell yeah' with the best of the redneck women last night."

Angel nodded. "Two helpings is his normal meal. Three would be embarrassing. I think he's showing off for you or Sally today. He never just eats one plate of homemade food."

"I'm saving room for extra cake," he declared.

Cathy touched the warm spot on her elbow. With Travis

wearing a flannel shirt and her in a thick sweater, surely vibes couldn't have shot through that much cotton. Her appetite disappeared and she could have strangled Travis. No man was worth losing her taste for ham and black-eyed peas. If she couldn't eat her portion of the cake, Travis Henry might really find himself on the business end of Granny Green's old blunderbuss. It could easily be his last day upon the earth, so he'd better eat very well.

She suddenly felt even more antsy than when she realized Travis was sitting in the living room. She wanted to rush back to the safety of the Honky Tonk. She felt like she was standing on the edge of a tall rocky cliff with a hurricane approaching. The wind was whipping around her in a frantic frenzy and she couldn't move for fear of falling. But she couldn't think of a single reason to run out right in the middle of a meal.

Dessert would be served and then there'd be coffee in the living room and the football game. Jezzy had gone to a lot of trouble to make the day special and Cathy couldn't be rude and disrespectful. She started running down a list of excuses why she needed to go home right after the final field goal was kicked or touchdown was made so she wouldn't have to stay for supper, too.

Jezzy pushed back her chair. "Looks like everyone is finished. I'll take away the dirty dishes if you'll bring in the cake, Sally."

Cathy gasped when she saw the cake. "My grandmother made cakes like that for Christmas dinner. I haven't had one in years. I'm having two pieces if it puts forty pounds on my rear end and thighs."

The feeling that she was about to be engulfed by a

hurricane passed and her appetite returned. The cake was every bit as good as the ones she had as a child, so she decided Travis could live another day.

"Y'all come on in the living room where it's more comfortable. We can have our coffee in there and watch the pregame show. Anyone want to put five dollars in the pot? I'm betting the Cowboys whip that sorry West Coast team by ten points," Leroy said.

"Could I put in an order for a cup of hot tea? And I'll put five in that the Cowboys whip them by at least two touchdowns," Travis said.

Cathy frowned. Travis Henry didn't look like the tea-drinking type to her. Beer, yes. Sweet tea, yes. But what did she know about the man? He might not even be a real cowboy. Maybe it was a weekend disguise and he wore three-piece suits to work like Amos did.

"Of course," Jezzy said.

"Make that two, then. Would you have green tea?" Angel asked.

"Yes, we do. Sally likes a whole array of teas. Personally I used to wonder how in the devil she woke up in the morning without coffee until she brewed me a cup of black tea. It was strong enough to fry the eyeballs out of the devil's mother-in-law. Sally, will you help me make coffee and tea? We'll bring the rest of the cake to the living room with the pretzels to nibble on while we root for the Cowboys."

Leroy pushed his chair back and led the way. "Pregame show starts in ten minutes. So when are you going to start with the soil samples?" he asked as he led the way into the living room.

A built-in cherry entertainment center with a flat-screen

television in the center covered the north wall of the living room. It was flanked on two sides and across the top with bookcases stuffed with fat mystery novels, paperback romances, cookbooks, and a full set of ancient encyclopedias. An overstuffed light brown, buttery-soft leather sofa with matching love seats on each end made a U-shaped conversation group with a coffee table in the center. Leroy sat on one end of the sofa with Merle on the other end. Cathy and Angel sat on the love seat to his right and Travis on the one to his left.

Travis leaned forward and asked, "Jezzy does have full mineral rights ownership of the land, doesn't she? Her two cousins will have to be talked to if she doesn't."

"Oh, yes, she bought it all and at a horrible high price. Made sure she owned it all the way to hell, as she said when she signed the papers that day. She didn't want them to ever come back on her for even a plateful of calf fries." Leroy laughed.

Angel touched Cathy's arm. "What are you frowning about?"

Cathy put on her best fake smile. "I was just thinking."

Angel lowered her voice. "You were frowning and you were looking right at Travis. He didn't mean any harm by the kiss. I've never known him to do something so irrational."

"Had he been drinking?"

"Not Travis. He's a one-drink-a-night man. Never seen him drunk and I've known him my whole life."

Sally brought the tea tray to the living room and set it on the coffee table. "Sugar and cream?" she asked Travis.

"Two of sugar and barely white," Travis said.

Sally fixed it and handed it to Cathy. "Would you please take this over there while I fix Angel's?"

It was filled to the brim so Cathy had to walk slowly. Travis's fingertips brushed hers when she handed it to him. She thought she had things under control, but his touch was as hot as the contents of the cup.

Stop it right now, she argued with herself. *It ain't happening. I won't let it. I'm not trusting a man again after Brad Alton, not even Travis. We are going to be neighbors. He'll be in the Honky Tonk buying a beer and there will be times when his fingers touch mine. This has got to stop.*

She got a warm feeling in the pit of her stomach and got angry because she couldn't make it disappear.

"Thank you very much," Travis said. She was one gorgeous woman and she'd be living right next door. But it was only for two months. Nothing could happen in that short length of time.

"You are welcome." Cathy started back to the love seat but Angel and Sally were side by side talking about medicinal qualities of green tea.

"Grab a cup of coffee and sit here. Kickoff in thirty seconds. Do you like football?" Travis patted the end of the love seat.

"I put five on the Cowboys to win by four touchdowns."

"You are my kind of woman," Travis said.

She sat down.

Sally handed Cathy a cup of strong black coffee. "I'll see your five and put five on the other team to whip the Cowboys by two touchdowns."

"You are speakin' treason," Cathy said.

"Oh, I'm a Cowboys fan but I've done my homework. They're goin' to get their plow cleaned today because they've gotten cocky."

"Everyone and everything in Texas is cocky. Why should they be any different?" Travis said.

"Be careful. You are in a room with a bunch of Texans," Cathy said.

"Not really. Leroy and Jezzy are both from Oklahoma. Angel and I are from Arkansas. Merle might be the only natural Texan here and she knows she's cocky." He locked gazes with Cathy and what fired up between them was hotter than the embers in the fireplace.

"And you're saying you're not cocky, with that belt buckle the size of a dinner plate?"

He grinned and touched the buckle. "It does make a statement, doesn't it? At least I didn't buy it at a pawn shop. I earned it. Made a little extra money doing some rodeo work when I was in college. Love ranch life. Momma has a horse ranch and raises some cattle on the side. I was more at home in the barn than anyplace else."

"And now?" Cathy asked.

"Now I'm too busy to rodeo and do much ranchin', but I miss it. Love the sound and the dirt of the rodeo and the people who go to them. And the peace in a hay barn sometimes calls my name. Ever been to a big rodeo?"

She shook her head.

"Well, someday you'll have to go."

"Back to the Cowboys. They've gotten cocky and it's going to cost them, I'm afraid," Angel said.

Travis grabbed his heart with his free hand. "Oh no! Was it something in the peas that poisoned you?"

Cathy chanced a sidling look at him. He was funny as well as handsome and he liked the Cowboys, so he wasn't a total washout. Maybe they could be friends and neighbors.

As long as she kept him out of her apartment. He was so damned handsome that having him that close to a bed would be far too much temptation for a lily-white angel straight from heaven.

And Cathy O'Dell was not a lily-white angel and she'd never had a halo, not even a severely crooked one.

CHAPTER 3

CATHY PUT A QUARTER IN THE JUKEBOX AND RONNIE Milsap was singing "What Goes On When the Sun Goes Down" as Tinker checked IDs and people came in out of the cold in groups of twos and threes.

"Where's Angel?" Garrett slung his leather jacket over the back of a barstool.

"Haven't seen her yet. Get you a beer?" Cathy asked.

"Bud, pint-sized. She said she'd be here at opening. I thought I was the late one."

"Maybe she'll be in later. How're things out at the ranch?" Cathy asked.

"Things are coming along. Come spring, we'll be ready to hit the ground running," he said.

Merle and three truckers came in fussing about the cold weather. Merle shivered and hung her denim duster on a hook beside the cue-stick cabinet. "Colder'n a mother-in-law's kiss out there. Set me and these boys up with a bucket of beers. I'll buy the first round."

"Where's Angel?" Garrett asked.

"Said if you came in tonight to tell you that she's workin' late. Bring that beer over here and show me that you've been practicin'," she said.

Disappointment showed in Garrett's face, but he picked up his beer and followed Merle.

Cathy wondered if the Double M Ranch was one of those lucky love places. Would the next couple to find their soul mates be Garrett and Angel? Her cousin and Jarod, who'd come from Cushing, Oklahoma, to help his Uncle Emmett through the last days of his life, had found love out there on the ranch. Now it was happening all over again.

The old jukebox with the forty-five records played music from Merle Haggard, Willie Nelson, Buck Owens, and Waylon Jennings. Songs were three for a quarter, just like they had been back when the jukebox went in the Honky Tonk in the early sixties.

The old songs were like a warm blanket around Cathy's shoulders on a cold night. They brought back memories of listening to country music cassettes as she and her father worked on an Oldsmobile F-85 that she'd used all her carhop money to buy the summer she was sixteen. Melancholy waves washed over Cathy as she drew up a Bud Light for a customer. She made change for a twenty, dropping a quarter and having to touch his hand when she handed it to him. Nothing happened. Not a single spark danced around like they did when her elbow brushed against Travis.

"Bartender looks pretty sad tonight," the stranger said. His dark hair was feathered back in a cut that probably cost more than she'd make in tips that night. He looked like a cowboy— well, almost. Most real honest-to-God cowboys didn't wear a diamond set in a wide gold-nugget band like the one on his right ring finger. His fingers were long and slim with nails that shined like they'd been buffed. And that ring hadn't come out of a McDonald's Happy Meal. She didn't know a real cowboy in the whole five-county area who got manicures.

"Little bit," she admitted.

"Country music will do that to you," he said.

"Guess so."

"How'd a pretty girl like you end up working in a place like this anyway?"

"That is a long story, mister. Where you from?"

"Dallas."

"What brings you to the Honky Tonk here on a cold night like this?"

"Came to talk to you, Miss O'Dell."

She raised an eyebrow. "Oh?"

"I've done my homework. You inherited the Honky Tonk from your cousin a few months ago. It's a lonely existence. Living in the back of the place. Running it by yourself with only that big bruiser of a man back there to help with the rowdies." He glanced back at Tinker.

She took a closer look at him. Creases in his jeans weren't even faded. The fold line across the pocket of the shirt said that he'd just bought it. She leaned over the bar and looked at his feet, not giving a damn if it was rude or not. Not a scuff mark on those new boots. If he was a real cowboy Cathy would do a striptease on top of the pool table.

The *bullshit* radar in her head sounded like a tornado siren in her ears.

"Who are you and why are you here? You just get out of prison, or did you suddenly decide that cowboys get all the hot women?" she asked.

He extended his hand across the bar. "Bart White."

She ignored it. Bart was too damned close to Brad, her abusive ex. Both names reminded her of that bastard.

He slowly laid it down on the bar and went on, "Ever see *The Godfather*?"

She nodded. "You got a dead horse head you're about to throw up here on my bar?"

"No, but I've come to make you an offer you can't refuse." He chuckled.

"I doubt that very seriously. Drink your beer and get on down the road, Mr. White. I'm not interested in a damn thing you are selling."

"I'm not selling, I'm buying."

Cathy's face flushed. "On that note, I reckon you'd better just get on out and not bother with the beer. Something tells me you don't drink beer anyway."

"You have misunderstood me, Miss O'Dell. I'm not asking to buy your body. I'm here to make you an offer for the Honky Tonk. One that you'd be a downright fool to ignore."

"Why?"

"Because I want it," he said.

"It's not for sale."

"One million dollars."

She shook her head. "Guess that makes me a downright fool."

"One and a quarter million," he said.

She glared at him. "Get out of my beer joint before I throw you out."

He eased off the barstool. "One and a half. Final offer. You've got twenty-four hours to think about it."

"Don't need twenty-four hours. Don't need twenty-four seconds. The Tonk is not for sale at any price, Mr. White. Not to you for a million and a half. Not to a beggar off the street for a dollar ninety-nine," she said.

"Mr. Radner will be disappointed," Bart White said.

Cathy shook her fist at Bart. "You tell Hayes Radner that the Tonk will never be his. I don't care if he buys up the whole state. This is *my* place and it's not up for grabs. Right now, I'd burn it down before I sold it to him."

Tinker looked her way.

She shook her head and he settled back into his chair.

"Mr. Radner gets what he wants, one way or the other. He wanted to start with the Honky Tonk. You will sell to him someday, lady, because there won't be anyone left to support the place. The rest of the area will be an amusement park. Only by then the price will be so low you'll feel like you're selling to that beggar off the street," Bart said.

"Hayes Radner can take his money and his highfalutin ideas and go to hell with them," Cathy said, raising her voice.

Bart White gave her a knowing smile and meandered across the floor, walking as if the new boots hurt his feet. Cathy hoped they rubbed blisters the size of half-dollars on his heels and he had to wear his house shoes to work the next morning. What on earth was he thinking? That she'd jump at the chance to sell the Tonk if he was dressed up like a cowboy? Well, he'd better butt his head up against a brick wall and get that shit out of his head.

Merle popped up on the barstool Bart had occupied and asked, "Did that drugstore cowboy ever touch this beer?"

"No, he did not. How'd you know he wasn't the real thing?"

"He walked like he had a corncob stuck up his ass when he came in here. It was the boots. If a man don't grow up walkin' in them, they have trouble. Listen to the Hag singing 'Everybody's Had the Blues.' I do believe he's talkin' about Garrett and Angel. She's workin' and he's got the blues tonight."

Cathy leaned on the bar. "So you like the old Hag, do you?"

Merle shook her head. "I don't like him. I love him. Lord that man could have parked his cowboy boots up under my bed any night of the week." Merle picked up the beer and tossed back half of it before coming up for air. "Little flat but it's wet."

"Garrett seems plumb smitten by Angel," Cathy said.

"He ought to be. She's smart, funny, cute, and can whip his ass in pool. What'd that fake cowboy want anyway?"

"To snooker me. My bet is he's some kind of fancy-ass lawyer and he thought he'd get on my good side by showing up looking like that. Hayes Radner sent him to buy the Honky Tonk from me. Crazy men ain't got any brains at all if they think I'll sell my home to them," Cathy fumed.

Merle picked up the beer and gulped down another inch before she came up for air. "Garrett just beat me fair and square. I swear I'm losing it, Cathy."

"It's probably the weather. Brings out idiots and lets amateurs win. Betcha there's a full moon out there."

"Wouldn't know. Can't see a damn thing for the clouds," Merle said.

"What's Angel working on tonight?" Cathy changed the subject. Merle only lost once in every sixth blue moon, but when she did it was because she let her opponent win so he or she would keep playing. Not often did someone really beat her, and when they did she pouted like a two-year-old who wanted chocolate candy five minutes before supper.

Merle sighed. "They are out there in that trailer talking about shale samples and how far to drill before they give up and all those important things. They're going to bring in the drilling crew for Jezzy's land next week. Looks to me like come five o'clock they could put it all away and forget it, but oh no! They've got to hash and rehash the whole thing a hundred times. She should be out here playin' a game or two with me, sucking down a few beers to loosen up, and maybe even seducing Garrett so he'll have his mind on sex rather than pool," Merle fussed.

"So she and Travis are cousins, are they?" Cathy asked.

"That's right, but best friends, too. She's always looked up to him like an older brother. Probably because his younger sister, Emma, was her best friend almost from birth. Most kids' first words are momma or daddy. Hers was Travis and she said it right plain. He's six years older than her and they've talked science since she spit out her first words. I'd never seen the boy until he showed up on New Year's Eve. It's a good thing they are cousins or I'd tell Angel to go after him. They've got everything in common," Merle said.

Cathy rounded the end of the bar and claimed a stool next to Merle. "So how'd they wind up here together?"

Merle downed an inch of beer, wiped her mouth with her hand, and said, "Travis has been workin' for Amos for several years. And I said something to Amos about Angel being at the top of her college graduating class. Guess Travis put in a word for her, too. And here they are. They always were interested in the same things. I always figured she'd end up with a rich oilman. Someone like Amos in his younger days. Don't see what that rancher has to offer, but she's free and over twenty-one and I damn sure can't talk sense to her. I'm going home before the roads get so slick I wind up in a ditch."

Cathy gave her a loose hug. "Drive careful and if you get in trouble, call me. I'll send Tinker to haul you out of the ditch."

"I appreciate it," Merle said. She stopped in the middle of the floor and wrapped her arms around Clark, a middle-aged truck driver who'd recently made the Honky Tonk his Monday night rest stop. The two of them waltzed through "Walk Me to the Door" by Conway Twitty before she left.

Cathy remembered when Buddy and Mac were the regular truck drivers on Monday night. Then Mac finally let his wife talk him into taking a day job as a dispatcher for a trucking company. And Buddy started driving the mail route between Oklahoma City and Dallas. Cathy missed them but not as much as Chigger and the Walker triplets. At least she still had Merle and Amos and her new friends Jezzy, Leroy, and Sally and now Garrett and Angel. She had no doubt that she'd see many customer changes if she stuck around as long as Daisy had.

At midnight a soft drizzle was turning everything that wasn't moving to ice. Most folks either wanted to get back out on the interstate or else to the safety and warmth of their homes. Not one person was left in the beer joint, so Tinker slipped his arms into his worn leather coat, unplugged the jukebox, and put his cooler on the bar.

"Stay in the Honky Tonk. You'll freeze," Cathy said.

"Naw, I'll just get onto my fire and stoke it up." Tinker smiled.

"I'll give you my bed and sleep on the sofa. I'm afraid for you to ride that cycle on the ice," she said.

"Don't you worry about old Tinker. I could drive that cycle through an iceberg or hell, whichever one was between me and my own pillow. Thanks for the offer." He pulled a ski mask down over his shaven head and disappeared out into the dreary night.

Cathy wasn't tired enough to prop her feet on a table and have a cold beer. She went back to her apartment where she took a warm shower, dressed for bed in an oversized sweatshirt and flannel pajama bottoms, and cuddled up with a frayed quilt and pillow on the sofa. She picked up the remote control, found the channel that played old movies all night, and settled in to watch *Steel Magnolias*.

"Back out easy and don't hit the brake if you start to slide," Travis warned when he helped Angel into her coat. "And call me when you are safe at home."

"I've driven on black ice before. Stop treating me like a kid."

"Just be careful," Travis said.

"I'll call."

He watched from one of the three oblong windows in the trailer door until the taillights of her small truck disappeared around the corner. Then his gaze went to the yellow glow from Cathy's living room window. The Honky Tonk was dark. The driveway empty. He checked the clock. It was only twelve thirty. Evidently the bad weather sent everyone home early.

A shadow moved across the window and he stepped back quickly as if she could see him staring across the distance into her private quarters. When he peeked out again the shadow was gone. He stood there for a long time wondering who Cathy really was. In the Honky Tonk she was a crackerjack bartender. After the New Year's Day dinner at Jezzy's place she was a loud cheerleader for the Dallas

Cowboys. And she whooped, hollered, and danced around when she won the pot in the middle of the coffee table. But what did she do when the Honky Tonk closed and she went home? Was she really alone or was that shadow he saw a man? Was that the reason she was so pissy about the kiss—she had a boyfriend?

He finally left the window and went to the bathroom where he took a warm shower, then changed into a pair of dark blue flannel pajama bottoms and a red thermal knit shirt.

He'd been in the trailer a week but everything was still strange, from the bed to the position of the light switch. By the time two months had passed he'd be able to maneuver in the dark and then it would be time to get used to a new place. He turned on a lamp beside his queen-sized bed and snuggled under a thick, dark brown down-filled comforter. It went with him on every job and had covered up more beds than he could count in the six years since he'd started working in the oil fields. It had been from Alaska to the tip of Maine and had made a swing through Nebraska and back to Oklahoma before settling down this time in Texas.

He'd been reading a thick mystery book by John Sandford, but he left it lying on the bedside table and laced his hands behind his head. He hoped like hell he'd made the right choice in coming to Mingus, Texas. Angel needed him in her first big step out into the real world, so when Amos gave him a choice between Mingus and the north part of the Texas panhandle, he'd quickly chosen Mingus so he could share her first victory or failure. Had it been a mistake? When he fell asleep the lamp was still burning brightly and the trailer was toasty warm.

Two hours later he awoke in pitch-black darkness, clutching the comforter to his chin. His nose was numb with cold and the hand that was outside the covers was freezing. He moved to the edge of the bed and shivered when he left the warm spot his body had created. The cold weather must have blown the breaker box because of the overload on the heater. His flashlight was in the truck, but surely he could make it from the bed to the hallway without a major catastrophe. He slung his legs over the edge of the bed and tried the lamp. Be damned if the bulb wasn't shot.

"Bedroom shouldn't be on the same circuit as the heater." He headed across the cold floor. Before he'd gone two steps he stubbed his toe on the footboard of the bed.

"Well, shit. That hurts like hell. I hope it's not bleeding all over the carpet." He hopped on one foot toward the door to turn on the light and ran into the doorframe, knocking himself backward to land on his back with his feet dangling off the bottom of the bed.

"Damn it all to hell!" he yelled as he grabbed his forehead. "I'm not going to freeze. I'm going to commit suicide by clumsiness."

The second time he shuffled across the floor and reached out like a blind man until his hands hit the wall.

"Finally." He flipped the light switch.

Nothing happened.

He tried again. Still nothing.

"What in the hell is the matter with this thing? It can't be on the same circuit as the heater. That thing has a breaker all of its own." Thirteen tries later he finally figured that the heater had overheated and blown the electricity in the whole trailer. He jerked the comforter around his shoulders, slipped his bare feet into the boots he'd left at the foot of the bed, and slowly made his way from the back of the trailer to the front. One peek out the window told the tale. Normally, lights flooded the parking lot at the Honky Tonk. It wasn't just his trailer that was in the dark; the whole area had no electricity.

"How does she have lights inside her place if everything else is out?" he asked.

He opened the door and heard the steady hum of a generator. Who'd have ever thought to purchase one of those in the middle of Texas?

"Looks like I've got two choices. Freeze or beg," he said.

He chose to beg.

———————————

Steel Magnolias was the saddest and funniest movie Cathy had ever watched and she knew the dialogue by heart. But she still cried like a jilted teenager every time she watched it. Discarded tissues cluttered the floor and she had poked a hole in the top of the second box when someone pounded on her door.

Her heart stopped. It was raining ice and the Tonk had been closed for hours. Electricity was out and she was running on a generator. Neither man nor beast would be out in that kind of weather. She tiptoed across the floor and slowly pulled down one slat of the mini-blinds on the window beside the door. One look and she let go of it like it was a red-hot poker and jumped back two feet. Bigfoot wrapped up in bearskin was standing on her porch. She peeked out again. It might not be Bigfoot but something big and brown and scary looking out there in the dark. Maybe it was a serial killer who preyed on single women who were vulnerable after watching sad movies late at night. But then it might be a homeless woman whose car had broken down and she needed to call a wrecker. Dear God, what if there were children in that car?

She made sure the chain was secure before barely opening the door an inch and keeping her distance in case it was a killer and he reached through the opening to snatch her bald-headed.

"Who are you and what do you want?" she asked.

If Bart White was trying to scare her into selling the Tonk, he'd best get his affairs in order, because he was a dead man. Crazy idiot fool anyway. First trying to buy her beer joint and then trying to frighten her. If it was him, he could sit on her porch and turn into a Popsicle for all she cared.

"I'm freezing," Travis said.

"No shit."

"Come on, Cathy. The electricity went out in my trailer and I don't have a generator. Can I please come in? I'll pay you to be warm."

She cocked her head to one side and frowned. "Travis?"

"Yes, who else would it be? I'll die by morning if I have to stay out there in that freezing tin can. I'll sleep on the floor. I brought my comforter and I can do without a pillow."

She shut the door.

He was about to turn around and head back to the trailer when he heard her moving the chain and the door opening.

"Thank you," he said.

"You'll have to stay in the Honky Tonk," she said. "You

are lucky I'm letting you walk through my place to get there and not making you go around to the front door. No men are allowed in here."

"But Amos was in here and I was, too." He clamped his mouth shut. Only a fool would argue with her when she had a generator.

She led the way through her living room and into the beer joint. "Claim as much floor space as you want. Or you can put two tables together and make a bed. If you wiggle around and fall off, though, don't beat on the door. I won't hear you."

"Could I charge a shot of whiskey? I didn't even think to pick up my wallet and bring money with me."

"I don't run tabs."

She stopped inside the door and he plowed into her back sending her forward with enough force that she had to grab the bathroom door to keep from tumbling on her face. "Good lord, Travis, be careful. I was turning on the men's room light for you so you can find your way."

"Sorry," he said sheepishly. "I didn't pick up my glasses, either, and I'm blind without them."

Every single contact he'd had with Cathy brought on a rush of hot desire. He'd always liked tall blonds, and blue eyes were a bonus. Delicate features were a plus. Being extremely intelligent was a must. Cathy fit all of those requirements except maybe the intelligence factor. It didn't take a doctorate in any subject to be able to mix up a piña colada.

But she was as prickly as a porcupine and very vocal about not being a bit interested in him, so why couldn't he control his desires? Why did he feel like a red-hot poker struck his heart every time he touched the woman? Or worse yet, why did his body react like he was a freshman in high school and had just touched a breast for the first time?

She made her way behind the bar in the dark. She picked up a bottle of Jack Daniel's and a pint jar. She poured an inch in the bottom and set it on the bar.

"I do not run tabs. I will give you a shot of whiskey to keep you from dying. God knows, I don't want to deal with a dead body tomorrow morning."

Travis tossed it back like an old gold miner in a Western movie from the fifties and wiped the back of his mouth with his hand. The warmth started at his throat and quickly spread all the way to his stomach. For the first time, he felt as if he might have a chance of surviving.

Cathy started back to her apartment. "Okay, you're on your own now. I'm going to bed. Don't even think about waking me. I do not do mornings so don't talk to me if I wander out here. Good night, Travis."

"Thank you, Cathy. I'll buy a generator tomorrow. This is a one night—"

"Sleepover!" she finished for him.

"I didn't mean to imply—"

"You've got warmth and a bathroom. Just one question—why didn't you drive to a motel?"

Travis slapped his forehead with his palm. "I was so stunned when I woke up freezing that a motel didn't even dawn on me. All I thought about was finding a warm place and your light was still burning. I'm sorry, Cathy. Thanks for the shot. Which way is the nearest motel?"

"Longhorn Inn is about ten miles back to the east of here," she said. "You are welcome to stay in the Tonk if you want. The roads are icy. It'll take a while to get there."

A wave of guilt washed over her. If the situation were reversed he would probably be a wonderful neighbor. He'd open the door, give her a blanket and pillow, and even share his home with her. She shouldn't be such a bitch even if she had just used up every bit of her compassion on a Hollywood movie.

"You are welcome to stay here," she said again.

He followed her back through the apartment. "Thanks, but I think I'd prefer a warm bed instead of a hard table."

"Are you sure?" she tried one more time.

"Thanks but no thanks," he said.

She'd tried three times and he'd refused. If he ran his truck off into a ditch and froze by morning it couldn't be her fault. Or could it? She hadn't been friendly and nice when she offered, and she'd been downright rude when she first opened the door. Why did she treat him like a leper anyway? The kiss wasn't enough to carry a grudge about. It had been damn nice.

"Thanks again. Stay warm," he said as he carefully picked his way back across the yard.

She sat down on the sofa and stared at the wall. It was a control issue. Her last boyfriend had been very nice and romantic right up to the time she crossed him and he started hitting her. If she lost her newfound control and let another man into her life, she might wind up with the same kind of situation. Two or three like that and she'd be one of those women who drew the wrong kind of men to her like flies on fresh cow patties. Even if she was attracted to Travis's type of cowboy and even if there was a possibility that he wasn't like Brad Alton, she wasn't willing to take the chance.

She sighed and went to bed.

Travis reached up under the body of his truck and felt around until his cold hands landed on the hidden key. He opened the passenger side door and grabbed the flashlight he kept in the glove box. The circular light on the frozen grass did not keep him from slipping and sliding, but it would give him light in the trailer, which had as many dangerous spots as the ice.

He dragged his comforter behind him like a frayed security blanket. The concrete steps were so slippery that he had to hold on to the handrail with both hands to navigate them. The brass door handle had a layer of ice around it and refused to turn until he chipped the ice away with his fingernails. When he was finally inside he made a wide sweep with the flashlight making sure there wasn't anything to trip him up on the way to the bedroom.

"Some neighbor Cathy is, anyway. She could have waited to make sure I was safe. I could've broke my neck and she wouldn't have known until morning. I was a fool to move to this godforsaken place. There's no oil here and if there was, it would be frozen. Texas is supposed to be hot and dry. What in the hell happened?"

He fussed and fumed all the way to the bedroom. He threw a few things into a duffel bag and reached for his glasses and wallet from the nightstand. He crammed a stocking hat on his head and slipped his cold hands into gloves, put his cell phone in his coat pocket, and found his pickup keys on the bar in the kitchen on his way out the door.

When he was safely inside his truck he heaved a heavy

sigh of relief. In half an hour he would be in a warm room with lights. Damn it all! He'd forgotten to pick up his book and he was wide awake, but he wasn't about to brave the journey back in to get it.

He inched along at a snail's pace past the Smokestack restaurant and out onto the interstate. The road had not been salted or plowed and one semi was already on its side in the median. Police cars and an ambulance lit up the dark night with their red, white, and blue flashing lights. Texans could survive hurricanes, tornadoes, grasshoppers, and blistering summers, but they weren't too good at driving on ice. Not that Travis was an expert, but he had lived in parts of the country where ice and snow were an everyday thing, so he could navigate fairly well.

What few cars were out at that ungodly hour were creeping along slower than a snail in molasses. He kept both hands on the steering wheel and wished he'd just slept on the Honky Tonk floor. The shot of whiskey made him sleepy so he kept his eyes wide open so long between blinks that they ached. What seemed like an eternity later he looked up to see the sign pointing to the exit to the Longhorn Inn. His shoulder muscles felt like he'd just stayed on a bull eight seconds when he pulled up to the office and got out of the vehicle.

The place was dark, but he hadn't expected it to be all lit up. He crossed his fingers like a little boy and hoped there was a room available when he hit the black call button beside the door.

A woman in a big thick robe with a stocking hat on her head opened the door. "We don't have a vacancy and we have no electricity. People are freezing here just like they would be at home. We won't be renting anything until the electricity comes back on." She shut the door in his face and disappeared back into the darkness.

Grown men do not cry in the freezing, drizzling rain. They don't kick the motel door down. They really do not throw themselves on the frozen grass and scream like a spoiled two-year-old. Travis wanted to do all three. He'd even pay the fine for vandalism if they'd give him his own cell in the county jail—one that had a bed and a wool blanket where he could curl up and go to sleep.

He stormed back to the truck and started the return trip back to Mingus. He would go to Merle's house. It wasn't but a couple of miles from the Honky Tonk, and she might cuss and rant about him waking them up in the wee hours of the morning but she'd understand when he told her the problem. He could sleep down in the bunker. It was stocked in case of nuclear attack with everything he'd need and even had a pool table in it, so you could bet your sweet ass she'd have a powerful generator.

When he reached the Smokestack his cell phone vibrated but he was too tense to try to drive with one hand. At the Honky Tonk parking lot he pulled off, rolled a few kinks from his neck, and looked at the phone. He'd missed a call from Angel but she'd left a text message saying that she and Merle were in a hotel in Ranger, Texas. The whole town of Mingus was without electricity. Merle's generator was out of gas. They'd been lucky enough to get the last motel room in the town.

Travis looked at the phone as if it were evil. Cathy was not going to be a happy woman when he woke her up. He got ready to beat on the door for five minutes and was surprised when she opened it the moment he hit it the first time.

She motioned him inside. "No vacancies?"

Thank the lord you are back. Now maybe I can go to sleep and get some rest without all that guilt trying to smother me. I can be a good neighbor even if I'm not willing for anything more than that.

Travis stepped into the apartment and shut the door behind him.

"You know the way into the Honky Tonk," she said. Guilt might keep her from sleeping, but he was not staying in her apartment. The way he jacked her hormones into overdrive she'd wind up losing more sleep than ever just knowing he was only a few feet away.

"I didn't bring a comforter this time," he said.

"Jesus, Mary, and Joseph! Just go to sleep on the sofa. There's a pillow and a blanket still there. I'm too tired to worry about it or you right now. Sorry, Ruby." She looked up at the ceiling.

He wondered who in the devil Ruby was and why she was apologizing to her for him sleeping on her sofa.

CHAPTER 4

"HOT DAMN," CATHY MUMBLED AS SHE THREW BACK THE quilt on her bed. The electricity was back on. The alarm clock flashed the same numbers over and over. Bright sunlight poured in the bedroom window and she could hear the drip from the roof as the ice melted.

She hopped out of bed and headed toward the kitchen to make coffee. The first cup took the beast out of her. The second one kept her from biting. After the third one she could pass for human.

The sofa was empty, so that meant Travis had awakened early, found the electricity working, and gone home. Life was so much better than it had been the night before. She picked up a few scattered tissues from the floor and tossed them into the kitchen trash before she started making coffee.

She hummed as she put extra grounds in the pot to make it stronger than normal. The battery operated clock on the kitchen wall said it was noon. No wonder she was so hungry. She reached up in the cabinets, pulled down a fresh box of strawberry Pop-Tarts, and tore open a package.

As soon as the coffee finished dripping she poured a cup and looked out the kitchen window. No deer. No rabbits. She hadn't seen the possum or even a stray cat since the trailer arrived.

A moan and movement not three feet from her made her slosh the hot coffee onto her pajama top and drop a

Pop-Tart on the floor. She jerked her head in that direction, adrenaline putting her into flight mode as it plowed through her body like a bulldozer through a kid's sandbox.

"Holy hell! You just scared the shit out of me," she said.

"Didn't mean to. I hope you're cooking a pound of bacon this morning." Travis sat down at the table and stared at her with big blue puppy-dog eyes. "I feel like hell and I'm starving."

"Electricity is back on. Go cook your own breakfast," she said when she could breathe again.

"Please. It was a tough night. If you were starving and you'd driven on the ice to a motel only to find no vacancies, I'd cook you breakfast."

He had a pitiful look on his face, which was even sexier without the wire-rimmed glasses.

She bit back a grin. He wasn't about to see her smile after keeping her awake most of the night—partly out of guilt and the rest out of nothing but pure lust. "Stop acting like you are dyin'. Where were you anyway? You weren't on the sofa."

"I *am* dyin'. I ain't got the energy to make it to the door much less across our yards and then cook my own breakfast. Nearly frozen and then starved. It's a sorry way to die. Reason I wasn't on the couch is the damned thing is too short. I curled up in the corner of the floor with the quilt and pillow. Call the undertaker. Tell the coroner that I died of starvation because you were too stingy to feed a hungry neighbor. God can decide whether to lay murder to your list of sins when you die," he said.

"How hungry are you?" she asked.

"Just shy of passin' plumb out."

She poured a cup of coffee and set it in front of him. "You can stay for breakfast but only because I don't want to drag your dead body out in the yard."

"You are an angel. A pound of bacon and six eggs over easy might keep me out of the undertaker's reach."

She set the box of Pop-Tarts in the middle of the table.

"That's not eggs," he said.

She opened it. "Pretend it's one of Denny's Grand Slam specials or a McDonald's sausage biscuit meal deal. I really don't care which. It will keep you from starving. I'm not cooking breakfast today."

He moaned again and tore into the package. "They're cold."

"Bitch, bitch, bitch. Coffee is hot. Dip 'em if you want a hot breakfast."

"You are mean," he muttered.

"Me? I let you sleep here when it was against the rules. I'm feeding you breakfast. You better play nice or I'll throw you out in the slush pit in your bare feet."

He dipped the strawberry-flavored pie dough in his coffee. Pretending couldn't make it bacon and eggs and he couldn't stretch his imagination far enough to make it a warm cinnamon roll straight from the oven, either.

"Talk to me while I eat this sumptuous meal," he said.

"I cooked. You talk."

"You already know about me. I told my family story at the dinner table on Sunday," he said.

"And you know mine. Daisy and I are all that's left of the family. Her dad died before she was born and her mother in a car wreck. Cancer got my dad. Heart attack got my mother. All died young. The end."

"How long you been a bartender?" he asked.

"Legally, since I was twenty-one."

"What does that mean?"

"Worked some dives that didn't ask me how old I was before I was twenty-one."

He raised an eyebrow. "How long before you were twenty-one?"

"I was sixteen. Momma got sick one night. She and Daisy's momma were both bartenders. I filled in for her. Anytime she was sick after that I worked. It just evolved."

Cathy wished he'd eat his pseudo bacon and eggs and go on home. It was too early to talk and way too early to answer questions.

"I couldn't live like that," he said.

"Hey, I don't want a pity party. I don't have a single complaint about the way I've lived. Well, maybe one, but it had nothing to do with what I do for a living. My dad was a wonderful man. He worked nights until he got sick and my mother was a great person. We weren't rich but we had a lot of love in our trailer house. So don't go judging me."

"I wasn't judging," he said defensively.

"Oh, honey, you were. Your eyes judged me even if your words didn't."

Travis pushed the chair back and stood up so quickly that his movement was a blur. "Thank you for breakfast and the use of your quilt and pillow. I'll try not to bother you again."

"Well, lah-tee-damn-dah, if he hasn't gotten his rich little underbritches in a wad. Pick up your trash before you go running off." She pointed at the pastry wrapper on the table.

He grabbed it and shoved it into his pocket. "You really are a bear in the morning."

"You were forewarned. You should have snuck out the door and left me alone," she said.

He whipped around at the door. "Know what tames a bear?"

"Sure, I do. Honey. But you haven't got enough and there ain't enough in the whole state of Texas to tame me, so don't go getting any ideas."

He stormed out without saying anything else. She opened up a second package of Pop-Tarts and carried the two strawberry-flavored pastries to the sofa where she picked up the remote and pushed the power button.

"I'm not feeling one bit guilty for being a bear, Mr. Travis Henry. Not one single bit. Take it or leave it."

CHAPTER 5

ON FRIDAY NIGHT EVERY ABLE-BODIED, BEER-DRINKING partier from Mineral Wells to Abilene was out looking for a good time. Toby Keith's "I Love This Bar" had folks on the dance floor. Cathy looked around as she drew up a beer. Toby was right. There were hookers if those women over there in the corner could be judged by their outfits and their wandering eyes. There were lookers, both good, bad, and ugly. Preppies sitting at the bar with Grey Goose martinis and hippies at a table with their tats and bandanas tied around their foreheads drinking their beer from Mason jars. And the thing that they all had in common was that they all loved the Honky Tonk and couldn't wait to get there.

Merle came in early with Angel but Travis wasn't with them. Cathy hid her disappointment and then got angry with herself for being disappointed anyway. Hadn't she decided once and for all that she was not going to be attracted to Travis Henry even if he was tall, blond, and sexy?

She consciously stopped frowning and smiled when Jezzy, Sally, and Leroy arrived. All she needed was for Jezzy to start her matchmaking. She was every bit as bad as Chigger's mother. If Cathy didn't know better she'd swear those two were in cahoots and working together to get her married off.

Tinker checked at least thirty IDs in a group of young people who came in right behind Jezzy's group. As soon as they were allowed in the place, they made a dash for the bar.

"Need some help?" Sally asked. "I'm not much good at mixing drinks, but I can sure draw beer and pop off lids."

"Yes, ma'am, and thank you," Cathy said.

She rounded the end of the bar, pushed the swinging doors open, and started serving beers. Cathy mixed two pitchers of hurricanes and set them along with six pint jars on a tray. A lady paid her and carried them back to a table where her friends waited.

"Pitcher of margaritas, please," a fellow at the end of the bar yelled above "Honky Tonk Life" by Darryl Worley. He sang about the girls there being prettier than any place they ever played and an atmosphere of blue-collar come-as-you-are. Cathy nodded at the man who wanted margaritas but she was really agreeing with Worley. She loved the blue-collar atmosphere of the Honky Tonk, too. If she didn't, she'd be sitting behind a desk crunching numbers.

Sally pulled the handle marked "Coors" and said, "That song about slow dancing with a memory sounds about right, doesn't it? I do that at night sometimes. I put on music and dance around the bedroom and pretend it's with Kirk."

Cathy barely nodded.

"Here comes Garrett with Merle's empty jar. Guess she's going to give him another lesson," Cathy said.

"Merle loves her beer almost as much as Jezzy. Jezzy calls mixed drinks jacked-up Kool-Aid and says that good whiskey should never be diluted with soda pop. I hear you parted with a shot of whiskey for your man during the ice storm," Sally said.

"How'd you find out about that? And he's not my man," Cathy protested.

"Gossip vine. Travis told Angel who told Merle who told Jezzy. So did you sleep with him?"

"I did not," Cathy said indignantly.

Garth Brooks started singing "Good Ride Cowboy" and a dozen lusty women hit the floor for a fast line dance. If Toby could sit at the Honky Tonk, he could easily write another song about them. There were the model-thin ladies in their skintight jeans and boots with barely enough on the top to keep them out of jail. Then there were the ones who'd either given birth or indulged in too many beers and had a chubby rim around their tummies that jiggled when they scooted up and down the floor in a line dance. There were those who barely had passed their twenty-first birthday and were still young and bright-eyed and those who'd never see fifty again, whose eyes told stories about living hard and fast. Yep, old Toby could sure enough tell a tale in song about the boot-kicking girls on the floor if he'd been there.

Cathy hummed with the music as she made a blender full of hurricanes for a middle-aged lady who was showing off for the younger crowd. When the song ended she paid for the pitcher and carried it and six pint jars to a nearby table.

"Don't Call Him a Cowboy" started playing and the woman hit the floor again, moving like a pole dancer without a pole.

Cathy sang along with Conway Twitty about not calling him a cowboy until she'd seen him ride. High color filled her cheeks as she thought of Travis and the way he looked that morning at her breakfast table. After a night of wild sex with him would she be able to truly call him a cowboy? Searing hot flashes set her on fire at a visual of him all tangled up in the sheets and her long legs.

"Now where in the hell did that come from?" she mumbled.

"What?" Sally asked.

"My mind was in the gutter."

"Who was in it with you?"

Cathy didn't answer.

"Was it Travis Henry?" Sally teased.

Cathy still didn't answer.

"Hey, it would make sense. He's the first man who slept in the apartment and you even gave him a shot of whiskey to warm him up. Cold man. Warm whiskey. Cold night. You really expect me to believe he slept on the floor?"

Cathy sputtered. "Yes, I do, and you know more than a little gossip. 'Fess up."

Sally laughed as she drew up two beers and handed them to Garrett. "He and Angel came to the ranch for soil samples. Ate supper with us. He said you were an old bear in the morning."

"She wouldn't be an old bear if she'd marry me. I'd treat her so good that she'd be a sweetheart in the morning," Clark said from the end of the bar.

"It'll take someone just as mean as her to tame her and you ain't that mean," Sally said.

"Well, thank you so much," Cathy said.

Travis grabbed a barstool when a cowboy left it for the dance floor. "She's speaking the pure gospel truth. I ain't never seen anyone bite as hard as her in the mornin.'"

Cathy jerked her head around from the blender and swore under her breath. How in the hell had he gotten in the door without her seeing him?

"Give me a Coors please. Longneck," Travis said.

Cathy wiped off a bottle and flipped the lid off. She set it on the bar in front of him. She wasn't taking chances on their hands brushing, not after those naughty thoughts that had danced through her mind. He handed her a five-dollar bill. She made change. He carried the beer back to the pool tables where Garrett and Angel were in a heated game. Clark followed him and picked a cue stick from the wall. Travis racked up the balls and took a long draw of his beer.

"You ever been bow huntin'?" Merle asked.

"Yes, I have," Travis said.

"Then draw that cue stick back like you was drawin' back a bow. And move your body into the shoot for more power. Scatter them balls so the pickin's will be easier," she said.

"Think Travis will beat Clark if he listens to Merle?" Cathy asked.

"Guess if he loses his shirt and his home and his truck, he can always sleep on your sofa," Sally said.

"It's too short. He slept on the floor," Cathy said before she thought.

"Shame on you. That sofa makes out into a bed. I know it does because I've heard you talk about sleeping on it until Daisy got married. I don't even like cowboys and I would have at least let him have the sofa."

Cathy shrugged. "He didn't ask."

Before Sally could shoot back a reply a lady popped a hip up on a barstool and said, "Martini, please."

Cathy sized up the newcomer. "Shaken?"

"Stirred, please," the woman said.

Cathy picked up the gin, vermouth, and the olive jar and set them on the work counter. The jeans were new, the Western shirt looked like one of Merle's creations, and the boots were scuffed. Had Hayes sent in a different buyer with hopes of getting Cathy to sell to a woman?

She set the martini in front of the lady. "Haven't seen you around these parts."

The woman sipped the martini. "Very good. Just right. You must be Cathy O'Dell?"

"I am and if you are here with intentions of making an offer for the Tonk you are wasting your time. It's not for sale."

The woman had brown eyes, straight black hair, high cheekbones, and a wide mouth. No doubt about it, she'd been dipped in an Indian genetic woodpile.

"This is a very good martini and I'm not here to buy this place. I just came in for a drink and a good time," she said.

"Are you a messenger from Hayes Radner?"

"I'm not a messenger for anyone, honey. What's he got to do with this place anyway?"

Cathy looked her right in the eye. "Hayes wants to buy the Honky Tonk and all of Mingus to build an amusement park."

The lady smiled. "And evidently you are not interested in unloading your beer joint?"

"Hell no! The Tonk is not for sale. It's mine and I don't give a damn if he offers me every bit of the rest of the state of Texas for this beer joint. It still won't be for sale. He can put that on his toilet paper and wipe his sorry ass with it."

"Well, I'm not here to buy anything for Hayes Radner. I've never met or talked to the man. I came in for a good martini and now I've got one."

"And you are?" Cathy asked.

"Larissa Morley."

"You ain't from these parts. Your accent isn't quite right and you don't usually wear boots and jeans," Cathy said.

Larissa smiled brightly. "You're good, girl. You ever think about doing detective work?"

"Comes from years of bartending. So what are you? A reporter doing a piece about women beer joint owners or something?" Cathy asked.

Travis leaned in between the woman and the man on the barstool next to her. "Hey, I lost the first game so give me a beer for Clark. He says he's spittin' dust."

Larissa's eyes traveled from his boots up to his pretty blue eyes. "Hello, handsome."

"Hi, who are you?" Travis asked.

"That's a blunt pickup line," she said.

"I ain't pickin' up. I'm playin' pool. You know how to play?" he asked.

"Not me." She shook her head. "I'm Larissa Morley—and you are?"

"Travis Henry. Nice to meet you, Larissa. Excuse me." He picked up the beer and carried it carefully to the pool table.

"Don't let him deflate your ego. He's not housebroken yet," Cathy said.

"Your boyfriend?" Larissa asked.

Cathy sputtered. "No, ma'am."

"Hmmmm," Larissa said.

"Where are you from?" Cathy asked.

"Mingus. I own a house right smack in the middle of town. Maybe I'll stop by another night." She downed the rest of her martini and set her sights for the door. A couple of cowboys asked her to dance on the way but she brushed them off coldly.

Sally poked Cathy in the ribs. "Did you see the way she was sizing up Travis?"

"Of course I did. I'm not blind. Why would anyone move to Mingus, Texas?"

"You did. Don't judge the woman. And don't judge Travis, either."

Cathy cut her eyes around at Sally. "You taking up for him?"

"I'm stating facts. You've been all pissy lately. That cowboy has flat out got under your skin, hasn't he?"

"Why are you asking? Are you interested in him?"

"No, I am not. I have a boyfriend who is in Iraq. When he comes home in six months we are getting married. Daddy doesn't like the idea of me marrying career military but it's my life. Larissa Morley don't look like she was used to wearing jeans and boots and those nails weren't used to hard work neither."

Cathy looked down at her hands. "Wonder who she really is or if that's her real name. Larissa? Sounds kind of fishy don't it."

"Sounds hoity-toity to me," Sally said.

In a few minutes Sally touched Cathy's arm and nodded toward the dance floor. Rudy, one of Garrett's hired hands, was showing Larissa how to two-step to "The Thunder Rolls" by Garth Brooks. She seemed to be picking up the steps easily and laughing good naturedly when she did something wrong.

Cathy frowned. "When did she come back?"

"Don't know. I'm going to get a beer and leave it with you. Things have slowed down," Sally said. "And I'd appreciate it if you didn't mention the idea of a summer wedding.

Daddy gets all riled every time I say anything about marrying Kirk."

"Thanks for the help, and your secret is safe with me." Cathy grinned.

Someone put more money in the jukebox and Billy Currington sang that God was great, beer was good, and people were crazy.

"Damn straight," Cathy said aloud.

"Damn straight about what?" Travis asked.

"That people are crazy," she said.

"You got that right. I need an apple martini for Angel. Merle's going to give me some more pointers while we shoot a game," Travis said.

Cathy made the martini and handed it to Travis.

She tried to ignore him by watching Rudy two-stepping Larissa around the room to a slow song. The two of them were as mismatched as... Cathy stopped herself from thinking as she and Travis were. Instead she told herself that Larissa was probably married to a rich man and they'd had a fight. Her husband was a two-bit cheating bastard and she was on the prowl to pay him back. Poor old Rudy might get lucky, but come morning she'd be right back in her little Porsche or Lexus or maybe even a chauffeur-driven limo sitting out in the parking lot, going home to her husband who had a fortune in oil money or owned an exotic resort island where she was really the queen.

Big and Rich began singing about being lost in the moment and Cathy felt sorry for Rudy. He might be lost in the moment with the rich lady who had her arms around his neck. Come morning, he'd be singing the blues worse than Hank Williams.

The movement of Tinker hurrying across the floor to a table in the far corner took her attention from Larissa to where two young cowboys were bowed up like a couple of old roosters, feathers all fluffed out and eyeing each other through bloodshot eyes, daring the other one to throw the first blow. Tinker waded into them like a father about to thump two little boys' heads together. He said a few low words and escorted them both to the door. He didn't care if there was a bloodletting after they were out of the Honky Tonk, but it was his job inside the beer joint to keep stains off the hardwood floors. Two tomcats having a pissing contest didn't faze him.

Cathy would love to know what he said to the rowdies that sent them outside without argument. Did he tell them how hungry the buzzards were back behind the Tonk and how they'd be right glad to eat pickled cowboy for breakfast?

Cathy saw that Larissa had traded Rudy in for another of Garrett's hired hands. Maybe Rudy wasn't tough enough for the citified martini-drinking woman who was out slumming that night. Jake did look a little more rough with his goatee and tattoo of a tiger peeking out from under the rolled up sleeve of his shirt.

At closing time Tinker made the announcement that the Honky Tonk would shut down in five minutes. What customers were left found their coats and were gone in a few minutes. He carried a six-pack of empty soda cans to the bar and picked up his paycheck.

"Been a rowdy night," he said.

"Yes, it has. What did you say to those men, Tinker?" Cathy asked.

A slight grin turned up the corners of his mouth. "Old

Indian secret. If I tell, it might take the magic away from it. See you tomorrow night, Cathy."

"You're not Indian," she called out as he crossed the floor.

"No I'm not, but my secret is Apache."

"Where'd you get an Apache secret?" she asked.

"My friend who was in Vietnam. Good night," he said as he pulled on his coat and left.

She popped the lid off a longneck bottle of Coors and carried it to the nearest table. For all the rowdiness the place wasn't in too bad of shape. Empty beer bottles had been pushed to the middle of the tables. Very little trash littered the floor but beer had been sloshed out of the jars in several places, so it would require a thorough mopping the next day.

She propped her feet on the table and tilted the chair back to the wall. She took a long draw on the beer and enjoyed the icy cold liquid as it slid all the way to her stomach. One more song was left on the jukebox so she listened to Jason Aldean sing about her being country from her cowboy boots to the songs she sings.

"That's my story," she said as she kept time with her foot. "I'm a hick to the bone. Nothing here for Travis Henry to be interested in, so why in the devil can't I get him out of my mind?"

Travis cussed the key into opening the door of his trailer. He hadn't been buzzed since high school. There was that night when he and the football boys had a secret party and he'd gotten really plastered. The next morning he had awakened with a headache and figured he was in big trouble with his father. But his dad had played dumb and told him at the breakfast table they would be cutting wood all day for the fireplace. The chain saw felt like it was cutting through his brain and he vowed never to get drunk again. He hadn't until that night and he couldn't even remember why he'd had more than one beer. It had something to do with Cathy, the bartender, looking so cute in that tight black top and those hip slung jeans. The way they hugged her rear end had made his mouth dry and his hands want to cup a hip in each of them.

Why had that one kiss affected him like that anyway? He was almost thirty years old and had been in three serious relationships. Not engaged but not far from it, and now a barmaid's kiss heated him up and set him to thinking thoughts that had no place in his world.

He left a string of clothing from the front office through the kitchen and down the hall. By the time he reached the bathroom he was naked and shivering. He leaned against the edge of the shower and turned on the water. Nothing happened. He frowned, cocked his head to one side, and twisted the handles on the sink. Nothing there either. Without thinking he flushed the potty. The water swirled away but none came back up.

All the beer he'd drunk hit at that moment and his bladder felt like it would explode.

"Well, damn it all to hell! First no electricity and now no water. I swear someone is trying to tell me to take my sorry ass away from here." He stumbled down the hall to his bedroom, then jerked on a pair of jeans and a T-shirt from off the dirty clothes hamper.

Cathy had just stepped out of the shower when she heard hard pounding on the back door. She hurriedly threw on a terrycloth bathrobe and headed in that direction. When she reached the living room it sounded as though someone was trying to tear the door off the hinges. She peeked out the window to see Travis hugging his body and shivering.

The first thing she did was check the electricity. It was on in her place and there was light showing in the trailer window. She slung open the door and he rushed inside.

"Damn, Travis, don't you have any better sense than to run around in your bare feet in the cold?" she asked.

"I'm buzzed and I'm not thinking straight and there's no water in my trailer. Can I use your bathroom?"

She sighed. "You know where it is."

He hurried down the hallway and shut the door with a bang. She sank down on the sofa and waited.

In a few seconds the potty flushed. The shower started and stopped ten seconds later. "Well, shit!" His deep voice carried to the living room.

Travis reappeared. "I forgot my pajamas. Got to run back out to the trailer and get them."

She frowned.

"It's either that or knock on your door every time I have to take a leak all night," he said.

"Then go get 'em. And put your boots on. You're going to catch pneumonia in your bare feet."

He gave her a thumbs-up and took off, leaving the door wide open.

"At least the storm door shut." She went to the door and watched him gallop across the yard and into the trailer. A minute later he was jogging back toward her with a bundle of clothing. He kicked off his boots at the door and frowned. "Crap! I forgot to bring socks."

"You can borrow a pair of mine. I've got white tube socks that'll fit you," she said.

"Thanks, Cathy." He grinned and hurried to the bathroom again.

She couldn't leave him out there in a trailer with no running water and she couldn't let him stay in the apartment. The rule said no men and it had served both Ruby and Daisy very well.

She sighed and looked up at the ceiling. "Okay, Ruby, it looks like it's time for us to have a sit-down. This rule about no men in the apartment worked fine for you and for Daisy. But neither of you had a neighbor living right across the backyard. So the rule has got to go. I can't let him freeze or live with no water, either. So are you going to sit on my bedpost and haunt me?"

No strange icy wind blew past her and no apparition knocked the sugar bowl or salt shakers from the table so she decided Ruby was all right with the idea. Travis was singing the song about a honky tonk badonkadonk when she passed the bathroom door on the way to her bedroom. She wondered what woman in the beer joint had brought that particular song to mind that night but couldn't come up with a single one. She put on a pair of red flannel pajama bottoms and an oversized sweatshirt, brushed back her wet hair, and picked up a set of sheets from the linen closet.

When he came out of the bathroom she had the sofa bed made up with an extra quilt folded across the bottom. He wore navy pajama bottoms and a gray long sleeved thermal knit shirt. Water droplets hung on his hair and his glasses were fogged over. Her hands went clammy at the sight of him standing there like some kind of mythical god. Her breath caught in her chest when the fresh scent of soap and shampoo wafted across the room.

He stopped in his tracks and stared at the bed. "Why didn't you tell me it made out into a bed?"

"You didn't ask. Need some coffee to get that buzz out of your head?"

"Do you have tea?"

"Not green. Have some plain old tea bags. Want me to put one in a cup and microwave it?" she asked.

"That would be wonderful and thank you."

She remembered that he liked sugar and cream and added both. She gave him his tea and sat down in the rocking chair. When he sat on the end of the bed their knees were practically touching. Close enough that he wanted to wiggle slightly and feel the warmth of her leg next to his, but touching her could send him straight back out to the trailer to live without water, so he adjusted his position.

"What happened to your water?"

"Don't know but I'll find out come morning. I hope the pipes aren't frozen. Amos will throw a shoe at some plumbers if they've frozen and burst. Maybe I ought to check them tonight?"

"It hasn't been that cold. You can figure out the problem when morning comes," she said.

They looked up at the same time. He moved forward a few inches to find her doing the same, and their lips met without any other parts of their bodies touching. The fiery embrace had them both panting before they finally broke away. She sat up straight in her rocker, sipped the

coffee—which was cold compared to the fire in her lips—
and seriously wondered if they'd shared a kiss or if she'd
imagined it.

"Damn!" he said.

"What?" she asked.

"That was hot!"

So it really had happened. She touched her mouth.
Blazes didn't burn her hand. It was really quite cool. "Yes, it
was, and now I'm going to bed."

"Okay, and thanks for giving me a bed and a bathroom."

"You are welcome." She set her empty cup on the table.
She shut her bedroom door and stretched out on her bed with
a book she'd been reading for more than a week. She hoped
the characters would take her mind off that steamy kiss, but
as luck would have it she'd reached the three-page sex scene in
the book. She read all the way through it, tossed the book on
the nightstand, and laced her fingers behind her head as she
replayed what she'd read, putting Travis in the hero's place.

"Damn, damn!" She swore as she sat up and beat her
pillow into a more comfortable position. She heard something that sounded almost like music. She cracked open the
door to hear Travis humming in his sleep. Or maybe he was
still awake. She hoped so. If she couldn't sleep then it was
only fair that his tea kept him awake, too.

Travis hummed "Honky Tonk Badonkadonk" and
thought about how often he'd stared at Cathy's cute little
fanny every time her back was turned. The words to the
song asked just how she did get them britches on? Travis
didn't care how she got them on; he wanted to take them
off. He pulled the covers up and shut his eyes and dreamed
of her again that night.

CHAPTER 6

"My head still hurts." Travis was sitting in the middle of the sofa bed with a beer in his hand. "Hair of the dog thing," he explained. "I left the money for it on the bar."

Cathy looked fine in her tight jeans and black sweater, but Travis's head hurt too badly to even think about her honky tonk badonkadonk.

"I'll make coffee. Want tea?" Cathy asked.

"And breakfast?" Travis asked.

"Don't push your luck. I've got Pop-Tarts and I could make cinnamon toast."

"Toast please."

The sound of truck tires crunching on the parking lot right outside the door made her start in that direction. She had the door open before Amos knocked. He held out a box of doughnuts. "You got coffee. I got pastries."

"Come on in. Travis didn't have water last night, so he stayed on my sofa. Ruby and I had a talk and I don't think she's going to practice any voodoo on me," she said.

"Doughnuts! Amos, you are a saint," Travis said.

"I'd say you had one too many last night if you're already drinking this morning." Amos sat down at the table and opened the box to reveal a dozen assorted doughnuts, long johns, and cinnamon rolls.

"On your way to the office?" Cathy asked. He wore an expensive three-piece suit and a bright blue tie.

"Yes, I am. Got time to talk?"

"What's on your mind?" Cathy filled three coffee cups and set them on the table. She picked up a cinnamon roll and dipped the edge in her coffee.

Amos looked at Travis. "You ask her?"

She looked up so fast her hand slipped and she dropped the roll in the coffee. She fished it out and hurriedly ate the part that was soggy. "Ask me what?"

Travis shook his head. "I wasn't sure you wanted me to."

She wiped her mouth with a paper napkin and said, "Please tell me you aren't putting more trailers in."

Amos shook his head. "Nothing like that. But I was tellin' Merle about my problem and she told me how you are doing her taxes. So I did some checking and was amazed at what I found."

"You want me to do your taxes?" Cathy asked.

"I want more than that. The accountant I hired to work for Angel had a car wreck last night. She was supposed to be here come Monday morning to start runnin' the office. Angel and Travis can't do that and keep up with the rig work. She'll be out of commission at least two months, so this is a temporary job. I'll pay you big bucks. You name the price. I thought maybe that was why Travis looked so down in the mouth tonight. I told him if we didn't find a bookkeeper he and Angel had to trade off days and stay in the office."

Cathy started shaking her head before the part about the big bucks. "Hell no!"

"Start at noon and be off by five. I wouldn't make you work mornings. It would be dangerous for the clients," Amos teased.

"Please!" Travis begged.

"No!" Cathy pulled an errant strand of blond hair back into her ponytail and shook her head again.

"You can work in your jeans and T-shirts. I wouldn't make you dress up. You can walk to work. No expenses on your part. Paycheck at the end of each week and a five thousand dollar bonus when Maggie is able to come to work."

"I'll leave candy and cookies on the bar and ice cream in the freezer," Travis said.

She hesitated before she spit out another no.

"I know you are a bartender, but I also know now that you are an accountant with a college degree in business finance," Amos said.

"Why are you runnin' a bar if you are a high-powered accountant?" Travis asked.

"It's a long story and I'm too busy to tell it tonight," she said.

"Don't make sense to me." Travis picked up a glazed doughnut. "Please come to work for us. I'll do anything up to and including cooking for you. Supper a couple of times a week. Breakfast every morning."

"What makes you think I can't cook?"

"Pop-Tarts!" He frowned.

"I can make my own food, thank you very much. What else have you got to tempt me with?" She considered it as she finished off the roll and reached for a chocolate iced doughnut. It would never work. The fire she had for him wasn't going away until she poured enough water on it to extinguish the flames. There wasn't that much water in Palo Pinto County. And the flames would set her on fire if she had to be close to him in a small trailer every day.

But the whole idea is that he'll be in the field and you'll be in the trailer alone all afternoon doing the paperwork. It's nothing more than you did in Mena, and you know damn well that you've missed that work. It's what you were educated to do. You can have both worlds for a couple of months.

"Want some time to think about it or is the answer a definite no?" Amos asked.

"It's a definite maybe hell no," she said.

"Good enough. If you want the job go to work tomorrow at noon. If you don't show I'll start interviewing temp applicants. Maybe I'll make Angel do the interviews for me." Amos brushed a bit of glaze from the lapel of his jacket.

"You think she and Garrett are getting serious?" Cathy asked.

"Oh, yeah. She stayed at the farm last night," Travis said. "So you going to take the job?"

She shrugged. "What kind of ice cream you got?"

"Whatever kind you want. I'll make a trip to the store and stock up. Name your poison. Are you really civil by noon?" He wished he could take the words back as soon as he uttered them.

"What difference would it make? You'll be in the field with Angel so I won't bite you," she said. Good grief, had she just made up her mind to take the job? First she tossed out Ruby's rule and now she was contemplating another job. Would that be Honky Tonk adultery? Was it a sin?

Another rapping on the door turned their attention that way. She laid her doughnut on a napkin and eased around the sofa bed. When she opened the door Angel walked in and headed for the kitchen table.

"Food and coffee. Life is good," she said.

"Help yourself," Cathy said.

"Be careful, though. She bites in the mornings," Travis said.

"Looks like she was good enough to let you spend the night on her sofa for whatever reason," Angel said.

"I'm only grumpy until my third cup of coffee, but I'm not *that* mean." Cathy was glad for Angel's diversion to give her time to think about Amos's proposition.

Travis pushed back a blond curl tickling his eyebrow. "Amos says she gets a rabies shot every year."

Amos threw up his palms defensively. "Hey, I'm trying to get her to work for me. Don't drag me into a fight between you two."

Cathy ignored him and looked at Angel. "What brings you out so early?"

"To see if Amos talked you into coming to work for us. I'm here to beg if you didn't say yes. Did I get here before you turned him down?"

"Just barely," Travis said.

Cathy shot him an evil look.

"You sure about that rabies shot?" Travis asked Amos.

"I told you to keep me out of this." Amos grinned.

Cathy set a cup of coffee in front of Angel. Her small dining area was full with four people. If anyone else came knocking, they'd have to sit on the floor.

Travis held up his cup for a refill before Cathy sat back down. "I was only teasing about the rabies shot, but she's surly until she's had a pot or two of coffee. Just remember that and you'll get along fine."

Angel frowned. "Stop teasing and tell me that she's going to work for us. I hate to be cooped up in the office as much as you do."

Cathy was warming up to the offer so quickly that it made her head spin.

"So?" Travis asked.

"What?" She needed more time. She couldn't bring herself to take it at that moment, yet she didn't want to close the door to the possibility.

"You going to take the job?"

"Why should I?"

"I hate being stuck in an office. It's like prison. I can't breathe. All I do is pace the floor and want out. I feel like a caged animal."

Their eyes locked in the middle of the table. Sparks danced around the crowded room like pole dancers in a strip joint. He could see flashes of color bouncing off her dark blue eyes. She felt like she was standing in front of an old open-face heater.

"Say something. Don't just stare at me like that," he said.

Her face began to burn. "I'm thinkin' about it."

"Hell, woman, spit out what's on your mind. You women are always beatin' around the bush. No wonder men don't understand you." He wanted to kiss her so bad his lips hurt. To taste the sweetness again, to see if it was as good as it had been the night before.

She whispered, "I am not a hard woman to understand. I just don't know if I want to take on a second job."

Angel tapped Travis on the shoulder. "What's going on here? You two drawin' a line in the dirt and spittin' on your knuckles?" She looked from one to the other so quickly that her kinky ponytail flopped back and forth.

Cathy stood up. "Give me time to think about it, okay?"

Travis drew his eyebrows together in a single line and pressed his fingertips to his forehead. Women! His sisters said they were from Venus and men were from Mars. Well, that wasn't so hard to understand. He'd be willing to bet that when little girl babies were born an ethereal being snatched their souls and took them to live on an all-female planet for thirteen years. When they hit puberty they slung them back to earth and men had to try to understand the impossible from that age on.

Angel waved a hand between them to break the tension. "Both of us hate to be cooped up in an office. Please come to work for us! We're working on a tight deadline and we're both needed at the rig. Believe me, you won't see hardly anyone in the office."

"Give me until tonight. I'll think about it until then," she said.

"Fair enough. Me and a bunch of the bikers are planning to come to the Honky Tonk tonight so we'll talk then," Amos said.

"Please," Angel whispered as she followed Amos out the door.

Travis grabbed another doughnut, put it in his mouth, and started making the bed.

"Get on out of here. I'll do that. You are probably already late for work," she said.

"Thanks," Travis said around the pastry and darted out the door in his bare feet.

The Honky Tonk was absolutely rocking an hour after they opened that night. The jukebox wasn't quiet one second and the dance floor always had at least a dozen people two-stepping or even more doing line dances.

Travis arrived at ten o'clock and hiked a hip on the last remaining barstool.

"Hey, good-lookin'. You from around these parts?" The girl next to him winked.

"Just for a couple of months. Where y'all from?" Travis asked.

"We're at a family reunion in Mineral Wells and had to get away for a while," she said.

"How'd you know about the Honky Tonk?" Cathy asked.

"One of the cousins is from down in Huckabay. He's been here before and said it's got the best dance floor around. Got a tray? I'll take them in two trips," she said.

"Hey, Travis, you up for a game?" Merle asked.

"No, my mind wouldn't be on it," he said honestly.

Cathy worked at the other end of the bar, barely keeping up with the orders. She wished Sally would show up and offer to draw beers while she mixed drinks. Maybe she should offer the schoolteacher a job on Friday and Saturday nights.

Yeah, right, can't you just see that? Schoolteacher working as a bartender in the Honky Tonk. That would send her superintendent and half the Bible-totin' parents of her students into a whirlwind.

She caught up just in time to start over. The kids who'd escaped the family reunion were ready for refills. The tall red-haired girl who had ordered the first round showed up with empty trays. She wore her jeans slung low and her skin-tight knit top short enough to show a belly button ring and was evidently the designated driver because she was not drinking. She delivered them to the table and two-stepped through "Broken Road" by Rascal Flatts with Rudy.

Cathy was working on a pitcher of hurricanes when she looked up to see the girl at the bar again. "Be with you in a minute," she said.

"I got to stay sober and drive these yahoos home tonight. Want some help? I'm twenty-two, got my bartender's card, and would rather be working than sitting," she said.

"You are hired," Cathy said.

"I'd have helped if you'd asked me," Travis said.

Cathy smiled. "Are you twenty-two and own a bartender's card?"

"I'm more'n twenty-two so that should make up for not having a card," he said.

The girl efficiently filled an order for a martini and then went to work on a tequila sunrise. "I'm Mindy. Live over in Mineral Wells. Used to work at the Lazy Circle Bar before it shut down."

"I'm Cathy and the whining cowboy is Travis," she said.

Travis narrowed his eyes. "I'm not whining."

"I think he's cute," Mindy said.

Travis grinned. "Thank you."

"Looks like that movie star, the blond one. What's his name? He played in *The Wedding Planner*. Matthew McConaughey. That's who he looks like."

Travis grinned bigger.

"Don't feed his ego," Cathy said.

Mindy giggled and set up a clean blender to make a piña colada.

"Want a job on Friday and Saturday nights?" Cathy asked.

"Not really. I'm usually out with my boyfriend those nights. He's off on a conference trip to Germany this weekend so I'm out partying with my rowdy Oklahoma relatives. I work all week at a computer consulting firm."

"I'll work for you on Friday and Saturday nights if you'll take the job for Amos," Travis offered. "For free. I might not be able to brew up whatever she's doing, but you can do that and I can draw beer. See, the handles are even marked so I wouldn't make a mistake."

"Deal," she said.

"Are you serious?"

"I am very serious. You work for me those nights and I'll work for Amos, but remember..." She looked up and almost lost her train of thought. "Just remember that Amos is my boss."

"I'll be your superior, since it'll be my house you are working in," Travis argued.

"And I will be your boss two nights a week and you will answer to me. Remember that if you get all cocky." She smiled again.

"I'd dang sure hire him if I owned a bar. Lord, the women would flock in here to buy drinks," Mindy whispered.

"Then they'd start fighting over him," Cathy said out the side of her mouth.

"What kind of secrets are you two tellin'?" Travis raised his voice above Garth Brooks singing about beer for his horses.

"We don't tell our secrets. It's a woman thing," Mindy answered.

Travis yelled across the room at Amos who'd claimed a table with his biker buddies. "She says yes."

"Well hallelujah. Make me a fancy martini and I will definitely celebrate," Amos said.

"What are you celebrating?" Mindy asked.

"Cathy is going to work for me. I won't have to waste time doing interviews," Amos answered.

"Then make me one, too. That's the best news I've had since… I can't remember when," Angel said from between Travis and Amos.

"What are you going to do for them?" Mindy asked as she shook a martini.

"Bookkeeping."

"But you are a bartender," she said.

"Yep, I am, but I can answer the phone and take messages," Cathy said.

"Don't let her fool you. She's got a resume that would knock your socks off," Amos said. "I'd hire her full-time if she'd take the job and put Maggie to work in the Dallas office. She didn't really want to move to Mingus anyway."

Cathy put up both hands defensively. "Oh no! Two months and then I'm finished."

"We'll celebrate with a movie out at the trailer after closing time. I'll make the popcorn," Travis said.

"What movie?" she asked.

"Your choice. I bring a box full of them with me to every new site. You can choose."

"Joint don't shut down until two."

"And you always watch a movie before you go to bed anyway," he said.

She smiled. "Ice cream?"

"Rocky road and pecan pralines and cream."

"My two favorite kinds. I'll be there."

CHAPTER 7

HE LEFT AN HOUR BEFORE THE HONKY TONK CLOSED. Dark clouds hung in the sky and he could almost smell rain. At least it wasn't cold enough to freeze again and the city had fixed the water problem. Lightning zipped through the sky and thunder rolled through the clouds down to the southwest. It was too early in the year for a tornado, but the sky had that strange, eerie cast to it like one was on the horizon and twisting its way toward Mingus.

He forgot all about the weather as he straightened up the kitchen and the living room and office combination. They'd have to sit in kitchen chairs and watch the movie on the small television set on the bar. The one in his bedroom was bigger and the bed would be much more comfortable, but he didn't trust himself to invite her back there. Not after the kiss they'd shared in her apartment.

Ice cream waited in the freezer and popcorn was ready beside the microwave. He made a pitcher of sweet tea in case she'd rather have that than a cold beer. He fidgeted with the DVD player and laid out four movies for her to choose from.

He splashed on a little more Stetson shaving lotion and combed his hair at two o'clock. When she knocked on the door ten minutes later his hands were sweaty and his heart was doing double time.

"Come in," he called out.

She eased the door open and looked inside. The whole living room area had been turned into an office with a desk and chair taking up most of the room. The place smelled like buttered popcorn and shaving lotion. Both sent her senses reeling.

"That smells wonderful. I'm hungry," she said.

"Ice cream, popcorn, ham sandwiches, or yogurt. Past that you'll have to find a can of soup," he said.

"Popcorn first. Ice cream later," she said.

He motioned toward the movies while he poured bowls full of popcorn from the microwaveable bag. "Your choice."

"You sure are being nice." She looked through the stack on the counter. "Do we have to watch one of these?"

"We don't have cable out here. I have a couple of series things back in my bedroom. I've got *Nikita* and the first two seasons of *NCIS*, but..." He let the sentence hang.

"*NCIS*," she said quickly. "I just got started watching that lately and I'd love to see the first episodes."

"Really?" he asked.

"Yes, don't you just love Mark Harmon? He's got the sexiest grin."

"I like Ziva better," he said.

She giggled. "I suppose you wouldn't think Leroy Jethro Gibbs had a sexy grin. Get a quilt and a couple of pillows from back there, too. We can make a pallet."

"Give me a minute," he said. He found the first season of *NCIS* in a box inside the closet, yanked the big brown comforter from the bed along with two pillows, and lugged it all to the kitchen where she helped him make a pallet on the kitchen floor.

"Now put the television on a chair and set it right there and we'll pretend we're at a drive-in," she said.

"Something tells me you've done this before." He

dragged a chair across the floor and put it where she'd pointed.

"I lived in a trailer. Sometimes Momma let me have a kitchen party while she read in the living room."

He put the first disc in the DVD player and turned to find her sitting against a pillow propped against the refrigerator door, her boots off and her mouth full of popcorn.

"Did you know from the beginning that you were going to work for Amos and you just drug it out to see what you could get me to agree to do?" he asked.

"Skeptical little fellow, ain't you?" she said when she'd swallowed.

"Tea or beer?" he asked.

"Tea."

He poured two tall glasses of tea and joined her on the comforter. "You didn't answer me."

"I like what I do in the Honky Tonk. I love the place, the people, and my hours. But sometimes I miss the oil business, too. I had to think about the time involved. I decided I could manage," she said.

"So do I still have to work for you two nights a week?"

"Damn straight you do," she said. "Shhhh, I can't wait to see the pilot episode."

At the end of the first forty-five-minute episode she was yawning but determined to watch one more. While the credits rolled she ran to the bathroom and hurried back to settle into her pillow. Travis picked up the remote and hit pause right when the music started.

"Why'd you do that?"

"Because if you want ice cream, you'll have to move," he said.

"I changed my mind." She reached for the remote at the same time he did. Both their hands closed on it and she looked up to find his lips only inches from hers. They met in a clash with one kiss leading to another and another, his hands under her shirt and on her bare skin, making her shiver in anticipation, and hers toying with the curls at the back of his neck and meeting him kiss for passionate kiss until they were both panting. She'd stretched out on the pallet and he had one leg thrown over hers when the next kiss made the trailer begin to rock.

"Pretty damn forceful making out," she mumbled and opened her eyes to see that the trailer really was moving from side to side.

"Damn!" He sat straight up. No kiss in his entire life had left him dizzy. Then he realized that the kiss hadn't sent him into a tailspin but that the wind was causing the trailer to shake.

"Tornado?" he said.

"I don't know, but I'm not staying in a tin can if it is. Grab your pajamas and let's go to the Honky Tonk. It's got more stability." She was already on her feet and headed for the door when he chased down the hall and shoved what he needed into a duffel bag and zipped it tightly. She had the door open when he returned and was watching the wind bend trees into pretzels.

"Hold my hand and run," he said. "Don't let go no matter what."

It sounded like a freight train moving across the sky above them. Black clouds swirled around with funnels dipping down and back up, picking up whatever was in their pathway and pulling it up to the skies to check it out. What it wanted it kept to sling back down to earth later on. What it didn't like it pitched right back like a child with toys he had grown bored with.

Rain and hail pelted down on them like bullets stinging their skin. Travis grasped her hand tightly and kept moving until they made it to the porch. It took forever for her to get the key worked up from the bottom of her tight jeans.

"Well, hell," she swore as the wind whipped the key from her hands.

"Hold on to the porch post and don't let go no matter what happens," he yelled. He braved the fierce wind and went after it, dropping his duffel bag in the mud when he did. He never let his eyes leave the thing for fear the storm would grab it and haul it up to the sky with the rest of the debris. He picked up his wet bag and held the key firmly in the palm of his hand until he reached the door. He shoved it into the keyhole, turned it, and rushed into the apartment behind her.

She threw herself onto the leather sofa. "I thought we were goners for sure."

He sprawled out beside her, both of them dripping cold water everywhere. "Me too."

He reached across the middle of the sofa and put his hand over hers. "Ice storm, no water, now a tornado. Do they have tsunamis in Texas?"

"In this state anything is possible." She shivered.

"You better head for the shower and get warmed up. You are shaking," he said.

"So are you."

An evil gleam flashed in his eyes. "Are you suggesting…"

She withdrew her hand and slapped his arm. "I am not.

You go first. If your pajamas are wet I'll pitch them in the dryer."

"The duffel is weatherproof. I think they'll be fine," he said. "Go on. I don't think I can move yet. That was a scary sumbitch." He scooted over slightly, tipped her chin back, and kissed her sweetly on the lips. "That's a relief. I thought your kisses were making the trailer shake around."

"You mean they don't?" she asked.

"Honey, they send my mind straight to the gutter. But if they made the whole trailer shake then we'd be in big trouble if we did anything more than share a few hot kisses," he said.

"On that note I'm going to the shower," she said.

She left her wet clothes on the floor and stood under the hot spray for a long time trying to sort out her feelings. When she got out and wrapped a towel around her body, she hadn't figured out a single thing.

"Shut your eyes. I'm on the way to my room and my robe wasn't in the bathroom," she hollered.

"Not on your life," he yelled back.

"Remember you are next," she said.

His laughter followed her the four feet from the bathroom to her bedroom. She pulled underpants, a sleep shirt, and pajama bottoms from a dresser drawer, ran a brush through her wet hair, and checked her reflection in the mirror. No makeup and slicked back hair made her look like a drowned rat. Add baggy pajamas and a knit shirt with Betty Boop on the front and there was no way her kisses would shake a rocking chair much less a trailer house.

The wind was still roaring outside when she went back to the living room. Travis hadn't moved an inch and was still dripping water. He shivered from his head all the way to his boots and she pointed to the bathroom. "Go now before you get pneumonia. I'll make up the bed while you are gone and you can get under warm covers."

Without a word he picked up his duffel bag and carried it to the bathroom. He didn't hum that night as he showered, and when he came out he was quick to get under the quilts she'd piled onto the sofa bed.

"Don't these things usually only last a few minutes?" he asked.

"I have no idea. Haven't ever been in one. But I did look out while you were in the shower and the trailer is still standing. The trees are still whipping around but not like before. I think the worst of it passed us by."

She sat down beside him with her legs pulled up under her. "Scared the bejesus out of me. Tinker told me about one that passed through here several years ago in the spring of the year and stripped the mesquite trees bare. Texas tornadoes aren't something you mess with. I'm glad it didn't pick up Amos's trailer and set it down in Oklahoma. Now go to sleep. What time do you have to go to work tomorrow?"

"Noon. I'm on the noon-to-eight shift every day. Angel is an early riser so she opted to work from eight to four. That way one of us is there all day. I hope the storm is over by the time she goes to work."

"She'll be fine." Cathy brushed a kiss across his forehead. The Honky Tonk swayed just slightly and she smiled.

CHAPTER 8

"Man, am I glad to see you," Angel said when Cathy opened the trailer door. "Desk, computer. Your password and ID is on that pad right there. Your set of keys is on the desk. Hard file cabinets are in the small bedroom. And Amos likes everything in hard copy. He'll never trust a computer. Says they are nothing but eyes for the government to spy on us. So each day we print the day's report at five o'clock in duplicate. Small bedroom has shelves. Put one there and leave one on the edge of the desk. Amos will pick it up. Sometimes they build up for a week before he gets here. I think that's all. I just came in to show you where everything is and to give you a set of keys. Now, I'm off to Jezzy's place. We're so excited we could dance a jig in a pig trough!"

"Been a long time since I've heard that expression," Cathy said.

Angel shoved her arms into the sleeves of her work jacket and waved as she went out the door. "Been a long time since I've been this excited!"

The trailer reminded her of the one that she'd grown up in back in Arkansas. A bar to the left separated the living room from the tiny kitchen which was barely big enough for a small wood table with four chairs around it. Beyond the kitchen was a hallway leading to an alcove for the washer and dryer, a bathroom, bedroom with the door open covered in shelving and file cabinets, and a closed door at the very end.

"Not enough room to cuss a cat without getting a hair in your mouth," she muttered as she did the two-minute tour.

The bathroom still had the faint aroma of Stetson after-shave and Irish Spring soap. The washer was empty but the dryer was full of towels. One cup, plate, fork, knife, and spoon were in the dish drainer. An oak desk that had seen better days sat right in the middle of the living room floor, facing the door. The walls were bare and the windows covered with mini-blinds that had been raised to let as much light as possible into the small room.

Cathy sat down in a padded, adjustable chair, raised the seat to accommodate her long legs, pulled up the screen, and got started. Basically it was the same program she'd used at Green's Oil Company in Mena, but there was no way she'd get all the work caught up in one afternoon. Maybe by the end of the week she'd have it manageable. Hopefully in two months Maggie wouldn't come in to a complete mess.

A whoosh of cold air hit her in the face when the door opened. She looked up half expecting to see Angel, but it was a tall, dark-haired man.

"Hey, Maggie… You're not Maggie," he said.

"Maggie will be here in a couple of months. I'm filling in for her. I'm Cathy O'Dell. What can I do for you?"

"I'm Rocky, the tool pusher. I'm pullin' my rig in and just stopped to tell Maggie…I guess to tell you…that I'll be taking the back slot. Got the sign-in sheet ready?"

Cathy pulled a sheet up on the computer screen and printed it. Rocky dragged a chair from the kitchen to face the desk. He removed his coat and sat down while he signed for slot number twenty.

"So tell me about this Honky Tonk thing out there. What kind of place is it? Open only on weekends?" he asked.

"It's open every night except Sunday. Monday night is oldies night. It's got one of those old jukeboxes that still plays three songs for a quarter and has Waylon, Willie, Merle, and Hank Williams, senior not junior, on it. Rest of the week it's usually music from the new jukebox," she said.

Rocky was somewhere in his early thirties with dark hair and roving eyes that settled on Cathy's breasts. He had wide muscular shoulders and hands that had seen their fair share of hard work. A thin white line down one cheek marked an old scar and Cathy wondered if it'd happened on the rig or in a barroom brawl.

"They don't ever have live bands? You been there?" Rocky asked.

"I own it and there's no live music. You want something live, go on up the road to the Trio Club," Cathy said.

"Why are you working here?" Rocky asked incredulously.

"Amos needed someone and I qualified."

"Where's Travis?"

"Out at the rig, I suppose. Only time he's got to report to me is Friday and Saturday night," she said.

"Why then?"

"Because those are the nights he's going to help me bartend."

Rocky's face fell apart when he laughed. "The Travis Henry. The almighty smart petroleum engineer of the century is going to work in a bar. Man, I'll be there Friday night just to see that sight."

Cathy slid the sheet to one side of her desk. "Why do you want the back parking slot?"

"Noise level. I work days so I get to sleep nights. I saw the

Honky Tonk. I want as far away from the noise as possible. And the whole thing is on first-come, first-served basis with Amos. I get here first every time so I can have my choice. Besides, back that far I might be able to catch a glimpse of a deer every so often. It's not often we get to park in places like this," he answered.

The door opened again. "Mornin'. I'm Bart, the driller. I want a parking spot in the middle. Fast Rocky here the only one who's beat me?"

Cathy nodded and handed him the sign-in sheet. Bart was somewhere between thirty and forty and had a mop of red hair and freckles all over his round face. He peeled off his coat and pulled up a chair next to Rocky on the other side of the desk. If they were going to sit around jawing all day, Cathy would never be caught up by the end of the week.

"This is Cathy O'Dell. She's temping for Maggie and she owns that Honky Tonk. And you'll never believe it, but Travis Henry is going to work for her Friday and Saturday nights," Rocky said.

"The Travis Henry? Well, hot damn. I'll be there on Friday night. Got any good-lookin' women hangin' around?" Bart asked.

"Sometimes," Cathy said.

Bart picked up the sheet and signed for slot three. "Hey, this could be the best job we've had in a while. Don't even need a designated driver to get us home."

"Thought you wanted a middle one," Cathy said.

"Changed my mind. Closer the trailer, less I have to walk," Bart said.

The next time the door opened a short, blond, brown-eyed man entered the crowded room. "Did y'all see that parking lot out there? Reckon Amos made a deal with the owner of that beer joint? Now this is what I call a real job."

Rocky pointed at the paper on the desk. "Parking slots are out back and this is Cathy," Rocky said. "She's temping for Maggie and she owns that beer joint. Choose a place and we'll get our rigs out of the way. The rest of the crew will be here in the next hour or so. We're supposed to be at the drilling site by two to look things over. Tomorrow we start putting it together."

"Mornin', Cathy. I'm Tilman Greeson."

She handed him the sign-in sheet and he chose the trailer space right beside Rocky. She'd thought she'd have the office to herself all afternoon with nothing but a computer and paperwork. But it sure seemed like the men were going to use the trailer for a gossip shack.

"Okay, guys, let's get set up. Roughnecks and derrick hands will be here soon. What time does that beer joint open?" Rocky asked.

"Eight sharp. Shuts down at two," Cathy said.

"Friday and Saturday?" Tilman asked.

"Every night but Sunday," Cathy said.

"Well, hot damn," Tilman said.

"But you won't get to see Travis Henry behind the bar because he's only helping on Friday and Saturday and you work most nights," Rocky said.

Tilman followed them out. "Don't matter if I see him or not. I'm off on Thursday nights and it'll be open, so I can at least see what's going on."

She was entering invoice numbers and amounts on the debit spreadsheet when the door opened again. She didn't even look up but pointed toward the sign-in sheet.

"I don't reckon I'll be hookin' up a trailer. I came by for the WHMIS and the Second Line BOP reports to be sure we are in total compliance," Travis said. Her hair had been set free from her usual ponytail holder and flowed to her shoulders. Her sweater was the same steely blue as her eyes. He shoved his hands in his pockets to keep from touching her face.

She finished putting in the last invoice and pulled up a screen tagged safety and regulatory details. A touch of the keypad and the printer spit out the two reports he asked for. She handed them to him, careful not to touch his fingertips.

"Anything else?" she asked.

He put the chairs back around the kitchen table and poured a cup of coffee from the percolator that she hadn't even noticed. "Want coffee? Did you find the ice cream?" He invented a reason to stay a while longer.

"Didn't look. Haven't had time. Would love coffee, but I'll get it," she answered.

She wound her way around the desk, the kitchen table, and to the cabinet. She brushed against his hip and mumbled that she was sorry. The next minute he had his fist on her chin and his eyes were looking into hers with a dreamy expression. He slowly leaned forward and brushed a kiss across her lips. She put an arm around his neck and tangled her fingers into his hair.

He pushed his luck with the next one, kissing her hard and passionately, letting it linger on and on as their tongues did a mating dance. Cathy kissed back. She tasted coffee, cold wind, and desire. The bones melted in her knees and for the first time in her life she actually felt faint. Just before the kiss ended she had the fleeting idea that she might swoon.

Travis hugged her tightly to his chest for a few minutes, listening to the rapid beating of her heart echoing his. "I've got to go back to work. See you tonight at the Honky Tonk." In four easy strides he was out the front door and gone.

Cathy touched her burning lips. "Holy shit! It happens every time he kisses me."

———————————

That evening Travis weaved among the hats and boots to the bar. Ladies bumped into him on purpose and smiled or winked when they had his attention. Men accidentally collided with him and quickly begged his pardon. The place was packed. Tables were staked out with beer bottles and coats hanging on the back of chairs. Both pool tables were in use with dollar bills out to pay for the privilege to play the winners. Hank Williams was singing about setting the woods on fire. From outside the joint it sounded like there was a live band playing and the singer was a ringer for Hank senior.

One fellow gave up his barstool when a woman in a short tailed dress and lots of gold jewelry asked him if he wanted to dance. Travis quickly claimed it, got Cathy's attention, and mouthed that he wanted a beer. She held up a finger and finished dumping ice around six longneck bottles of Coors in a bucket, then picked up a pint jar and filled it with draw beer.

Mickey Gilley's "Bring It on Home to Me" invited a different kind of dancing. The women did a glorified bump and grind that looked like they needed a pole, a stage, and a little less clothing. Travis pictured Cathy dancing like that in one of those strapless tops that stopped above the belly button and hip slung jeans.

She set the beer in front of him. "Here you go."

Her voice startled him back into reality. "Thanks. Busy night, ain't it?"

"I don't know where they all came from," Cathy said breathlessly.

Larissa leaned in between Travis and the cowboy sitting next to him. "Need some help? You look run ragged."

Cathy nodded. "Ever done any bartending?"

"I'll help," Travis offered.

"I'll take Larissa," Cathy said.

Travis locked gazes with her. "Why?"

"Because I have to pay you with five days a week in the oil office to get you to help on Friday and Saturday nights. I can't afford your price." She smiled.

He winked. "I might make a deal that didn't involve the oil office."

Cathy blinked and looked away. A quick vision of how she'd pay him didn't do a thing to stop her breathlessness. The infatuation was about to drive her as crazy as a drunk toad frog.

Larissa slapped Travis on the shoulder. "Don't be flirting while she's busy, cowboy. How do I get back there? Do I have to crawl over the bar?" She wore tight designer jeans and a red knit shirt with a cutout at the neckline. Big red hoop earrings showed when she tucked her hair behind her ears.

Cathy pointed. "Through the swinging door at the end of the bar."

Larissa wasted no time taking a place behind the beer

machine and drawing beers while Cathy took orders for mixed drinks.

"I'm hurt," Travis teased.

"Oh, hush and drink your beer. Go talk Merle into a game of eight ball," Cathy said.

"She's playin' with Clark," Travis said.

A fast song by Emmylou Harris cleared out the barstools and put almost everyone in the beer joint on the dance floor for a line dance. The way they were moving reminded Travis of a can of wiggling fishing worms, but he would gladly be out there on the floor with Cathy if she'd dance with him. He could imagine her arms wrapped up around his neck and that cute little fanny moving seductively against him at belt buckle level.

"Where'd they all come from?" Travis asked.

"Who knows? Maybe they heard about the oilmen. I swear something put the word out and they don't even seem to care that this is oldies night. I've never had a night like this, not even New Year's Eve and that night was a good one."

"I need two pitchers of piña coladas," a young woman shouted above Emmylou's voice. "I love this music. It's what my momma played the whole time I was growing up. You play this all the time?"

"Only on Mondays." Cathy filled the order and set them on a tray with empty jars for the woman.

"What's on the other nights?"

"The new stuff," Larissa answered. "But it's just as good. Come on back tomorrow and see which you like best."

"You can bet on it."

"Where y'all from?" Larissa asked.

"My group is from Fort Worth," she said. "We been to

everything over there and besides, we got this friend named Mindy who said this was a neat place. She was right."

Don Williams's voice said that he wouldn't want to live if she didn't love him.

"Ever have someone in your life you would die for?" Larissa asked.

"Nope," Cathy said. "Where'd you learn to bartend? Please tell me one more time that you aren't here to try to buy this place for Hayes Radner."

Larissa filled six quarts and set them on a tray, collected the money, and made change. "One more time and that's it. I'm not here to buy your beer joint. I moved to Mingus because I wanted to live here. And you are changing the subject. Anyone can pull a lever and fill up a fruit jar with beer. How old are you, Cathy?"

"Twenty-eight." Cathy started two more blenders of piña coladas.

"And you never loved anyone enough that you wouldn't want to live without them?"

"Ain't no one in this world that I'd want to die for," Cathy answered.

"Looks like we've got something in common. I've got two years on you in age, but neither one of us has been led down the daisy path, have we?"

"I didn't say that. The daisy path and I are very well acquainted. That's why I wouldn't die for a man. Basically, they're all alike, aren't they? Ever hear that old saying about burn me once, shame on you. Burn me twice and shame on me. Well, that's the story of my life. I ain't livin' a 'shame on me' life."

Larissa kept filling jars, icing down beer in buckets, and

making change. "Someday we'll have to discuss that when we can sit down and not yell over the music and people."

The tables and stools cleared out again when Kenny Rogers starting singing about knowing when to hold 'em, when to fold 'em, and when to walk away or when to run. Four long lines of people covered the dance floor in a line dance yelling "Fold 'em" with Kenny when he said the words.

"That's my brand-new favorite song," Larissa said.

"How come?"

"I'm learning that folding them isn't such a bad thing. I'm beginning to think I was a winner when I thought I was the biggest loser in the whole world. We'll talk about that later, too," she said.

"What makes you think we'll be friends and talk about anything other than beer and piña coladas?"

"Hey, you want to dance?" Travis yelled the minute the song ended.

The second he hollered a rare moment of silence filled the joint. His voice echoed in the stillness and everyone looked at him.

"Which one of us you talkin' to, cowboy?" A girl in a laced-up-the-front white blouse that dropped off her shoulders in an elasticized neckline sidled up to him and laid her hand on his thigh.

"The bartender?" Travis blushed.

"Are you talking to me? No thank you. I'd lose my job." Larissa laughed.

Someone plugged more quarters into the machine and Marty Robbins began singing about his wife. Dancers were stuck to each other and moving slowly on the packed floor.

Travis was jealous. That's the way he'd like to be hugged up to Cathy, not sitting across the bar from her with no possibility of anything but their hands touching.

Cathy stopped in front of him to replenish the pretzel bowl. "Thanks for asking me to dance, but I don't dance with customers or while I'm working. And even if I did, it's too dang busy for me to leave the bar even for one song. But thanks anyway."

He reached for a handful of pretzels just to touch her fingertips. Hot vibes between them created something akin to a kid's sparkler on the Fourth of July.

Larissa touched Cathy on the arm. "What would it take to make that song your favorite song?"

Cathy pulled her hand back from the pretzel bowl. "My song is Gretchen Wilson's 'Redneck Woman.' You're just now discovering country music and you think every one of them is written just for you, don't you?"

"Hell yeah!" Larissa smiled.

"You're getting into this, aren't you?" Cathy asked.

"Been listenin' to country music all day while I cleaned up my yard. That storm shook every loose leaf from my trees. I've got enough of a pile to make a bonfire for a wiener roast. Listen to the song. What would it take to make you someone's woman?"

Cathy listened to the familiar words. "Guess he'd have to be willing to give me his share of heaven," she said.

"Well said, sister," Larissa said.

Travis was figuring out how a person made a deal to give up their share of heaven and when Angel tapped him on the shoulder he almost dumped his beer in his lap.

She giggled. "I didn't mean to cause a disaster, darlin'.

Come dance with me until Garrett gets here. Oh, there he is. You're off the hook."

Angel grabbed Garrett in the middle of a fast Jerry Lee Lewis tune and they danced not far from where Tinker had set up post. Garrett ran the tips of his fingers down her sides and she moved seductively against him.

Cathy wished for a long breath of fresh, cold winter air. The blend of shaving lotion, perfume, smoke, and liquor mixed together was enough to singe a billy goat's nose hairs. And watching Angel and Garrett with glazed eyes only for each other as they danced like they were the only two people in the whole Honky Tonk didn't do a thing for the heat inside her body. She looked over at Travis to find him mouthing the words to "Hello Darlin'" with Conway Twitty. Travis's blue eyes met hers over the bar when he sang about letting him kiss her and hold her in his arms one more time. She forgot about the fancied-up bodies in the place and cigarette smoke hanging in the air and even Angel and Garrett. All she thought about was his kisses. She had to hold both her hands behind her to keep them from her mouth to see if it was as hot as it felt.

"I need two pitchers of hurricanes and a single tequila sunrise," Larissa hollered from the other end of the bar.

Cathy blinked her way back from imagination kissing to bartending. She glanced back toward Travis. He smiled and held up his beer in a toast.

Barbara Mandrell was the next jukebox star to sing. Another line dance formed with both men and women participating. Rocky was pretty damned agile and that didn't surprise Cathy. But Bart did. She'd figured he'd be clumsy but he knew exactly when to kick back, two steps forward, kick forward, and twist and turn three times before starting again. He never missed a beat and looked like a ballerina the whole time he danced.

Waylon Jennings sang "Luckenbach, Texas" next and kept the line dancers on the floor.

Travis meandered over to the pool tables to talk to Garrett while Angel and Merle set up a game.

"If we could change that to Mingus, Texas, instead of Luckenbach, it would describe me," Larissa said.

"You had never ever been in a bar before you walked in the Honky Tonk, had you?" Cathy wiped trays and stacked them up for the next run.

"Not like this. Went to my share of nightclubs in New York City and Dallas and Houston and been to Vegas but not a honky tonk. Did it show that much?"

"Yep, it did."

"That's another long story," Larissa said.

"This your first experience with country music, too?"

Larissa nodded. "And my first time to drink beer and two-step."

"Mercy sakes, you ain't been livin'. You just been existin.'" Cathy laughed.

Travis listened to Garrett talk about Angus, but his eyes never left the bar. Cathy was beautiful when she smiled. Bits of her laughter floated across the smoke-filled room to his ears and sounded like harp music or maybe the tinkling of a Floyd Cramer piano. What had Larissa said that had brought it on, anyway?

Larissa poured peanuts into the bowls on the bar. "You are right about living and existing. But I'm learning my way around this kind of life."

"What'll you have, cowboy?" Cathy asked a rancher who was panting so hard from dancing that he couldn't catch his breath.

"Give me a bucket of Millers."

Cathy reached under the bar and set a galvanized milk bucket on the bar, slipped six bottles of cold Miller beer into it, and then shoveled in two big scoops of ice.

He handed her a wad of crumpled bills. "Keep the change."

"Thanks." She straightened the money and made change. What didn't go into the cash register she handed to Larissa.

"What's this?"

"Pay. Whatever tips come in this evening belong to you," she said.

"I'm not working for money," she protested.

"What are you working for?" Cathy asked.

"Because you were too busy and it's too crowded for me to dance. I'm not good enough to dance with that crowd," Larissa said.

"Me neither," Travis said.

"Where'd you come from?" Cathy asked.

"Garrett and Angel have a table staked out soon as those two cowboys finish their game and they don't want to lose it so I'm here to buy beers for them."

"Why aren't you comfortable dancing with the crowd?" Larissa asked.

"I just don't like to get in the middle of that much movement."

"Darlin', pretty as you are the womenfolks wouldn't care if you were dancin' standin' straight up or layin' down on your back. Hey, listen to this song." Larissa pointed to the jukebox.

Tanya Tucker was singing a song that asked if he would lay with her in a field of stone.

"Every single one of the songs has a meaning," Larissa said. "Lord, I love this music. Why wasn't I listening to it my whole life?"

"Would you?" Travis's eyes locked with Cathy's.

"Would I what?"

"Listen to the words. Would you do that?"

"I'm too damn busy to listen to the words of every song that plays on the jukebox. They're just songs, Travis. I don't look for hidden meanings in them. Go shoot some pool with Merle. She looks lonesome," Cathy lied.

Her pulse quickened and her mouth went so dry she wished she didn't have a rule about not drinking while she was working. A shot of Jack to steady her hands would be very nice even if it did burn the hell out of her ulcer.

Travis didn't believe her. She *was* listening to the words. If he'd had to answer the question, he would have said yes, that he would lay with her in a field of stone at the base of a mountain or even in the sands of a desert with no water for miles and miles.

Larissa set two beers in front of him. "I would lay with you in a field of stone, darlin', but something tells me you done got your eyes on someone else to fill that position."

He raised an eyebrow. "Oh?"

"Don't play dumb with me and I won't tell her," Larissa said.

"You got a deal." He carefully toted the beers across the room to the pool tables where Garrett and Angel took time for a long drink before they picked up their cue sticks.

Larissa filled two buckets and set up a dozen beers on

two trays before she got a break. She touched Cathy on the arm and asked, "You got a thing for that cowboy, don't you?"

"Afraid so, but I *will* get over it," Cathy said.

"Good luck," Larissa said.

"Hey, could we get some beers down here? I need a bucket of Coors." A cowboy slid onto Travis's vacated barstool.

Larissa set up a bucket. "You betcha."

"You're a quick study," Cathy told Larissa as she worked up three pitchers of margaritas.

"That's what they say," Larissa said.

"And who would they be?"

"A story for a day when we're not working our tails off. Not complainin'. This is more fun than I've had in years," Larissa said.

George Strait's voice filled the joint with his song about pure love. Cathy looked across a sea of dancing and drinking people at Travis, who raised his glass when Strait sang about it being pure love, milk, and honey and Cap'n Crunch and her in the morning. She remembered giving him the toaster pastries and a cup of coffee. Pop-Tarts, coffee, and arguments were not sexy, so why was he remembering that it was?

"Who is that man singing? God, I love this song. It's just moved up the charts to be number one in my book," Larissa said.

"That is George Strait. Every song that's played tonight has been your new favorite," Cathy said.

"Wait a minute. Who is this? Wow!" Larissa asked.

"That's Don Gibson." Cathy made the mistake of looking over at Travis when Don sang about his sensuous woman. Travis raised his jar again and winked.

She inhaled deeply and pretended she didn't see the wink. She put a pitcher of Coors and six pint jars on a tray for one of the girls dressed in a black leather corset-type top laced up both the front and back. It wasn't easy to keep her eyes off him and on her work the next few minutes. She wanted to look back and see if he'd wink again, but she wouldn't let herself get drawn into a flirting game while she was working.

"This is one jumpin' place. Love the old music. Is it like this every night?" the girl was asking, but Cathy couldn't remember what she was supposed to be saying or doing.

"Just Mondays," Larissa answered. "Rest of the week it's just as jumpin' but it's the new country music. No rock or even alternative here. Just pure country like George just sang."

Cathy could have hugged Larissa. If she'd have had to speak or burn down the Honky Tonk after Travis's wink, Tinker would have had to strike the match and watch her cry as the old place burned to nothing but a pile of ashes.

"My crew will be back another night then. We love to line dance and two-step."

"Where y'all from?"

"Breckenridge."

"Well, come on back down here. We'll be right here." Larissa gave her the change in quarters. "Three for a quarter tonight."

She pocketed the change. "I done put in a dollar but my songs aren't up yet."

"Sorry about buttin' in. You looked a little pale. What happened?" Larissa asked Cathy.

"Nothing," Cathy said.

"Honey, only thing that makes a woman lose her ability to

talk is a man. Either they make her so mad she can't speak or else they do something that makes her think of the bedroom and she can't say a word because her mind is in the gutter."

"You are so right."

Charlie Rich started singing about his baby making him proud by never hanging all over him in a crowd but when they got behind closed doors she made him glad that he was a man. Cathy didn't dare look at Travis for fear he'd wink or blow her a kiss.

Several months before, Daisy had complained that every blessed song on the jukebox reminded her of Jarod. During that time Cathy thought she was out of her mind in love or headed for the insane asylum, one or the other. That night Cathy knew exactly what she had been talking about. Everything a country music artist sang seemed like a Cupid's arrow pointed straight for her heart. She found herself hoping that Travis would be in the oil field the rest of the week. That way there would be no excuse to get tangled up with him in the kitchen and wind up setting a wildfire in Palo Pinto County. Hopefully the songs on the new jukebox wouldn't make her want to fall backward on a big soft bed and drag that cowboy down on top of her.

At midnight Travis set his empty jar on the bar and waved at Cathy before he weaved through the people and went home to his trailer. The Fort Worth girls whooped and hollered through one more line dance then disappeared past Tinker in a flurry of giggles.

By one o'clock things had slowed down enough that Larissa asked Cathy to make her a martini. She carried it to the other side of the bar and sat down. "That was fun. Can I do it again? I made a hundred bucks in tips."

"Don't know how I would have handled it without you. Thanks for helping me."

"Hey, want to shoot some eight ball when the doors are shut?" Larissa asked.

"Not tonight. You any good?" Cathy asked.

"Fair. Been tryin' to get up enough nerve to ask Merle to play," Larissa said.

"Where'd you learn?"

Larissa shrugged. "London. There was this earl who liked his billiards."

"Are you serious?"

"As a heart attack, and he was fine looking, especially behind closed doors. We played a few times in the nude. Hey, you heard that new song called 'Skinny Dippin''? I'm going to try that when summer gets here. By then I'll have my own good-looking cowboy to go with."

"Yes, I've heard it," Cathy said. She didn't say that she'd already imagined doing just that with Travis Henry. "Tell me, how did you go from an earl to Mingus, Texas?"

"I have trouble staying in one place, with one thing, or with one man for very long. I get bored easy."

"Going to get bored with the Honky Tonk and Mingus in a few weeks?"

Larissa sipped the martini. "Best martini I've ever had and that includes all of them. And I don't know if I'll get bored in Mingus or not. If I do I'll be here three days past the boredom day."

"Three days?"

Larissa's eyes glittered. "Yes, it'll take me that long to get a moving van in and to call Hayes Radner to sell my house to him."

"You wouldn't!"

"I might if I was bored. So you better not throw me out of the Honky Tonk."

"Don't tease me about Hayes Radner. That man is evil with a bank account."

"Okay, okay. I won't tease you about him. Who's that singing?"

"Emmylou Harris. And the song is 'Two More Bottles of Wine,'" Cathy told her.

"I've been there and done that. Like Emmylou says, I've got two more bottles of wine, only mine is two more beers."

"Hey, pretty lady, you want to dance?" Bart asked.

"You one of Cathy's oilmen?"

"I am."

"Married?"

"Divorced."

"I'm not very good at dancin' to this music but you look like you'd be a hell of a teacher." She stood up and wrapped her arms around his neck and he two-stepped her right out into the middle of the floor.

Dolly Parton sang about her man bringing her the sunshine when she was in darkness. Cathy had a soft place in her heart for that particular song. Her mother had loved it and had danced around the living room with her father every time it came on the radio and she could corner him in some part of the trailer.

Larissa was panting when she claimed her seat again after half a dozen songs. "It's time for this Cinderella to go home. I'll be back tomorrow evening. Maybe I'll make another hundred dollars in tips?"

"If we're as busy as we were tonight I'd love the help. I'd pay you if you'd agree to work for me."

Larissa shook her head emphatically. "I got a job and I sure don't want to be tied down to anything. If I'm here and you are busy I'll work for tips. If I want to dance with a good-looking cowboy or oilman, then by golly I want to be free to do it. Agreed?"

"Agreed," Cathy said.

At two o'clock Tinker sent the last dozen people home and Cathy locked up behind him. The Kendalls finished up the night with a song that said heaven was just a sin away. The singer said that way down deep inside she knew that it was all wrong but his eyes kept tempting her.

"You got that right," Cathy said.

She wouldn't even have to get the car out of the garage to find sin. The way Travis held up his drink and winked at her said that he'd be more than willing to help the devil take her to heaven any night of the week. All she had to do was walk across the backyard, knock on the door, and kiss him. Heaven would be waiting in his arms. Only trouble was come morning it would be hell to pay and she wasn't willing for another broken heart.

"Hey, did you see those two yahoos sitting over there in the shadows all evening? They had shifty eyes. One went to the bathroom and came back and then the other one went and they kept looking around like they were casing the place. Never drank a single beer or danced with anyone or watched a pool game. Mostly they watched you and Larissa," Tinker said.

She shook her head. "It was so busy and full tonight I almost counted heads to make sure we weren't over limit. I didn't notice them. Why do you reckon they were here?"

"Might have to do with Larissa. She's new in Mingus.

Come in here and bought a house and don't appear to go to work anywhere. Maybe they're stalking her."

"Well, they wouldn't be stalking me." She laughed.

"Just keep your eyes open and be careful," Tinker warned. "Lock up behind me and be sure to keep your windows locked. The way they were actin' don't feel right."

"Maybe they were religious and trying to figure out a way to save my wayward soul or maybe they were Hayes Radner's men trying to figure out a way to talk me out of my beer joint," she told him.

"No, neither one of those seems right. They show up again, I'm going to confront them."

"Point them out to me if they do." She followed him to the door and locked it behind him. She set her empty beer bottle on the table, turned out the lights, went into her apartment, and headed straight to the shower.

CHAPTER 9

CATHY ROLLED HER EYES WHEN SHE LOOKED AT THE stack of papers on the desk to be entered into the computer. Another stack of forms to be noted for future use and then filed away waited on the other side of the computer along with the payroll time sheets. They had a bright purple Post-it attached to them with doodles of daisies in the corners and a note that they should be finished before the next shift. A second Post-it, this one neon orange, said that someone would be by to pick them up before three, so the men could clock out.

"Forget about getting caught up today," she growled.

She entered the information from the time cards into the computer, rubber banded them together, and set them to one side. Then she started on the stack of data-entry papers that had sprung up like mushrooms in a rainy spring. The second day of work in an office convinced her that running a beer joint was her calling, not working for an oil company.

The door opened and she looked up to see a stranger. "Can I help you?" she asked.

"Name is Cal Anderson. I'm a derrick hand and I'm down for the eight-to-eight night shift starting tonight. Got a parking list for me to sign in?" he asked.

Cal was a short, round man somewhere between twenty-five and thirty. There was a white line where a wedding band had been until recently. His baby face was as round as his waistline, but his arms stretched the fabric of his coat.

Cathy handed him the list and he put his name on the number four slot. His writing had a feminine flare that looked out of place with the other scribbles.

"So what's the story on that old beer joint out there? Is it closed up?" he asked.

"No, it's open from eight to two every night but Sunday. I own and operate it," she said.

"Well, if that ain't the sorriest luck. If I'd have known that we had an on-site beer joint I'd have put in to work days. My shift's from eight to eight Tuesday through Saturday. Only night I can go for a cold beer will be Monday. You reckon you could open it in the daytime for us who work nights?"

"No, sir. Six hours at night and this job is plenty for me," she said.

"Then save me a barstool on Monday. Don't expect you've got live bands except on the weekends, do you?"

"Don't ever have live bands. You want that you go on up the road to the Trio Club. We have oldies night on Monday. That means the old three-for-a-quarter jukebox is plugged in. Rest of the week we have the new jukebox with the new artists. Guess you'd better like the old stuff if you're only coming out on Monday," she said.

"Love it. Cut my teeth on Marty Robbins and Conway Twitty. Granny listened to them. Grandpa listened to Dolly Parton and Crystal Gayle. Got any of them folks croonin' on that old jukebox?"

"Every one of them," Cathy told him.

"Then I'll be there. Save me a dance, too." He grinned.

"Can't do it. Don't dance with customers," she said.

"If it wasn't for bad luck..."

She held up her hand at the cliché. "I know, you wouldn't have no luck at all."

He started out the door with a loud, make-believe sigh. "What's your name, honey?"

"Cathy O'Dell and I'm just temping for Maggie," she said.

"Like I said...bad luck...no luck at all." He waved.

She went to work and when she looked at the clock she was surprised to see that two hours had passed and her neck was in a cramp. It popped when she rolled it several times. She inhaled deeply and caught a whiff of strong coffee still in the percolator. Her stomach grumbled so she went to the kitchen to see if Travis had really put ice cream in the freezer.

She snooped around in the cabinets and found a dozen kinds of soup, two loaves of bread, and peanut butter along with a package of soft chocolate chip cookies and a bowl filled with Butterfinger candy bars. The refrigerator had cheese, apples and oranges, twenty containers of yogurt, and milk. Four kinds of ice cream and a dozen man-sized frozen TV dinners were in the freezer.

She picked up a container of strawberry yogurt and opened three drawers before she found the spoons. She leaned against the bar and ate slowly. She'd forgotten about computer kinks and aches. Bars had their own set of pains at the end of a shift that involved sore legs and throbbing toes. Computer work put kinks in the neck and lower back. She ate a bite and rolled her neck; ate a few more and did a couple of squats; another couple and did a dozen knee lifts. She had just put the last bite in her mouth when Travis stepped into the office.

He looked at the desk then down the hall and finally his eyes came to rest on her standing there with an empty yogurt container in one hand and a spoon in the other. "I'm here for the time sheets."

She motioned with the spoon. "On the desk with the rubber band around them."

He removed his caramel-colored canvas work jacket and dark brown leather gloves and laid them on the kitchen table. He rubbed his hands together to generate warmth, poured a cup of coffee, and wrapped his fingers around the hot mug instead of drinking it. The north wind was bitter cold that morning and the nerves in his face and nose tingled as the warm air brought them back to normal temperature.

"That's interesting," he muttered aloud.

"What? That I stole one of your yogurts?" Cathy asked.

No way was he going to tell her the interesting thing was that his insides were hot as fire while the outside of his body was cold as ice cream.

"That you like strawberry. It's my favorite, too. Mind if I have a taste?"

"I just ate it all," she said.

He took two steps and was so close to her face that he could smell strawberries.

"It's all gone," she said.

"Not quite. Your mouth will still taste like strawberries."

"Oh?" she said.

He inched so close that his chest met hers and his nose was only three inches away. His eyes crossed and he wrapped his arms around her waist. He leaned in and pulled her mouth to his in a soul-searching kiss that went on until they were both breathless.

"Darlin', that is one fine way to taste yogurt," he whispered.

She reached up and brought his lips to hers again. He slipped his cold hands under her sweater, feeling the warmth of the soft skin below her bra strap, and she unbuttoned enough of his shirt to run her hands over his muscular chest.

The noise of a pickup right outside the trailer caused them to jump back as if they were fourteen years old and had gotten caught making out on the sofa in the dark. Travis hurriedly buttoned his shirt, picked up the coffee mug, and was sitting at the table when the door opened.

Cathy adjusted her sweater and had her back to the door when Rocky came into the trailer. The crimson blush in her cheeks matched the fiery feeling in the pit of her insides. Another minute and they would have been fumbling with zippers as they headed down the hallway toward his bedroom. And all without locking the front door!

"Got any coffee? Texas ain't supposed to be this damn cold," Rocky said.

"It's been made since breakfast but it's hot and strong," Travis said.

"Just like I like my women." Rocky laughed. "You hot and strong, Cathy?"

"That question could be considered sexual harassment," Cathy said.

Rocky brushed past Travis on the right. "You get up on the wrong side of the bed this mornin', woman?"

Cathy shrugged and headed back to her desk and started to work. She'd have much rather been kissing Travis than entering numbers into the computer screen, and she'd be willing to do a dance in the middle of a rainstorm if Rocky would suddenly turn into a frog and hop out of the trailer so she could go back to running her fingers over Travis's hard chest muscles.

Now why in the hell would I think something like that? I've vowed to run from this, not right into it. But maybe if we had a romp in the sheets it would cure me of the infatuation and I could get him out of my mind.

"What do you need other than hot, strong coffee?" she finally asked.

He threw up his palms as if she was about to attack him. "If I answer that you'll have me up on harassment charges." He grinned.

"Get your mind out of the gutter and tell me what brought you to the trailer other than coffee and warmth," Cathy said.

"You are a hard woman, Cathy O'Dell. Amos would do well to put you on the full-time payroll the way you keep us in line. I need a printout of the crew. We are going to hire one more roughneck," Rocky said. He removed his coat and hung it on the back of a chair before he sat down with Travis.

"You were right. It's damn hot and damn strong. It's only a little less thick and black as the oil."

"It'll warm you up," Travis said. "Think we'll hit something in two months?"

"It don't matter whether we do or not; this place is warm compared to where some of us will be headed by the end of February," Rocky said.

"Ain't it the truth," Travis said.

Cathy stopped working and stretched her neck so she could see across the bar separating the office and kitchen. "What are you talking about?"

"Alaska," Rocky said.

Travis chanced a glance in her direction. His gaze locked with hers and blistering hot sparks danced between them. If Rocky weren't the best tool pusher in the whole business he'd fire him on the spot for interrupting what was happening between him and Cathy.

"Alaska?" she finally asked without blinking. She'd known it was a two-month gig, but Alaska? That just put the icing on the cake as far as letting desire win the race with common sense. If she did sleep with him and it caused her to fall for him, then he'd be gone and she'd be in a world of big-girl hurt.

Travis forced himself to stop undressing her in his mind. "Amos is willing to sink two million into this venture while he makes a deal in Alaska, but that's his limit. We're cuttin' corners as much as possible. It's one of those situations where if we hire too many to get the job done in the time slot then we overextend our budget. Without the men, we can't finish in two months, so it's like we're working with one of those old balance things. Men on one side; money on the other. And keeping them perfectly balanced isn't easy."

"What about Angel? Does Merle know about Alaska?" She hoped her voice didn't sound as hollow as her heart felt.

"Angel told Amos that she'd go to Alaska or the moon, and of course Merle knows," Travis said.

Cathy hit the right buttons and the printer spit out a list of the crew members with possible recruits' names on the bottom of the page. She reached up and laid them on the bar.

Rocky picked it up and studied it before handing it to Travis. "What do you think?"

"Luther can't be beat."

"He still married to that cute little filly who wants to travel with him?" Rocky asked.

"Last I heard they were divorced. He came home early and caught her with the driller. Sounds kind of dirty and the men made a lot of jokes about it, but Luther didn't think they were funny," Travis said.

"You sound like you are talking about a soap opera," Cathy said.

"It gets that way. Men who travel with their wives are askin' for trouble. It's different if it's a permanent situation, but most of this isn't. We travel a lot as you can see by the parking list. Women living in cramped quarters get antsy and that makes trouble," Rocky said.

"So what about the men who are married and away from home for weeks on end?" Cathy asked.

"Some of them couldn't be shook away from their wives and families with a blast of dynamite. Others fall off the true-blue wagon the first time a honky tonk momma makes a pass at him." Rocky finished his coffee. "I'll call Luther and see if we can get him down here by tomorrow."

"Where does he live?"

"Up in Ardmore, Oklahoma, right now. He's been in Biloxi for a few months but he's back on his folks' ranch until Amos finds him something pretty close. I think he'd move this far. Can't see him going to Alaska, though," Travis said.

Rocky looked across the bar at Cathy. "I can't wait until you see Luther."

Cathy squared her shoulders. "Why? What's the matter with him?"

Travis chuckled.

She shot a look across the bar. "What does that mean?"

Travis stood up and slipped his arms into his coat, pulled his gloves on, and winked at Cathy. "I'll just let Luther be a big surprise. Come on, Rocky; let's go fight the deadlines."

"You are a…" Cathy couldn't think of anything vile enough to call him.

He stood back and let Rocky leave before him and then bent down to kiss her on the ear lobe. "I'm a what?" he whispered.

"A right fine kisser," she said. *And fast becoming my friend. Do friends knock each other's socks off when they make out? I never had a guy-type friend before, so I'm swimming in unfamiliar territory. But here lately when anything happens my first thought is that I can't wait to see Travis and tell him about it. Does he feel that way about me, I wonder?*

Travis lined up the time sheets in the pockets above the clock. The rig shack was a portable building, eight feet square with a time clock on one wall and a small table pushed up against the back wall. It held a coffeepot that was never to be empty. Whoever took the last cup would start a new pot. Leaving a completely empty pot was an unforgivable sin and could get a man fired quicker than being careless on the rig. The walls were covered with papers, maps, seismological reports, and changes to regulatory details. If it was important or they might want it in a hurry, it was tacked to the wall.

It wasn't Travis's job to do such menial labor but he'd been going to the trailer the day before for the WHMIS report, so he'd volunteered to pick them up. He could have had Rocky pick them up when he went in for a new copy of the updated report but Travis wanted to see Cathy, so he'd volunteered.

He touched his lips. So she thought he was a right fine kisser, did she?

He smiled. That was funny because he thought the same thing about her, and the more he knew her the more he wanted to be around her. Whether it was helping her in the Honky Tonk or sleeping on her sofa. He couldn't wait to tell her about his day or what happened at the rig site. She understood his language when he asked for a WHMIS report and didn't hesitate when he asked for time sheets. Damn, he'd found a friend and a damn fine kisser. Exactly what he was going to do with either or both was a mystery, but he'd worry about all that later.

"Are you sick?" Angel asked so close to him that he jumped.

Was everyone out to sneak up on him that day? First Rocky barged in and broke up the make-out session with Cathy. And now Angel was disturbing his sizzling memories as well as his profound discoveries about Cathy. If he and Cathy ever did make it to the bedroom, would the devil open the door or would real honest-to-god angels with halos block it?

"What makes you think I'm sick?" Travis asked.

"You looked kind of glassy-eyed like you were getting a fever. Honey, if you are, suck it up; we're working twenty-four hours a day on this. I'm damn sure not wanting to go to Alaska and leave Garrett, so we've got to cuss some oil out of that Texas dirt out there," Angel said.

"I'm not sick. I was just thinking, that's all. We need more time and men," Travis said quickly.

"Rocky said he was calling Luther. I've heard a lot about him. Is he as big as they say?"

"I'm hoping that he'll be here in the morning and you can see for yourself," Travis said.

"Good, I might talk Amos into a few more dollars but I don't think he'll spring for one more day. If we hit pay dirt one of us gets to stay in Mingus and set up permanent shop. Buy leases. Keep the crew. If not, you know what's next and I'm not so sure I can do it, Travis. Not since I've met Garrett. I'm in love," Angel said.

"Does Garrett know?"

Angel tore a piece of paper off the south wall and put up a new one. "If he doesn't it's not my fault. What am I going to do? I didn't come to Mingus expecting to fall in love. Hells bells, I planned to ride the oil rigs for ten years before I even thought about settling down. Now here I am at twenty-three thinking about a white dress and baby booties."

His head jerked around like one of those folks in the scary movies who are possessed by a demon. "Baby booties?" He gasped.

"I'm not pregnant, but that's where my mind is going. I want to live on the ranch and have babies, and I want to do this, too. What's the matter with me? Am I crazy?"

"I don't know why you couldn't have it all. Amos has a permanent office in Fort Worth. Bet he'd be glad to put you to work in this area even if we don't cuss oil out of that sorry old Texas dirt," Travis said.

"But what if he says Alaska or nothing? You've been with him all these years. You can negotiate. Right here at first I should do what I'm told," Angel said.

"What you should do is follow your heart. If it's not happy then you'll be miserable wherever you are." Travis hugged her before he went back out into the cold to oversee the derrick going up.

What about his heart? If they failed at bringing in a productive well, what would happen between him and Cathy? She'd never leave the Honky Tonk. Was he ready to take the Mingus office if Amos offered it to him? Or did he really want to go to Alaska?

A few hot and steamy kisses and I'm thinking of the future. What in the hell is the matter with me? I'm not a teenager. I'm thirty years old and I've been in love more than once. So what makes this one so different? Whoa, boy! I'm not admitting or saying that L word. No sir. Kissing that big tall blond is one thing, and admitting that she's becoming my good friend is all right, too. We're two adults, so if it leads to more than a few kisses, that would be fine. But I'll fight the idea of falling for her. She's a barmaid and I'm a wandering oilman. Her business is tied down firmly to a dance floor and a bar. Mine could move at any minute and I love it that way.

When he started home that evening the moonlight transformed bare mesquite tree branches into arms beckoning him to hurry. He parked in front of the trailer and checked Cathy's living room window to find it and the Honky Tonk both dark. He'd never seen the whole place with no lights on at seven o'clock in the evening.

He headed out across the grassy area between his trailer and the Honky Tonk to see what was going on. Music filtered through the night air. At first it was barely audible but with every step it became louder. By the time he was halfway across the lawn he could hear the thump of the steel guitar and beat of the drums. He stood still and cocked his head to one side and then followed the sound to the garage located just south of the Honky Tonk. The door was cracked; he slipped inside and a loud blast of old country music blaring from a radio in the corner hit him in the face.

"Anyone home?" he yelled.

No one answered.

The only life in the place appeared to be from Highway 101 singing a song right out of the eighties and the bare light bulb swinging from the ceiling. He closed the door and leaned against it. A big Harley-Davidson motorcycle was parked at the end of the garage—shiny black with red leather seats and not a smidgen of dust anywhere on it— with just enough room beside it for Tinker's ride. A burgundy Chevrolet Silverado pickup was parked next to the cycle and a red Cadillac sat beside it. He walked down the length of the garage, wondering which vehicle belonged to Cathy. Surely she didn't own all three. Why would she need a car, a truck, and a cycle?

When he started back a movement in his peripheral vision startled him. He looked between the truck and the Caddy, expecting to see a cat or a mouse or some small animal. A bright orange creeper eased out from under the truck a few inches at a time. He leaned on the hood and waited.

"What the hell?" Cathy gasped when she looked up from her back.

"I might say the same thing. What are you doing?"

She made no effort to get up. "Changing oil. What are you doing in here? You scared the shit out of me."

"You change your own oil?"

"You don't?"

"Hell no. I take my truck to the Chevrolet house and they service it for me," he said.

"Well, little rich boys can do that. Little poor girls learn to change their own to save a buck," she said.

He ignored her barb about rich boys. "You going to get up off that thing?"

"When I'm ready. It's draining. When it gets done I'll replace the filter and drag the tub of old oil out. Ain't no use in getting up until it's finished. Won't take but a minute longer."

She wore a pair of stained blue coveralls that zipped up the front. "Harry" was stitched above the breast pocket. Her hair was braided into two ropes and she wasn't wearing a drop of makeup. Travis thought she was absolutely stunning.

"Harry?" he asked.

"They belonged to my father. He taught me how to change oil, spark plugs, and tires. Said girls who didn't know how to do jack shit had to marry early so they'd have a husband to do it for them. He didn't want me hookin' up with someone just because I couldn't take care of myself."

She slid back under the truck. What did he think he was doing, coming into the garage uninvited? She'd gone to the garage to work on her truck to take her mind off him and his kisses. She hadn't had much luck in getting him out of her mind, so maybe there was something to that old adage about thinking of the devil and he would appear. She put in the new oil filter and carefully dragged the plastic pan of used oil out with her when she was finished.

"So how was your day?" she asked.

He leaned on the truck's fender. "Busy like usual. I like

to be busy, so it's not a complaint. Why do you listen to old music? I'd think you'd get enough of that on Monday nights."

"When Daddy and I worked on his old truck or my old car he always had that old red radio up on the porch. I inherited it when he died and it's one of my prized possessions. It was tuned to an oldies station and heaven help the person who changed the dial. Of course, it's not the same station here in Texas but it's still an oldies station that plays the same kind of tunes. Even Momma knew better than to touch it. If you'll move, I've got to raise the hood and pour in the oil now."

He extended a hand to pull her up and she took it. The electricity between them didn't shock her as much as it did that first time he kissed her in the Honky Tonk, but it was still there. He pulled and when she was on her feet, he gave a little jerk that landed her right in his arms.

When he kissed her he smelled oil and tasted spearmint chewing gum. The weird combination was strangely heady. He inhaled deeply when the lingering kiss broke and drew her to his chest just like he'd done in the kitchen.

"I've got to go back out to the rig at midnight and stay until morning, so I won't be at the Honky Tonk tonight. I just wanted to find you and see how your day had gone. Now I know," he said.

"You don't have to be there until Friday." She was amazed at the calm tone of her voice. It should have come out all breathless.

"Luther is coming tomorrow, so that should speed things up. He does the work of three men and he's good-natured. But I wanted to come to the Tonk tonight," he said.

She wiggled. "If you don't let me go, you are going to be covered in dirt."

He held on tighter. "It's worth it. I'll wash and so will my clothes."

She felt an odd peace in his arms. Every nerve tingled. The emotional roller coaster was speeding along at a breakneck speed. The excitement between them glued her to the garage floor in a red-hot melting pot of desire. But in among it all there was peace.

"I've got half an hour to finish this and get the Tonk opened. Tinker will be opening that big door on the end any minute. After that near miss this morning when Rocky barged into the office, I don't think my nervous system could stand another, so I'm going to step back and you are going to leave. I'll see you sometime tomorrow."

"That's not very nice," he said.

"That's life. I hear a motorcycle engine coming across the parking lot."

"Tinker won't care if I'm in the garage."

"Maybe not. But I don't want to deal with him or anyone else tonight," she said.

She stepped out of his embrace and the garage door rumbled on its way up. He brushed a hurried kiss across her lips and eased out into the darkness at the same time Tinker parked his cycle.

CHAPTER 10

CATHY DIDN'T OPEN TRAVIS'S BEDROOM DOOR. SHE wouldn't invade his privacy. It wasn't that she hadn't wanted to take a peek inside his bedroom, but she'd been good all week. Every single time she went to the filing room or to the bathroom she'd fought the temptation and emerged the victor at the end of the day. However, that afternoon when she went to the filing room the first thing she noticed was that his door was cracked two inches. She went back to work because that blasted righteous angel whispered in her ear that she wouldn't want him prying in her bedroom.

She ate three yogurts and a dip of chocolate ice cream in an attempt to appease the curiosity. None of it worked, so finally she gave in to the devil and tiptoed down the hallway. She promised God if no one caught her invading his privacy that she would only peek inside through the small crack. She wouldn't even sneeze on the door to open it a bit farther. Propping her hands against the doorjamb, she leaned forward and peeked inside with one eye.

There was a book on the nightstand along with his wallet, keys, and cell phone. His boots and jeans were in a pile beside the bed. She could see the edge of the big brown comforter dragging on the floor. Then a foot dangling off the bed. She jumped back and grabbed her heart with one hand and her mouth with the other.

Wild horses couldn't have dragged her back into the office at the front of the trailer without another peek. If it was only open one more inch she could see better, but she'd vowed that she wouldn't open the door. She had to stand to one side and turn her head to an almost-break-the-neck angle but she finally got the full view.

One hand was behind his neck; the other dangled off the bed. He slept in the nude and the sheet barely covered the necessities. What was it Cal said? If it weren't for bad luck, I'd have no luck at all? She squinted to see more. His eyelids quivered and she wondered what he was dreaming about. His blond curls were mussed and he needed to shave. Six feet two inches of muscles all begging to be touched and she couldn't take a step inside his bedroom. If the door was cracked a bit more and if she had the courage she could slip inside the room and into bed with him.

And what then? Why do you torment yourself by looking at what you should not have?

She backed away from the door and blinked a dozen times on the way back to her desk but couldn't erase the image of him. She'd barely gotten settled into her chair when the front door opened. Her first thought was that she was glad she hadn't had the nerve to crawl into bed with him or she'd have been caught. Her second was to take off down the hall and beg Travis to protect her from the man in the doorway.

A complete eclipse blocked the light and the man between her and the bright sun was as big as an army tank. He had to duck to keep from hitting his head. His arms were bigger than Dolly Parton's bust and his chest would have to be measured in acres instead of inches.

"Afternoon, ma'am. I need the sign-in list for the trailers. I'm Luther." His deep voice bounced around in the trailer like drum beats in an old metal building during a barn dance. She didn't want to be around if he ever got mad and started yelling. The driller who'd slept with Luther's wife had to be a complete idiot.

She picked up the list and handed it to him. "Chairs are in the kitchen. Can I get you a cup of coffee?"

"No, ma'am. Never drink that stuff. It'll rot your pipes. Rocky tells me you own that beer joint. Need a bouncer on weekends?"

"Got one," she said.

"You got pool tables?"

She nodded.

Luther bent over the desk and scribbled his name in lot number eighteen. The pen was a toothpick in his big paws. He had a mop of black hair and pecan-colored light brown eyes. His face was as round as a basketball. He should have been playing fullback for the Dallas Cowboys instead of signing in as a roughneck.

He pulled a chair from the kitchen and sat down. "So you got anyone who's any good at eight ball in these parts?"

Cathy expected the chair to smash but it didn't. A vision of Luther in the Honky Tonk playing pool with Merle was too much for her brain. She shook her head to get it out and he took it as a no.

"So there's no competition around?" he asked.

"I'm sorry. Must've been a hair on my neck. Thought it was a bug," she lied. "We've got Merle Avery."

"He pro or just likes to play?"

"Merle isn't a he. Merle is a woman who is past seventy and she'd probably whip any pro you could line her up with. Her niece, Angel, is every bit as good. Merle says she's even better but I think it's a draw."

"I haven't met with Angel yet but I heard of her. Didn't know she was good at pool. Where's Travis?"

A slow burn started on her neck and rapidly rose to her cheeks. "Asleep. The trailer is both the office and his home."

Luther tucked his chin into his chest and his whole body rocked in laughter.

"That funny?"

"Little bit," Luther said.

"Why?"

"Travis usually has a fancy apartment."

"Luther?" Travis said from the hallway.

He'd pulled on a pair of flannel bottoms but his chest was bare.

Cathy was speechless.

Luther held up a big hand. "Mornin', Travis. Amos did good this time, didn't he? Puttin' us right here beside a beer joint. It's probably some kind of test to see if we can work and party, too."

Travis yawned and rubbed his eyes. "I wouldn't know. Maybe Amos is givin' you boys a good site since he's going to put you in igloos if this one don't pan out. What was so funny that you had to shake the whole trailer and wake me up?"

"You livin' in this trailer with the office. I'm goin' to get set up and go take a look at the site. I hear the woman out there is a sassy bit of baggage but she'll give you a glass of sweet tea anytime you show up at her door."

Travis squinted at Cathy and spoke to Luther. "That's right. Her name is Jezzy."

"Can she cook?"

"Oh, yeah."

"How old is she?"

"Midforties," Travis said.

"Well, I could get interested in an older woman. I'm pleased to meet you, Miz Cathy. Rocky says you're hot as a two-dollar hooker." He smiled.

She stood up and leaned across the desk right into his face. "Are you insulting me?"

Luther raised an eyebrow. "Whew! She is a tall one, ain't she, Travis? No ma'am, I'm not insulting you. I'm teasing Travis. Livin' in a trailer with a pretty thing like you in the front room all the time. I wouldn't be wastin' my time sleepin' if you was this close to me. You dating anyone?"

"Why are you asking?"

"Honey, I'd be honored to take you to dinner any night of the week," he said seriously.

"I work every night but Sunday. Doesn't leave much time for dating."

He stood and she looked up.

They locked gazes and she refused to blink. No man was going to intimidate her again.

Luther refused to let a woman stare him down and narrowed his eyes to make her blink.

"If y'all are going to fight, take it outside," Travis said.

Cathy shot him a dirty look. "Don't tell me what to do. If me and Luther want to fight right here and tear this damn place down it's not your call."

"You tear it down and I will move in with you and I won't sleep on the sofa, darlin'. You decide," Travis challenged.

Luther set the chair back in the kitchen. "Whew! You might have to call the Mingus Volunteer Fire Department if the sparks take a hold in this trailer. Looks to me like y'all need to either kill each other or kiss and make up. Take it from me, the kissin' is a lot more fun."

"This is our fight," Cathy said.

"And darlin', I got no doubt you can finish anything you start. Hope to see you both later." Luther whistled as he left.

Cathy glared at Travis the minute the door was shut. "Why aren't you at work?"

"I didn't get in until ten this morning. We had a problem and I stayed at the rig all night working on it. What business is it of yours anyway?" he snapped.

She smiled. "And you think I'm a bear in the mornings?"

"You are," he protested.

"Go put on a shirt and I'll make you some breakfast."

He folded his arms across his chest. "I don't want a cold Pop-Tart."

"I'll cook a real breakfast."

Travis spun around and headed down the hall. Another minute in her presence and he'd pick her up and stumble toward his bed. He pushed the door open and caught a whiff of her perfume. He whipped around but she wasn't there and he heard pots and pans clattering around in the kitchen.

He slammed the door, peeled off his pajama bottoms, folded them, and quickly put the room to rights before he got dressed. When he opened a dresser drawer for a pair of socks he caught a glimpse of Cathy's picture. He frowned. He didn't have a photo of her.

When he looked at it the second time he realized it wasn't Cathy but the cover of the second season of *La Femme Nikita*. He carried a few seasons of his favorite television series with him to the sites, since he never knew what hours he would be working. He'd learned to be prepared for hours of boredom between shifts. The actress who played Nikita wasn't as tall as Cathy, but they had the same face shape, the same wide lips, narrow nose, and long blond hair. Peta's eyes were lighter than Cathy's, but they both had long legs that started on earth and went all the way to the pearly gates. Cathy and Nikita were both kick-ass women. Travis had never seen anyone, male or female, bow up to Luther. Nikita wouldn't even be that brave.

The aroma of bacon and coffee drifted down the hallway and into the bedroom as he dressed in soft jeans and a dark green thermal long-sleeved shirt. He picked up the DVD box and looked at the cover. Peta was pretty but Cathy could beat her, hands down, in any contest.

"Can you cook? Well, Cathy can. I can smell bacon and Jezzy told me she makes an amazing chocolate cake." He laid the box down and headed back to the kitchen.

The table was set for two with an arrangement of salt, pepper, jelly, butter, and syrup clustered in the middle. Travis poured a cup of coffee, leaned against the cabinet, and sipped it while she made omelets. When she started making pancakes he peered over her shoulder and said, "That smells wonderful. If you'll cook for me every day I'll work an extra night at the Honky Tonk."

He smelled like Stetson and looked like sex on a stick. The majority of Cathy's determination plunged to the bottom of the deepest gutter. The warmth of his breath on her neck shoveled dirt on what little willpower was left. She wanted to forget breakfast and lock the front door.

Rocky poked his head in the door and followed his nose to the kitchen where he pulled out a chair and sat down. "Food?"

"My food," Travis said.

"I'll fight you for it, and as hungry as I am, you will lose," Rocky said.

Cathy shook her finger at them. "Oh, stop your pissin' contest. I've got enough cooked for the Confederate army if the South wanted to rise again. Travis, put another plate on the table. Rocky, you can pour your own coffee. It'll be ready when I flip these last pancakes."

The little guardian angel that she hated sat on her shoulder and whispered that Rocky was her salvation, not a demon. He kept interrupting things because she and Travis were headed down a highway straight into trouble. Friendship was fine and dandy. Anything past that would never work.

But what if he's the devil in disguise and just keeping me from my soul mate? Tell me that, would you? And while you are at it, go rustle me up a handful of straight pins and one of those little voodoo dolls that looks like Rocky.

She flipped the last of the pancakes onto a platter and set it in the middle of the table, along with a second platter piled high with bacon, cheese omelets, and toast.

"I can't believe you made me eat cold Pop-Tarts when you can cook like this," Travis said.

"When did that happen?" Rocky heaped pancakes and bacon onto his plate.

Travis slipped two omelets, toast, and bacon on his plate. "She froze me then wouldn't even feed me and she knows how to cook. I'm not sure she can get into heaven after committing sins like that. Saint Peter might give her one of them do not pass go, do not collect two hundred dollars, and go straight to hell cards."

"You played too much Monopoly in your life," Cathy said.

"Way I heard it is that she's mean as an old arthritic grizzly bear with a toothache in the mornings," Rocky said.

Cathy buttered a piece of toast and opened the strawberry jam. "Did you both forget I'm sitting right here, and if I'm that hard to live with I could take all this food and dump it in the trash? And who told you I was mean?"

"Luther didn't let his coattail hit his hind end before he was in the shack tellin' everyone who would listen that you was ready to take him on in a fistfight, but Travis stepped in to stop it. He said that he'd marry you tomorrow mornin' but that you must already be in love with Travis because you wouldn't even go on a date with him. I ain't never seen nobody tell Luther no. Are you in love with Travis?" Rocky asked between bites.

"That man would scare a rattlesnake out of an outhouse. It wasn't guts that told him no, it was pure old fear. And I'm not in love with Travis. We are just very good friends. What did that driller think he was doing making a play for Luther's wife?" Cathy swiftly changed the subject.

"Well, Luther thinks you'd kick a rattlesnake out of an outhouse and not even flinch. He was plumb impressed by you, darlin'. He said if Travis don't hurry up he's goin' to beat his time with you. We all got bets laid as to which one will get you to go on a real date first."

Cathy swallowed quickly to keep from choking. "You might as well take your money back because it will set in the pot until it rots into dust. I'm not interested in marriage. Tell me about the driller who hit on Luther's wife. Did he have a case of acute stupid or a death wish?"

Rocky put a second stack of pancakes on his plate. "We'll

see about that money. I betcha it's in somebody's pocket by the time we hit oil. And about the driller. He won't ever work with one of Amos's crews again. Not only was he messin' around with Luther's wife, he was playin' around with Bart's on the side, too. Plus he was lookin' the other way while his sorry nephew stole equipment."

She ignored the bet issue and kept the subject on Luther. "What'd she look like?"

"Skinny as a rail. Black hair. Nothin' special but Luther thought she was some kind of angel. I'll marry you tomorrow if you'll cook for me," Rocky said.

"No thanks," Cathy said.

Two men now had made the comment that they'd marry Cathy. A pang of pure old green jealousy stabbed Travis in the heart. He finished off his eggs and forked a stack of three pancakes to his plate. They were delicious but not as good as one of Cathy's kisses. He wouldn't marry her for her cooking but for the way she sent his senses reeling every time he looked at her. He didn't even have to touch her or kiss her for his body to heat up.

"I think I'll work late every night if you're going to make breakfast," Travis said.

"I'll make sure there's lots of Pop-Tarts in the trailer. I've got to go grocery shopping after work today. You got any particular flavor you are partial to? You could dip them in yogurt," she said.

Rocky shuddered. "That is gross."

"I need to shop, too. How about I go with you?" Travis asked.

Rocky looked up with a gleam in his eye.

Cathy put up a palm. "It's not a date. It's two business associates and friends going shopping for Pop-Tarts."

"Well, dang. I was ready to tell Luther that Travis had beat his time. Then we could lay bets on how long Travis could keep all them pretty white teeth."

"You are all crazy," Cathy said. "I'm not talking about dating anymore. Why did you come into town, anyway? I don't think you could smell bacon frying all the way out to Jezzy's place."

"I need a copy of all the roughnecks and their current status with safety protocols. Inspector is coming around in a day or two. I want everything in order," he said.

She left them to finish their midafternoon breakfast and carried her coffee to the computer. She brought up the right forms, printed them, and stapled them together. "There you go."

"So is everything up to code?" Travis asked.

"Oh, yeah. Amos would shell out the pink slips if we lost a day because of some minor regulatory infraction. He doesn't abide stupidity."

"He did with that driller," Cathy said.

"Yes, but he corrected it in a hurry. I got to run. Thanks for the food. You ever change your mind about marriage you call old Rocky. I'll do right by you, I promise. But if you got a mind to make me eat them toaster things, I'll divorce your sorry hide."

She waved without looking up from the computer screen. "You are welcome. I won't change my mind. And you don't have to worry about a divorce. You got to have a marriage first and it ain't happenin.'"

Travis looked at the clock on the microwave. It was a quarter past four. It would take ten minutes, tops, to do the dishes. What in the hell was he going to do with the other thirty-five minutes? He could instigate a make-out session and see where it would lead, but he'd only feel cheated. Thirty-five minutes was barely enough time to get warmed up. Hell, he could cuddle that long before and after with the middle lasting a heck of a lot longer than a mere thirty-five minutes. With a soft sigh he started straightening the kitchen.

"I'll help with that after five. I want to get this last report done in case Amos comes in tonight. Especially if there's an inspector on the way," she said.

"You cooked. I'll clean. Are we really going shopping after five?"

"I am. You can go with me if you want. What time do you have to be back to go to the rig?"

"I'm on from ten tonight until five in the morning. I'll be asleep when you come in to work tomorrow. If Luther comes in don't let him laugh," Travis said.

"If anyone tried to keep Luther from laughing he'd blow up and the trailer wouldn't be anything but a pile of rubble anyway," she said.

She heard the door shut and looked up to find Travis gone. One minute he was in the kitchen cleaning up and the next he was gone. She was both angry and relieved—angry that she couldn't see him and relieved for the same reason.

Travis stared at the picture of Nikita again on the DVD box and saw Cathy rather than the actress. What had brought him to Mingus anyway? He didn't believe in coincidence or fate, either. Amos told him he'd hire Angel but only if Travis would go to Mingus to be her mentor. He'd come close to refusing but Angel needed a toe in a good company and Amos was the best. He rationalized that it was Angel then that brought him to Mingus. It wasn't that spunky, smart, and beautiful bartender who could make a nun have dirty thoughts.

The picture of the actress stared at him as if she knew something he didn't.

"What?" he muttered.

Why don't you admit you've got a thing for her that goes way beyond friendship?

He picked up the novel on his nightstand and propped a few pillows against the headboard. He read ten pages and checked the clock. He couldn't remember a single word he'd read but it had passed off ten minutes. He threw the book to one side and laced his hands behind his head. He didn't need a picture of an actress to remind him of Cathy. All he had to do was shut his eyes and there she was: in the kitchen with an egg turner in her hand; behind the bar at the Honky Tonk; changing oil in her car. And in every single scenario she was sexy as the devil.

It took three days past eternity but finally the clock numbers said 4:59. He rolled off the bed, put on socks and boots, grabbed his coat from the closet, and carried it to the office.

———————

Cathy worked up the reports and watched the minutes tick off the clock so slowly that she wondered if the electricity had gone off. Finally she heard him shuffling around in the bedroom, checked the clock, and shut down the computer at a minute until quitting time.

Her heart did one of those skips like a little girl who was

set free from school after a long day of multiplication tables and verbs and couldn't wait to prance all the way home. When Travis stopped in front of her desk, it forgot about skipping and went into a full-fledged race that set her pulse into a thump like the drum rolls in a rock band.

"You ready?" he asked.

"Soon as I take this report back and file it. Got Amos's all stapled and ready." She pointed to the one on the desk.

"I'll file it." He reached.

"Thank you," she said stiffly.

She slipped her feet back into the boots under her desk and was standing at the door when he returned.

"Where do you buy groceries?" he asked.

"Walmart in Mineral Wells. If they don't have it in Walmart then I don't need it," she said.

"So does that mean you aren't a high-maintenance broad?"

"It means I'm a redneck broad," she said. "I'll get my coat out of the apartment and meet you at the garage."

"We can take my truck," he said.

"I'm driving. Does that hurt your male pride?"

"Depends. I refuse to ride behind you on that Harley," he said.

"There's not enough room in my saddlebags for groceries. We'll have to take the Caddy or the truck. Since it looks like it could rain, we'd best go in the Caddy or else everything will get wet."

"I suppose my male pride can handle being chauffeured in a Caddy. Do I ride in the front or the back seat?"

"In the front, but you aren't driving," she said.

"Okay then. I'll meet you in the garage."

She made a hasty trip through the apartment and into

the bathroom where she touched up her makeup, applying a fresh coat of lipstick and a dab of blush before she brushed her hair. After that she grabbed her coat from the bedroom closet and hurried out to the garage.

Travis leaned against the side of the Caddy. "I'd have started it and had it warmed up for you but I forgot to ask you for the keys."

"A knight in shinin' armor." She smiled.

He opened the door and made sure her coat was tucked in before he shut it. "Nope, just a cowboy whose momma taught him to be nice."

She pushed the button on the remote garage door opener and waited for it to roll up. "What else did your momma teach you?"

"To say please and thank you," he said.

She started the engine, drove out of the garage, and pushed the remote to close the door.

"So your momma is still alive?"

"Oh, yes, alive and raising horses. She's the horse rancher. Dad is a lawyer and wouldn't know a good horse from a swayback mule."

She pulled out of the Honky Tonk parking lot and drove south to the interstate where she hung a left and set the cruise control on seventy-five. "Where do they live?"

"Fort Smith. I was born and grew up there right on the ranch. Momma's people were all horse ranchers. Dad's were all corporate people. It was the story of opposites attracting each other. But they've made it work for thirty-five years, so it must be true."

"Is that all she taught you, to say please and thank you?" she asked.

He smiled. "She said that my smart brain would take me far in life but charm would get me anything I wanted. What'd your momma teach you?"

"To work my tail off, to make good grades for a scholarship to the university, and to never think any man was better than no man," she said.

"There's nothing about nice and please and thank you in there," he said.

"Nope. My granny taught me that and my daddy taught me to change oil and fix cars, like you already know."

"What else did your momma teach you?"

"To respect her. Momma was a woman who demanded respect. She wasn't my best friend. She said I could kick any bush in Mena, Arkansas, and find a best friend and they'd change as often as I changed my mind about my hair or clothes, but I'd only get one momma and her place was to be a mother. I worked my hind end off in high school, was valedictorian of the graduating class, and got a good scholarship. Went to the university and bartended for extra money even though I wasn't old enough. Fake IDs are cheap. Then came back home to Mena and worked at an oil company."

"So did you believe her about the 'any man, no man' thing?"

"I sure did. It was the best advice she gave me."

"Then you've never been married?"

She shook her head. "Almost once."

"What happened?"

"He got mean. I got gone."

Travis's gut clenched up. "Someone hit you?"

"His name is Brad Alton. We were engaged and he let his temper go past knocking a hole in the wall or throwing a hammer through the windshield of my car. When he hit me, I left. It's in the past. I've moved on."

"Did you hit him back?" Travis asked.

"Hell yeah. Now let's change the subject. We've only got an hour to shop because if I'm there any longer than that Tinker will be out lookin' for me. He's never come to the Tonk and not found someone there."

An uneasy feeling prickled the back of her neck while she shopped. Twice she saw two men dart around a corner too fast and once she noticed the same two lingering far too long in the tea aisle without putting a single thing in their cart. She tried to get a good look at them to compare notes with Tinker that night after hours but they were always looking away or moving too fast. So she added two boxes of green tea to her cart and went on, completely forgetting about them when Travis smiled at her purchase.

Wednesday night was church night in the Bible Belt. God might forgive a body for succumbing to the wild call on Friday and Saturday nights after a hard week's work, but He did not forgive folks for going to the Honky Tonk when the church doors were thrown wide open and there was an opportunity to repent for the weekend slide from grace. There were folks in and around Mingus who liked to sow wild oats through the week and sit in the front row of church on Sunday and Wednesday to pray for a crop failure. Then there were those who didn't care if the wild oats made a bumper crop. Those were the ones who often frequented the Honky Tonk on Wednesday night.

Jezzy and Leroy were there but Sally stayed home to grade papers. Merle found Luther and they laid claim to the closest pool table. Rocky and Tilman ordered a bucket of beer and carried it to a table where a couple of ladies had come in with flirting on the brain.

"Hey, Cathy, can we plug in that old jukebox? Remember us? I'm Betsy. We were over here Monday when it was so crowded we couldn't even wiggle," one of the women shouted.

Cathy nodded at Tinker who lumbered over to the jukebox, plugged it in, and put a quarter in to start the music. The Nitty Gritty Dirt Band played an instrumental called "Cannonball Rag." The women pulled Rocky and Tilman out on the floor and had them doing a fast waltz by the time the second guitar lick sounded.

They held on to their dancing oilmen when the song ended and Charley Pride started singing about loving her a long, long time. Betsy melted against Rocky so tightly that there wasn't room for a breath of fresh air between them. If she could fry bacon he might have just found a wife.

Jezzy propped a hip on a barstool. "How's the job going?"

"Which one?"

"I can see how this one is going. I'm talkin' about the one out there in the trailer. Does it make you want to go back to accounting and forget this bartending?"

"Hell no!"

"I heard that you locked horns with Luther." She giggled.

"I can't hiccup without everyone in Palo Pinto County knowing what I had to drink after I shut down the Tonk."

"That's about right," Jezzy said. "That Luther is one big man. Sally's eyes about popped out of her head when she saw him. If I was twenty years younger I'd take him on. I always did like 'em big and burly. I heard you and Travis went grocery shoppin' together. That sounds serious to me."

"Well, it's damn sure not serious," Cathy said.

Larissa claimed the stool next to Jezzy. "What's not serious?"

Jezzy filled her in on everything that had happened, then told her the story of how Cathy had stood up to Luther. "Way I hear it is that he proposed to her on the spot and she refused him."

"Is that Luther over there with Merle?"

Jezzy nodded.

"Lot of man," Larissa said. "Draw me up a Coors, darlin'. Who're those men over there with the Fort Worth hussies?"

"That's Tilman who's a roughneck like Luther and Rocky who is the tool pusher," Jezzy said. "See how fast I'm learnin' the oil business. If I could learn about Angus cattle as fast, it would make Leroy right happy."

"Well, those women don't have any right to take up the best dancers in the place. I can't learn if they don't dance with me," Larissa said.

"Want me to go trip 'em? If they got broke ankles they won't be rubbin' all over them men," Jezzy said.

"I don't care if they rub on them. Hell, they can have sex standin' up for all I care. I just want them to be nice and share. They can even take them home and sleep with them when the place closes down. I just want someone to dance with," Larissa said.

"Larissa!" Cathy said.

"Well, it's the truth."

Luther left the pool table, leaned on the bar, and winked

at Cathy. "Give me a quart of Coors, please, honey. I been thinkin' that Sunday evenin' me and you could go to Abilene and catch a movie and have dinner together. You say the word and I'll tell Amos I want the day off."

"No, thank you." Cathy shook her head.

"You going to play hard to get and make me work for a date? That don't seem fair, since you told Rocky you and Travis was just good friends. If that's all you are then why can't you date me?"

"I'm not playing hard to get but I'm not going out with you," Cathy said.

Larissa tapped him on the shoulder. "Hi, cowboy. Can you dance?"

"I can dance the leather off them boots you got on, lady, if you're willin' to give it a whirl." He grinned.

"I thought you were shooting eight ball with Merle?" Cathy asked.

"Angel's got a game going with her until her boyfriend, Garrett, gets here so I'm free for a while. You serious?" Luther asked Larissa.

She wiped the foam from her mouth before she handed the jar to Cathy and motioned for her to put it under the bar for later. "I am very serious."

The beat of Waylon Jennings singing "Amanda" was conducive to a nice slow two-step and Luther was light on his feet in spite of his enormous bulk. Larissa was a midget compared to him but he was holding her at arm's length. If he'd have pulled her up to his chest in a chest-to-chest dance, she would have been looking at his belly button.

Cathy watched them dance while she drew up half a dozen beers. Luther wasn't as handsome as Travis but he wasn't butt ugly. Travis hadn't asked her out on Sunday night and Luther had. So why didn't she go? Dinner and a movie didn't mean a trip down the aisle and a three-tiered cake. Cathy didn't feel a bit of remorse or regret. He might be a nice fellow but he could be someone else's nice fellow.

Rocky was back in the shadows with one of the Fort Worth hussies in his lap. They were either in a serious lip-lock or else they'd figured out a new way to share a beer. Tilman and the other Fort Worth hussy were on the dance floor hugged up tightly to each other swaying to a Tammy Wynette tune.

"You been gettin' any good lovin'?" Jezzy asked when Cathy made her way back down the bar to where she sat.

"Have you?" Cathy shot right back.

"Lord, girl, don't you ever answer a question?"

"Not if I can get out of it. Go dance with Leroy. He's gettin' antsy. Why don't you marry him?"

"Can't. I'd feel like I was commitin' incest on the weddin' night. He's always been my big brother. Besides, if I married him we'd kill each other before the honeymoon was over. But I will go dance with him."

"Stop worryin' about me and Travis."

"I'm not worryin'. I just hate to see you pass up something good. Don't judge him by other men in your life."

"How'd you know I was?"

"Been there and done that." Jezzy waved as she crossed the half-empty dance floor and made Leroy two-step with her.

Cathy kept check for new customers in the long mirror across the back of the bar as she cleaned a blender. One minute everything was going smoothly; the next she looked up into Travis's clear blue eyes. He smiled and her knees went weak.

"I thought you had to work," she said without turning around. He still wore his heavy work coat and his cowboy hat was on the bar in front of him.

"I do in half an hour. Thought I'd run by and see how things were going. Looks like Rocky is fixed up for the night. At least he's down on the end of the lot," Travis said.

Cathy whipped around to face him. "What's that mean?"

"Think about it. Ever see that old bumper sticker that says, 'If this trailer is rockin', don't come knockin'?"

"Jealous?" Cathy asked.

"No, ma'am. Not one bit."

If Rocky had been dancing with Cathy then he would have had to answer yes, definitely. What would it be like to make a trailer rock with Cathy when a tornado wasn't licking the front porch steps?

"Are you blushing?"

"Yes, ma'am, I am. That remark was crude and I shouldn't have said it in front of a lady. It's from workin' with a bunch of foul-mouthed oilmen all the time. Don't excuse it but it helps explain it. Forgive me," he said.

She almost dropped the blender pitcher. "Okay."

He picked up his hat and settled it on his head. "Thank you for that. I'll be leavin' now. See you tomorrow. Remember, you promised to keep Luther from laughing."

"I did not promise you any such thing. I'm a big girl but I'm not big enough to keep Luther from laughing. You ever hear the joke about the five-hundred-pound gorilla?"

"No, what is it?"

She propped her elbows on the bar. "Okay, tell me where does a five-hundred-pound gorilla sleep?"

"I have no idea," Travis said.

"Any damn place he wants to. And that's the way with Luther. I imagine he laughs any place he wants to laugh."

"You got that right." Travis left whistling along to Don Williams singing a song about the hard part being over and the loving part was beginning.

"Yeah, right," Cathy mumbled. "The hard part ain't but barely started and I'm not sure the loving part will ever begin."

"Who are you talkin' to?" Jezzy asked.

"Myself. I was talkin' to Don Williams about his song," she said.

"You've got to get laid, girl," Jezzy said bluntly.

CHAPTER 11

WHEN THE HONKY TONK LIGHTS STARTED FLASHING, the noise of slamming pickup and car doors sounded like the first day of deer season. Tinker checked IDs as they filed into the beer joint and Cathy kept the handles down on the draft beer handles as every lusty, thirsty drinker in the whole area bellied up to the bar.

Travis pushed through the swinging doors at the end of the bar. "I'll take over the beer business. I'm not too good with heavy machinery so I'll let you run those pesky blenders."

Cathy made change for a bucket of beers. "Where'd you come from?"

The man took the change and said, "From Dallas, darlin'. We heard this was a good place to party. Some friends of ours are into vintage country and said Monday night was a real hoot. We thought we'd see what was happening when it ain't vintage."

"Enjoy your beers." Cathy looked up at the next customer. "What can I get you?"

"Pitcher of hurricanes and one of piña coladas. You mean Monday is the only night you play the old stuff?"

Cathy nodded at the preppie wearing pleated slacks and a pearl-snap Western shirt.

"Well, damn! Guess we'll have to come back on Monday." He waited on his order and carried it to the table.

Cathy touched Travis's shoulder. "I was talking to you

when I asked where you came from. I figured you got called out to the rig and wasn't going to work here tonight."

"Sorry about being late. I was out there at eight o'clock when the lights went on but I couldn't get through the doors." He drew up six pints and put them on a tray for a woman wearing barely enough hot pink spandex and lace to keep her out of jail.

"Thanks, darlin'. You on call after hours to play doctor?" she asked.

"No, ma'am. I flunked out of medical school," he answered.

"Too bad. I make a real cute nurse. Even got one of them fancy little costumes and a hat."

"Never was much for nurses," he said.

"I'm not sure if that was an insult or not, but I'm not going to let you rile me. I've got a night out and I'm going to enjoy it." She carried the tray of beers back to a table where five of her friends waited.

The jukebox was completely hidden with people gathered around it. The new jukebox flashed all its pretty colors and songs went at fifty cents a pop or three for a dollar.

"Been busy out at the rig? Didn't see you yesterday." Cathy mixed a pitcher of tequila sunrises.

"I didn't come in. Caught a few winks of sleep in the pickup. Today I finally got away at five thirty. Took a long shower and a short nap and here I am," he said.

She put the pitcher and six empty jars on a tray, collected money, and made change. Travis looked more like a bouncer than a bartender in snug-fitting Wranglers and boots with a black T-shirt stretched over his broad chest. But his bloodshot eyes behind those thick lenses looked horrible.

She touched his bare arm and said, "Go home and get some sleep. I can handle it or else get Larissa to help if she wanders through the place."

"And miss all this fun? No thank you. I've been waitin' all week to get behind this bar with you, Cathy O'Dell. I'm not leaving until the last dog has died, the last song has played, and the lights are off. Can you believe she's trying to run me off, Jezzy? I bet she don't want to work on Monday mornin' and if I leave she'll have an excuse. Can I get you a beer?"

"Hey! I didn't see you come in. How are things out on the ranch?" Cathy asked.

"I want one of them martinis that Larissa's been braggin' up. Why would you try to run Travis off? Looks to me like he's pretty good help. Besides, every woman in the place is going to be up here orderin' beer just to get a look at him," Jezzy said.

"Then why are you orderin' a martini?"

"Larissa says you make a mean one. Thought I'd give it a try."

Cathy shook one up while Travis filled Mason jars with beer and bantered with women who kept downing them as fast as he could draw them. Maybe she should redo the billboard out on the highway and put his picture on it wearing that black T-shirt and tight jeans. That alone should bring in half the lusty women in central Texas. Hells bells, it might cause such an uproar that she'd have to knock out the south wall and build a bigger dance floor.

She set the martini in front of Jezzy and waited. Jezzy took a sip and nodded. "Damn good. Used to be my drink of choice back when but that's a story for another day."

"Don't tell me you played billiards in London with Larissa," Cathy said.

"No, in Paris." Jezzy laughed.

"You knew her before she moved here?"

"Hell no. I was yankin' your chain, darlin'. And if it had been in Paris it would have been Paris, Texas. I'm from Bugtussle. McAlester, Oklahoma, was like going to another world to me."

A fast song put the bravehearted on the floor for a line dance and gave Travis and Cathy a lull behind the bar. They grabbed rags and wiped up spills then refilled the pretzel and peanut bowls. Every time they moved they bumped into each other or brushed against skin. Even a slight touch of fingertips reaching for a dry bar rag generated more passion between them than all the dancing out on the floor.

"Get ready for it," Cathy said.

"What? To have the woman I love layin' in my bed like Darius is singing about?" Travis teased.

"Wouldn't know about that, but I do know that as soon as this one is done there'll be a beer run. Look at all that sweat."

"Makes you glad for the smoke, shaving lotion, and perfume, don't it?"

"Amen," she answered.

Two slow songs played and a few folks ventured out for two-stepping but the line dancers guzzled beer. Cathy wound up putting the jars on the trays and taking money while Travis used both hands to fill them.

Larissa edged in between two big burly ranchers wearing pearl-snap shirts. "Hey, Cathy! When you get time, draw me up a Coors."

"Want to dance, darlin'?" One of the ranchers touched her shoulder.

"Soon as I get this beer and take a few gulps," she said.

"He can't dance. Tell him no and dance with me," the other one teased.

"Hey, Rissa, you ready to do some two-steppin'?" Luther lumbered across the room.

"Got the next one promised to this feller right here, but you can have the one after that," she shouted back.

Cathy set her beer on the bar and the fellow on her right quickly paid for it. "Let me buy you that drink, sweetheart. Maybe it'll convince you to dance all night with me rather than that ox. Bet he'll step all over your toes."

"Darlin', that man could probably do the ballet, he's so smooth, so don't be callin' him an ox. And thanks for the beer but it won't keep me from dancin' with Luther," Larissa said.

Luther stopped at the end of the bar. He towered over everyone on stools and pointed at a quart of Coors that Travis was drawing up. "One of them, please, Miz Cathy."

She leaned over to tell Travis that the next one belonged to Luther. Her warm breath made his hands so clammy that he had to stop and wipe them on the legs of his jeans before he filled a quart with Coors.

"Getting tired?" she asked.

He put a quart of Coors in her hands and shook his head. Yes, he was tired, but not too tired to want to take her to bed. And yes, he'd caught a whiff of her perfume and he would love a long sexy kiss. He probably wouldn't be worth a damn for anything more than that anyway.

Larissa led her rancher out to the dance floor and wrapped her arms around his neck. Cathy kept an eye on them to see if the man could dance. He wasn't too clumsy and Larissa had come a long way from the first night she'd showed up at the Honky Tonk. She'd said that why she was in Mingus was a story for a time when they could sit together and have a long talk. Cathy's curiosity was piqued to the point that she was eager to hear the story.

Luther drank a fourth of his beer and handed it to Cathy. "Put this under the counter for me. I'll come back for it soon as me and Rissa get tired. She's learnin' fast for a newbie."

"And I thought you were in love with me. I'm hurt. First filly out of the chute that asks you to dance and I have to take the back seat. You ready to trade me in for her?" Cathy teased.

"Honey, you or that woman—either one is too much woman for old Luther, but it don't hurt to look at the merchandise or dance with it neither. See you later." He caught Larissa by the hand as soon as the song ended.

"You like to dance?" Travis asked Cathy.

"Love to but don't get much chance. All the cowboys go home at two o'clock and I'm damn sure not interested in going to a different joint on my one night off," she said.

Travis grinned. "Want to dance behind the bar? I'm not a customer. I'm the hired help."

"Could I get two buckets of beer over here?" the woman in hot pink spandex and lace asked.

"Guess you don't have to answer that question," Travis said.

Rocky waved at Cathy to catch her attention. "Coors in a bottle."

"Are you just gettin' here? Your sweet little honey from Wednesday night has been watching the door for you. I was afraid she was going to throw you over for that rancher over there in the blue shirt," Cathy said.

"Had to clean up after work. Can't catch a date smellin' like oil and sweat," he said.

"Oh, I don't know." Betsy sidled up next to him and clamped a hand on his thigh. "I like those two smells just fine, but you look damn fine all cleaned up, too. Bring that beer over to our table and we'll talk about the first thing that pops up."

Rocky grinned at Cathy. "This is my lucky night."

"Rockin' trailer?" Travis whispered in her ear.

She slapped at his biceps with her semi-wet bar rag.

He grabbed the rag midair and used it to pull her to his side. His eyes zeroed in on her lips and were headed in for the kiss when a customer asked for a Jack and Coke.

"That'd be your job," he whispered.

"Guess it would," she said. Damn but she'd wanted that kiss even if it was the wrong time and the wrong place.

At closing time Tinker pulled the plug on the jukebox and pointed at the clock. He set his cooler on the bar and tossed his Dr Pepper cans in the trash as the last of the partiers went home.

He picked up the envelope containing his paycheck from behind the cash register. "Been a good week."

"Best we've had since I took over," Cathy said.

"I'm glad you had some help back there," he said.

"Me too. Travis did pretty good for a green hand, didn't he?"

"I reckon he did. See you tomorrow night," Tinker said.

"I'll be here," Cathy said.

Travis looked around at the messy beer joint. "Now what?"

"Grab us each a beer and we prop up our feet. You look like the only crippled chicken at a coyote convention, Travis. Don't worry. I never clean it up until the next morning, and besides, your end of the bargain didn't involve sweeping and mopping."

"Coors?" he asked.

She nodded.

He pulled two out of the ice and carried them to the nearest table. She had already propped her feet up when he handed her a bottle. She downed half of it before she came up with a loud burp.

"Pardon me. My redneck woman gene just surfaced," she said.

He propped his aching feet up on the table. She was beautiful even at the end of a busy shift. Her ponytail was a little limp, her makeup sweated off, and there was a stain on the front of her shirt. Even after working all night she could have walked down a model's runway and had every photographer in the joint vying for a picture of her. A hint of cleavage started his testosterone boiling as if he hadn't been sleep deprived. He looked over at the jukebox.

Maybe a couple of slow ones. Mercy, who would have ever thought that bartending could suck even more energy out of a man than putting up an oil derrick.

He pulled a handful of change from his pocket.

"You don't pay for your beer after work. It's part of the deal," she said.

He set his beer down and headed toward the jukebox. He plugged in the old one and put a quarter in the slot. "Didn't intend to pay for it."

Travis walked across the floor and held out his hand to Cathy as Ronnie Milsap started singing a slow ballad.

She slung her feet off the table and wrapped her arms around his neck. "I thought you couldn't dance."

"Love to dance but I hate all that crowded business. My idea of dancin' is two people, one dance floor, one bedroom floor, one big old barn, or even one grassy lawn," he whispered.

Cathy laid her head on his shoulder and wished she could stay there in his arms for eternity. Brad was the last man who'd held her in his arms for a dance and that had ended in a blaze of fireworks that had nothing to do with passion and everything to do with anger.

He kept her in his arms when the second song started. "I don't think Mickey Gilley sang 'City Lights' first. Wasn't it Ray Price? My grandpa loved him."

"My dad did, too," Cathy said. "What'd you pick for your third song?"

"It's a surprise." He tipped her chin up and brought her lips to his for a lingering kiss. "Behind Closed Doors" played as the kisses went on and on.

"But I really am too tired to say 'I want to,' like Charlie Rich is singing," Cathy whispered.

He kissed her eyelids and her forehead before going back to her lips. "For tonight this is enough."

When the song ended he led her back to the table. "Thank you for the dances."

"You are very welcome, but now it's my turn." She removed a quarter from the cash register and headed for the jukebox.

Travis tipped up his bottle of beer and took a long draw. He watched her punch the buttons and use her forefinger to motion him to join her in the middle of the dance floor.

She wrapped her hand around his neck and she moved to "Marie Laveau" by Bobby Bare. He put his hands on her ribs and ran them slowly down the length of her body all the way to her ankles and back up as they kept time to the music. When he reached the top again he whipped her around and put both hands on her shoulders and began something between salsa and dirty dancing.

She'd thought she'd show him a thing or two about dancing, but his hands on her body and his eyes locked with hers made her wonder who the teacher was. When the next song started she whipped a pretend skirt tail around her legs and did a seventies-style bebop dance to "Bright Lights, Big City" by Sonny James. He stood there with his arms crossed over his chest and a big grin on his face. He reached out and took her hand and spun her around four times. If she'd been wearing a cotton skirt over a big cancan slip, it would have been standing straight out by the time he let her go. He spread out his legs and slung her between them and back again. Then he pulled her into his arms and put one arm around her waist and one on her shoulder to finish the song.

"Where'd you learn to dance like that?" She panted.

"My grandma. We used to go there on Sundays and Grandma would get out her old vinyl records. My great-grandma could do the Charleston and the jitterbug. I grew up dancing."

"You been holdin' out on me cowboy," she said.

"Got to keep a few surprises to keep you interested."

Her last song was an old Elvis Presley song, "Can't Help Falling in Love." Travis drew her to his chest and barely moved as they listened to Elvis's smooth voice.

"Am I supposed to be thinking about you or the words to this song? Did you choose this to send me a message?" Travis asked.

"I'm not sending messages," she lied.

The last piano note echoed off the paneling on the Honky Tonk walls and still Travis held Cathy. He hummed the Elvis tune softly in her ear as he moved her around the floor a few more times. Finally, he leaned back and said, "I'll put a dollar in if you'll keep dancing with me."

Cathy shook her head. "You've got to work tomorrow and it's late. Let's call it a night."

He slipped an arm around her waist. "Let's go out and look at the stars before we go to sleep."

She kept in step with him, their boots and the beat of their hearts the only sound in the Honky Tonk. The cold night air hit her in the face when she unlocked and opened the door. A quarter moon hung in the midst of a million stars like a king surrounded by his subjects and she could have stood there forever with his arm around her waist.

"They are almost as beautiful as you are." Travis softly kissed her one more time.

She leaned against a porch post. A movement in her peripheral vision made her turn to the left and watch a van slowly drive out of the parking lot. The windows were dark and the license plate muddy. She attributed the crazy prickly feeling on her neck to the feel of Travis's arm when he slipped it around her and forgot all about it when he brushed another kiss across her forehead.

Cathy awoke at ten o'clock and sat straight up, planning to get the Honky Tonk put to straights and go to work at noon. When she realized it was Saturday and she didn't have to open the office that day, she rolled over and picked up her cell phone. She hit the speed dial number for her cousin, Daisy.

"Daisy, I miss you," she said when she heard the familiar voice on the other end.

"Hey, girl, come and see me. Guess what—I'm pregnant," Daisy said.

"You rat. You beat me to the altar and now you get a baby before I do. Is this payback for totaling that old junky car of yours?" Cathy asked.

"I told you I'd get even, but it took me twelve years to do it." Daisy laughed.

"Morning sickness?"

"Not a bit."

"Now I am jealous. You get the handsome dark-haired cowboy, the ranch, the job you love, and a baby with no morning sickness. Have you been kissed by the good luck fairies?"

"I believe I have. Speaking of babies, Chigger called last night. She's due any day. I'm coming down there when the baby is born."

"Now that's the best news I've heard," Cathy shouted.

Daisy giggled. "Don't bust my eardrum. It'll be next week probably. I'm waiting until she calls to start that way. I've already got a whole basket full of cute little pink things I bought for the new baby."

"I'll make a trip to the baby store and get my present ready. There's so much I've got to tell you but I'm not doing it over the phone if you are coming next week. Is Jarod coming with you?"

"Yes, and we'll be staying out at the ranch with Garrett.

Suppose you already know that he's plumb smitten by Angel," Daisy said.

"Yes I do. You could stay here. I'll give you and Jarod my bed and I'll sleep on the sofa," Cathy said. Travis could stay at home a few nights. Lately he'd shown up at her door almost every night. It started with ice, no water, a tornado, and lately just to talk for an hour or two. They'd share what they'd been doing all day, kiss a couple of times, and then make out on the bed. But if Daisy was coming he could sleep in the trailer.

"Thanks, but Garrett has lots of room. Jarod and Garrett will be all involved with the ranch business so we'll be free to spend the days together. Now get up, clean the Tonk up, and go shopping. I'm hearing through the grapevine that Travis Henry has his eye on you," Daisy said.

"We'll talk about that when you get here," Cathy said.

"Yes, we definitely will. I sure miss that place. Goodbye."

"Goodbye, and tell Chigger I wouldn't mind her havin' that baby a few days early." Cathy threw the covers off the bed and danced around the room like a sugared up six-year-old after a visit to Grandma's house.

She made coffee and carried a cup into the Tonk with her. The place was messier than she'd ever seen it, but the stuffed cash register made up for the job of putting everything to rights. By noon she had it cleaned and her weekly bank deposit ready. That involved a quick drive to the bank in Stephenville and back.

Twice she looked up in the rearview to see a van following her, but when she slowed down or pulled over to one side, it sped past her. By the time she got to the bank she'd convinced herself that it was all her imagination anyway.

Then on the way back to Mingus she noticed the same color van sitting on the side of the road with the windows down. Two men were inside. They didn't appear to be talking but cigarette smoke was drifting out the driver's side window. She'd have to remember to ask Tinker that evening if he'd seen the two shifty characters he'd mentioned again and if one of them smoked.

When she got back to the Smokestack in Thurber it was the middle of the afternoon and she was starved. She parked the red Caddy on the far reaches of the lot and wondered if she shouldn't have parked closer, since a sprinkle of wintry rain hit her in the face as she hurried inside out of the cold.

"Well, look who's here," Amos said from a table right inside the door to her left.

"Hi, Amos! You eatin' alone today?"

He motioned toward the chair on the other side of the small table. "Not now. Come sit with me. Tell me everything you know while we have our dinner and supper combined."

Her eyes twinkled. "Ordered yet?"

"We don't even need a menu, do we?"

Amos held up two fingers to the well-known waitress.

"Coconut pie?" she asked.

"Yes, ma'am," Amos said.

Cathy pulled her arms from her leather jacket and let it fall back on her chair. "What brings you to Thurber today?"

"Had to check on the well out at Jezzy's place. It's lookin' promisin'," Amos said.

"And if it comes in good, does that mean you'll be buying mineral rights to other property?"

"Don't know. Never count my chickens before they're hatched. I'm still working on a deal up north. Depends on where I can make the most money. I been hearin' things about Angel and Garrett. You got anything on that?"

She'd held her breath when he said he'd been hearing things, afraid he was about to ask for a report on her and Travis. "Ask Angel."

"I will but first I'm askin' you. If I take the crew to Alaska is she going with me or has Garrett McElroy stole her heart?"

"Angel is a damn fine engineer, Amos. If she decides to stay in Texas with him, put her in charge of the wells in this area. She can handle it even if she is young and green. She's got a nose for oil and she's not afraid to get her hands dirty," Cathy said.

"That's good advice. I wish you'd sell the Honky Tonk and come to work for me. You've got a nose for oil too, only in a different way, and you keep your fingers on the pulse of the staff. Name your price and I'll double it," he said.

"The Tonk is not for sale," she said seriously.

"I'm not talking about that beer joint. I'm talking about salary."

"No thanks. I left that line of work behind me. I'm just doing you a favor. Answer me a question. How did you get your hands on my resume?"

"I called Daisy. She knew where you worked so I called them and said I was interested in hiring you. They faxed the resume with enough letters of recommendation to make the president of the U.S. of A. sit up and take notice."

"No thanks, still," she said.

Amos waved at someone coming through the door. "Well, look who's here. Hey, Travis, come on over here and join us. I'll buy your dinner if you haven't eaten yet."

He pulled up a chair beside Amos right across from

Cathy. "Haven't had a bite since breakfast and that wasn't anything but a doughnut on the run. I've been out at the site and came in to get cleaned up and grab a few hours' sleep before I do my shift at the Honky Tonk."

"What are you doing here then?" Amos asked.

"Coming back from a fast run to Stephenville. We looked everywhere for a V-belt and couldn't find one, so I ran into town and bought a dozen. Thought I'd grab a burger before I took them out there. They won't need them today but we will the first of the week." He didn't admit that he'd spotted the red Caddy as he drove past, made an illegal U-turn in the middle of the road, and drove back.

"Don't order a burger. Get the chicken-fried steak," Amos said.

Travis looked doubtful. "Any good? I hate a bad one."

Amos leaned back in his chair and crossed his arms over his chest. "Tell him, Cathy."

"Best you'll ever put in your mouth. Amos is paying so give it a try."

"I'm a connoisseur of good chicken fry."

"So am I," Cathy said. "And this place makes them almost as good as my grandma's, and honey, that's a compliment worth havin'."

Amos got the waitress's attention and held up three fingers and nodded when she mouthed "coconut pie." In a few minutes she brought their salads and garlic bread.

Amos dug into the salad. "We were just talking about Angel. What's your take? You think she'll go to Alaska when I move the crew up there?"

"Don't know. Ask Angel. Don't know if they raise Angus cattle in Alaska or if Garrett would want to relocate."

"Pretty serious, is it?"

"They don't know it yet, but it's serious. Keep her in this area and give her a shitload of responsibility. She's tough. She can handle it."

Amos ate slowly, savoring every bite. "What about ranchin', husbands, babies, and the oil business all combined?" he asked.

"She loves her job and she's got enough energy to do it all."

"And you?" Amos slipped the question in slyly and kept his eye on Cathy more than Travis.

"Give me an opportunity to move to Alaska and I'll have my bags packed in ten minutes. Only I want to go permanently, not on a six-month turnaround. I want to buy a chunk of property and live there."

The set of Cathy's jaw told Amos that she had no notions of living in Alaska.

"Ever been up there?" Amos asked Travis.

"Oh, yeah. My first job as a petroleum engineer back before I signed on with your company was mainly in that area. I did a six-month turnaround in the Prudhoe Bay area and said if anyone ever said I had to go back there I'd shoot myself first. Then I did a turnaround near Anchorage. Not right in the big city but on the outskirts. Fell in love with the place. That is where you are negotiating, isn't it?"

Amos nodded. He didn't want Cathy to move to Alaska and he wondered just how much Travis would like it there without her.

CHAPTER 12

TRAVIS HAD TO PUSH HIS WAY TO THE FRONT OF THE line and listen to snide remarks about cutting when Tinker let him into the Honky Tonk on Saturday night. All the barstools were filled, tables were claimed, games were going on at both pool tables with people waiting to play the winners, and the dance floor was so crowded he had to pick his way to the bar. "Come On In (The Whiskey's Fine)" by Mark Chesnutt had line dancers and two-steppers taking up every square foot of room.

"Sorry I'm a little late." He went right to work taking orders.

Cathy's blond ponytail swung back and forth as she hurried from customer to customer. Sparkling rhinestones in the shape of a heart lit up every time the light hit her black T-shirt. Her hip slung jeans were tight and her boots scuffed and worn. His pulse was testimony that it was going to be a long, hot night and he'd be ready to sleep in the beer cooler by the time Tinker shut the place down.

Cathy pushed the button on the blender to make a pitcher of hurricanes and took time to look at him. He had rolled up the sleeves on a black T-shirt showing biceps that flexed every time he pulled the handle to fill another Mason jar. She sniffed and got a noseful of Stetson above the smoke and perfume. It would be so damned easy to fall for Travis or even just to fall in bed with him. She'd have to be very, very careful.

"The lot was full when I opened up. They were lined up halfway to the highway and have been coming in as fast as Tinker can check their IDs. I'm beginning to feel like we're runnin' one of those fancy joints in Dallas. I've never had to worry about the maximum load but tonight could be the first," she said.

"What is the max?" Travis asked.

Cathy checked the plaque on the wall beside the mirror for an exact number. "Three hundred, but I've never seen that many."

He set two buckets on the bar and filled them with bottles of Miller and ice. "It looked like you had more than that on New Year's and twice that many last Monday night."

She smiled. "We were just a little backwoods beer joint six months ago. What in the hell has happened?"

"Twitter, Facebook, email. It's like a small band that finally gets their foot in the door and everyone wants to say that they were following them when they were nobody. Somebody has put out the word there's a quaint little joint over in Palo Pinto County that's rockin' with oldies music." Travis set four quarts of Coors on a tray and made change for a lady with a black lace, skintight top held up by thin straps. Didn't those women know it was cold outside? What would Cathy look like in a getup like that? How long would it take him to peel it off her body? Would she knock him cold on the floor if he tried?

A man snapped his fingers in front of Travis to get his attention. "I'm next. I want a bucket of Coors and two piña coladas."

Travis jumped. "Sorry, sir, I didn't hear you above the noise. What was that again?"

"Two piña coladas and a bucket of Coors," he said.

"Comin' right up. Cathy?" He looked over his shoulder.

"I heard him. Soon as I finish these tequila sunrises I'll be right on it."

Betsy, the lady who had been hitting on Rocky the past few nights, waved between two cowboys to get her attention. She'd traded in her pink spandex and lace for fake black leather and satin that night. Her blond hair had come straight out of a bottle but didn't look bad in the dim lighting.

"We heard we could get the vintage songs and even at the old prices. Think we could get some of that? We can hear the new stuff any old time on the radio."

"This is Saturday night. The new bands play tonight. Old stars are up on Monday," she said.

"Please," Betsy whined.

"I'd like to hear some old Hank or Merle Haggard," one of the cowboys said.

"Put it to a vote. Those who want the vintage can stay. Anyone who doesn't like it can go up to the Trio or The Boar's Nest," Travis suggested.

Cathy unplugged the jukebox just as Gretchen Wilson finished asking for the last "hell yeah."

"Hey, what're you doin'? We can't dance without music," Bart said.

"Can I borrow your chair for half a minute?" Cathy asked.

He dragged it across the floor. She stood on it and clapped her hands twice. The place went silent. "We're takin' a vote. Usually Friday and Saturday nights this new jukebox is what we listen to. But some of the customers have asked us to use the old one tonight so they can listen to vintage country music. How many of you want to listen to the old music like we have on Monday and how many want the new songs? Vote by a show of hands, please," Cathy said. "New?"

A dozen hands went up.

"Old?"

The place looked like a wave at a Cowboy's football game. The whoops and hollers were louder than Gretchen Wilson's "hell yeahs" had been.

"The customers have spoken. Anyone who hates this kind of music is welcome to leave and let some of the folks outside in." She hopped down and plugged in the old jukebox, took a quarter out of her pocket, and got the night started with Tammy Wynette's "Your Good Girl's Gonna Go Bad."

"That surprised me," Cathy told Travis when she was back behind the bar.

"Not me. It's a new novelty. Kind of like going back in a time machine. Remember when Barbara Mandrell sang about being country when country wasn't cool?"

"She was talking about me. Were you country when it wasn't cool?"

"Oh, yeah. From my hat down to my boots. How about you?"

"From birth. Cut my teeth on Hank Williams, Porter Wagoner, and Dolly Parton."

He filled another bucket with bottles of beer and shoveled ice in on top of them. "Me too. Grandma and Grandpa loved those old artists. I bet if my grandpa was still alive and he found out there was a jukebox like that still around he'd be your best customer."

Cathy took an order for three margaritas. "Then how come you'd never heard of Marie Laveau?"

He ran a hand down her rib cage. "Don't have any idea but if you'd like to dance to it again, I'm game."

She shivered. "I believe that's harassment."

"It wasn't last night."

"After hours plays by different rules," she said.

"Yes, ma'am. Then save me a dance after hours."

"You askin' or demandin'?"

Luther claimed a vacated barstool. "Askin' what? Did you say you'd go out with him? Did he end up being more than your good friend after all? The Hag didn't do this one first, did he? Seems like I remember Ray Price singing 'Silver Wings' when I was a kid."

"I didn't say I'd go out with Travis yet. And I think you are right about Ray singing that song. So you listened to the old guys, too?" Cathy asked.

"You bet I did. Granny and Grandpa, Momma and Daddy, and even my big brother loved country. Still do."

"Big brother. Surely you mean in age?" Cathy said.

"Both age and size. I'm a midget compared to Harlin. He's six foot seven and outweighs me by fifty pounds."

"What does he do for a livin'? Wrestle or pro ball?"

"He's a football coach up in northern Oklahoma. He's got a good team that usually goes to state," Luther said. "Y'all seen Rissa? I want to dance and can't find her out there in that can of wigglin' worms."

"She's usually here on Saturday night. Go shoot some pool with Merle. She looks like she could use some competition," Cathy said.

"Will you send her over there when she gets here?" Luther asked.

Travis nodded. "Want a beer while you wait?"

"Quart of Coors," Luther said.

At midnight a few people left and Larissa was one of the dozen that Tinker let inside. She went straight to the bar, got Cathy's attention, and ordered a martini. Her black lace blouse had flowing sleeves with ruffles at the cuffs and white pearl buttons down the front.

"Luther's been waiting for you," Travis said.

"What happened to this place? There's fifty people out there just waiting for someone to leave so they can come inside. They're dancin' in between the cars in the parking lot to the music that's coming out through the cracks. If they could get a bucket of beers they'd probably be as happy out there in the cold as in here," she said.

Cathy set the drink in front of her. "It's a fad. Next week we'll be lucky to draw in a hundred on weekend nights."

"I wouldn't count on it." Larissa waved as she weaved her way through the noisy crowd to the pool tables. She said something to Merle who nodded and pointed at the edge of the pool table. Larissa set her martini beside Merle's beer and Luther waltzed her out onto the dance floor to a couple of old tunes by Charley Pride followed by a Bill Anderson ballad.

Someone must have been tired of slow songs because the next one out of the jukebox started off with "Great Balls of Fire," by Jerry Lee. That put everyone on the floor in a line dance. Luther showed Larissa the dance steps and the second time everyone crooked their leg, slapped their boot behind them, and shuffled forward two steps, she had it down.

"She's a natural," Cathy said.

Travis looked up from the beer section and asked, "Who?"

"Larissa. She's only been coming in here a few weeks and she's already got two-stepping down and look at her on that line dance. She's as good as Luther."

"Wonder what she did before she moved here? Maybe she ran a dance studio that taught ballroom dancin'," Travis said.

"I have no idea what she did. She just showed up here one night. I thought she was one of Hayes Radner's henchmen," she said.

"Who's that?" Travis asked.

A woman reached across the bar and touched Travis on the arm. "Hey, good-lookin', I'm Randa. I need two buckets of Millers and two pitchers of piña coladas. We just got in and we got to make up for lost time."

Travis grabbed two buckets from under the counter and loaded them with bottles and ice while Cathy blended and filled two pitchers and put them on trays with empty pint jars.

"I love this music. How long have you been here? What's your name? How come y'all ain't got name tags? Y'all open any other nights?" Randa asked Travis.

"The Honky Tonk has been here more than forty years. I'm Travis and this is Cathy and we don't need name tags," he said.

"Well, hot damn. We thought it was brand new and only open on Friday and Saturday. Wait 'til we get back home and tell everyone what we done found. We love the old country music," she said. "Hey Brenda, come help carry this stuff. I only got two hands. Guess what—this place is forty years old. Can you believe it?"

Larissa breezed through the swinging doors into the bar

area. "Luther is making the rounds gathering up trays. I'll wipe them down and stack 'em up. You are getting low."

Luther set a three-foot stack of trays on the end of the bar. "Busy night, ain't it?"

"Keepin' me on my toes for sure. Thanks," Cathy said. "If the fad doesn't die out I'll have to hire some extra help."

Travis grabbed a clean tray and filled four quarts with Budweiser. "I'm your hired help. Don't be givin' my job away."

"Honey, I'll let you help yourself to anything you want if you'll quit your job and work for me," Randa said.

"Rule is the hired help can't dance or drink with the customers," he said.

"I'll pay you big bucks." She winked. "If you change your mind, there's six of us over there in the back corner who you can help all night long."

"I'll remember that." Travis grinned.

Cathy slapped him on the butt with a wet bar rag. "Stop flirting."

"Why? I can't flirt with you. That's harassment during working hours. And I do believe if I checked the handbook that touching my butt is considered harassment, too."

"I'll harass you, darlin', any time of the night or day." Another woman flirted from the space Randa left.

"Sorry, boss says I can't," Travis said.

"Tell the boss to go to hell. Honey, if I could take you home with me, I'd chain you up and never let you out of my sight."

"Other than that, what can I get you?"

"I guess a bucket of Coors. I can use the ice to cool off my hot little body," she said.

Travis filled up a bucket and the woman handed him a fifty-dollar bill.

The woman leaned over on the bar and let a piece of ice sliver down four inches of cleavage. "Get that out for me and you can keep the change."

"That's a lot of money," Travis said.

"It's melting fast and it's a long way down there," she teased.

"Gotta pass. Here's your change." He laid the money on the table and looked down the bar at the next customer.

"I'd have paid her to let me get that ice," the man said.

"If you hurry, you might catch her before it's all melted," Cathy said.

"That tone was colder than the ice in the woman's boobs." Travis laughed.

Cathy shot him a dirty look.

"I can't help it if they flirt. This is a different crowd than you usually have," he said.

"If you'd have gone for the ice I planned on breaking your fingers, so keep that in mind."

"Broke fingers couldn't draw beer. You keep that in mind. Don't you just love this sound?" He changed the subject.

The guitar music, drums, and steel were definitely old country. From the first guitar lick to the last note it had an unmistakably county beat. Cathy was reminded of the song that Alan Jackson sang about murder on music row that said in today's world the old singers wouldn't have a chance. Looking out over that crowd of hooting and whooping people, she wondered if it wasn't making a comeback. Maybe it hadn't been murdered on music row but just shot in the leg.

Luther kept Larissa on the floor through Buck Owens,

Dolly Parton, and Johnny Cash. When Bobby Bare started singing about Marie Laveau, Travis grinned at Cathy.

He held out his hand. "Could I have this dance?"

She took his hand and did a couple of sexy bumps and grinds against his side. He looked as if he'd been poleaxed.

"Shocked you, did I?" She laughed.

"You broke the rule," he teased.

"Yep, I did. Some rules just have to go out the window. Get ready for the next wave. That song sucked the sweat out of them. They've got to have beer or we'll be sweeping up dead bodies when we clean up in the morning," she said.

"Where'd you get that 'we' business, woman?" Travis's eyes glittered.

"You mean you're not going to volunteer to help me put things in order tomorrow morning?"

"No, ma'am, I am not. I've got to be at the rig site at nine o'clock and there's no way I'm waking you up that early."

"That's probably wise," she agreed.

He hummed along while Loretta Lynn sang about being someone's Kentucky girl. Cathy could be his Alaska girl, but the way her business was booming she'd never leave the Honky Tonk.

My girl! When did that happen? I've kissed her a few times. I haven't even made love with the woman. So why do I think she's my girl?

"What are you thinkin' about?" Cathy set six Jack and Cokes on a tray.

"As many times as I've leaned on these handles, I'm wondering whether we're goin' to run out of beer. How much you got in the cooler?" He wasn't about to tell her that he'd been entertaining notions of her being his girl.

"There's enough to last until closing. I may have to call the distributor and ask him to make an extra run on Monday to get through the first of the week. But right now we're in good shape," she answered.

At one o'clock part of the crowd called it a night and Tinker let the rest of the folks who'd waited in the yard inside. They hit the bar for buckets and Mason jars of beer and fresh energy pushed its way right out onto the dance floor. At one thirty it thinned out a little and at five minutes until two Tinker unplugged the jukebox right after Conway sang "Lonely Blue Boy."

A lady yelled, "Ah, man, we only got an hour."

"Come early on Monday night. We'll open at eight," Tinker said.

"I'll be the first one in line if I have to camp out on the doorstep all night," she said.

The place was empty at two when Tinker set his cooler on the bar, and for the first time since Cathy had been in the Honky Tonk it still had two unopened Dr Peppers in it.

"Didn't have time to drink much," he said.

"It's just a crazy fad," she said.

"Busier than I've ever seen it. If it keeps up we might need to hire Travis or Larissa full time. I thought I saw those two men again tonight. They were out in the parking lot leaning on a car. Things was busy so I didn't get out there to put them going. I expect they're stalking Larissa because when she left they did, too." He waved goodbye and left.

Travis picked up two beers and headed for a table. "What's going on with two men?"

"Tinker thinks there are a couple of stalkers hanging around. At first he thought they were looking at me but now he thinks they are after Larissa. Don't know what or who she was before she came here. Maybe she knows them." She didn't tell him that she'd had the uncanny suspicion they were following her in the Walmart store or to the bank.

"Show them to me the next time they're here and I'll find out what they're up to. Now…" he held out a hand, "want to dance?"

"Hell no." Cathy slipped her boots off behind the counter and followed him in her stockings. "I want to put up my aching feet and guzzle a beer."

Travis sat across the table from her. He tipped back his beer and took a drink. Lord, it tasted good after that six-hour run. He set it down and looked at her long, long legs. He leaned across the table and took her left foot in both his hands and began a deep foot massage.

"Oh God, don't stop," she moaned.

"That sounds like more than harassment," he teased.

"Honey, what you are doing feels so damn good you can sue me. Hell, I'll give you half my kingdom if you'll do that for an hour," she said.

"What would I have to do for all your kingdom?"

She'd never known that icy blue eyes could have fiery hot embers in them, but his did. They could have set the Tonk on fire if it had been physically as hot as the vibes they shared.

"More than rub my feet," she said. "Don't ask me things like that tonight, Travis. I'm too tired to be rational."

"Then how about going out with me tomorrow night for dinner? You name the place. A real date. I'll pick you up at six and we'll do dinner and then a movie." He started on the arch of the other foot.

She leaned back and shut her eyes tightly. "If you won't stop for the next ten minutes the answer is yes."

"Can you stay awake for ten minutes?" he asked.

"Probably not. Wake me up when it's over."

He laughed.

"No sexual connotation intended," she said.

"Let's curl up on your sofa and just cuddle together until we fall asleep?"

"Can't do it."

"Why not?" he asked.

"Because I'd want more and I'm too damned tired to enjoy it," she said honestly.

"Then there is a tomorrow?"

"Maybe." She pulled her feet down. "You sleeping on the sofa tonight or going home?"

"I sleep better on the sofa. You seen any more of those stalkers?" He finished his beer, stood up, and brushed a kiss across her forehead. If he kissed her lips he wouldn't be able to stop.

"Not lately. I can't even be sure that they ever followed me the first time. It all could have been my imagination, since Tinker and I'd talked about them. Nerves talking instead of common sense," she said as she locked up, turned out the lights, and followed him to the apartment.

He pulled his duffel bag from the coat closet, removed a pair of clean pajama bottoms, and made a mental note to repack it the next day. Lately, he'd spent more nights at the apartment than he had in the trailer. Most mornings he was long gone before Cathy awakened, but he enjoyed that hour of company they shared after the Tonk closed. When he did go home before closing, he watched for the parking lot to empty, Tinker to go home, and the light to appear in her window. That was his cue to traipse out across the grass and knock on her door.

While she showered he peeked out the window. No slow-moving vans. Maybe Tinker and Cathy had both been wrong. Shady characters often hung around beer joints. He dropped the mini-blind slat when he heard the shower stop.

"Your turn," she called out.

He washed the smoke and day's grime from his body, donned faded pajama bottoms and a T-shirt, and went back to the living room where she waited on the sofa with a cup of hot chocolate in one hand and one of green tea in the other.

"So tell me, you going to get that oil to come up out of the ground in the allotted time? Are you really going to Alaska?"

He reached out and took one of the cups and sipped the chocolate. "I hope so on both counts. You ever been up there?"

She shook her head. "I've seen pictures on the internet."

"It's not the same as seeing the place. You live a lifetime in Texas and see maybe two or three bald eagles. In Alaska you'd see that many in a week. Lighting on telephone poles and looking like the king of the clouds. And the peace is unreal." He sat down in the rocking chair.

"To me this place is peace," she said.

He raised an eyebrow. "A noisy honky tonk?"

"That's right. Peace is the condition of the heart, not the place the body abides." She didn't say that lately her heart hadn't known a moment's peace or that most nights she fell asleep wondering what it would be like to awaken all curled up in his arms.

"Want to watch a movie tonight?" he asked.

"No, I'm wiped completely out. I've got to get up in the morning and balance the cash register and then drop a deposit at the bank, so I'm ready for bed."

"On Sunday?"

"I usually make my biggest deposit on Sunday. There's a night drop at the bank, so it's no big deal. But it takes me a while to get it ready and on Sunday I don't have to rush. What's your day looking like tomorrow?"

"We're on schedule but I'm going to put in some hours out at the rig. Want to go out tomorrow evening for dinner and maybe a movie. A real date?"

"How much of your money is in the pot?" she teased.

"Enough to buy dinner and a movie. But I'll give it all to Luther if you'll go with me," he said.

She nodded on her way to her bedroom. "I'd love to. Good night, Travis."

He carried both cups to the sink, rinsed them, and put them into the dishwasher. He thought he heard a vehicle moving slowly through the parking lot but he was already half asleep and didn't leave his warm spot to check it out.

The next morning Cathy found the sofa put to rights and the covers folded in the rocking chair. She called Daisy while she ate a Pop-Tart and coffee breakfast but only got her answering machine. She left a message telling her that she'd call later in the week and went into the Honky Tonk, took all the money from the cash register, pulled the tape, and sat down to balance them.

Lately she'd been bringing in twice what she did in the first days when she took over the joint. If the fad built into a steady thing she'd have to consider hiring full-time help. Her zippered bank bag was full of cash and credit card receipts when she finally got the money and register tape to agree.

She still wore her flannel pajama bottoms and a T-shirt but she didn't need to be dressed up to drop a bag of money through a slot. She thought about putting on a hooded sweatshirt or a jacket but the truck would warm up quickly and then she'd be too hot, so she tugged on her cowboy boots, stuffed her cell phone into her pocket, and headed out to the garage. From the edge of her vision she caught sight of a van going down the road too slowly.

"Tinker, you've got me seeing demons on every corner." She sighed. She kept watch in the rearview mirror as she drove to Stephenville but only saw a pickup truck with an elderly couple talking with their hands and one of those new station wagon vehicles with several children in the back seat.

She made her deposit, stopped by the Sonic for a cherry limeade, and headed home. When she reached the turnoff to go to Garrett's ranch, she slowed down and seriously considered going for a visit. Then she remembered what she was wearing and changed her mind.

She rolled up the garage door with the remote and backed the truck inside. When she stepped out two men rushed inside. She scarcely had time to blink before one had her around the neck and the other was pointing a pistol at her head. She kicked the gun from out of the red-haired man's hand and elbowed the one trying to strangle her. Gun man made a dive for her feet and she planted a boot in his shoulder, sending him sprawling against the pickup.

"Get the hell off my property," she shouted.

Neck man jumped on her back and she leaned forward and then threw herself backward against the Cadillac parked next to the truck. She heard a whoosh as the air left his lungs and he slumped to the ground. The banty rooster in front of her went for the gun and pointed it at her again. She plowed into him like a bulldozer over an anthill, cussing and ranting like a madwoman. The gun went off in the melee and ricocheted around in the garage, hitting an empty metal gas can and rattling around inside until it came to a stop.

The red-haired man was on the ground, with her knee in his chest and her fingers around his neck. She was enjoying the beautiful sight of his face turning blue when something stung her neck. She could endure a bee sting if she could watch the man turn one more…shade…of…

Suddenly the man's face was entirely too close. Why would he try to kiss her when she was strangling him? Her hands went slack and she couldn't convince them to press any harder. The garage walls danced toward her and everything went black.

———————————

Cathy's eyelids felt like they were made of those heavy rubber bands. She'd open them and then they'd spring back shut. She forced them open and listened to her captors. Why weren't they dead? Why were they still talking? She'd choked one and smashed the other.

"So you think we'll be there by nightfall? I hate that place after dark with all those weird sounds and the rats. God, I hate rats," one said.

"Stop your bellyachin' and look back there and make sure she's still sleeping," the other answered.

"Stop worryin'. She's out for twenty-four hours. Ain't no way she'll wake up after that shot. Damn she's a big woman, ain't she? We shoulda brought one of them stretcher things. It woulda made the job easier."

Cathy blinked several times. Her nose itched but when she tried to scratch it she couldn't move her hands. They were both asleep and she was lying on them. She never slept with her knees drawn up but they were all cramped up under her and she couldn't straighten them. She inhaled deeply and tried to stretch but neither her legs nor arms would move. The strong smell of hamburgers, onions, beer, and smoke filled the room. In the dizzy darkness she wondered what those aromas were doing in her bedroom.

"Don't know why in the hell he wants someone that damn big. Ask me, a little woman is a lot easier to control. Slap her once and she knows who's boss. That big old horse of a woman ever hits him back and he'll be on the floor whinin' like a pissy little girl."

She was in the middle of a hellacious nightmare and couldn't wake up or move. Where was Travis? Had he awakened early and left the television playing when he left for work? Was she meshing whatever dialogue the actors were saying into her dream? She tried to swallow but her mouth was so dry it felt as if it had been packed with sand. She looked around the blurry room. Only it wasn't a room. She was in Travis's trailer house and it was rocking worse than it had during the tornado. Had they made love and she'd slept through it? Then someone started talking again.

"She made him mad when she lied about being married

to that redneck rancher. He said he'd get even. And then his uncle said that if he didn't settle down with a woman like her he was going to be out of a job. I guess some women at the oil company filed a sex harass thing against him. His uncle got him out of it but said he had to get a wife and be 'spectable. It's probably the truth about him comin' on to the women. That boy never could keep his zipper up even when we was all kids. If it was a girl it was fair game. He reckons that by the time she spends a few days in that fishin' shack she'll be softened up and ready for him to rescue her. She'll be so damned grateful to be out of there that by fall she'll be engaged to him again. Then the old man will be happy because he always did like her more than he liked Brad anyway. At least that's what he told me. Did she kill off all your brain cells when she put that choke hold on you? I done told you this once."

"You reckon he'll settle down?"

"Brad? Hell no! But she won't know it. He's a sneaky bastard."

She forced herself to focus on the wall. Her eyes adjusted and she realized her knees were bent and short chains went from cuffs on her ankles to those on her wrists. Her first reaction was to scream and fight. She arched her back and had her mouth open with a string of cusswords that would fry the slime off a frog's ass, then clamped it shut.

"You sure you gave her enough to knock her out for a whole day? I damn sure wouldn't want her to know who we are."

She relaxed. She was in the back of a van. Two men were talking in the front seat. The passenger was eating a hamburger and onion rings. The driver had a beer in his hand

and took a swig every few minutes. But why was she there and what did they want?

"Stop askin' me that question, you moron. I'm smart enough to know how much juice to give a horse to drop them in their track. I gave her enough to keep her quiet for the whole trip. Hell, she ain't goin' to wake up until some-time tomorrow. She'll wonder how in the hell she got from Mingus to Jefferson, Texas. Not that she'll know where she is. He wants her to think she's in hell for a week before he sweeps in there and rescues her."

"She won't just think it. She will be in hell in that place. When he comes to rescue her, she'll be so glad to see him she'll marry him on the spot."

"That's what he's hopin' for. His uncle said the next time he messes up he's out of the business and he's sure got used to that big money. Remember when we was kids and he always said he was going to have an office with lots of pretty girls all around him?"

"Did his uncle really say that he only had six months to settle down?"

"If he didn't, would we be drivin' a horse of a woman to an old fishin' shack?"

Her eyelids drooped but she forced them open. Maybe they would keep talking and she could figure out what in the hell was going on.

"Hell would be heaven when she wakes up and finds herself in that old fishin' shack on the bayou. Put that Larry the Cable Guy CD in the player. I could use a good laugh. This is a boring damn ride. If I'd a known how far it was over to that gawdforsaken hellhole I wouldn't have gone over there."

Cathy tried to get comfortable as Larry the Cable Guy had the two men guffawing with his country comedy. Her legs cramped, yet if she tried to straighten them the metal cuffs cut into her wrists. She held her eyes open until they were so dry they hurt as bad as her legs. Finally she couldn't do it anymore and her eyelids snapped shut. As darkness closed in around her she repeated what they had said over and over. *Jefferson. Bayou. Fishing shack.* Only four words but she had to remember them.

CHAPTER 13

CATHY NAMED THE ONE IN THE DRIVER'S SEAT BEER and the passenger Hamburger because that's what she could smell. She had no idea how long she'd lain in that position but every bone in her body ached like she had a severe case of the flu. Nothing was real. She was only lucid a few minutes at a time before the effects of whatever they'd shot her with put her back into la-la land.

They'd gotten into a discussion about Brad Alton during one of her clear moments and whether he'd pay them or not. Beer said if he didn't pay them, he was going to set the woman free and tell her where to find him. Hamburger said if he didn't pay up, they'd best keep their mouths shut because Brad could be a mean sumbitch. She wondered how much he offered them to tie her up like a calf at a roping arena but drifted back to sleep before they admitted anything.

"Put that pillowcase over her head. If she wakes up we don't want her to see our faces," Beer said.

"Damn it, Duroc, I told you I give her enough to knock out a horse," Hamburger snapped.

"Do it anyway or else give her some more juice. I ain't takin' no chances. Sheriff in Jefferson gets his paws on me again he'll send me to prison, Oscar."

She didn't know if they'd been driving thirty minutes or thirty years. She might look in the mirror later that day and see an old woman looking back at her. Whatever was in that bee sting of a shot sure put her in an episode of *The Twilight*

Zone where time had no meaning. In the past fifteen minutes she'd managed to stay awake enough to realize they were going through a town and hitting every red light. After that Hamburger said something about crossing a bridge and being glad it wasn't frozen over yet.

She drew her eyebrows down as she tried to remember the night before. Or was it a month ago? Travis had kissed her and she went to bed. She awoke that morning and went to the bank. When she returned two men rushed inside the garage and attacked her. She was killing one of them with her bare hands when a bee stung her.

You sorry bastards. You shot me with a tranquilizer. That's why the garage started spinning and I lost my grip. I'll tear you apart limb by limb if you ever take these cuffs off me.

She wanted to bite and scream when they opened the double doors at the back of the van but she made herself pretend to be asleep. Cold drizzling rain blew in on her bare feet and hands but she played dead. Which wasn't easy when it was so cold and she had to keep the shivers at bay. Hamburger grabbed the chain and pulled her to the edge of the van floor like she was a dead deer he'd shot. She was angry enough to spit but there was no way she could run or walk if she did get free—not until she got feeling back in her hands and feet.

"Keep them chains on her. We can get her to the boat. It ain't but ten feet from here," Beer said.

Hamburger slipped his hands under her arms and lifted. "God, she's heavy. I'm glad the dock is right up to the water."

"Don't seem too heavy to me," Beer said.

"Well, by damn, next time you get this end."

They eased her down in the boat. She waited for the

engine to start but it didn't. When the boat began to move she fluttered her eyes enough to see that they were rowing. If she didn't have chains putting her in a reverse fetal position she would have beat them both with the oars until they were blue and tossed them into the cold water for the alligators to feast upon. Or crocodiles or water moccasins or any other varmint that could survive cold water and had a good healthy appetite. She opened her eyes and tried to memorize details to give the sheriff but all she saw was their backs. They were both medium height and thin built but they wore gray hooded coats and heavy boots. There was no way her description could ever help catch the sorry bastards. She did remember the one she was choking was red haired and neither of them were nearly as tall as her so that would put them below six feet. Their names were Oscar and Duroc. Evidently Duroc was the red-haired little piglet and Oscar the chubby one with bad breath that smelled like chewing tobacco and beer.

"I'm glad it ain't but a mile down here. My arms is already sore from haulin' that big ox of a woman around all night," Hamburger said.

"I hear you, Oscar."

"Stop using my name. She might hear it even in her sleep. You moron, Duroc."

"Well, you just called me by name, and besides, I'm not ig'nert. I filled up that needle good. She ain't going to hear shit the way she's sleepin'."

Finally, they docked on the other side of the water and wrapped a rope around a rotting tree stump.

"It's your turn to get her arms," Hamburger said.

"It'd make it easier to get her in the cabin if we was to loosen them chains. Ain't no way we're goin' to carry her up them stairs with her all bent backward. Keep the cuffs on her feet and arms. If she was to wake up then she couldn't get far before we'd catch her and give her some more of that stuff," Beer said.

Was Oscar or Duroc the one she'd named Beer? Which one was Hamburger? She wanted to open her eyes but she didn't dare take a chance of another dose of medicine, so she went completely limp.

Hamburger fiddled with the chains. "You get her up under her arms and I'll get her feet. It ain't but a hundred yards back to Brad's grandpa's old shack. We can do this. Pretend it's two of them hun'erd-pound sacks of deer corn."

Cathy did not weigh two hundred pounds. A fit of anger stiffened her body.

"Is she dead? Feels like rigor is settin' in. Brad will shoot you dead if she ain't alive in a week. Good God, did you give her too damn much of that horse tranquilizer?"

Cathy went limp as a wet dishrag.

"She ain't dead. She musta been havin' a nightmare. I don't guarantee my shots will make them have sweet dreams, just that they'll sleep."

One man slipped his hands under her arms and grunted when the other pulled her feet up out of the boat. Twice on the way to the cabin they almost let her fall. The next time Beer lost his grip on her arms she almost arched upward to keep from getting any wetter but relaxed at the last minute.

"Shit, man, I can't keep this up. Trade ends with me," Beer said.

"You ain't nothin' but a weaklin'. Lay her down and we'll swap. I'll be glad when this job is done. Next time Brad wants something done he can do it hisself."

She was only on the cold wet earth a minute before they picked her up again and trudged on toward the cabin, but it was long enough to chill her entire backside. She lolled her head to one side and opened one eye just enough to see what was ahead. She'd seen outhouses that looked better than that place. Surely they weren't going to leave her stranded there for a whole week. If she got free, Duroc and Oscar were about to find themselves cuffed to the porch post of that horrid-looking shack. She pictured them shivering in nothing but their tighty-whities. As angry as she was she might not even leave them that much to keep them from freezing. With their IQs they didn't need to reproduce anyway.

They were both panting when Beer kicked the door open with his foot and heaved her onto a bed. It squeaked and bounced twice then everything was quiet. Hamburger unlocked the cuffs from her arms and Beer fiddled with the ones on her leg.

Cathy opened both eyes wide.

Hamburger took a step backward. "Man, you better hurry. She's wakin' up too early," he said.

She kicked as hard as she could but was a second too late as she heard the click of the shackle snapping around her ankle. She connected with something because Beer grunted, squealed, and headed for the door in a bent-over position. Quicker than a gnat can blink, she swung hard with her right hand and caught Hamburger in the nose. Blood sprayed all over her T-shirt and his shirt as she came up fighting like a wounded mountain lion. Both men took off out the front door with her right on their heels. Her legs were rubbery and running was tough, but if she caught them she swore she'd find the strength to kill them both. Hamburger fell to his knees out in the yard beside Beer who had rolled up in a fetal position and was moaning like a fire siren.

"Damn you, I told you to give her plenty of that horse stuff and now look at us. She's liable to break that chain. Does that shit make a horse strong and mean when it wakes up from it?" Beer panted between groans.

Hamburger blubbered through a bloody nose, "Hell, I don't know. I never stayed around long enough to see how they come out of the shit. Let's get out of here."

"I will soon as I can walk, you idiot."

"That woman is a hellcat. Brad is the idiot. She's going to kill him." Hamburger wiped his nose on his coat sleeve but it didn't stop bleeding.

"Don't talk to me," Beer said in a high, squeaky voice.

Cathy made it to the front door when the chain ran out. Like a short bungee drop, the forward motion came to an abrupt halt and sent her backward to land on the floor with a loud thump. "You sorry sumbitches. Get in here and let me go or I'll chew this damned chain in two and beat you to death with it."

"I'm goin' to kill you long afore you chew the chain in two," Beer yelled through the blubber.

Cathy looked around the room for something to fight with. All she saw was a bare mattress on top of metal springs on a rusty old iron bedstead. If she could get Duroc and Oscar back in the house she could smother them with the mattress or knock their heads against the bedstead until their brains looked like burned scrambled eggs. She was sure God wouldn't even write down the sin of killing them in his little logbook. He might even put a gold star beside her name.

Two stained blankets were tossed on the floor on the

back side of the bed. Maybe she could wrap them up in the blankets and beat them until they were cold with her bare fists. A toilet and sink were in the far corner with a tattered muslin curtain for privacy. She eyed the rectangular cover on the back of the toilet. She could heave it like a discus at the first one through the door and flatten his face like a real Duroc hog. A chain attached to a thick shackle on her right ankle was affixed to a pivotal eyebolt in the floor. If she could pull it up out of the floor it would be a good weapon to use for a garrote. She grabbed it and pulled with all the might she could muster but it didn't budge.

Duroc and Oscar were still out there in the yard and it didn't look like they were too damned eager to come into the house or get out of the rain. The one curled up was still weeping and holding his crotch; the other one was trying to stop the blood dripping off his chin. She paced to get her legs back into working order. If it hadn't been for the medicine they'd pumped into her, she'd have kicked Beer's teeth in, but she couldn't get her foot that high. That's why her foot landed so much lower. Once she got her muscles to stop trembling she'd show him a thing or two.

"You ain't goin' to kill her. I am!" Hamburger's voice gurgled through his hand as it caught blood still flowing from both sides of his nose. "I bet she broke my nose and I know my eyes is both black as hell."

"You big boys come on in and we'll see who is dead when the bloodlettin' is over. Y'all ain't nearly as mean when I'm awake, are you?" She rattled the chains.

"Go give her another one of them shots." Beer whimpered like a six-year-old girl.

"Hell no."

"Here kitty, kitty, kitty," Cathy tormented them.

"We was goin' to leave you some food but we could change our minds. We ain't comin' back until late tonight if we do decide to let you have something to eat. And you better be nice to us or you can starve," Hamburger said.

"You get close to me, I'll tear your arm off and eat it raw," she shouted.

"I told you we shoulda handcuffed her to the bed," Beer said.

"What in the hell does Brad want with a hellcat like that anyway?"

"I don't know, man. He might want to give her two weeks, or hell, even a month. It's goin' to take more'n a week to soften her up."

"Y'all tell Brad that hell is about to crawl up his ass and fry its way all the way through the top of his head." She tugged at the chain but whatever they'd anchored it to under the house didn't budge.

"She knows. She heard us in her sleep just like I told you. Damn, he's goin' to be mad. I ain't tellin' him nothin'," Hamburger said.

"Me neither. I ain't a scared of him but I am of that big old ox of a woman. He can take care of her all by hisself when he gets here next weekend," Beer said in short raspy sentences.

"Let's go get some food and give it to her and then get the hell out of Dodge until deer-huntin' season. You want that hun'erd dollars he promised to give us next week?"

"Hell no. Let's take off for Las Vegas for a few months. I got a cousin out there who cleans up the bathrooms in a casino. He can get us a job," Beer said.

"You think I can't find you in Las Vegas? I'll hunt you

both down if I have to go in every men's room in the whole town, and when I find you…"

"She means it, don't she?" Hamburger whispered.

"Let's go get that food and start drivin' west. I'm tired of this cold, wet weather anyway," Beer said.

"We can go up to the grocery store and put it on my momma's ticket but I ain't takin' it in there to her. Are you?" Hamburger asked.

"Hell no! I reckon we can use a fishin' pole to open the door and push the food in through there. I ain't about to go in that place."

"Y'all turn me loose and I'll give you each a thousand dollars," she yelled.

"That's a lot of money," Hamburger said.

"She'll kill us. We won't never see a bit of money," Beer told him.

"I won't harm a hair on your heads. You just walk in here and undo this shackle, and I'll go to the bank and get each one of you a thousand dollars. Then you can leave and I'll take care of Brad."

Cathy waited but neither of them said another word. They disappeared like two shadows into the foggy afternoon. She heard a thump and swearing as they got into the boat. She was so cold and angry that she couldn't quit shaking. Even though the blankets looked like something a bag lady wouldn't touch on a dumpster-diving expedition, she wrapped one around her shoulders and sat down Indian style on the floor in front of the door. If they came back she fully intended to jerk them into the shack and shake the keys to the shackle out of their pockets. The wind picked up and blew rain in through the holey screen wire and she scrambled back toward the bed. She couldn't afford to get any wetter. If she caught pneumonia she'd die right there in that godforsaken place.

She yanked and pulled on the bolt again with all her might but it wouldn't give in. She looked around for a wire or a hairpin—anything to use to pick the lock on the ankle shackle. She snarled at the idea of even sitting on the stained mattress, but it was dry so she fell back on it and stared at the ceiling.

Brad was insane. She'd found it out after they were engaged, but this even went beyond what she'd thought. How in the hell did he ever figure he could talk her into going back with him just because he'd rescued her? The man was certifiably goofy.

They'd worked together, fallen in love with each other, moved in together, and were going to get married. Then they had their first big argument. He threw the first punch and caught her on the lower jaw with his fist, jerked his belt off before she had time to catch her breath, and began to swing. She curled up in a ball on the floor for about sixty seconds then came up like a tornado out of a sunny Texas sky and fought back. After she'd kicked him in the crotch and boxed both ears until they rang like out-of-tune cowbells, he took off out the front door, his belt flapping in the wind behind him.

She moved to Mingus and thought it was all over until she looked up one night and there he was in the Honky Tonk. Bless Billy Bob Walker's heart—he'd told Brad that he and Cathy were married.

She felt a movement on the bed and looked to her right. A rat the size of a housecat eyed her hungrily. She glared at him and bounced once but he didn't move.

"You got a choice. You can attack and die or you can slither off with your pride and skin intact," she told him.

Rat licked his paw and washed his face, glancing over every few seconds to see if he'd scared her into a screaming hunk of fresh blood. When she glared back and growled, he turned tail and took his time about jumping off the bed and disappearing through a hole in the floor.

That's when the tears welled up and spilled down her cheekbones. She hated roaches, rats, and mice. If Oscar and Duroc brought food she'd have to stay awake to protect it or Rat would come back with an army of his friends. She'd also have to be very careful not to cut herself because if Rat smelled blood he wouldn't be so easily scared away.

"What in the hell am I going to do?" she whispered.

Without a clock she didn't know if it was two hours or six days past eternity when she heard them whispering outside the cabin. The front door, which was nothing but a flimsy framework with screen wire tacked to it, opened enough for a cardboard box to slide inside.

"That's all you get. Make it last or you'll go hungry," Hamburger shouted.

"You sure you don't want a thousand dollars each? It's a hell of a lot more money than Brad was going to give you," she hollered.

"Naw, we talked about it. Brad is our kin. Shirttail cousin by marriage. We'd piss off our momma if we was to go agin him. You make that last and don't die."

"If I die they'll hunt you down like snakes and charge you with murder. I'm going to prick my finger and write your names on the wall. Oscar and Duroc, isn't it?"

"God Almighty, she *was* awake. I told you that one shot

wasn't enough. She'll tell the sheriff and he'll send me down forever and I won't never get to go deer huntin' again."

"Well, I expect we'd best get on the way to Las Vegas, hadn't we? They've surely got deer huntin' somewhere out there. If they ain't we can hunt whatever they've got. I always wanted to hunt one of them big rabbits like I seen on them postcards."

"Goodbye," Hamburger yelled.

"I'm a voodoo queen and I'm putting a curse on both of you. You're about to have so much bad luck you'll come back to Mingus, Texas, and beg me to kill you both with a fish filletin' knife. My curses are horrible and they never fail. I've already killed a rat and hung it on the porch to rot. When it gets ripe then the curse starts to take effect. Everywhere you go rats are going to hunt you down because of the second part of my curse. Want to know what that is?"

"What?" Hamburger asked then clamped his hand over his mouth so hard that his nose started oozing blood again.

"Boils are going to break out all over your balls and start oozing blood and pus. That's when you'll be afraid to go to sleep for fear the rats will sneak up on you and chew their way under your britches and have a party on your balls."

"I don't believe you," Beer said.

"I picked that rat up by the tail and slung him against the bedpost. I don't reckon the animal rights people will get too worked up over one dead rat. Anyway, he's dead and the words have been said over him. I tied two little balls of cotton out of the mattress around his neck to represent your balls. Want to see him? Come on up on the porch and take a look. You'll see I'm not lyin'. You'll start to itch in about two days. All you got to do is unchain me and I'll take the curse off."

"Damn it all, I knowed we shouldn't have listened to Brad. Now ain't neither one of us goin' to find a job in Vegas," Hamburger said.

"Then let's go down to New Orleans and find us another voodoo woman to take the curse off us. It's a hell of a lot closer anyway."

"We need to call up Brad. Tell him that we left her food but we ain't stickin' around," Hamburger said.

"You call him. I ain't tellin' him shit."

Hamburger pressed the right numbers and leaned against a willow tree. "Brad, you know who this is so I ain't sayin' no names. We got her in the shack but she's a wild one and you got your job cut out for you. No, man, she don't know nothin.'" He looked over at Beer and winked.

"Sure, man, you can count on us. We'll have her up there in two days. You want us to put her where?" Another wink.

"On Tuesday? You got it. You'll pay us then? Just leave the money on the back of the toilet. Reckon we'd best get on out of the area for a few days after that. Okay, then, goodbye. I only got five more minutes on this phone. Have to buy a new one. I'll call you on Tuesday when we get there."

Beer slapped him on the shoulder. "Why did you do that? He's goin' to be mad as hell when we don't show up with her and I'll be damned if I try to get close enough to dose her up again."

Hamburger hit him back. "It give us enough time to get to New Orleans without him wonderin' where we are. He wants us to bring her up to Arkansas on Tuesday and put her up in the mountains in an old huntin' trailer, but we'll be long gone. I told you, I ain't dumb."

Beer chuckled. "Well, let's get the hell out of here then."

Cathy kept the blanket around her shoulders as she walked barefoot across the dirty, cold floor to the door. Six inches less chain and she wouldn't have been able to reach the cardboard box. It was filled with small cans of Vienna sausage, peaches, and beans in flip-top cans and six boxes of cheap saltine crackers.

She opened a can of sausage and ate them with her fingers. When she finished she kicked the door open and slung the can as far as she could out into the yard. Rat could lick it clean out there if he was interested.

Her feet were freezing so she went back to the bed and huddled down in her blanket like an old Indian woman. Where were her boots? She distinctly remembered putting on her boots with her pajamas to go to the bank that morning.

"Those sorry bastards left me barefoot in the middle of winter. Damn them to hell for all eternity. Why would they do such a mean thing? That's why the one I kicked can still walk at all. It's because all he got was my bare foot and not my boot."

Her legs went to sleep and she stretched them out using the second blanket to cover her feet. Suddenly she had an idea. She opened another can of sausage, hurriedly ate the tiny morsels and sent the can flying out the door to join the other one. Then she used the sharpened edge of the can lid to cut a hole in the middle of the better of the two blankets.

She slipped her head through the hole and made a poncho that hung almost to the floor. She carefully cut two squares and two long skinny strips from the other nasty blanket. She tied the squares around her feet with the strips. She tossed the rest of the blanket on the bed. Should she cut a hole in the middle for a second poncho or keep it to use as a cover at night?

She looked closely at the sharp metal but couldn't figure out a way to use it to jimmy the shackle lock. However, it might come in useful later, like to cut Brad's liver out when he came to rescue her, so she laid it on the floor right beside the bed. He might come before the week was out and she'd be ready for him.

She paced from one end of the chain to the other several times before she finally sat back down on the bed. After a while her eyelids drooped and she dozed, only to awaken with a start to loud squeaking noises. Her eyes darted around the bed expecting to see a whole army of rats trying to talk each other into attacking her. The noise was coming from the door, where they'd dragged the sausage cans back up on the porch and were fighting over the cold jelled liquid.

One stuck his ugly head through a hole in the screen and locked in on her box of food. She grabbed it and carried it back to the center of the mattress. She picked up her sharp lid and posed, ready to defend her rations. They could attack in numbers or one at a time. All she had to do was nick one of them and the rest would go crazy after the warm blood.

It was while she was hovering over her basket of food that she thought about the bedsprings. They were made up of wires and held together with smaller wires. She leaned over and looked under the mattress. She could see any number of slim wires small enough to pick a lock. She slid off the bed, set her food box on the toilet, and yelled at the rats.

"Don't you dare sneak in here while I'm working at this.

I swear I'll kill you with my bare hands if you so much as look at my food."

They ignored her but she didn't trust them so she carried a box of crackers to the door, kicked it open, and slung rats and crackers both ass over teakettle out into the yard. They were scrambling over the crackers like flies on a fresh cow patty when she went back to the bed, threw the mattress on the floor, and set about the job of working a wire out of the springs.

It was dark before she finally succeeded in untangling one small enough to use. And that's when something began to vibrate against her leg. She thought a rat had snuck into her pocket and jumped up, jerked it out, and slung it across the room before she realized it was her cell phone.

"Well shit!" she said.

It was against the far wall and her chain wouldn't reach that far, so she stretched out on her stomach and reached as far as she could, but it wasn't enough. She stood up and went back to the bed where she bent the end of her picking wire and tried again. Rat darted across the floor and sniffed the phone while she reached.

"You touch that phone and I'll poke your eyes out with this," she threatened.

He reached a paw out and touched it.

"I mean it. You're supposed to be outside eating crackers, not my cell phone. Damn it all, why didn't I remember it was in my pocket?"

He pulled it an inch further out of her reach and licked the edges.

"I hope it electrocutes you." She finally got the wire hooked into the speaker hole.

The rat reared up on his hind legs and bared his teeth.

"Why do you want it? You can't call for help. Let me have it and I swear I'll give you every cracker in that basket." She grabbed it and hurried back to the bed. Rat lumbered down the hole in the floor and went out to fight for soggy crackers.

She had part of one bar which meant if there was service in that area she might make one call. She sat there for a long time trying to decide who to call. Daisy or Travis?

Travis was closer and could get there faster.

"But Daisy and Jarod have access to an airplane. They could be here in an hour and I don't have any idea how far I am from Mingus." She remembered Jarod's parents owned a small plane.

She noticed that she had several messages and listened to Daisy explaining that she and Jarod had been to church that morning when Cathy called. Evidently they were playing phone tag but for Cathy to call late that night if they didn't connect sometime during the day. There was a message from Travis saying that he had to work late and they'd have to put off dinner and a movie.

Tears welled up in her eyes as their voices played in her ear. She held the phone to her heart as if it was a real person. When she looked at it again she noticed the blinking little battery notification at the top right-hand corner. She had enough power for one call if she was lucky.

She dialed Travis's number and waited while it rang five times. Then his voice said that he wasn't available, to leave a message. She groaned and was about to push the button to hang up when she heard the first little beep telling her that her phone would be powerless in a few seconds.

"Travis, I'm in Jefferson, Texas. Cross the bridge, down the bayou or river or whatever water is there, about a mile, in an old fisherman's shack. Don't call the police. Just come get me. I've been kidnapped and I'm chained to the floor and…"

Her time was up. She hoped he listened to his voice mail that evening. If not, no one would even realize she was gone until Monday night when she didn't open the Honky Tonk.

"Well, Cathy O'Dell, you don't have anything else to do other than fight with rats until then, so get busy on the lock," she said.

Travis awoke late on Sunday morning. He rolled out of bed, ate a bowl of cereal, and got dressed. He was supposed to check things out at the rig site and then be done for the day, but Rocky either got food poisoning from his honky tonk woman's cooking or else a flu bug from kissing her and couldn't work with his head in the toilet every twenty minutes. So Travis filled in for him and worked until six on Monday morning.

It was midmorning when he got home and reached in his pocket to call Cathy to tell her that he was going to sleep at the trailer, since she would already be up and around. But his cell phone wasn't there. He patted his shirt pocket and it wasn't there, either.

"Must've dropped it in the truck. I'll get it later," he mumbled and went to bed.

He awoke at one o'clock and listened carefully. The place sounded and felt empty. He checked the clock again. Cathy should have been there at noon. He hoped she hadn't con-tracted the same flu bug that had put Rocky on the ground. He went to the hall and peered out toward the Honky Tonk. The skies were gray and the day dreary. There should be lights on in her apartment and there were none.

That prickly feeling he only got when something was very, very wrong inched its way up his neck. He threw on a pair of jeans, socks and boots, and a T-shirt and darted across the wet grass separating the trailer and the back door of the Tonk. He beat on the door for two minutes but no one answered. He peeked in the window at the garage and all three of her vehicles were there. He went back to the door to thump on it and yell for another five minutes.

When she didn't answer he jogged back to his truck and found his cell phone on the floor. He dialed her number and it went straight to voice mail, then he dialed the Honky Tonk and it went to the answering machine.

"Maybe she went shopping with Jezzy or Angel or even Larissa and lost track of time," he rationalized.

When he noticed that he had messages he pushed the right button and put the phone to his ear. The first one was from his mother saying that she missed him. The second from his sister, Emma, saying that he should call more often. The third one made the hair on his neck stand straight up. It was Cathy and her voice was frantic. The bad connection created a crackling background and he had to listen to it four times before he finally got the whole message pieced together.

He hit the door of the trailer at a dead run. The Honky Tonk. What to do about it? He had no idea where in the devil Tinker lived or how to get hold of him and he'd tear up the whole state of Texas and start on Louisiana if Cathy wasn't there.

"Jezzy!" he said aloud as he threw clothing, shaving gear, and socks into a duffel bag. He drove like a bat from the bowels of hell's back forty acres all the way to Jezzy's place and slung gravel everywhere when he braked hard in front of her house.

Jezzy opened the door before he knocked. "Come on in and have some coffee with me and Leroy. We're arguing about whether to buy more cattle or put in more wells if this one is a good one."

"Where in the hell is Jefferson, Texas, and how do I get there, and will you and Leroy take care of the Honky Tonk tonight?" he said all in one big breath.

"What is going on?" Leroy asked.

Travis explained in as few words as possible. Jezzy pulled an atlas out of the book rack beside her recliner while he talked. She had the town circled with an ink pen when he finished and handed the book to him.

"Catch I-20 east to Marshall and then go north on Highway 59 right into Jefferson. You sure you got that message right?" Jezzy said.

"I'm very sure. I'm going after her. I just need y'all to run the Tonk and tell Tinker to stay put until I call or get back. He's got keys to the place so if you're there when he arrives he can let you inside. I don't know if it's been cleaned up or not," Travis said.

"Between the three of us we can make it decent in a few minutes," Leroy said. "You don't worry about that end. Just go get her."

"You should be there before it's time for us to open up

tonight. If you call and say she's safe we'll just tell Tinker that she's at Daisy's place for a couple of days."

"I'll call soon as I've got her safe. You got a hacksaw?"

"I'll get one out of the garage," Leroy said. "She's a strong woman. Who in the hell kidnapped her and why? Or better yet, how in the hell did they kidnap her? I wouldn't tangle with that woman."

"I don't know but I'm about to find out. Jezzy, how far is it?"

"Probably four hours. You can be there before dark, and be careful. I'm writin' my cell phone down for you. I want to hear from you as soon as you get there."

"Call Amos for me." He and Leroy headed for the garage.

"How about the Jefferson police? They might know where she is and have her rescued before you get there."

He shook his head. "Let me try first. She didn't want me to call the police."

CHAPTER 14

SMALL PIECES OF BROKEN WIRE WERE PILED UP TO ONE side of Cathy on the bed. She tried to spring the lock in the shackle around her leg all night. At daylight when the seventh one broke tears streamed down her face. She gave up and threw herself back on the bed, resolved to the fact that she was stuck until Brad, damn his sorry soul to hell for eternity, came to rescue her. She fell asleep and awoke to the rustling sound of Rat and two of his friends helping themselves to the box of food she'd put on the toilet seat. That proved that rats could indeed scale a glass wall on a rainy day because there they were climbing up and down the slick porcelain like it was a grassy knoll.

"Get away from my food, you ugly bastards," she screamed hoarsely. Her mouth was so dry the words barely came out. She needed water and there was plenty in the form of rain, but her chain wouldn't let her get far enough to open her mouth and get a drink straight from the clouds.

She stomped across the wooden floor. "I will tear your damn tails off and use them to unlock these shackles."

They scattered but didn't leave the room. She carried the food to the bed and hovered over it. "Might as well give it to them. Three days without water and they'll get it all anyway."

She had no concept of time: how much had passed, how long she'd been asleep, or even if it was Monday or Tuesday. She had called Travis. Maybe he'd called the police. No, she'd told him not to call the police. Why had she done that? Because at the time she really thought she could sweet-talk Oscar and Duroc into taking her money and letting her go, and she'd told them she wouldn't tattle. If the police knew about the kidnapping they'd go after Duroc, Oscar, and Brad. She didn't give a rat's ass about Duroc and Oscar but she wanted a chance at Brad Alton before the law got to him.

She shivered beneath her blanket poncho. "I can whine or I can try again. I'm not a quitter." Saying the words gave her the willpower to work another piece of wire from the bedsprings and try again.

She pictured Brad in his posh office on the second floor of Green's Oil in Mena. He'd best enjoy the smug confidence up on the top of his self-made pedestal because when the lock gave way she intended to bring it crashing down. If he broke a leg or arm or messed up his pretty face in the explosion, that was his problem.

Deep in her soul she knew that Travis would find her. Maybe not today, but he wouldn't let her die in a cabin full of rats. Not Travis. He wasn't like Brad Alton and she'd been a fool to judge him by that yardstick.

"Just like the damn rain," she muttered. "Water all around me and I'm dying of dehydration. Travis was there all around me and I couldn't get past Brad to see him. Damn, this is no time to get philosophical. Open, damn it."

It didn't.

She remembered an episode of *NCIS* she'd seen on late-night television a few weeks before. One of the agents had used two pieces of wire to pick a lock. Of course, that was make-believe and the shackle was very real, but anything was worth trying. She inserted a second wire into the lock.

"If I hold this down and move that to one side then abracadrabra bippity boo." The wire broke and the lock did not open.

"Every time I lose the battle, you are giving up a tooth, a ball, or an eye, Brad. I might even let you decide which one." She worked another wire from the springs and started all over.

The lock popped and she sat in the middle of the bed staring at the shackle until another rat darted across the floor. She jerked her foot free and picked up the metal and heaved it at the toilet, hitting the box of food and sending the contents all over the floor.

"You can have it all. Chew your way through the cans." She opened the door and inhaled a lungful of freedom. She ran through the wet grass to the water's edge where she slipped and fell headlong into the muddy embankment. She pulled herself up to a sitting position and leaned her head back, catching beautiful raindrops on her tongue. If the bayou hadn't looked like chocolate milk she would have buried her face in it and drunk until she was full.

"Start walking, Cathy." Her mother's voice was so clear that Cathy jerked her head up and did a quick scan of the area.

"I'm tired," she said.

"You'll be dead if you don't get out of here."

Cathy stood up. One foot at a time she picked her way through the fallen limbs and rocks as she followed the bayou back toward the bridge. She had to stay alive to make Brad pay.

"Cross the bridge, down the bayou or river or whatever water is there, about a mile, in an old fisherman's shack,"

Travis said aloud as he drove through Jefferson, Texas. In the dreary, cold mist not even a dog walker was out on the sidewalks. One lonesome-looking police car slowly made rounds. He made a right turn at a big corner building and passed two old white frame hotels, one on either side of the road, but he didn't cross a bridge. He turned the truck around in a church parking lot and drove back to the library. He made a right-hand turn and drove across the Big Cypress Bayou Bridge. He slowed down on the other side, not sure what to do at that point, and noticed a muddy lot that must be used to park or put fishing boats into the water.

He stopped the truck and got out. She'd said down the river or bayou. Which way was down? He hunched his shoulders inside his lined denim coat and noticed the wooden boat tied up to a rotten tree stump. It had a speck or two of green paint shining in the dull winter evening. The benches were rotted but the oars looked fairly new.

Cathy walked a few hundred feet and sat down on the wet ground to rest. She told herself that she couldn't stop. She saw Duroc and Oscar behind every tree. A fish sloshed out in the bayou and she thought it was them rowing the boat back to the fishing shack to kill her. She hid behind a tree until she was sure they were gone.

It was late evening when she saw the bridge up ahead. It was time to swim across the bayou to the other side and that water looked damn cold. It wasn't far and it didn't look deep, but still, to put her bare feet out into it was more than she could do. A voice drifted across the water and she squinted. Surely that wasn't Travis. She had to be seeing things.

"I hope this damn thing holds my weight," Travis said.

"Blasted piece of junk. If I fall in this cold water I'm going to tear this thing apart with my bare hands."

It was a hallucination just like her mother had been. Nothing more than a trick of a dehydrated, hungry mind in a state of severe shock.

"You are not real," she shouted.

Travis looked at the apparition across the bayou. "Cathy?"

"Are you really there?" she asked.

"Be still. I'll bring this thing across and get you."

"Okay," she said slowly and cocked her head to one side expecting him to disappear.

He crossed the narrow bayou and she stood there staring at him blankly. "Cathy, come over here and get into the boat. I'll take you home, honey."

"If I do I'll drown. You aren't real," she said.

He grounded the small boat, kept the rope in his hand so it wouldn't float away, and stepped out onto marshy, wet ground. He held out his hand and she put hers in it.

"You aren't a ghost," she whispered.

"I'm Travis and I'm real." He put her into the boat and quickly rowed to the other side. Her hair was plastered to her head. The blankets around her smelled like urine. The soles of her feet were red and bare beneath ratty bits of cloth tied to her ankles.

"Are you all right?" he asked.

"I will be. I'm so thirsty and so dirty, Travis. Just take me somewhere where there's water to drink and hot water to get this stench off me, please."

He tied the rope to the dilapidated wooden dock and led her to the passenger side of the truck. His arms were freezing in the raw drizzling rain. He couldn't imagine how cold she had to be.

"I saw a motel on my way into town. We'll go there first and get you cleaned up," he said.

Warm air poured in the minute that he started the truck. Her nose twitched and her stomach knotted up. She swallowed several times but it didn't keep the nausea at bay.

"I'm going to be sick from the smell of these blankets," she said.

He pushed the gas pedal and the pickup lurched ahead. He hoped the cop would catch him speeding and lead them to the station where she could make a formal complaint.

She gagged and clamped a hand over her mouth. "Pull over in that parking lot. There is a Dollar Store still open. They'll have a bathroom. I can buy clean things," she said.

"We're going straight to the motel and I'll come back to the store while you take a bath."

"Thank you," she whispered from behind her hand.

He braked to a screeching halt under the awning in front of the motel, bailed out, and ran inside the lobby. She gagged again and tasted Vienna sausage. She wouldn't ruin the inside of Travis's truck. She unlocked the door and got out. The clean rain and the aroma of dryer vent drifting from behind the hotel filled her nostrils. She took several deep breaths and the nausea subsided.

"Cathy?" he said at her elbow.

She took two steps backward and her eyes widened.

"Don't be afraid. It's me. Travis. Our room is two doors down with an outside entrance. I'll carry you."

"Don't touch me. I'm filthy."

"Then follow me," he said.

She started yanking the poncho up as he opened the door. "I hate rats," she said.

He put a hand on her shoulder. "Not yet. We need pictures."

"No!"

"We need them for proof. Let me take them."

She let the blanket drop back down around her shoulders and looked blankly at him as he snapped several pictures.

"Send those to my computer." She rattled off her email address and jerked the poncho off.

Travis sent the pictures as she tossed the rags and her pajama bottoms out the bathroom door. He longed to hold her, brush back those nasty strands of hair plastered to her face, but the empty look in her eyes said he'd better give her some space.

"Will you be all right here alone while I go back to the store?" he asked through the door.

She giggled nervously. "There's no rats and there's a lock on the door and water in the faucet. I'm so thirsty and I'm afraid to drink because it'll make me sick."

"They didn't leave you water?"

"Oscar and Duroc didn't have enough brains between them to think of that."

A pair of wet underpants and a pajama top flew out the door. He picked them up and shoved them into the plastic laundry bag provided by the hotel along with the rest of the smelly rags. He carried them outside and shoved them down into the locked toolbox in the bed of his truck.

The Dollar Store was located a couple of miles from the hotel and offered gray sweats long enough for Cathy's legs. The sweatshirts all looked too short in the arms so he bought three Christmas T-shirts from a sale rack. She liked flannel pajama bottoms so he looked for those, but the only size left on the shelf was small and they wouldn't come to her knees. Finally he found a rack of nightshirts that said one size fits all so he bought two of those. He had no idea what size underpants or what style she wore. He checked the back, tried to figure out how many inches it would be around her bottom, and finally settled on size six. He tossed a package of six pairs of assorted colors in the cart.

He noticed socks next to the underwear and picked up three pairs along with a pair of fluffy pink house shoes. He thought about a bra but shook his head. He wouldn't even know where to begin. He made a run through the toiletries, throwing in a toothbrush, toothpaste, hairbrush, shampoo and conditioner, and shower gel.

Cathy closed the lid on the toilet and sat down, naked and wretchedly dirty. Her hands shook as she started water running in the deep Jacuzzi tub. Her eyes locked on the clean, clear water and she couldn't force herself to blink. Finally, she put her head in her hands and wept silently. It was five minutes before she got control and opened the door, filled a small hotel cup with cold water, and drank slowly.

She stared at the woman in the mirror.

How do lips get so parched when it's raining? Look at me. God, I'm a mess.

"Fifteen minutes." She touched her dirt-smeared face and her filthy hair.

That's all her mother gave her to pout, whine, or cry. If life gave her pissy friends or a bad day, then she could bitch and moan for fifteen minutes. After that she had to forget about it and get on with living. Well, she'd had her time and she would get on with it—right after Brad Alton had his fifteen minutes. A picture of what she intended to do to him was the single thing that kept her sane enough to go back into the bathroom and crawl into the tub.

She laid back and ducked her head into the water. She felt as if she'd been baptized a second time when she came up with water sluicing off her face, turning the water brown as it cleansed away the dirt and mud. She poured all the entire bottle of hotel shampoo onto her head and built a mountain of bubbles.

Even with the smell of shampoo and clean water, the stench of the rats stayed in her nose. She poured shampoo into the palm of her hand and sniffed so hard that she sucked some into her nostrils and coughed up bubbles. She washed her body with the small bar of soap so many times that it was nothing but a thin sliver and still she felt dirty.

She flipped the lever to drain the tub, stood up, and turned the shower. Long after the shampoo was gone from her hair she stood under the hot water. She was alive. Nothing had frozen. There was a purple circle on her ankle and a few cuts and bruises on her feet but they would all heal. Her fifteen minutes were up so why didn't she feel right?

Travis looked down at the clock on his pickup dash as he pulled into the Dairy Queen parking lot.

"Well shit!" He flipped open his cell phone and hit the right buttons.

Jezzy answered before the first ring had finished. "Is she all right?"

"She's in a motel room taking a bath. I had to go into town and buy clothes. They grabbed her in nothing but pajamas and she didn't even have shoes. She'd tied an old blanket around her feet to keep them warm and it stunk like rat piss. They gave her a box of food but no water. I'm so mad I could rip someone's head off with my bare hands. I'm thinking we'll be home in the morning after she has a good night's sleep. Tell Amos and Tinker she is alive. And Jezzy, thanks for working the Honky Tonk for her tonight."

"That's good news, but I'm telling everyone that she took two days off to go see Daisy. She can tell them about this if she wants. Other than Amos no one else is going to know a blessed thing. And Travis, get a hold of that temper. She needs a broad shoulder, not an avenging angel."

"Thanks, Jezzy."

"She'd do the same for me. If she pitches a fit and wants to come home tomorrow, bring her after she files charges. If she needs another day to get it all sorted out, come home on Wednesday. Me and Leroy have the place covered until then."

"I'll call tomorrow with an update."

"Take care of her. Even the strong fall apart after an ordeal like that."

"Yes, ma'am," Travis said.

He went inside and ordered two chocolate malts, three double meat cheeseburgers, a triple order of fries, two cups of coffee, and two Dr Peppers. The Dairy Queen was right across the highway from the motel so the food was hot when he carried it into the room. She was still in the bathroom so he set it on the table and went back to get the Dollar Store bags.

When he returned the second time, Cathy was standing in the middle of the floor like a lost, wounded soul. A towel was wrapped around her body and a second one around her hair. He dropped the bags on the floor and gathered her into his arms.

"I was scared and I don't like to be afraid," she whispered.

"Anyone would be scared," he assured her.

She laid her head on his broad chest. "Hold me for a long time."

Without loosening his hold on her, he backed up and sat down on the king-sized bed. "Do you want to talk about it?" he asked.

"The rats came and ate my crackers and I tore up the springs for wire to pick the lock on the shackles," she said.

His jaws worked in anger but Jezzy said she didn't need an avenging angel that night. Later, when she was settled, after she'd made a police statement, there would be time for his rage and whoever caused her pain would pay.

"They said he was going to leave me there a whole week. I barely stood it a day. I'd have been crazy in a week. The rat tried to run away with my phone. Did I tell you thank you for coming to get me? I'm sorry," she said softly.

"Shhh." He kissed the soft clean skin on her long neck. "It's all right. I've got you and they're gone now. We'll take care of everything."

She leaned back and looked deeply into his blue eyes. She could trust Travis Henry. He'd never let anyone else harm her.

"Kiss me," she said.

He leaned forward and brushed a soft kiss across her lips.

A strange feeling surrounds a person when they've faced

death and fear and endured both. It's indescribable but definite and demands a token of life. Something that says, "I'm still alive." Cathy broke away from the kiss and looked up at Travis. His eyes were so soft. He was so kind and had rescued her.

"Make love to me," she said.

"This isn't the time. You are vulnerable. We'll save that for later," he said.

"What if there is no later? What if right now is all we get?"

"You are safe, Cathy. It's over. You are hungry and sleep deprived." He wasn't sure if he was trying to convince her or himself.

She snuggled down into his arms even deeper. "You are a good man."

He brushed a sweet kiss across her forehead.

"I'll brush your hair and then we'll eat," he said.

She clamped a hand over her mouth. "Brush? I need a toothbrush."

Damn, she'd just asked a man to make love to her and her breath probably smelled as bad as the blankets and the shampoo mixed together.

"There's one in the sacks. I bought a hairbrush and toothpaste and everything else I thought you might need."

The first thing she found was the package of panties. She removed one pair and tugged them on up under the towel and then pulled out a nightshirt. She ducked behind the partition separating the bedroom and vanity and dropped the towel. She wanted him to make love to her and now she had a sudden bout of modesty that put a smile on her face. Everything was still surreal.

She removed the tags from the nightshirt and jerked it over her head. The plain old knit felt like silk against her skin.

Travis laid all the Dairy Queen food on the table for two in the corner. When she'd brushed her teeth and her hair a virtual banquet waited.

"That looks so good. I will never ever eat Vienna sausage again."

Travis bit into the cheeseburger. "Why?"

"That's what was in the box of food." She went on to tell him the whole story from the time they said good night to the time she thought she was seeing ghosts across the bayou.

He laid the cheeseburger to one side. "Did they hurt you physically? Are you up for talking to the police now?"

"If you are talking rape, no. I tried to kill both of them but I was a second too late and they had already locked the shackles. If I hadn't been drugged they'd be out there in that cabin when Brad arrived next weekend. And we aren't calling the police."

"Why?"

"We've got a bunch of dirty clothes in a bag and there's a cardboard box of food out there in an old shack. It's my word against theirs and they're off to New Orleans to find a voodoo woman to take my curse off them. Brad is up there in Mena, Arkansas, doing his job and he will have an airtight alibi."

"You're just going to go home and forget it?"

"I did not say that. How'd you know I liked chocolate malts?"

"You like hot chocolate, and you are changing the subject."

She leaned across the table and kissed him hard. The taste of burgers, fries, and chocolate was absolutely wonderful. He drew the back side of his hand down across her jawline. When it reached her lips she grabbed it and held it to her lips to kiss each finger tip.

In one swift movement she was sitting in his lap. She leaned back far enough to get a good angle and pulled his head forward. Lips met in a flash of passion that set them on a course that would not be denied. Vulnerability and common sense took a back seat to desire and want.

"You taste like heaven," she said.

"So do you," he whispered.

She inched her fingers under his shirt and laid her palms on the broad expanse of chest. "You are so warm and strong."

He groaned. "One more minute of that and I won't be responsible."

"What will a whole night of it do?"

"It will make a perfect night with a perfect woman." He picked her up and laid her on the bed.

She pulled him down on top of her and tugged his shirt up over his head. "If it weren't for that little mole right there"—she kissed his chest right above his left nipple—"you would be perfect, too."

"Thank God for that imperfection," he groaned as she kissed every square inch of his muscular chest.

"And now it's my turn." He slipped the nightshirt over her head and tossed it toward the chair where she'd been sitting. Holding back the eagerness to make love to her, he trailed kisses from her neck to her toes, stopping along the way to nibble and taste.

She touched his hair, grabbed his shoulders in a fierce grip when she could stand no more, and still he continued to kiss places that had never been touched before. "Travis, I'm ready."

"But I'm not, sweetheart. Something this good has to be savored and appreciated. Not swallowed whole and forgotten." He kissed her lips again in a clash of sparks that lit up the room in an array of bright colors.

Realizing that he was still fully dressed and nothing was going to happen until she took care of that, she unbuckled his belt and pulled it through the loops without ever taking her lips from his. A whiff of leftover Stetson fired her senses even more as she unzipped his jeans and tugged them off. She jerked his boxers off and slung them behind her, pulled his sweater over his head and flung it in the opposite direction, then rolled over on top of his naked body. She grabbed the edge of the bedspread bringing it up to wrap them like a cocoon.

"Nice?" she murmured in his ear, nibbling at the lobe as she talked.

"Very." He rolled with her, keeping them inside the spread and taking it to the final level at the same time.

"Oh, my," she groaned into his neck.

He began a slow rhythm that sent every thought other than pleasing her straight out the window into the cold Texas night air. He buried his face into her damp hair and whispered love words in her ear, telling her how sexy she was and how much he wanted her from the first time he kissed her.

She kicked the covers off and wrapped her long legs around him and brought his face to hers for a kiss that lasted until he tried to say her name. Nothing but a moan came out as he collapsed, bringing her with him in fireworks that would rival any Fourth of July celebration.

Cathy opened her eyes only to see the hotel room ceiling and Travis's blond hair all bound up in an aura with fuzzy edges and soft music off in the distance.

"My God," she moaned.

He rolled to one side taking her with him. "Me too."

She snuggled down into his embrace and pulled the spread back over them. If being vulnerable got that kind of treatment, she'd have to order up another dose of it. She strung soft kisses up and down his neck and shut her eyes. Just a few more minutes to enjoy the glow settling around them and then she'd get up and find that nightshirt.

At midnight she awoke with a start, her eyes darting around the room. They'd come back and were holding her down so they could cuff her hands to the iron bedstead. She flailed against them but they were so much stronger than they'd been at first. When she opened her eyes Travis had a leg thrown over her, one arm hugging her next to his side and the other hand had laced itself through her fingers.

She inched out of his embrace so he wouldn't wake and padded to the bathroom. She'd barely gotten wet when he pulled the curtain back and joined her. He had a bottle of shampoo, conditioner, and shower gel. She inhaled deeply when he opened the shampoo.

"Be still and enjoy," he said. He lathered up her hair and massaged her scalp until her whole body tingled. After he rinsed it, he repeated the process with conditioner and then he began to bathe her using nothing but his hands and the shower gel.

"Okay, now that you've got my hormones singing, it's my turn," she said.

She shampooed his hair, kissing him on the neck and back every few seconds as she dug into his scalp.

"You've got four hours to stop that," he said hoarsely.

"What? This?" She massaged harder.

"Or this?" She kissed lighter.

"Either or both," he said.

"Ever made love in a Jacuzzi?" she asked.

"No, but I've got a feeling my luck is about to change."

"Yes it is." She flipped the shower switch down and let the water fill the tub.

When they awoke the second time, they were naked under the covers on the king-sized bed and it was seven in the morning. Cathy moaned and expected to open her eyes to one hellacious sex hangover but instead it was to Travis's face right next to her. His blue eyes were open and his arms were around her; his hands rubbed teasing circles on the small of her back.

"So how do you wake up after a night of love making? Still biting?"

"I do not bite after a night like we just had, but I would love some coffee."

"Breakfast is served in the lobby from six to ten. Want to put on your new sweats and join me?" he asked.

"I'd wear my nightshirt to the lobby for food and coffee."

"Before or after?" he asked with a gleam in his eyes.

"It'll have to be after if it is at all. I don't have the energy for a good morning kiss right now. You may have to dress me."

He shook his head and bounded out of bed. In all that gorgeous naked glory he reminded Cathy more of a Greek god than a cowboy. "Honey, you will have to dress yourself.

There's no way I'd ever be guilty of putting clothes on a body as perfect as yours. Now, taking them off is another matter."

She giggled and threw a pillow at him.

"Aha, a night of pure old lusty sex tames the beast," he teased.

She rose up out of the bed like a medieval siren and went to the mirror over the vanity. "I look like hell."

"You are beautiful, Cathy O'Dell."

"You are a liar. Don't put your glasses on until I get my hair fixed and some clothes on." She tugged a new pair of panties up over her hips and tore the tags from the sweat bottoms. They were too big but long enough and they did have a drawstring. The T-shirt was soft and warm and the sleeves too short so she pushed them up. Then she pulled on a pair of socks and the house shoes.

"They feel safe," she said.

"Safe?" he asked.

"That's the only word I can use to describe them. Being left barefoot in the cold was as devastating as being shackled. These make me feel warm and safe, like I do in your arms," she said.

He smiled. "Thank you. Are you ready?"

"Give me a minute to brush my hair. When we leave here I want to stop at the first mall."

"Yes, ma'am," he said.

Hand in hand they walked to the lobby, Travis in jeans and a Western shirt and boots, Cathy in gray sweat bottoms, a red T-shirt with a Christmas tree on the front, and pink house shoes. She felt like a queen coming down a winding staircase into a ballroom.

The aroma of bacon and coffee rushed out to greet them when they opened the double doors. "Hot damn, that smells good. I'm starving," Cathy said.

"Worked up a little appetite, did you?"

"I did not. I worked up a big, humongous appetite. They better have two cooks still working in the kitchen. That buffet looks like it was made just for me."

She filled a plate with biscuits and gravy, added a dozen pieces of bacon on the side, and carried it to a table. Then she went back for a glass of milk and a cup of coffee. She sat down and started eating while he was still waiting on waffles to cook. By the time he pulled out a chair she was half finished and eyeing the doughnuts.

"Those are lemon poppy seed muffins. I'm starting with half a dozen when I get through here," she said.

"You always this hungry after a two-act play?" he asked.

She looked at him with a question in her eyes.

"What?"

"Think, Cathy."

"Ohhhh!" She made a perfect O with her mouth. "I wouldn't be able to answer that seeing as how I've been to very few two-act plays. Most of what I attended was a one-act that had a severe time limit on it."

He grinned.

"But I never apologize for my appetite, whether it's for plain old food or something much, much better," she said.

"I'm not sayin' a word, sweetheart."

"Not only is he handsome and sexy as hell but smart, too. What more could a woman ask for?"

"You sure you don't want to at least talk to the police? You don't have to press charges since you don't have much proof. But they could be aware that these two bozos are out there," Travis said.

"I'm very sure. I've got a plan. Do you have a map in the trunk?"

"Got Jezzy's atlas," he said.

"Oh, my God, I forgot about the Honky Tonk! Tinker is going to…"

"I took care of it. Jezzy and Leroy ran the bar last night. The story is that you went to Daisy's for a couple of days. Amos is the only other person who knows the truth, and I had to tell him because he's my boss."

"Thank you one more time. When we finish eating I'd like to look at that atlas, please."

"Why? I know the way home from here."

"We're not going home, Travis. We're going to Mena, Arkansas. I'm going to finish this business once and for all. I refuse to live in fear the rest of my life."

CHAPTER 15

"I don't think this is a good idea. You should go home and recuperate before you take on Brad," Travis said as he pulled out onto the highway and pointed the truck north instead of south.

"Maybe not, but it's what I'm going to do. Like I said last night, I have no evidence and I could have just pulled Oscar and Duroc's names out of my ass. Brad could say that I'd met them both because they are related. He's very good at lying and deception. You've got pictures but they could have been staged," Cathy said.

Travis tried to poke holes in her theory all the way to Linden but she was right. The two kidnappers were gone and their association to Brad hung by a single weak thread that any first-year law student could rip to shreds.

Cathy pointed to a highway sign. "Take that one. It's a smaller road but it's shorter. In Foreman, Arkansas, we'll get 41 and hook back up with 59 in De Queen. That way we'll easily be in Mena before noon."

"Reason you want to be there any particular time?"

"No, but if we are there before noon, I can take care of my business before he goes on his lunch break. I don't suppose we'll be back in time for me to open the Tonk tonight, will we?"

"If we drove like hell, we might," he said.

"Did you call Jezzy and Amos this morning?"

"I did and they said that things were under control. Jezzy

said the Honky Tonk was booming last night but they'd cleaned it up before they left. They are going to work tonight and Larissa is helping out behind the bar, too. I'm expected back at work for the evening shift tomorrow. Amos said you can catch up whenever you get there. Phone's right here if you want to call anyone." He tapped his shirt pocket.

She shook her head.

"You want to stop and buy something to wear? At least some shoes?"

She shook her head again.

"Cathy, I've got money. You can shop if you want to."

Tears welled up behind her eyes but she refused to let them spill down her cheeks. "I'd like to stop but only if there's no chivalry when I pay you back."

"Deal," he said.

In Maud he pulled over at a convenience store, filled the gas tank, and bought two large coffees. He put three packages of sugar and two containers of half-and-half into his cup, slapped a lid on both, and carried them out to the truck.

"Thank you," Cathy said.

Traffic was light when he got back on the road. They passed a couple of trucks and one Texas Highway Patrol car. Travis wanted to ask a million questions but Cathy needed time to figure out what she wanted to do once she was face-to-face with her ex. Had it been Travis, he would have shot first and asked questions later, but it was Cathy's problem and for her own peace of mind she had to take care of it herself. However, no matter what she did or how mad she made him, Brad would not lay a hand on Cathy. Travis would step in if he did and be glad to take care of the bastard.

"You got any particular kind of place you want to stop? Size of these towns we're going through hasn't got much in the way of a shopping mall."

"Western wear would be nice. I'll start looking for signs. Sometimes they advertise out on the highway. You're not very talkative this morning. You regrettin' last night?" she asked.

"Are you?"

She cut her eyes around at him. "I won't ever regret last night."

"Why? Was it payback for the rescue?"

Anger filled her dark blue eyes. "It was not payback for anything. What was it for you? Pity?"

"Hell no. A man would be crazy to pity you. Hell, woman, I have no doubt you would have chewed through that chain if you couldn't get the lock undone. And you would have slaughtered the rats if they'd have pissed you off two days in a row. Pity? What in the hell put that damn notion in your mind?"

"Well, we got that figured out, didn't we?"

She leaned back in the seat and watched the winter landscape go past at seventy-five miles an hour. Travis thought she was a strong woman, did he? Well, he hadn't seen her go to pieces when she thought she was going to have to stay in that rat-infested hellhole a whole week. And he hadn't heard the sobbing session behind the bathroom door the night before while she tried to wash the smell and dirty feeling from her body and soul.

Travis listened to music on the soft country station as he drove. Late tonight or tomorrow they'd be back in their own worlds. Would the night they'd had in the Jefferson hotel make a difference in their lifestyles? It would be so easy to fall for Cathy; he was already halfway there. But in a few weeks he would be on his way to another location and she'd still be at the Honky Tonk. Even if he stayed right there in Mingus and bought a place to settle down, he would never be comfortable with the idea of their blond-haired sons going to school and telling everyone that their mommy owned a beer joint.

"There's one." She pointed.

"One what?"

"A sign for a Western wear store up ahead in New Boston. It's supposed to be right off this road if I saw the directions right."

"Then that'll be our next stop. What have you got in mind?"

"Jeans, shirt, boots. Turn here. I see the sign. Park right there."

"I'll get you up close to the door and then park in the lot. Want me to carry you inside?"

She spun around in the seat. "You'd do that, wouldn't you?"

"I would."

"Thank you but I can walk six feet on the sidewalk. Look, it's not even wet."

She opened the door and hopped out. She felt a little like Julia Roberts did in the old movie *Pretty Woman* when she walked inside and the young sales clerk snarled her nose. At least she didn't call the manager and ask that Cathy be kicked out the front door for coming inside their store in her sweats and house shoes.

"Can I help you?" she asked curtly.

"First I need a pair of jeans. Think you can fit me…
Josie?" Cathy read the girl's name tag pinned right above the
company logo embroidered on her blue chambray Western-
cut shirt.

She looked at Cathy's long legs. "I can fit you but they
won't be cheap."

"I don't think that's a problem," Travis said from the
door.

Josie looked at Cathy and back at Travis. Maybe this was
one of those consumer tests to evaluate how well the clerks
waited on the customers. That had to be the explanation
because those two definitely did not belong together. He
was so handsome and she looked like she'd been dumpster
diving for her clothes behind a dollar store.

"Okay… I'd say you are a size seven," Josie said.

Cathy smiled. "That's sweet, honey, but I'm a size nine
with extra-long length."

Travis leaned against a wall and listened to Mark
Chesnutt's "When I Get This Close to You" on the local
radio station piped into the store through several strategi-
cally placed speakers. He tapped his foot to the beat of the
song and wished he could ask Cathy to dance with him.

When Cathy picked out a pair of designer Western jeans
that cost almost a hundred dollars, Josie's kindness jacked
up.

"Would you like a shirt to go with those?" she asked.

"Maybe a lightweight sweater and then I'll need boots,"
Cathy said.

Josie pulled one from the rack that had wide stripes in
two shades of blue. "Right over here. This one is the same
color as your eyes."

"Do you sell bras?" Cathy asked.

"Just sports bras."

"I'll try on one in a thirty-four, this sweater, and these two shirts." She pulled two shirts from a round rack and added them to the jeans. "I'll decide which one works best and then we'll look at boots."

Travis flipped through a rack of belts. If she bought the blue plaid shirt, the belt with silver lacing would look really good. And if Brad got sassy, the big rhinestone buckle would be right handy to beat the shit out of him.

Cathy put the jeans on and looked at her butt in the three-way mirror. They fit well and she could justify the price by saying that she hadn't bought a new pair of dress jeans in six months. She wasn't really crazy about black jeans but they were damn cute. She wiggled a few times to the song on the radio. The sweater was a little too short in the sleeves so she opted for a long-sleeved black Western shirt with lace ruffles on the cuffs and collar. Besides, the sports bra didn't give her nearly enough uplift to wear with a sweater. She folded her sweat bottoms and T-shirt and walked out of the dressing room in the black outfit.

Travis's mouth went as dry as hot sand when he saw her. Even with her hair hanging straight and no makeup she looked like a runway model. Why would any idiot ever hit something that looked like that? Brad had cow chips for brains.

Cathy handed Josie the sweats and the tags from the jeans, bra, and shirt. "I'd like to look at boots now."

"Black?"

"I think so."

"Baby Phats?"

"No, roach killers. Size eight."

Josie passed the popular round-toed boots and went straight to the exotics. "Smooth gator and plain leather and a new shipment of Lucchese Mad Dog black goat leather." She picked up a pair of good-looking black leather boots and handed them to Cathy.

Cathy ran her fingers over the soft leather. "This is goat?"

"Yes, ma'am." Josie smiled.

"Do they run true?"

"Pretty much."

"Bring out an eight and an eight and a half. I'd like to try both."

Cathy tried the size eight first and walked around the room on the carpet in both boots before she put on the eight and a half. "They're a snug fit across the instep but these feel a little too long. I think I'd rather have the eights."

"That's the way they're supposed to fit. They'll mold right to your foot," Josie said. "Never had a single pair brought back, but we guarantee them."

"How high is this heel?"

"Inch and a half."

"I'll take them. All right if I keep them on?"

"Yes, ma'am. I'll just put the box on the counter with the tags from your other purchases. Anything else?"

Travis handed her a black leather belt with a big silver buckle encrusted with rhinestones. "Lace this through your loops."

Cathy flipped the belt over and looked at the numbers on the back. "How'd you know my size?"

"Easy, darlin'. I spanned your waist a few times while we were...dancin.'"

Cathy giggled.

Josie pretended she didn't hear the hesitation before Travis's last word. "That's the same goat leather as the boots. It'll look good with them. Need a hat?"

Travis nodded. "I believe she does and maybe that duster hangin' on the mannequin in the window if it's the right size. You're missin' a loop in the back, honey. Here, let me help you."

The feel of his hands burned through denim and cotton underpants to sear her skin. Maybe she should make an excuse to take him to the dressing room. It would be a tight fit, but hey, there were three mirrors to make it interesting.

"Penny for your thoughts," he whispered softly in her ear as he wrapped his arms around her waist and finished lacing the belt.

She told him exactly what she'd been thinking.

"I'll pay Josie to guard the door if you'll really do it."

"We'd never make it to Mena if we did," she teased.

Lord, it was amazing how much better a woman felt all dressed up than she did in sweats and house shoes. But then sweats were so much better than tattered blankets that smelled like rats, so it was all relative.

"You wanted to look at black hats?" Josie returned from the sales counter.

Cathy pointed to one.

"That is bull hide and will look really smart with the outfit you've put together. Are you going to something special?" Josie asked.

"Yep, I'm going to a first-class ass kickin'," Cathy said.

Josie laughed. "You are funny. Really, are you going to be a rodeo queen or something?"

"Nope, just the queen of the ass kickin'," Cathy assured her.

Josie handed the hat to Travis. "Would you please put this on her? I'd have to get a ladder."

A leather hat band decorated with a turquoise conch in the front and brass studs on the underside of the upturned brim decorated the black hat. When Travis set it on her head he brushed a few blond hairs back behind her ear and kissed her on the tender skin right below her earlobe.

"Much more, darlin', and you'll be taller than me, and you look like sex on a stick," Travis said.

She blushed. "You don't know how many times I've thought the same thing about you. Do I look ten feet tall and bulletproof yet?"

Travis folded his arms across his chest and studied her. "Ten feet tall, yes, ma'am. Josie, you go get us that black duster up there in the window and we'll make her bulletproof."

Josie scurried away to get the coat from the window but the sleeves were too short and the shoulders too narrow. Her face was a picture of disappointment. The Scully duster would have sent her sale close to a thousand dollars.

"I've got a long leather coat back there made by the same company that would probably look better than the duster and you'd get more wear out of it."

"Well, let's take a look," Travis said.

"You got that much money?" Cathy whispered.

"Yes, I do." Travis slipped the coat on Cathy.

Josie clapped her hands. "You are going to be the queen of that ass kickin' for sure. That's black boar suede and it hangs just right. The shiny beading looks good with the lace cuffs peeking out, don't you think?"

"What do you think?" Cathy twirled around so Travis could see all the angles.

"Buy it," Travis said hoarsely.

"Anything else?" Josie asked.

"I don't reckon there's anything else we can hang on me, is there?" Cathy laughed.

"I do have some fine-lookin' turquoise earrings that would set off that hat band real good," Josie said.

"Well, let's look at them," Travis said.

Josie led them to the jewelry counter where Cathy picked out a pair of short dangles studded with turquoise stones and put them into the holes in her ears. She almost backed out of the whole sale when the girl rang up nine hundred fifty-three dollars and forty-nine cents. She could do without the coat, the hat, the belt, and the earrings. But Travis had a card out and the items paid for before she could say a word.

"That was fun," Travis said when they were back in the truck and headed north again.

"That was very expensive," she said.

"You don't have to pay me back. It was worth every dime to see Josie's face when she realized you weren't a bag lady shoplifter."

Cathy slapped his shoulder playfully. "I got to admit, I did feel like Julia Roberts when she went shopping in *Pretty Woman*, but I will pay you as soon as we get home and there will be no discussion about it."

"Never saw that. My sisters think it's a classic. Tell me why it made you think of that movie."

"Julia is a hooker and Richard Gere has hired her to stay with him. He gives her money and sends her shopping for something nice to wear to dinner that evening. She was wearing thigh-high plastic boots with a pin holding up the zipper and a short skirt with a skimpy top and she really looked like a hooker. But this shop clerk treated her like dirt and she went back to the hotel in tears."

"Did she wear that getup to dinner with him that night then?"

"No, the hotel concierge took pity on her and made a phone call. She looked fabulous by the time Richard Gere came home from making millions that night."

"And Josie made you feel like that?" Travis frowned.

"At first."

"I'm glad I didn't know. I would have had her manager ring up the sale and put it on his commission," Travis said.

Cathy smiled. He was willing to rescue her, take up for her, finance her pretty things until she could pay him back, and deal out revenge to anyone who hurt her feelings. It would be so easy to fall in love with a man like Travis, but Alaska was a long way from Mingus, Texas.

CHAPTER 16

GREEN'S OIL COMPANY WAS LOCATED ON A SIDE STREET in Mena, Arkansas, in a brick building that had originally been a bank. It had been painted soft yellow and the logo was engraved in a huge plate glass window overlooking the sidewalk.

"You ready for this?" Travis asked when she hesitated at the door.

"Oh, yeah, I'm more than ready." She opened the door and marched inside with Travis right behind her.

"Is that you, Cathy O'Dell? Good lord, girl, you sure do look fine. And who's that behind you? You get him off a Marlboro ad?" Tina Green came from behind her desk to hug Cathy. Tina barely came up to Cathy's shoulder. She wore high-heeled shoes and a black-and-white polka-dotted dress that stopped at her knees. Neither did much for her overweight figure, but her eyes were bright and her smile genuine.

Cathy motioned toward Travis. "This is Travis Henry. Travis, this is Tina. Her uncle owns the company and we were pretty good friends while I was here."

Travis extended his hand. "Pleased to meet you."

"Me too. But we were only friends after the lunch break. No one messed with Cathy in the morning. Now tell me, what you are doing in Mena? I didn't figure you'd ever come back this way again." She kept his hand a second longer than necessary.

Cathy smiled. "I still growl before noon and no one messes with me before my third cup of coffee. We were passing through and I thought I'd stop in."

"Through to where? You look like you just came off a Western wear runway, girl. The beer joint business must be really good," Tina said.

"The Honky Tonk has been very good to me. How are things around here?"

"Same as ever. Uncle Mark misses you. Had to hire two people to do your job. Brad hit on both of them the first week but I put a bug in their innocent little ears. He's not speaking to me for it but who gives a shit. He never was my favorite cousin anyway. Now if you'd have married him, you might be my favorite. I heard through the grapevine that Uncle Mark has given him six months to settle down and stop causing problems, and you know what kind I'm talking about."

"So he's still here?"

"God, yes. I'd rather he was in the cemetery but you know how it is with family. Uncle Mark told his momma he'd take care of him when she died. Blood is thicker than common sense. Have a seat or else let me take you both to dinner."

Cathy shook her head. "Can't stay long enough for either. Come see me in Mingus and we'll talk all night. Is Brad in his office?"

"No, he's in the conference room with Uncle Mark." Tina frowned. "You sure you want to go up there?"

"Yes, I am. And I meant it about driving down to Mingus to see me. Bring your friends and you can dance all night with the pretty cowboys and sleep in my apartment." Cathy headed for the stairs.

"No elevators?" Travis followed.

"Had one but it broke down and Tina said we should use the stairs for exercise. When Mark gets too old to run up and down them, he'll have the elevator fixed. Don't fuss about it. Brad did enough of that to last a lifetime," she said.

He touched Cathy's arm. "Don't ever compare me to that fool. Don't even say my name in the same sentence with his. I hope he does something really stupid so I can beat the shit out of him. I'll even pay the assault fine just to get to do it."

She stopped halfway up the steps. "You'd do that?"

"Oh, yes, and enjoy every minute. I'd write the check in his blood."

"Well, thank you, Travis. But I can take care of him all by myself and then it will really be over." She stopped and kissed him hard on the lips and then wrapped her arms around his neck for a second softer kiss.

"For that kind of treatment I might just whip his ass for the fun of it," Travis said when she broke away.

"Let me take care of it. I need to," she whispered.

He reached for her hand and squeezed slightly. "I'm here if you need me."

A door to the left of the stairs opened at the same time Cathy and Travis got to the top. Drillers, roughnecks, and engineers, along with Mark and Brad, pushed out into the hallway. They all stopped in their tracks and stared slack-jawed at the six-foot woman in front of them.

Mark opened his arms. "Well, I'll be danged, if it ain't Cathy O'Dell."

She walked into them for the hug but kept her eyes on Brad's face. It had gone a dull shade of ashy gray and his eyes darted around the hall like a cornered one-legged chicken at a coyote convention. Travis blocked the stairs and the oilmen kept him from getting back into the conference room, or he would have made a quick excuse and taken off to hide until she left town.

Evidently he'd been expecting to see her in totally different circumstances and surroundings. Every single dime of the money spent on the outfit was worth it when he scanned her from boots to hat.

"What brings you to Mena? I thought you were runnin' a beer joint in Texas," Mark said.

She stepped back out of his embrace. "I am. And doin' a little moonlightin' for Amos Lambert. I hear you faxed him my resume."

Mark's grin smoothed out part of the wrinkles in his face. "I told you if you wanted to get back into the business to call me." He turned to a pair of lingering engineers. "You boys shoulda been here when Cathy worked for me. She never made a mistake. Had an audit once and the IRS couldn't find a penny in the wrong place. She's worth her weight in gold. If I'd been a smart man she wouldn't have ever left me. And if my nephew had been smart he would have never lost her."

"Why did she leave?" One of the men flirted with his eyes.

"She and Brad got crossways. They were engaged and broke it off. She said she couldn't work with him. I offered to fire him but she'd have none of it. So she went to Mingus, Texas, to her cousin's place and hasn't been back until right now," Mark said.

"Good God!" Brad exclaimed.

"It's the truth." Mark chuckled.

"I'd like you to meet Travis Henry," Cathy said.

"I know Travis. I tried to steal him from Amos a couple of years ago. How are you, son?"

"Doin' pretty good, sir. Y'all still finding oil up here?"

"You almost went to work here?" Cathy asked.

"No, he didn't. He wouldn't leave Amos for anything. I just saw him at an oil convention in Dallas and made an offer. He refused and that was that, and yes, son, we are still making a profit," Mark said. "Got time for lunch? I'll take you two out and see if I can steal both of you away from Amos."

"No, we're just passing through. Brad? A minute please. In your office? In private?" she asked.

"Well, it's good to see y'all," Mark said.

"Thanks. If you're ever in Mingus stop by the Honky Tonk. I'll make you the best martini you've ever had," Cathy said.

"I remember your martinis. You boys should've been around the last Christmas party she was here. Not only could she keep an immaculate set of books, she's the best damn bartender in four states. And one of her martinis would make you slap your granny, it's so good. Darlin', just talkin' about them makes me thirsty. I might show up there sometime. Come on, boys. Let's go get some lunch. Brad, I guess you're on your own today since the lady wants to talk," Mark said.

"It's good to see you, Cathy, but I've made plans to have lunch with someone else," he said icily.

She stepped up so close to him that her hat brim brushed his hair. "Change them. We are going to talk."

"Looks like she's a handful," one of the oilmen said to Travis.

"She can be," he said.

"You want to go with us to eat while she and Brad have a visit?" Mark asked.

Travis shook his head. "Naw, I reckon I'll stay here. When she gets finished we need to be going on home. We got a beer joint and an oil company to run."

"You ready?" Cathy asked Brad.

She was glad that Travis had insisted on the outfit because she felt like King Kong on cocaine. She would have beat the shit out of him in her gray sweats and bare feet, but the intimidation in his eyes when she looked over Mark's shoulder was worth every cent she'd spent on the outfit.

"Sure!" he said with too much bravado.

His office was right beside the conference room. He slung the door open and stood to one side. She walked right in and hiked a hip on his desk. He was as bad as a fussy old maid in an eighty-year-old house. Chairs were made to sit in. Nothing touched his immaculately clean desk except his blotter, phone, and whatever else he happened to be working on. No extra papers. No pictures. No dust.

She took off her hat and set it on his desk blotter and pulled up a knee to prop a boot heel on his chair. "Sorry I didn't think to bring some dirt from the Big Cypress Bayou so you could have a little taste of home."

He gave her a go-to-hell look and slammed the door.

Travis sat down on the top step and waited. If Cathy needed him he'd gladly kick the door down and throw the son-of-a-bitch out the window. If he heard so much as a gasp from Cathy, Brad would need a new door and possibly a casket.

Brad took two menacing steps toward Cathy. "Get off my desk and get your feet out of my chair."

She smiled. "Oscar and Duroc send their love. They said to tell you that they don't want your hundred dollars and if you want to buy them a beer, they are in New Orleans until deer season next year. Guess you were expectin' to see them today instead of me? Nice little fishin' shack you got down there on the Big Cypress. Right cozy. Is that your retirement condo?"

"Are you crazy? I don't know anyone named Oscar or Duroc." Brad's voice sounded hollow.

"Ah, they'd be hurt to hear you say that. They had such respect for their shirttail kin." She stood up and in a few easy strides was face-to-face with him.

He raised a hand to push her back.

She grabbed it midair. "Don't you dare."

"You can't prove a damn thing. I was right here and I have a perfectly good alibi," he growled.

"You got that right."

"So what are you doing here?"

"Making sure you understand that I'm not afraid of you or your shirttail kin and to make sure you will leave me alone the rest of my life. I don't want to see you, smell you, or any of your relatives."

"And if you do?" he asked through clenched teeth.

"Don't test me to find out, darlin'." Cathy moved so close that he leaned back.

Brad circled around her and sat down in his chair like a king on his throne. He shoved her hat off on the floor and gave her a daring look. "Why'd you lie to me and say you were married to that country bumpkin? I suppose now you're goin' to tell me that cowboy out there is your husband?"

That was the straw that put the proverbial camel on the ground. Her boots hit the top of his desk with a thud as she bounced up on top of it and started kicking. Blotter, telephone, and a folder of papers scattered all over the office. He was standing up to protest when she planted the bottom of a boot in his chest and sent him flying backward on the floor. He was gasping for breath when he looked up to see her straddling him. She openhanded slapped him across the face.

He drew back and she grabbed his hand. It was arm wrestling in the air and he lost quickly. She held on to his fingers even after she'd pinned them on the ground. "Don't you ever make trouble for me again or the next time I'll fill you full of shotgun holes and watch you bleed out. Do you understand me? You can settle down with whatever woman you can find to please your Uncle Mark, but it damn sure won't be me."

He gripped her hand with all the force he could muster and tried to break her fingers. "I will kill you instead of marrying you," he growled.

She shook free of his hand, reached back, and grabbed his thigh. "Two inches higher and you and Duroc can sing in the same choir. Is it over?"

"Okay, okay. I'll leave you alone," Brad said.

"I've got pictures and dirty clothes for evidence. I've got Oscar and Duroc's names. I know where to find them and they'll squeal like little girls if we ever walk into the courtroom. That is if it ever gets that far. You remember my bouncer, Tinker? Well, darlin', we might just bypass the law-and-order thing and go straight for vengeance. And if he gets tired of knockin' heads together Travis will step in for him. I'm tired of this and it's over." She moved up an inch and squeezed as hard as she could. He reached down and tried to pry her hand from his leg but she hung on like a bulldog with a soup bone.

He wanted to toss her cold dead body out the window. But Mark would never ever believe she committed suicide or that she fell by accident. Neither would that big bruiser of a cowboy waiting on the steps, and Brad had no doubt if she screamed the lock on the office door wouldn't keep him out in the hall.

"Okay," he whispered.

She crawled off him and picked up her hat. "Appreciate your Uncle Mark. He's the only good thing in your life. Settle down and be a real man. Don't hit on your wife and don't mess around on her."

"Go to hell. I was a fool to ever get mixed up with you anyway." Brad righted himself and brushed at his suit. He combed his hair with his fingertips and looked around with a bewildered look on his face.

"One more thing. If you think you're going to continue this war, check your computer in the morning before you make another move. I'm sending some pictures and a complete report of everything I can remember so you'll know exactly what happened out there. If I see a shadow that looks like you it will all go straight to Mark. Your resume won't be worth anything but toilet paper," she said.

"Get out of here. I never want to see you again," he hissed.

"That's exactly what I want to hear. You should put a better door on the fishing shack. Word on the street is that you won't ever find a decent job if he fires you, but you can always share your fishing cabin with the rats and roaches, not to mention Oscar and Duroc. And pray that I have a long and happy life. Because if my cousin, Daisy, or Tinker smells the faintest hint of foul play at my death, Mark gets the files. Goodbye." Cathy settled her hat on her head.

"I really thought you were special. Guess I was wrong," he said.

She slapped him hard. "Don't try to play on my sympathy. I don't give a damn about you. That's for knocking my brand-new hat to the floor. Tell Mark that you fell and hit your face on the desk." She left him holding his nose.

"Is it finished?" Travis asked.

"It is. I'm hungry. Let's go get some pizza and then head home. Want to go through the Talimena drive? It's not as pretty this time of year as it is in the fall, but it's a nice drive. Then we could have dinner tonight between here and home and maybe stay in a hotel," she said.

Travis took her hand.

She winced.

"What?" he asked.

"Little finger hurts but he looks worse than me."

Travis's laughter rang throughout the whole building.

CHAPTER 17

Sunrays filtered down through big white marsh-mallow clouds that hung so close to the top of the mountain that Cathy could almost touch them. To have a clear sky with no haze in February was a miracle in the Ouachita Mountains. It was an omen that everything was right in her world. She'd taken care of the Brad issue once and for all. Tomorrow he'd get the story and the pictures. She hadn't been whistling "Dixie" out her naturally born redneck ass when she told him she would file it away for insurance. If he got another wild hair up his hind end they would help him remember what was at stake.

"So why do you like this mountain drive?" Travis stopped the truck at a scenic parking spot.

"I always imagine that it's Montana. I've always thought I'd like to visit there. Never been anywhere but Oklahoma, Texas, Louisiana, and Arkansas," Cathy said.

"Amos has had me all over the place in the past few years. You'd love Alaska, Cathy. We've talked about it before but I wish you could see it."

So do I, but... Those four words confused the hell out of her. She'd found peace in Mingus, Texas. How could she be yearning to see Alaska? It felt as if she'd married the Honky Tonk and thinking of leaving it was the same as cheating.

She changed the subject so she didn't have to think about Alaska or seeing it with Travis. "Did you go to work for him right out of college?"

"No, I worked for a Tulsa-based company for a year, but

then Amos offered me a good deal and I took it. Never been sorry. Someday I'd like to have my own company but that'll be on down the road."

"Why?"

"Why what? That I want my own company or that it'll be on down the road?"

"Both," she said.

"It's expensive to start a company and when I do it means I hang up my wandering hat and settle down," he said.

"When do you plan on doing that?"

"Not for a while," he answered. *Not until I find a woman who turns my world upside down just like you do. And who'll go anywhere in the world with me. Someone as beautiful as you but not tied to a damned beer joint like you are.*

Thinking of Travis leaving plunged Cathy into a mood worse than what she'd experienced in the fishing shack. She'd let him get under her skin when he bulldozed his way into the Honky Tonk with that kiss. Sitting on the top of the mountain and looking down into the valley below, she realized that he'd carved a place out in her heart. The only trouble with that was that he had wings and flew all over the world; she had roots and they were grounded in the Honky Tonk in Mingus, Texas.

"You've gotten serious," he said.

"My mind was drifting," she said.

He pulled the truck back out on the road and started the descent down the mountain. "So tell me, what would you do if you could do anything in the world?"

"I'm doing it."

"Running the Honky Tonk? Don't you ever want to get away from it?"

"After that fishing shack back there on the bayou, I'll just stay at the Tonk, thank you very much," she said.

They came down out of the mountains in a tiny settlement called Page at a place where Highway 259 went north or south. Cathy had the atlas in her lap and pointed to the south.

"We'll be home in about six hours. Not in time to open the Tonk but long before bedtime," she said.

"Or we could be in Fort Smith in one hour." He pointed north.

"Why would we... No, it's not even an option." She shook her head emphatically.

"You wanted to go to Mena and the pickup went north instead of south. Seems only fair that it does it again, don't you think?"

"But?"

"I haven't seen my folks in weeks and I'm this close. What would you do if it was your folks?"

She winced. Maybe his mother would be the only one at home. His sisters and father would be at work in the middle of the afternoon. It wouldn't be a big deal to run in for an hour. If her mother was alive and she was that close, wild Missouri mules couldn't keep her from seeing her.

"Of course," she said.

"Good. You'll love Momma. She's the rancher in the family. Dad still goes to the construction office every day but she runs the ranch. I'm going to call her and tell her we're on the way," he said.

He spoke briefly, never mentioning that he'd been the knight in shining pickup who'd rushed to her rescue. He just said he was in the area and had a few hours to spare. And he hung up right after he told her he was bringing someone with him so put on a pot of coffee because Cathy didn't drink tea.

It was the longest sixty-six miles she'd ever ridden. She fidgeted with her hair and wished for her purse so she could put on a bit of makeup. Her jeans were too tight and her belt had too much bling. She should have bought the plainer boots and not spent so much on the suede coat with the sequins. His mother would think she was a glorified hooker. She saw a sign that said Fort Smith was ten miles away. How could a trip that took so long be over so quickly? Travis tapped his thumbs on the steering wheel, keeping time with one song after another from an Alan Jackson CD. How could he be happy when she felt like she was sitting in a bed of red ants? He made a few turns and then slowed down to turn left into a lane with a white fence on both sides penning in horses of every size and color.

"Momma is partial to paints but she raises all kinds," Travis said.

Cathy didn't answer but clasped her hands tightly. *Good lord, woman, you are twenty-eight years old and you've met parents before. What are you so blasted nervous about? Loosen up. It's one woman and it's an hour at most. After that you can make him take you straight back to the Honky Tonk where you can hole up for the rest of your life.*

He parked in front of a rambling white clapboard ranch house. Big roomy rocking chairs were scattered down the length of a wide porch. Dormant crape myrtles waited for spring in the flower beds in the circular driveway.

Momma met them at the door and Travis bent to hug her. She was a petite blond with green eyes and she wore faded jeans and a red plaid flannel shirt.

Travis stepped to one side. "I'd like you to meet Cathy O'Dell. Cathy, this is my mother, Odessa Henry."

Cathy extended a hand. "I'm pleased to meet you, ma'am."

"I... I'm in shock. You are so beautiful," she said bluntly. "He's talked so much about you on the phone but I never asked what you looked like. I just assumed you were short. I have no idea how I got that notion in my mind."

Travis chuckled.

Cathy blushed.

"I'm sorry. Where are my manners? Come on in. Myrna has a ham in the oven. I called your sisters and your dad is on his way home. They'll all be here in an hour and we'll eat early. Y'all can stay the night, can't you?"

Travis looked at Cathy. "We have to be in Mingus by tomorrow afternoon. We can have supper and a visit, but then we'd better get some miles in."

Cathy was barely inside the house and the walls began to close in. She had an acute desire to turn around and run all the way to Mingus. She followed Odessa and Travis into the living room but every step was a chore. She was too antsy to sit so she walked over to a huge stone fireplace with glowing embers covering the north wall. Pictures of children on the mantel captured Cathy's attention and gave her an excuse to keep from sitting down.

Odessa joined her. "Those are the children when they were little. Travis, Gwen, Rose, Emma, and Grace. Travis is the only one who got my blond hair. The girls were always jealous. Gwen and Rose keep theirs blond now, straight out of a bottle. Emma and Grace learned to live with plain old light brown hair like their father."

"Hello! I heard the prodigal son is home." Homer

Henry's body matched his big, booming, deep voice. He met his son in the middle of the room in a bear hug. He was the same height as Travis but fifty pounds heavier. His light brown hair was cut very short and his blue eyes looked huge behind wire-rimmed glasses. Put blond curls on his head and he was Travis in thirty years.

"Dad, this is Cathy O'Dell. Cathy, this is my father, Homer."

Cathy extended a hand and Homer shook it firmly.

"I see where Travis got his blue eyes," she said.

"And his glasses. Neither of us can stand the idea of putting something in our eyes so we aren't candidates for contact lenses. Dessa has to hold us both down to put eye drops in during allergy season," Homer said.

"Don't be givin' away my secrets." Travis laughed.

"It ain't a secret. It's a failing," Homer said. "What brings you two to Fort Smith? Y'all out scoutin' for new territory?"

A gray-haired lady in jeans, a red T-shirt, and an apron brought in a tray with coffee, tea, and cookies. "Come over here and give me a hug, boy. You been gone too long this time. And why didn't you call me earlier so I coulda made you a peach cobbler? I could whip you all over the yard for sneakin' up on me like this. How is Angel? Why didn't you bring her along?"

Travis hugged Myrna and introduced her to Cathy. "This is our head cook and the person who keeps the house running. We couldn't make it without Myrna."

"Hello," Cathy said.

"I expect you'd best make the sacrifice and hug me too, young lady. I know I'm short but you're young and bendable," she said.

"Yes, ma'am." Cathy bent low to hug the small lady.

"Now y'all don't ruin your supper. We'll have the last of that chocolate cake I made yesterday and ice cream for dessert, but next time you'd best be callin' me the day before so I can make your lady think we're somebody."

"I will," Travis said.

"Come sit with us. You haven't seen him in a month, either," Odessa said.

"Maybe for a little bit. Bread is made up into rolls so I've got a few minutes before it goes in the oven. Miss Grace likes her hot rolls with ham and baked beans." Myrna sat down and propped her feet on the coffee table.

Travis remembered that she'd asked about Angel so he gave them a quick rundown on her new romance with Garrett.

"So what are you doing in this area?" Homer asked.

"Let's save that story for the supper table when everyone is here," Travis said.

Cathy slipped out of her coat and laid it on the back of a rocking chair and joined Myrna on the sofa, but she didn't have the nerve to prop her cowboy boots on the coffee table. And she was damn sure not telling these people who she'd just met the story of her life or the one about how their son had rescued her, either. Did he want her to tell them that he was a damn fine lover and that just thinking about what he could do to her body made her break out in hives?

"Then tell me what's goin' on in Texas. Did you strike oil yet?" Homer asked.

Travis put two sugars and a tablespoon of cream into a cup and filled it the rest of the way with green tea. His mother did the same. Myrna poured black coffee in two cups and handed one to Homer.

"You're not a tea drinker, are you?" she asked Cathy.

"No, black coffee, but I'll fix it."

"You take this one and I'll pour myself another." Myrna handed her the filled mug. "Me and you, we'll get along just fine."

Travis shook his head. "We haven't hit the pocket yet but it's down there. We've got two more weeks to bring it in and then one way or the other Amos will probably send me somewhere else. He's got some negotiations going on in Alaska."

"I hope you aren't going that far!" Odessa said.

Travis patted his mother on the shoulder. "There are planes that fly out of Anchorage every day just like they do in Dallas."

"Yes, but it's the idea of you being halfway around the world that's scary. Texas is far enough. Tell Amos you want to drill in our backyard," Odessa said.

"There is no oil in our backyard," Travis said.

"Who cares? I'll pay you big bucks to come home and take care of the horses. Do you ride, Cathy? You can help him exercise them every day."

"Cathy is an accountant. She works for Amos in the afternoons. I doubt she'd want to leave Mingus to come ride horses all day." Travis laughed.

"I'm also a bartender. I own and operate the Honky Tonk beer joint. Amos was friends with the original owner, Ruby Lee. That's how I got to know him. The accountant job is just part-time until his other lady gets back on her feet after a wreck," Cathy said.

Myrna patted her knee. "Well halle-blessed-luyah. I thought you was another one of them fancy women that couldn't work because they might break a fingernail. That's the kind he usually brings home."

"You really own a beer joint?" Odessa asked.

"I really do and your son is helping me bartend two nights a week," Cathy said.

She figured Travis would either kick her out the door or at least shoot her a drop-graveyard-dead look but he did neither. He just winked at her and blew her a kiss behind his parents' backs.

The sound of car doors out in the yard sent Myrna to the kitchen and Odessa and Homer to the living room. Travis crooked his finger and motioned for her to stand beside him. She started to refuse but it was his party and she did owe him big-time for the rescue and the shopping trip.

When they all trooped into the living room he had her pulled up to his side with his hand around her waist. In five minutes she'd gone from one-night stand to girlfriend. She didn't have time to think about what all that entailed but she'd play along.

Introductions between Cathy and Emma, Grace, Rose, and Gwen were made. Emma was taller than her sisters but she still didn't reach Cathy's shoulder. She'd come straight from school and wore a denim jumper with a plaid shirt under it. Cathy reached out and brushed a bit of Play-Doh from her hair after shaking her hand.

"I've got a friend in Mingus who teaches kindergarten. She's all the time coming home with that stuff stuck to her," Cathy said.

Grace was the spitting image of her mother. Short, cute, and green-eyed. She wore a black power suit and high-heeled shoes.

"I'm glad you called because I've been starving for Myrna's ham," Grace said. "The only time we get invited is when the fair-haired glory man-child comes home."

"Oh, stop it. Cathy's not going to feel a bit sorry for any of you," Odessa said. "All you have to do is call Myrna any day of the week and she'll have supper on the table for you and you know it."

Gwen wore a baby blue sweater the same color as her eyes. She had her father's hair and face shape and her mother's eyes. She sat down on the sofa, poured a cup of coffee, and propped her feet up. "I'm exhausted. I thought I was going to have to beg off but at the last minute the little boy's fever broke so we didn't have to hospitalize him."

"Well, wait until you hear about my day," Emma said. "It was a nightmare. You know nowadays that every kid in school has at least four parents and enough grandparents to populate a small third-world country. And if the kid doesn't like the teacher they all come to bitch and moan."

"Hey, girl, you should work at the courthouse and you'd see what happens when they all get mad because their sweet little darlin's getting put in jail for smoking pot on school grounds. Your little kindergarten devils turn into our delinquents," Grace said.

The best place in the whole world to hide out is in the middle of a big family. All Cathy had to do was listen to the conversations between them as they talked about their varied experiences and finally got around to asking Travis about what was going on in his world. They set up a howl when he told them he might be going to Alaska.

"How do you feel about that?" Grace looked at Cathy.

"I haven't decided," she said.

"Supper is on the table," Myrna yelled from the kitchen.

Everyone headed for the dining room and to their permanent chairs around the table. Travis pulled out a chair for Cathy and bent to brush a light kiss across her neck. The jolt made her pulse take off like a NASCAR race car jacked up on high test fuel.

When he sat down she reached under the tablecloth and squeezed his thigh. Two could play the flirting game. "Sweet tea, please," she said.

"Yes, ma'am." He poured for both of them as well as Myrna.

"We've been pretty rude. It's just that we don't all get together nearly often enough and this is such a surprise. So tell us, Cathy, what do you do other than look like a model? God, I'd kill a senator for your height," Rose said.

"I own a bar called the Honky Tonk."

"That one in Mingus that's getting all the hype on Facebook and Twitter?"

"That's the one, but I didn't know it was getting any free advertisement," she said.

"It is. They're saying it's the in place for old music and two-stepping. I'd love to go there," Emma said.

"You're a teacher!" Travis said.

"So? I like to dance and I like a good cold beer every so often just like you do."

"I bartend for her on Friday and Saturday nights," Travis said.

Emma spewed tea across the white tablecloth. With just a little more force she would have hit him right between his pretty blue eyes, but it stopped just short of that and stained the white tablecloth.

"Thank God for bleach," Myrna said.

"Are you shittin' me?" Emma asked Cathy.

She shook her head.

"It's the gospel truth," Travis said.

"Is it?" Rose asked.

Cathy nodded.

"It's payment so she'll work for Amos and I don't have to spend time in the office," he said.

"That explains it," Gwen said. "This boy hates to be cooped up."

Homer clicked his tea glass with his spoon and looked around the table. Cathy expected him to give a toast of some kind and got ready to raise her glass. Was it someone's birthday? Had they been saving an important family announcement until Travis was home?

"Okay, listen up. First of all, welcome to our home, Cathy O'Dell. We are glad to have you. And second, we have always enjoyed the time around the supper table. It's when we talk about our day. Tonight you've promised to tell us what brings you and Travis to Fort Smith. So we are all ears and the microphone is yours."

She could have slapped the grin off Travis's face. "You tell them."

"Oh no, it's your story. Don't leave out a bit of it. Gwen is a doctor. She won't mind hearing about rats while she eats. And Grace and Rose used to try to make me sick at the supper table, so if there's something really gory you left out when you told me, be sure to include it this time," he said.

"Okay, then, here goes. Is this a once-upon-a-time story or a mystery?"

"It's a true crime story," Travis said.

She smiled and started at the beginning when she and Brad had the big fight and she decided to move to Mingus to get away from him. Then she went on to tell about the time when he came into the Tonk and Billy Bob claimed to be married to her. That brought on some discussion about Chigger and Jim Bob with Travis putting in a character description or two about Jezzy Belle and Tinker. Then she told about the kidnapping, up to and including driving to Fort Smith and being nervous about meeting Travis's family. But she didn't tell them about the bedroom scenes or the Jacuzzi.

"I'd like to get a hold of that sorry sucker," Rose said. "I bet I could figure out a way to make charges stick to him."

"Probably not," Grace said. "Cathy was right. With those two kidnappers on the lam and her not being able to really pick them out of a lineup it would be her word against his. She did the right thing. Only she should have taken it to the next level and at least crippled him."

Travis sat back with a big smile on his face. A couple more visits and she'd have them all eating out of her hand, but then why shouldn't they? She was pretty, smart, intelligent, and she could tell a damn fine story.

"Okay, don't jump and run. Grace, you come and help me with dessert. If your brother would have gave me more notice there'd be peach cobbler so if the cake is stale, blame him," Myrna said.

Dessert was a scoop of vanilla ice cream on top of a square of chocolate cake drizzled with chocolate syrup and sprinkled with chopped pecans. Cathy moaned with the first bite.

"Sheet cake?" she asked.

"That's right. Myrna makes them once a week," Grace said. "How'd you know?"

"I make them for special occasions."

"Don't tell Travis. He'll glue himself to your side and follow you around like a little puppy dog. He loves chocolate sheet cake," Myrna said.

"What else does he love?" Cathy asked.

Odessa waved a hand. "Don't get Myrna started. She thinks the reason the sun comes up in the morning is to shine on his blond curls. She's spoiled him her whole life. If I'd have known my way around the kitchen when I married Homer we wouldn't have hired Myrna and Travis wouldn't be nearly so spoiled."

"Oh, don't be giving Myrna the medal for spoiling the fair-haired boy child. You and Daddy had him rotten before us girls were ever born," Grace said.

That set off the fireworks with everyone talking at once. Cathy ate her cake slowly, enjoying the big family atmosphere as much as she did the cake. It would be so easy to fall in love with him and the family, to fit in with all the good-natured bantering and fun.

But Travis had his heart set on an Alaska adventure, and even if she could hold him down, he'd come to hate her for it when his wandering soul wanted to sprout wings and fly again.

CHAPTER 18

RIDING AFTER DARK IS BORING AND MONOTONOUS. Cathy couldn't see the scenery of the countryside, even if it was nothing but miles and miles of dormant scrub oak trees and rolling hills. Dash lights did little to light up the cab of the truck and Travis had been unusually quiet for the past three hours. She'd been left alone with nothing but her own thoughts and they were on a continuous loop, going nowhere, solving nothing. She could see a glow in the sky giving testimony that they were coming up on Durant, Oklahoma.

The Toby Keith CD Travis had in the player ended. He took it out and handed it to her. "Pick out something else. We're fixing to go through Durant. Are you tired or do you still want to drive until the wee hours of the morning?"

Cathy yawned. "I'm exhausted. Everything is surreal. It seems like a month since last Saturday night. I've been on a three-day adrenaline high and it hit bottom a ways back. I could sleep for a week."

"Me too," he said. "There's a sign for a Hampton Inn. It's right off the highway."

"I could... No I couldn't. The Hampton is fine."

"What were you about to say? You want to stay in a different motel? There are several to choose from."

"I almost said that I could sleep in a broom closet but after that fishing shack, I'm not saying it. Have I thanked you for everything today?"

"Maybe a dozen times."

He stopped the pickup under the awning at the hotel. Cars zipped up and down the main thoroughfare to the south of the hotel. A steady stream of traffic slowed down for the red light before turning west into the Walmart parking lot. Brakes, horns, sirens, a couple of early-bird crickets, and a lonesome old tree frog combined to sound like bad rock music. Cathy gladly got out of the truck and stretched, moving her neck from side to side and loving the noise of a busy college town not yet ready to turn in for the night. It sure beat squeaking rats and rusty bedsprings.

She pointed at the brass luggage carts in the foyer. "Guess we didn't bring enough to need one of those, did we?"

"Thank goodness. I'm too tired to deal with that much baggage," Travis said.

The young lady behind the desk looked up from a book she'd been reading. Her eyes glittered as if the hero pictured on front of the fat romance book had suddenly miraculously materialized in front of her.

"What can I do for you?" she sing-songed.

"We need a room," he said.

The glitter faded when Cathy leaned out from behind him.

"King-sized, please," Cathy said.

"Yes, ma'am. Love your coat," she recovered quickly.

"Thank you."

"We have a Jacuzzi suite still open."

"We'll take anything." Travis dug his credit card out of his wallet and laid it on the counter.

"Just a plain room is fine. We're too tired for Jacuzzi tonight. Is that coffee fresh?" Cathy nodded toward the counter behind them.

"It is and the cookies and apples are for our customers. Breakfast is from six to ten in the morning in the dining room behind the coffeepots there. The pool is closed for the winter but the exercise room is open."

"We won't need that tonight," Cathy said.

The girl handed Travis a paper to sign. "Checkout is eleven. Just leave your key at the desk. Room three hundred fifteen. Elevators are straight ahead to your left."

Travis gave the key to Cathy. "Go on up. I'll park the truck and bring in the bags."

She went straight to the coffee bar, found green tea bags and hot water as well as decaf and dark roast coffee. She unwrapped a bag, put it in a Styrofoam cup, added two sugars and a teaspoon-sized container of half-and-half, then filled it with hot water and put a lid on the top. Then she filled a cup with coffee, covered it with a lid, and carried them to the elevators.

When she reached the room she balanced two cups in one hand while she opened the door. She went straight to the desk to set them both down before looking around. There was a flower arrangement on the coffee table in front of a love seat, a plasma-screen television, microwave and small refrigerator, big bathroom, and a fast-speed internet connection. None of it appealed to her like a king-sized bed covered with a fluffy white duvet and four big soft pillows plus a neck roll pillow that all looked like heavenly clouds. She sat down on the love seat, pulled off her fancy new boots, and wiggled her toes. When Travis knocked she opened the door and stood to one side to let him tote the baggage inside. Her shirt was unbuttoned and her jeans unzipped.

"Wow!" he said.

"Don't be gettin' your hopes up. I'm so tired you'd have to wake me when it was over," she said.

He set his duffel bag and three plastic Dollar Store bags on the floor. "Honey, you'd have to wake me to get it started. I'll just be happy to have a shower and cuddle up in that bed with you. I was wowing because you look so danged sexy."

"Thank you. I'm headed for the shower." She hung her shirt and jeans in the closet, tossed her bra on the shelf, and padded to the bathroom in white cotton panties.

The bathroom was as large as the kitchen in her apartment and a small elephant could easily fit in the shower. She waited until the water was hot and adjusted it. She'd barely gotten her hair wet when Travis popped his head inside. "It's big enough for two. Want some company?"

"It's big enough for an orgy. Too bad we're both worn out." She lathered up her hair with the hotel shampoo. "Duck under the shower and get your hair wet and I'll wash it for you, since my hands are already soapy."

She poured what was left of the shampoo on top of his hair after he'd gotten it wet and gently massaged his scalp. He bent forward slightly and braced himself by putting his hands on her waist.

"Part of me is willing; the other part is too tired," he moaned.

"We need sleep more than sex. Now turn around and I'll wash your back."

"I think the willing part is winning the race. That feels wonderful. You've got three hours to stop and when you are done I will return the favors," he said.

"If you touch me, my willing part will win the race and we'll never wake up in the morning. You'll lose your job."

"It would be worth it." He grinned.

"For a week and then you'd be sorry. We're about to fight. I feel it in my bones so I'm going to rinse this soap out of my hair and brush my teeth while you finish your shower."

She was dressed in a nightshirt and was applying hotel lotion on her legs and arms when he came out of the bathroom. His hair still had water drops clinging to it and the only thing between her and that sexy body was a loosely wrapped towel.

"Wow!" she said.

He grinned. "Thank you."

"You are very welcome. Did I tell you lately that you are sexy as hell? Oh, I forgot, I made you green tea. Hope it's still hot enough to taste good."

He picked up the cup and took a long sip. "Not bad. Did I tell you lately that you are sexy even in a Dollar Store nightshirt with Rudolph on the front?"

She smiled.

Looking at you in nothing but a loincloth would probably make men all over the world start drinking green tea if they thought it would give them a body like yours.

He sat down at the desk. "When did you make this?"

"They have a coffee and tea bar down in the lobby for customers. I bypassed the apples and cookies," she said.

"Well, damn. Were they chocolate chip?"

She nodded.

He looked down. "Think I could get away with going after one wearing nothing but a towel?"

"If you can run faster than that sweet little thing behind the counter. I thought she was going to spread cookie crumbs on your body and have you for a midnight snack. And then she saw me and her world collapsed," she said.

He raised an eyebrow. "Jealous?"

"No, but she was." Cathy smiled.

He finished his tea and tossed the cup in the trash before standing up and dropping the towel on the floor. He pulled back the covers and crawled naked into the bed.

"You coming to bed soon?" he asked.

"Right now." She curled up next to him with her face on his chest.

He sighed, rolled to one side, and wrapped both arms around her. "Good night, Cathy."

"Mmmm," she mumbled, already in the first stages of sleep.

The rats were back only this time they weren't interested in the food basket. She'd cut her arm on the lid from the sausage can and they could smell the blood. She wiped it on the mattress and got as far away as the chain around her ankle would let her but the wound wouldn't stop dripping. They followed the blood drops from the bed to the corner. She wrapped her arm in the blanket poncho but it dripped through and one rat licked the floor. Another stood on his hind legs and squeaked at her. A third's evil eyes locked in on her arm and he began to climb up the poncho.

She screamed at the varmints and kicked out at the brave ones who were coming in for the kill. Duroc's high squeaky voice cackled over by the door. Oscar said she was getting what she deserved.

"I will kill you both," she yelled.

Then Duroc threw a rope around her and pinned her to

the floor. Rats ran in every direction but she'd rather fight the rats than the man.

"Wake up, Cathy. It's me, Travis!"

Duroc yelled lies in her ear while he held her down. Travis wasn't in the shack. He was in Mingus. She raised a knee but a hand clamped down on it.

"No, no!" she screamed.

"Cathy, wake up!" Travis said.

She opened her eyes and tried to see the whole room at one time. Where was Duroc hiding? She'd kill him if he wasn't out of reach of the damned chain. Where did the soft pillows and comforter come from?

"Breathe," Travis demanded.

She spoke between short sobbing gasps. "It was so real. They were there trying to bite me and he was holding me down."

He hugged her close. "It was a bad dream, a horrible nightmare. You'll probably have them for a while. I'm here, honey. Nothing is going to hurt you ever again."

"Promise?"

"I promise."

Travis kept his eyes open long after she relaxed. Henrys kept promises that they made and they didn't give their word lightly. Would he be around to keep her safe forever?

"Travis?" she whispered.

"I'm right here."

"Thank you," she murmured.

The next time she awoke she was alone in the bed and the room was too quiet. "Travis?" She raised her voice slightly so he'd hear her if he was shaving.

Nothing.

She bounded out of bed and pulled the curtains back. Bright sunlight blinded her for a few seconds until her eyes adjusted. She checked the clock to find that it was eight o'clock already. They should already be on the road to Mingus. Travis was going to be late and Amos had already been patient about him missing work. Her mind ran in circles as she hurriedly dressed in her new jeans and a T-shirt. She was putting on socks when the door opened.

"Good morning," he said.

"Where have you been? We should have been driving an hour ago. Why didn't you wake me?"

"Whoa, darlin'. It's all right. I called Amos. He's all right with me being a little late if we don't get home right on the hour. Here's coffee. I didn't have breakfast yet but it looks pretty good. When you are ready we'll eat and go. What woke you up anyway? I was going to let you sleep as long as you wanted since you had a restless night."

She took the coffee. "I'm starved. What's on the breakfast menu?"

"Fruit, waffles, omelets, bacon, cereal, yogurt." He got his things from the bathroom and put into the duffel bag. "So does that sound good?" he asked.

"It sounds just fine," she quipped.

"Drink more coffee."

"I thought I was being sweet," she said.

"By the time you get to the bottom of that second cup, there's the possibility that you might be."

"You have a split personality. You were all sweet last night and now you are picking a fight."

"Me? We're talking about me?" he asked.

"Well, we sure aren't talkin' about me. My personality is

the same every day. I make no bones about it. I'm not nice until I've had three cups of coffee in the mornings."

"How did that Brad fellow or anyone else work with you? You did go to work at nine, didn't you?"

"Eight. And no one bothered me until after lunch. You'd be amazed how much work an old bear can do in the mornings when she's left totally alone. It was the secret to my success. While everyone else was gossiping over the water cooler about me, I was getting two days work done behind a closed door."

"You've been faking it. You aren't mean in the morning. It's a facade to get people to leave you alone."

She shrugged. "If anyone ever finds that out I'm blaming you. I've got a reputation to uphold. Let's have breakfast and give them the room key so we can go home."

He picked up the bags. "You ready to get rid of me?"

She stopped so quickly that he ran into her. She spun around and put her hands around his neck, pulling his face to hers for the first passionate kiss of the day. His hands were filled with bags so he couldn't hug her or even control the kiss by touching her face.

The bed was there and the key wasn't turned in yet. His energy level was up to par. He dropped one bag and wrapped his arm around her waist.

She pulled back. "That answer your question?"

"I believe it does. You sure you want food? We don't have to check out until eleven," he said hoarsely.

"Yes, I do. Amos has been patient enough with us. If we get home by noon or even a little after I will have only missed two days at the office. I'm already so far behind it'll take all week to catch up. So pick up the Dollar Store

Samsonite and let's go have breakfast." She marched out of the room and toward the elevators.

On the ride down to the first floor he dropped the bags and cornered her for more steamy kisses. When the doors opened she opened her eyes to see an older couple staring right at them.

"Going up?" Cathy asked.

"Oh, yes, darlin' and I hope it's the elevator that causes that," the woman said.

"It sure is. When you touch the button it fires up your passion."

The woman laughed and pushed the button.

"I'd like to be a fly on the wall when she puts one on that man. He's liable to think he's died and gone to heaven," Cathy said.

"He did have a twinkle in his eyes when she reached out to push the button. I'll take these things out and put them in the truck. Go ahead and get started. I'll be right back," he said.

She loaded one plate with omelets, bacon, and toast and another with a Belgian waffle. When Travis returned she was sitting at a table for two in the middle of the dining room.

He made green tea and had a yogurt and a waffle with a side order of bacon.

"You sure you didn't eat breakfast before you woke me up?" she asked.

"I didn't wake you. You were up and raring to go when I got back to the room," he said. "And no, I didn't eat anything. I had a cup of tea and watched the early morning news."

"Are we fighting? Our tones tell me we might be. Maybe it's a good thing if we are."

He propped both elbows on the table and stared at her. "And why is that?"

"Because it would prove that we aren't right for each other. The old familiarity-breeds-contempt thing. Maybe it's to show us that we can only stand each other for three days before it all falls apart. That once we gave in to the heat between us and had sex, everything was finished. Can we still be good friends even if we don't have sex anymore? I'd miss you if we weren't friends."

"You really believe that?" he asked.

Their eyes locked somewhere above the waffles and sparks flickered around them like confetti.

"No, I don't. Not when you can still make me hot as hell's flames by just looking at me," she said.

He went back to his yogurt and tea. "Then we will last a while longer because I get hot every time I see you."

"It can't go anywhere, Travis. The excitement of the next oil rig and whether it will bring in a gusher will always be in your blood. It's what drives you and makes you happy. You have wings. I have roots in the Honky Tonk and they go really deep like an old oak tree. The two don't mix."

"I'll chew on that a while and get back to you on it before we get home, but I believe a person can have wings and roots at the same time," he said.

"Are you sure or are you just avoiding the inevitable?" she asked softly.

"I'm very sure, honey. Eat up. The wagon train leaves in a few minutes. You don't want to miss it."

She didn't press the issue but she didn't expect him to come up with anything profound on the trip to Mingus, either. He couldn't explain his feelings any more than she could hers.

CHAPTER 19

CATHY GRABBED HER CELL PHONE WHEN IT RANG, HELD it with one hand, and filled pretzel bowls with the other. She barely got out a hello when Daisy started.

"Where in the hell have you been and why haven't you answered your phone and don't you ever listen to your messages? Tell me you are well and all right and that the Honky Tonk didn't burn down or terrorists aren't holding you hostage or you didn't marry that Travis Henry and not even invite me to the wedding. I told you to talk to me. Did you do something so crazy that you don't even want to talk to me about it? And why haven't you called me back?"

Cathy took advantage of her cousin running out of air to begin. "The story is that I spent a couple of days with you. I've got thirty minutes before the Tonk opens and that's barely long enough to tell you but I'll talk fast. First thing is that my cell phone went dead and I only got it charged up a little while ago. And I couldn't call you but your voice on that one message I heard was what helped me get through the ordeal."

"With that sentence you'd better talk fast," Daisy said.

When she finished Daisy started again. "Are you sure Brad won't come back around to finish the botched job? And those two sumbitches that took you? What happens if they come back and try again? And I'm calling Tinker as soon as he gets there and telling him to start living at the Honky Tonk to be your bodyguard. Good lord, Cathy, they could have killed you."

"I've got it under control. I'll send you a copy of the tape and you will send it to Green's Oil Company in Mena if he does anything else. He sure doesn't want his uncle to know what he did. Trust me. It is finished," Cathy said.

"I'll be down there next week. I want the details when I get there," Daisy said.

"I can't wait to see you. All the old crowd will probably come when they find out you are here," Cathy said.

"No, they won't. We've all moved on and in different directions but I'll be glad to see Amos and Merle and meet your Travis Henry."

"He's not my Travis," Cathy protested.

"Yet." Daisy hung up.

Tinker came in ten minutes early, got his normal six cans of cold soda ready, and plugged a few coins into the jukebox so music would be playing when the first customers arrived.

"So how was Daisy?" he asked.

"She's fine," Cathy said.

Tinker leaned on the bar. "And where were you and Travis really at?"

Cathy looked up from the dishwasher. "What did you say?"

"You didn't go to Daisy's. You didn't go anywhere because you wanted to go. Something happened that you don't want everyone to know about. So tell me."

She couldn't lie but she only told him that she'd been kidnapped, chained to a floor, and that Travis came to her rescue. She'd called him because she hit redial.

He nodded when she finished. "Them two that took you to that place—were they the ones that were casin' the Honky Tonk?"

"I think they were. They were trying to figure out what I did and where I went so they could kidnap me," she said.

"I'll get one of them throwaway cell phones tomorrow. Something ever happens again you call me," he said.

She nodded.

"Only person that'll have the number is you so if it rings I'll know you're in trouble. If those two know what's good for them they'll stay in Louisiana. They show their faces here again, them or that ex feller of yours, I'm takin' care of them."

"Thank you, Tinker," Cathy said around the lump in her throat.

"Going to be a good night. We had a bumper crop on Monday. Larissa helped Jezzy and Leroy back behind the bar. Takes three to do your work. Last night was busy but not like Monday. Time to open the doors." Tinker picked up his cooler and headed for his post. Oscar and Duroc would do well to keep their distance from Mingus, Texas.

Jezzy and Leroy were the first ones in the doors and didn't stop until they were behind the bar. Jezzy grabbed Cathy in a hug. "We were so worried until Travis called. You've got to come to Sunday dinner and tell us all about it. Travis won't talk. He just says that you were already on your way out of the place and you took care of things," Jezzy said.

"Who were they? I'd like to chain them to the floor of a cold shack in the middle of a cold drizzle and leave them there for a while," Leroy said.

"All I know is Oscar and Duroc. Why would anyone call someone a hog's name? He did have red hair. That's about all I remember about either of them."

"Maybe he had little beady eyes and a big nose," Jezzy said. "You need us to help?"

"I can handle it. You'd best go lay claim to a table. It looks like another busy night."

Merle was sitting on a stool when Cathy turned around.

"So how's Daisy? Heard she is pregnant. That right?" she asked.

"It is. What can I get you?"

"The truth," Merle said.

Cathy looked across the bar at her. "That is the truth. Daisy is pregnant and she is very happy."

"But you ain't seen her and neither has Travis. This bar was barely picked up and ready for customers on Monday night and Jezzy and Leroy were so jumpy it was awful. Daisy didn't ever leave for a two-day vacation and neither would you. You can fool some people but not me. So where in the hell were you?"

Cathy leaned over the counter and whispered, "Kidnapped and chained to the floor in an old fishing shack over on a bayou. Travis rescued me late Monday evening. My ex-fiancé caused it."

"That sounds enough like a crock of shit that it's probably the truth. Where do you want the bodies buried or do you want their ashes left in the fishing shack?" Merle asked.

Cathy patted her arm. "Thank you but all I got was a couple of names and one of those has to be a nickname. They were Oscar and Duroc and my ex-fiancé hatched the idea. He was going to rush in and save me when my defenses were down, I was half starved, and almost dead. It was all a big plan to get me to go back to him so he could keep his job. He's been in a bunch of trouble with his boss who is also his uncle. Evidently he's got six months to settle down. Guess he thought he could scare me into going back with him. Kind of like ride in on a white horse and save the princess so she'll believe anything you say and put up with anything you do."

"We'll start with him. With a little persuasion he'll give up those other two clowns' full names. He likes that shack so much his sorry ass spirit can live there forever. I'll expect the whole story at Jezzy's on Sunday. Give me a beer and I'll go talk Luther into a game while I wait on Garrett and Angel. That Garrett is getting pretty damned good. He might even give Angel some competition in a few years."

Cathy quickly changed the subject. "So you think they'll be together that long?"

"Honey, those two were made for each other. I don't know why they have this pretense of meeting here and then going to the ranch. She ought to just go there from work. It would save a lot of time. Got to admit, though, I like a game or two while they are flirting around with each other." Merle picked up the cue-stick case with one hand and the beer with the other. "Might as well get a quart of Coors ready for Luther. I'd take it to him but my hands are full."

When Luther reached the bar Cathy set a Mason jar in front of him.

He grinned. "It don't take you long to know what I like. I missed you, darlin'. I thought it was right strange that you and Travis was both gone at the same time but then I heard about your cousin needin' you. So I'm not givin' up on that date just yet."

"Could I get a pitcher of whiskey and Coke down here?" a lady asked from ten feet away.

"Gotta go," Cathy said.

"I'd like a bucket of Coors and one of Miller," another woman said.

Larissa pushed the swinging doors and set two buckets on the counter. "I'm glad you are home. Things ain't the same around here without you."

"Thanks. Want to work tonight?"

"Only if after closing we can sit down and have a visit," Larissa said.

Cathy grimaced.

"That's the deal. Take it or leave it."

"Visit about what?" Cathy asked.

"Where in the hell you've really been and why Travis was gone at the same time. I'm nosy as hell and I want to know. So do I draw beer or not?" Larissa popped her hands on her hips.

"Deal," Cathy said. She might as well tell the story one more time. It wasn't going to stay under covers forever anyway. And while they were visiting, Larissa was going to answer some questions, too.

"Good, I've been on pins and needles ever since Monday night when I came in here and found Jezzy and Leroy in a tizz behind the bar. You shoulda seen the place. There wasn't room to shake a booty without hitting someone else."

Tinker didn't have to turn anyone away from the door but it was a busy night, especially for a church night. At ten minutes until two the jukebox was featuring Blake Shelton's "I'll Just Hold On." The lyrics said something about the girl having a gypsy soul and that he didn't know why he was falling for her.

"You like this song?" Larissa loaded the dishwasher and set the dial to start.

"It hits home pretty good right now," Cathy said.

When the song finished Tinker unplugged the jukebox and pointed toward the clock.

"Ah, man, it can't be two already," a woman said from the shadows where she had a biker cornered.

"We'll be open tomorrow at eight. Come on back then," Tinker said.

The night was over. Travis was gone. Tears welled up behind Cathy's eyelids but she held them at bay. She wouldn't cry. She should have followed her gut instead of letting her heart get in the way.

Tinker set his empty cooler on the bar, tossed his cans into the big trash can, and checked both bathrooms before he left. "See you tomorrow night."

Larissa threw her rag on the bar, opened a longneck Coors, and carried it to a table where she propped her feet on an empty chair.

Cathy did the same.

"So where were you?" Larissa asked.

"Why did you move to Mingus?"

"We'll get to that. You go first."

"I had an ex named Brad Alton. He got mean and thought he could whip me one night. Anyway, he got in a few good licks before I came to my senses and fought back," Cathy said. She told the story for the umpteenth time. It had begun to feel like a fairy tale instead of reality, like it had happened to another woman and she was merely telling it after the fact.

"Ex? Boyfriend or husband?"

"Boyfriend," Cathy said.

"Was it cold in the shack?" Larissa asked.

"Oh yeah, and there were rats the size of possums."

"Did you sleep with Travis?"

"What's that got to do with anything?" Cathy blushed.

"Guess you did. Okay, before we start on my story, I want you to promise when you and Travis get together permanently that I get first crack at buying the Honky Tonk from you."

"I told you the first time I met you that this place is not for sale and never will be. It's mine and I'm going to work it until the day they—"

"I know...carry your dead body out. But in case you change your mind, I want it. I'll pay you double what Hayes offered you and sign a contract that says I will never ever sell it to him," Larissa said.

"Okay, if I ever sell it, which I won't, then you can have first crack at the sale. Now why are you in Mingus?"

"It's a long story. I'm hungry. Let's go find an all-night restaurant in Stephenville and have some breakfast while I tell you," Larissa said.

"Better idea. Let's go back in my apartment and cook something. How about fettuccine Alfredo and garlic toast?"

"You cook?"

"You don't?" Cathy asked.

"I'm learning. It's part of the find-myself-in-Texas deal. I'm also going to put in a garden this spring. Know anything about that?"

"Not a blessed thing other than put the seeds in the ground and hope like hell it rains." Cathy led the way back into her apartment, turning out lights and checking both bathrooms one more time on the way.

"Nice place you got back here. Never figured it to look like this," Larissa said.

"Have a seat. Want a glass of tea while I cook?"

"No, I'll just finish my beer. Can I help? I really am trying to learn."

Cathy took a package of chicken breast from the freezer. "I'm going to thaw this in the microwave and cook it in a cube of butter."

"Real butter?" Larissa asked.

"I like real butter. As little as you are, surely you don't have to be careful of calories and fat grams?"

"Hell no. I could eat a whole cow and not gain a pound. I just want to get this right. I love Alfredo. Used to order it when…" She paused.

"You don't have to tell me every detail but I want to know why in the hell you are in Mingus, Texas, with your background. It's plain as the nose on a big old hog that you came from money, so talk while I cook."

The microwave bell dinged. Cathy removed the chicken and diced it into small pieces on a thick wooden cutting board while a cube of butter melted in a cast-iron skillet. She'd raked the chicken off in the hot butter before Larissa started.

"I grew up in northern Oklahoma, near Perry. My grandfather had the money and I was his only grandchild. It was put into a trust fund when he died to be given to me in monthly allotments until my twenty-first birthday, at which time they had to turn the whole nine yards over to me. I was eight years old when he died and Mother was the trustee of my funds. She had gotten wild in her college days. I was the result of that. She married the boy but it didn't last. Grandfather paid him off when the divorce came down. That's where my Indian blood comes from. Mother is a redhead and would remind you of Jezzy."

"She still up around Perry?" Cathy set a pot of water on a back burner for the fettuccine noodles and buttered four pieces of thick sliced bread with garlic butter.

"No, Mother travels. She has a house in Paris. France, not Texas. One in Italy. A place in London. She's only fifty and looks thirty so there's plenty of men and excitement in her life."

"Anyone left up there?"

"Just the house and a small staff that keeps it in order for if either Mother or I ever want to go home. It's over between Orlando and Perry, way back in the country. You'd never see it unless you were looking for it and never get inside the gates without the right words," she said.

"Miss it?"

"Can I set the table while you do that?" Larissa asked.

"Are you avoiding the question?"

"No, I don't miss that place. It's just stones and glass and lots of land. Home should be more, don't you think?"

"Go on." Cathy slipped noodles into the boiling water.

"Okay, I graduated from high school in Perry, went to college at OSU because it was close by. When I was a little girl my mother traveled a lot and I had a nanny and the house staff. Looking back I think the people I went to school with thought I was part of those folks instead of the ones who owned the place. Anyway, when I was twenty-one Mother transferred the funds. I set out on a holy quest to find myself. Kind of like a hippy but with funds."

"Did you?" Cathy asked.

"What?"

"Find yourself?"

"I'm thirty this summer. I think I'm close."

"Took you nine years?"

"It has."

"Where did you go to do it?"

"Started with a trip around the world that took five years. I didn't just visit places. I lived in them. Egypt. Jerusalem. Russia. England. Even a month in China back in a remote area in a convent." She hesitated.

"And?"

"And in December I was back home in Perry and nothing felt any more right there than it did in Cairo or Moscow. Christmas was just around the corner and my old nanny had put up a tree and Mother had sent small presents. You know what's in small presents, Cathy? I'll tell you. Expensive jewelry. There it all was coming together for me. Turkey dinner, presents. And no family or friends. My heart and my soul weren't satisfied. So I got out the map of the United States. Actually it's hanging on the wall in the library along with maps of every place in the world. So I didn't get it out but I pulled it down and played pin the tail on the donkey with it. I picked up one of those tacks that has a big plastic head on it, shut my eyes tightly, and decided to move wherever I stuck the pin."

"Good God! Mingus, Texas."

"You got it, honey. Lord, that smells good. Can you make it hurry?"

"It's almost done. So what did you do?"

"I came down here and fought with myself. Stayed in a motel in Stephenville for a week and drove over here every day. It was horrible. I was about to decide to go to Italy and spend a month with Mother but something kept saying that I'd be sorry. So I drove through the whole damn town a dozen times a day. Finally, one day a Realtor was putting a sign on some property up there a block from the post office. I stopped and asked about the house. It's a two-bedroom built in the thirties and sits on four lots. The old couple who were selling it had to go to a nursing home. There's a garden out back and a place for chickens but I haven't gotten that brave yet. A stray cat came up and I adopted him. He's black and white like that old Sylvester cat in the cartoons. I named him Stallone and he's fitting in well."

"So how long are you really going to stay before you figure out Mingus isn't where you left your soul in another life?" Cathy asked.

Larissa smiled. "I already figured it out. I'm at home."

"You say that this week. What about next week when you get really bored?"

"So far, so good. I'm happy here. Even Mother says she hears it in my voice. I get bored some days but there's always the Honky Tonk to look forward to in the evenings. And when spring comes and I start gardening I won't have time to get bored. Plus, you're going to sell me this place in a few months and then my soul will really be at home."

Cathy drained the noodles and added them to the creamy chicken mixture, quickly browned the toast in the oven, and set both on the table. "Don't get your hopes up. You ever heard that old thing about not having wings and roots both?"

"Heard it. I'm living proof." Larissa dipped deeply into the skillet and loaded her plate. "God, this is wonderful. And it didn't look so difficult to make."

"Nothing to it. Brown the chicken in butter, add a jar of already prepared Alfredo sauce from Walmart, and pour it over cooked noodles. You can make this standing on your head and cross-eyed. So if Hayes Radner came in here and offered you a million dollars for your land and house to get a toehold in the place, you wouldn't sell?" Cathy asked between bites.

"Honey, God could offer me the keys to His kingdom and I wouldn't sell my place to Him. So what chance would Hayes Radner have? I'm at peace and I'm at home. I do not intend to sell and I'll fight Hayes Radner until eternity dawns to keep Mingus out of his hands. He wants an amusement park, he can hustle his rich little ass on down the highway to a different town. I'll buy the whole town right out from under him and not change a thing before I let him have it," Larissa said.

"Mingus?" Cathy still couldn't believe that Larissa would live there forever.

"Imagine how I felt when I drove down here and saw it the first time."

"Like you'd fallen off the edge of the world straight into the flaming bowels of hell?" Cathy asked.

"That's about it. You must've felt the same way."

"Oh, yeah! I couldn't believe my cousin actually liked the place and wanted to be here. It took me about six weeks to stand still long enough for roots to grow under my feet. Travis has wings. I have roots. It's like shaking up oil and water. They do fine for about half an hour. Then they separate out again," Cathy said.

"You got to figure that out for yourself. Can't no one else do it for you. Listen to your heart and if it says for you to pull up your roots and fly then call me and I'll write you a check," Larissa said.

Travis worked until four thirty, went home and took a shower, and crawled into his bed. The pillow wasn't soft so he beat it into submission. The comforter was too hot so he threw it off the side and then got too cold and had to put it back. He read for ten minutes but when he looked up from the pages he couldn't remember what he'd read. He used the remote and watched an episode of *Nikita* but couldn't keep his mind on the plot.

He didn't hear the key in the lock or the footsteps down the hallway with the television noise but when his bedroom door opened and Cathy stood there in her cowboy boots and faded pajamas, he threw back the covers on the other side of the bed and patted the sheets.

"I couldn't sleep," she said as she curled up in his arms.

"Me neither."

"You don't have to..." she started.

He kissed her softly on the forehead and shut his eyes. "I don't even want to right now. I just want to feel you next to me. Good night, darlin'."

She threw a leg over him and slept without dreams.

CHAPTER 20

BRIGHT, BEAUTIFUL SUNRAYS FILTERED THROUGH THE spaces in the mini-blinds leaving stripes across the brown comforter and Cathy's blond hair. She slept with her knees drawn up and one arm up under the pillow. Heavy eyelashes rested on her cheekbones. Travis watched her sleep and wondered how he could have ever thought she looked like the *Nikita* star. Her features were softer; her upper lip had a deeper dip in the middle. Her hair was a shade darker and she was much more beautiful.

He waved a cup of black coffee under her nose. "Sit up and drink, darlin'. When you finish that one I'll go get another. Three cups, you said, and you are in a decent mood."

She sat up, took the cup and sipped it, making appreciative noises the whole time. "Three cups and I don't bite. Noon and I'm decent."

"Or three cups and wild passionate sex?" he teased.

"Are you making an offer? If so, I'll take the WPS now and finish the coffee later."

He took the cup from her hands and slipped under the covers with her. "That's an offer even the Godfather couldn't refuse," he murmured into her neck.

"I want long, slow kisses like in the song and I don't intend to get out of this bed until I have to go to work at noon," she said.

He slipped an arm under her and the other over her,

rolled to one side, and looked at the clock. It was already eleven o'clock. If the lady wanted long, slow kisses then that's what he'd deliver, but if she thought they'd stop with only that much, then she'd best think again.

Starting at her lips and working his way down, he developed a brand-new respect for Trace Adkins's song "Long, Slow Kisses."

"Sorry the bedroom candles aren't lit but the telephone has an answering machine." He began to hum the song as he made love to her whole body with his long, slow kisses.

When he found her lips the second time she was panting. "You're pretty damn good at this," she said.

"It's easy to be good when you've got someone as lovely as you to work with," he whispered softly in her ear.

His warm breath caressed the soft skin on her neck and he worked his way from ear to eyelids, the tip of her nose and down to her mouth. Sweet green tea was wonderful when she could have it in that form.

Cathy found a sensitive zone in the crook of his neck and made him groan with her soft kisses. "Woman, if you don't stop that this party is going to be over a lot sooner than noon."

She nibbled on his earlobe. "I forgot to allow time to get dressed so that's okay."

He rolled on top of her and started a rhythm so slow that the bed didn't even rock or squeak. "Have I told you in the last five minutes that just looking at you makes me hotter'n a coal of fire in hell's furnace?"

"Have I told you that you are makin' me hotter'n a two-dollar hooker?"

He smiled and his eyes twinkled.

Her roots were shaken in the severe wind of falling in love with Travis Henry.

Cathy took one more swig of cold coffee and braced herself for the cold north wind when she opened the trailer door. She had ten minutes to dart across the lawn in her flannel pajamas and new goat skin cowboy boots and get dressed for work. She didn't have time to run smack into Luther on the porch.

He looked her up and down with a serious expression on his big round face. "Was it a real date?"

She shook her head and kept walking.

"Then I'm still in the runnin'," he said.

She could still hear his laughter after she'd closed the door to her apartment. She'd never dressed so fast in her entire life. She jerked off her pajamas and boots, threw on a pair of jeans and a T-shirt with a bull rider on the front, and ran a brush through her hair before putting her boots back on. The clock said she still had five minutes so she took time to slap on a bit of eye makeup and apply a touch of blush to her cheeks.

At exactly noon she opened the door to the trailer to find Travis eating cereal for breakfast and Luther sitting at the table with him. Rocky and Tilman had drawn up the other two chairs to face the desk.

"Are we having a party?" Cathy asked.

"Angel hit her first well half an hour ago so I guess we are," Luther said.

Cathy was supposed to be happy. Now the people of Mingus wouldn't think about selling their property to

Hayes Radner for an amusement park. They'd all be climbing on the oil wagon and wanting a black pumper setting in their front yards to hang Christmas lights on every year.

But she wanted to cry. The only logical thing for Amos to do would be to put Angel in charge of finding more and send Travis on to the next site. This place didn't need two petroleum engineers and Angel was very much in love with Garrett. Roots and wings were about to be separated just when Cathy had finally admitted that she had fallen in love with Travis.

"So I guess part of us will stay and the other part will go on," Travis said. His voice sounded hollow in his ears. Alaska didn't look nearly as inviting as it had a few weeks before when Mingus was just a temporary stop on his way north.

Rocky pointed at the computer. "I need the latest crew list so I can do evaluations and give Amos my recommendations about who'd serve best under Angel's new leadership. I've already got an idea of who all is willing to brave the cold weather up north with Travis, but I want to go over each one."

She nodded without saying anything.

Tilman piped up, "And I need a requisition form for a couple of gear reducers. I'm on my way to Dallas to the warehouse."

She looked at Luther.

"I came to bring the good news and to tell Travis and Rocky there ain't no way I'm going to that cold country. I'm staying right here so, darlin', there's still a chance for us," Luther said.

She pushed buttons on the keyboard and the computer spit out the forms Rocky and Tilman needed. "Does it look like it's going to be a good one?"

"Oh, yeah. Jezzy is so excited she's talkin' about selling the Angus cattle and growing oil wells. I swear she's like a little kid at Christmas," Rocky said.

"And Leroy?" Cathy asked.

"He says he hopes she does. Says that he's sick of this place and ready to move on. He's thinking that he'll go wherever Sally moves with her new husband this summer. Says he wants to be a part of his grandchildren's lives," Tilman said.

And us? She wanted to ask Travis but there was no need. She couldn't even look across the bar at him for fear he'd see the hurt in her eyes.

"Is Amos out there yet?" Cathy asked.

"He's on the way. Says it surprised the hell out of him and he's a believer now that Angel has the gift," Luther said. "Hurry up, man. You can ride out there with me. We're all takin' a few hours off tonight and hittin' the Honky Tonk soon as it opens to celebrate."

"Want to come along?" Travis asked Cathy. His heart was a lump of stone in his chest and it was difficult to breathe around it. She hadn't made any gesture toward him when she came back. Luther had known they'd spent the night together and teased him unmercifully until they heard her on the porch. What were the last few days to her? What were they to him? They'd both known from the beginning he'd only be there a couple of months. How had things gotten so complicated?

"No, it's y'all's party. Go on. I'll work here until quittin' time and then get the Honky Tonk ready for a blowout," she said around the lump in her throat.

"Hurry up, man. Don't you remember how you felt the

first time you brought in a well? And here she is just out of the chute, high on love and everything is working out for her. We need to be out there to congratulate her," Luther said.

Travis made a trip back to his bedroom, shoved his feet into work boots, and put on his old stained work coat. The bed was still a tangled mess and the room smelled like her perfume. He touched the pillow where her face had left an indentation and a lump the size of a grapefruit closed off his throat. Why did this have to happen today? He'd prepared himself that they'd have to separate but it was supposed to be two weeks down the road, not today. Not after they'd made love and after he'd admitted to himself that he'd just plumb fallen in love with her.

"Did you go back to sleep?" Luther called down the hallway.

"I'm on my way," he said when he wanted to say that he wasn't going anywhere without Cathy.

She had her eyes glued to the computer when he got back to the office. "Tell Angel I'm very happy for her."

"See you tonight." Travis stopped and kissed her on the forehead.

She was glad that he hadn't wanted to talk. Words would have brought tears and he would not see her cry. She'd known from the beginning that the job wasn't permanent and neither was Travis. Why didn't that stop her from falling in love with him?

The Honky Tonk was alive with energy that night. All the rig workers were there, along with Amos and his bikers who'd heard that his crew had sunk a good well in virgin territory. Garrett and Angel were walking around with their feet six inches off the ground and spent the whole evening wrapped up in each other's arms on the dance floor instead of wagering bets on the pool table.

Larissa took her place behind the bar to help make drinks and draw beer. It was midnight before she or Cathy had a two-minute stretch of time to talk about anything but piña coladas, margaritas, buckets of beer, and who had time to unload and reload the dishwasher.

"Hey, you got a minute?" Travis asked from the end of the bar where he'd been sitting since right after ten.

"Yes, but it belongs to me," Larissa said. "But I'll be nice. Go on, darlin'. Take as long as you need. I'll man the bar a few minutes by myself."

Cathy propped her elbows on the bar in front of Travis. "What time did you get here? I've been so busy I didn't know straight up from backward."

"Just a few minutes ago. I've been watching you. Larissa took my order. Y'all didn't even realize that she worked this end and you got the other one. You do well together."

Cathy smiled through the pain in her heart. "So do we."

"We do, don't we? Well, maybe you'll come to Alaska to see me? I'll call often and email you. We aren't going to lose touch, Cathy. I'll be back when Garrett and Angel get married."

"Do you know something I don't?"

"No, but it'll happen. They're in love," he said hoarsely.

She nodded toward the jukebox where Mark Chesnutt was singing "Old Country." The lyrics said that she used to want to climb the walls and had never been loved at all until old country came to town.

"You sayin' I should come around every now and then?" he asked.

"I reckon it would be nice. When are you leaving?"

"In about ten minutes."

Ten minutes! The room spun around in psychedelic waves of color as she held on to the bar to keep from fainting. God Almighty, she was going to fall to pieces right there in the Honky Tonk.

"Want to dance?" he asked.

"Don't dance with customers. Remember?"

"I'll be at my folks for a couple of days and then I'll fly to Anchorage." Their gazes locked in the middle of bittersweet sparks.

Mark's song played on the jukebox for the second time. Dancers were swaying to the music. A few were kissing; some were talking. Merle and Luther were in a heated discussion over a pool shot. Tinker kept watch over the whole bunch. Everything was completely normal so why was Cathy's heart shattering like a glass window breaking when a baseball hits it?

Travis tossed back the last of his beer, leaned across the bar, and brushed a soft kiss across Cathy's lips. "You are something special."

She touched her lips. "To hell with rules."

She pushed through the swinging doors and walked into his waiting arms. "Dance with me one more time?"

He wrapped his arms around her waist and she laid her face next to his chest. She had less than four minutes to make enough memories to last forever. Seconds ticked off the clock with each word and left her heart in pieces as the song came to an end. When it was over he kissed her hard just like he'd done on New Year's.

"Hell yeah," she whispered.

He laid his fingers on her lips. "You've got my cell phone number."

"And you've got mine."

He looked deeply into her eyes and then walked out of the Honky Tonk.

Cathy watched until the door closed then spun around and went back to drawing beers behind the bar. It was over, severed quickly and abruptly. The pain began when he disappeared out into the night. The reality of him being out of her life would come later.

"Well, you broke one rule," Amos said. "Give me one of those martinis that Larissa says is so good. Might as well celebrate being wrong."

"About what?" Cathy said.

"Many things for many years. You are a hell of a lot more like Ruby than I figured, girl. You just might stay here like she did until they carry your body out. Just remember that brag don't come free. It's costly."

"Amos, I don't only know it, I feel it. Now what are you wrong about other than my love life?"

"Mostly, we'll celebrate the fact that Travis was right when he said Angel was a damn fine petroleum engineer. She's going to be a big asset to my company. And now she and Garrett can set a date for their wedding. I'm going to leave the office where it is for a few months, then decide whether to put the permanent office in Mingus or Gordon. We'll see which way the new findings take us. Oh, and Maggie refused to come to Mingus. She said I could fire her before she'd live in a place this small. She's got two little boys who have violin lessons and play soccer and all those things. Anyway, there's a lady in my Dallas office who said she would love a change of scenery so she'll be here starting Monday. Her name is Tessa and I expect she'll be in and out of the Tonk since she likes to dance. Matter of fact, I'm pretty sure the Honky Tonk being this close is what's bringing her to the area. She'll be moving into the trailer. Tomorrow can be your last day and you can go back to your old routine."

"Sounds good to me."

Amos sipped the martini. "Larissa was right. This is a good martini."

"Hey, could I get a pitcher of Coors down here?" A man waved from behind two ranchers who'd been sitting at the bar most of the evening.

"Gotta go," Cathy said.

"Bonus will be attached to your paycheck tomorrow night," Amos called out.

Angel had Garrett by the hand and was dragging him to the bar when Cathy had time to look up again. "Congratulate us, Cathy. Garrett just proposed to me. We haven't even called our parents yet. Look." She hung her hand over the bar and the lights picked up the sparkle on a diamond ring.

Cathy set two beers on the bar. "These are on the house and congratulations. And the ring is gorgeous."

"Can we have the wedding here in June?"

"At the Honky Tonk?" Cathy asked.

"It's where we met and it'll be romantic," Angel said.

"Of course you can, darlin'. By then I'll own the Honky Tonk and it'll be wonderful advertisement," Larissa answered.

"You will not!" Cathy said.

"Of course I will, but you'd let them use it for a wedding anyway. It's a perfect place. Lots of parking. Bar for drinks. Bathrooms and lots of room for dancing. I love it," Larissa said.

"Thanks. We'll pay for it. Momma will have it decorated with acres of tulle and roses," Angel said.

"You are welcome, but it'll have to be morning or afternoon. Can't see a wedding with this kind of crowd, and you won't pay for the use of the Tonk. It'll be a wonderful excuse to get Daisy and Jarod to come and visit," Cathy said.

Angel laughed and pulled Garrett back to the dance floor for another slow dance.

Larissa threw her arm around Cathy's shoulder. "Feelin' it, ain't you?"

"Yes, I am," Cathy said.

"Go after him."

"I can't. It hurts but I can't clip his wings. I don't want him to change and I can't be anything other than what I am. I'll get over it," Cathy said.

"I don't think so, darlin', but who am I to give advice? I'm just now finding myself."

CHAPTER 21

CATHY THREW HER COAT ON THE TABLE, TOOK A DEEP breath, and went straight for his room. The brown comforter that had made him look like Bigfoot during the ice storm was gone. There were no boots on the floor, no book on the nightstand; nothing but the lingering aroma of Stetson to prove that Travis Henry had ever made love to Cathy in that room. She stopped in the bathroom on her way back to the office and found an empty bottle of Stetson sitting on the vanity. She carried it with her to the kitchen and slipped it into her coat pocket. Four containers of strawberry yogurt were all that was left in the refrigerator. Cathy hoped Tessa liked that flavor. She'd never be able to eat it again without crying. She sat down at the computer and vowed that she wouldn't leave the place until it was completely ready for Tessa to take over Monday. When she locked the door at quitting time that day, she would never come back to it. She couldn't bear facing the emptiness echoing the feeling in her heart.

Angel was surprised to see her when she breezed through the office at nine o'clock. "It's not noon," she said, glancing at the clock.

"I wanted to get completely caught up. She doesn't need to come in to a mess," Cathy said.

"Travis made it home all right. He called this morning and left a message on my phone," Angel said.

"That's good," Cathy said.

"I thought you two would end up together. I'd never seen him so taken with anyone."

"There's a lot of distance between Alaska and the Honky Tonk."

"So that's it. I'll miss having you here. They say Tessa is good, but you are like family."

"Thanks," Cathy said. She wanted to ask Angel what she meant by the comment about *that was it* but was afraid the answer would make her weepy again. She'd had to use cold compresses on her eyes that morning to get the swelling down after a two-box tissue night.

"Well, I'm off to make Amos and Jezzy lots of money. We're ready now to buy some mineral leases to other properties. Want us to drill on the Honky Tonk parking lot? Might be a cute little conversation piece to have a black pumper right out there."

"No thanks. My insurance would be out the roof trying to cover drunk cowboys riding the walking beam like a bull," Cathy said.

Travis awoke in his old room in his parents' house with a start. He reached for Cathy but she was hundreds of miles away, probably still asleep. He picked up his cell phone from the nightstand but there were no missed calls. He dug around in his duffel bag for clean socks and underwear and brought out a package with two pairs of cotton panties. He held them to his chest and remembered the way she'd clung to him in that Jefferson hotel, fear still hanging to her even though she'd washed the stench of the cabin from her beautiful body. Carrying around ladies' panties was perverse so he tossed them into the trash can beside his bed, got dressed, and went to the kitchen.

"Easy over or omelets?" Myrna asked.

"Easy over. Is that pancake batter?"

"Yes, it is. Why didn't you bring that pretty Cathy woman with you? I liked her better than any of the ones you've drug in here before. And she's an Arkansas born and raised girl. You can't go wrong there."

Travis poured water over a tea bag. "She runs a beer joint, Myrna."

"So? There's beer joints all over the world. Way I hear it is if two people get together and want to build them a town, first thing they do is put up a church and right after they get a place to get saved, sanctified, and dehorned, they build a beer joint. That way they have a reason for the saving and dehornin'. She could run a beer joint anywhere your oil business takes you. That ain't no big deal."

"It is to her. She loves the Honky Tonk."

"Looked to me like she loved you when she looked at you with them funny-lookin' blue eyes."

"Sometimes love ain't enough," Travis said.

"Hmpphh," Myrna snorted.

On Saturday morning Cathy checked her cell phone a dozen times for messages as she cleaned the beer joint; she even picked up the phone in the Honky Tonk to make sure the phone was working in case he tried to call that number. When she had the place in order she cleaned her apartment and then paced back and forth, across the dance floor, behind the bar, back through the living room and bedroom, making the circle a dozen times before she threw herself on the sofa and opened another box of tissues.

Finally she went out to the garage, fired up the Harley, put her helmet on, and headed east. The air was chilly but the sun was out and the roads were dry. She pushed the cycle above the speed limits trying to outrun the pain but it didn't work. When she reached Gordon she made a U-turn in the middle of the road and started back home.

She made it as far as the turnoff to Jezzy's place but couldn't slow down in time to make the sharp right turn. A half a mile down the road she stopped, did another turn-around, and went back. She'd go look at the oil well and see for herself what could be so exciting that it could lead Travis around by the nose.

When she reached the house, Jezzy and Merle were on the porch. They waved at her to stop and motioned her inside the house. She pulled up outside the yard fence, hung her helmet on the handlebars, and followed them inside.

"I came out for a midafternoon snack. Jezzy made a pan of cinnamon rolls and hot rolls stuffed with cream cheese and ham," Merle said.

Jezzy led the way into the kitchen where Leroy and Sally were already eating. "Come on in and eat with us. We've been dying to know about the kidnapping. You can tell us all about it."

The food had better be as good as the smell of cinnamon and yeast promised because she'd been out on the Harley trying to outrun memories, not relive them again with the kidnapping story. "What do you want to know?"

"All of it. How in the hell did anyone get you tied up? Damn, I would have expected you to fight them tooth, nail, hair, and eyeball," Jezzy said.

Cathy picked up two warm rolls and put them on her plate. "I put up a fight but one of them popped me with horse tranquilizer while I was trying to choke the other one."

"So when did you wake up?" Leroy asked.

"First time was in the van. They'd cuffed my ankles and my feet then chained them together behind my back," she said and went on to tell them the story. All except the part about sleeping with Travis.

Sally made her retell the part about the curse twice and laughed so hard she cried both times. Leroy wanted a repeat of the rat and the telephone story. Jezzy and Merle agreed that if they hadn't shackled her leg to a chunk of concrete that she would have killed them with the chains.

It was late afternoon when she crawled back on the Harley. When she got back to the Honky Tonk she realized she had forgotten to drive down to the rig site. While she told the tale, Travis had been there beside her, his blue eyes sparkling behind wire-rimmed glasses. She parked the Harley and went back to her empty apartment where the only thing left of Travis was the lingering aroma of Stetson in her coat pocket.

Travis exercised horses all day on Saturday. The whole family would be in for supper that night so they could be together again before he flew to Alaska. Chances were it would be summer before he had time to come home and then every-thing would be fizzed up with Angel and Garrett's wedding.

The day had produced entirely too many hours to think about Cathy. He'd gone over every detail from the time he kissed her the first time to the last kiss, right after the dance. What would he have done different? If he could go back and redo any moment, what would it be?

"Not one thing other than begging her to leave the Honky Tonk and go with me. She said in the hotel that night that I'd be happy for a couple of weeks and then I'd resent her. Well, that's why I didn't ask her to leave her life. I'm afraid she'd resent me and I'd rather hurt now than later. I called her once and it was so awkward and hurt so bad I can't do it again. If I hear her voice next time the first words out of my mouth will be 'I love you' and she doesn't need to hear that," he whispered to the horse.

"Hey, you going to talk to yourself all day or come in and visit?" Emma asked from the stall door. "And where's Cathy? I liked her, Travis. Is she going to join you there?"

"I don't think so and I was unselfish. I couldn't ask her to leave her beer joint. She might have done it but she'd hate me later on. Is everyone else here?" He hung up the brush and threw a blanket over the horse's back.

"You are changing the subject and everyone isn't here. Travis, unless you tell her how you feel, she won't know. She can't read your mind, but as your youngest and of course favorite sister, I can sure read your eyes. You are in love and you are miserable."

"Let's talk about something else. Talking about Cathy hurts too bad." He slung an arm over her shoulder and led her out of the stables toward the house.

Cathy put in the movie *Lucky Seven* and set a big bowl of popcorn between her and Daisy on Sunday night. Daisy and Jarod had flown down earlier that evening. Jarod was out at the ranch where he and Garrett were talking cattle and Daisy had come into Mingus to spend the evening with Cathy.

"I want to hear the whole story, beginning to end," Daisy said. "Start with the time he kissed you on New Year's."

"But you already know that."

"Tell it again. I want to hear it while I look at you."

"But I can't tell it and watch the movie both."

Daisy picked up the remote and turned the movie off. "We can watch that another time. This has to do with your life and your heart. Talk, cousin."

Surely telling the whole thing time and time again would eventually exorcise it from her heart, but it didn't. When she got to the part about the boat and seeing Travis, the dam let loose and she told the rest through tears. She didn't even leave out the part about him being the best damn lover in the world or how the vibes between them almost set two motels and the bedroom out in the trailer on fire.

"You love him," Daisy said.

"I didn't say that."

"You don't have to say it. It's written in your misery."

"Well, I'll have to learn not to love him. Maybe that's what happened to Ruby Lee. She fell in love with the wrong man and the Honky Tonk became her love to replace him." Cathy let the tears flow freely.

Daisy handed her a tissue. "She never said but it makes sense. But you are not Ruby Lee. You are Cathy O'Dell, and you can do something about this. Pick up the phone and call him."

"I can't. Remember that old saying about if you love something you have to let it go. If it comes back then… I can't remember the rest," she said.

Daisy hugged her as she tried to dissolve the pain with tears.

Cathy and Daisy stood in front of the nursery window with Jim Bob and stared at the eight-pound, red-haired baby girl in the bassinet. The baby had been born on Sunday morning and the old Honky Tonk crew gave the Walkers time to enjoy her for a day before descending upon the hospital on Monday like a swarm of bees.

"You want one of them kind?" Cathy asked Daisy.

"I do but I won't complain if it's a boy," Daisy said.

Jim Bob threw a loose arm around both of them. "Ain't she beautiful? Wasn't for that red hair, she'd look just like her gorgeous momma. I'm already in love with her and I can hold her in one hand almost. Can you imagine how much I'll love her in a year or how much it's goin' to hurt when she leaves home?"

Cathy could well imagine. In the days that Travis had been gone she'd paced the floor, listened to old country music, cried to the lyrics until her eyes were swollen, and lost five pounds because food gagged her. He'd called once but the conversation was stilted and neither of them could say the words that lay between them like a barbed wire fence.

"Just enjoy her every day," Daisy said.

Cathy thought about enjoying the days with Travis. She'd enjoyed the banter, the flirting, working together, all of it up to and including that last dance. Most of all she'd enjoyed snuggling in his arms after making love and the soft, warm glow that wrapped them up together like a cocoon and telling him all about her day, then listening to him talk about his. Sharing not only bodies, but emotions and feelings. She missed him as a lover but she also missed him as her best friend.

"Hey, hey, where is she? I heard she had red hair," Merle called out as she and Angel came down the hallway to the nursery.

"Is it going to be curly?" Angel asked when they peered through the window at the chubby little girl baby swaddled in a pink blanket.

"Looks like it could be," Merle said. "Ain't she cute? When are you and Garrett going to make one of them for me to spoil?"

"Nine months after the wedding vows if I have anything to say about it," Angel said.

Daisy threw an arm around Cathy's waist. Looking at them from a distance no one would believe they were cousins. Daisy was shorter and had long dark hair, and her Indian mother had given her a face with high cheekbones and angles. Cathy's mother had been a tall blond and she'd dipped into that gene pool. Up close it wasn't difficult to believe they were kinfolks because they shared blue-gray eyes inherited from their fathers, who had been brothers.

"You ready? Honky Tonk opens in an hour," Daisy said.

"I am. She's beautiful, Jim Bob," Cathy said.

The sun was bright and birds were singing when they

walked out of the hospital. Spring was definitely on the way. Larissa had brought seed catalogs to the Honky Tonk and had been poring over them after hours.

Daisy fastened the seat belt in the red Caddy. "I remember the first time I saw this car. I was sitting in the parking lot at the Smokestack with a busted radiator. Ruby Lee drove up in this and bought my dinner. She offered me a job and I kept it seven years before Jarod walked into my life."

"More like collided into your life," Cathy reminded her.

"You got that right. One minute I was takin' a tray back to the bar and the next I was flat out on the floor with him on top of me. I understand you got into trouble taking a tray back to the bar, too. Maybe that's the curse or the omen?" Daisy said.

"Could be." Cathy swallowed hard. "He'll do for a romp every so often when he comes to town. Remember that Mark Chesnutt song about when a cowboy called old country came to town? Remember it says that she'd never been loved at all until old country came to town."

Daisy nodded. "You satisfied with that?"

"He's still flying and I've put down roots."

"You ever been to a tree nursery?" Daisy asked.

"What's that got to do with anything?"

"They transplant those big old trees and they don't die. I thought I'd die without my security blanket, which was the Honky Tonk. Sometimes I still get the itch to bartend. When I do, Jarod takes me to this little dive up there in Payne County and I get a taste of loud country music and dancing. It's been two months now since the last time. The urges are coming around less and less."

Cathy started the engine and drove north toward

Mingus. "I can't do it, and besides, Jarod asked you to marry him. Travis danced with me and walked out the door without looking back."

"Did you call out to him? God, girl, I went out to the ranch in the worst getup in the world. My house shoes didn't even match and I told Jarod exactly how I felt."

"Travis knows."

"Does he?" Daisy asked. "Or does he think you'll never leave the Honky Tonk?"

Travis flew to Dallas and boarded the two-thirty flight to Portland, Oregon, where he'd have a two-hour layover and then an eight-hour flight to Anchorage.

An elderly gentleman with gray hair and a thin mustache sat down next to him. He wore a three-piece suit and a red-and-white striped tie. "What's your name, son? Did you just come from a funeral?"

"I'm Travis Henry. On my way to Anchorage, Alaska. Been wanting to live there my whole life and no, I didn't come from a funeral."

"I'm Mason Albertson. I'm on my way home to Houston. Been visitin' with the grandchildren. Had a wedding today and didn't have time to change from this monkey suit into my jeans before the flight. I see you're a cowboy by them jeans and boots. What in the hell you going to do in Alaska, son? Look on your face says you want to stay right here."

"I'm a petroleum engineer. I sniff out places to drill for oil."

"Ain't your nose any good in warmer country?" Mason asked.

"It could be."

"Guess it takes all kinds to make up the world. Some of us stay where there's hurricanes and take our chances. Some of us live in Tornado Alley and wouldn't move if there was a class-five whirlwind comin' right at us. Then there's those like you out huntin' an adventure," Mason said.

"How many grandchildren do you have?" Travis tried to change the subject.

"Eight grands. Sixteen great-grands and one great-great. I'm eighty-five years old. My wife died five years ago. She'd have liked the weddin' today. She liked gettin' all dolled up and steppin' out on the town. That woman loved to two-step and I believe she'd have left me for Hank Williams if he'd of lived long enough and she could have got a chance at him. Pretty as she was he might have give up that drinkin' for her. I was a lucky man."

"Sounds like you got a nice family," Travis said.

"I do and I did. Had the best of both worlds. When Gracie was alive I was the king of the mountain. Now I'm all alone with my memories, but let me tell you they're fine memories," Mason said. "You married?"

Travis shook his head. "No, sir."

"What's her name?"

"Who?"

Mason poked him on the arm. "You know who. The one you let get away here lately. What's her name?"

"What makes you think I let one get away?"

"Son, your face is a picture of sadness and you tell me you are off on an adventure so it ought to be happy as hell. Only a woman could put that hurt in your eyes and you're about to make a mistake. Alaska is too damn far from Texas."

"Cathy. Her name is Cathy."

"Why ain't she goin' with you?"

Travis looked out the window so long that Mason figured he wasn't going to answer the question.

"She owns a beer joint in a little town and she loves it. She says she's not ever going to leave it," Travis said without looking back.

"You ask her?"

Travis shook his head.

"How'd you know she won't leave it if you don't ask her? Maybe she didn't plan on leavin' it until you come along. Maybe she changed her mind but she's too much of a lady to ask you to take her with you. Maybe she wants you to stay close by rather than runnin' off to dig up frozen dirt in Alaska," Mason said.

"I didn't have to ask. I know the answer," Travis said.

"Young folks today sure are different than we were. We wanted an answer, we asked the question. We didn't sit around lookin' like the world was about to come to an end," Mason said. "I'm going to take a nap. If I don't hear the captain tell us to buckle up for the landin' you wake me up."

Travis nodded.

Mason was wide awake when they landed. When they were off the plane and everyone was meeting someone in the rush, Mason sat down in the nearest chair. "My daughter is comin' to get me. She ain't never been on time for anything in her whole life. I reckon she'll be late for her own funeral. You got to rush or you got a few minutes to spare?"

"I got two hours. Want a cup of coffee? I'll go over there to the McDonald's place and get us a couple," Travis said.

"And two of them little apple pies?" Mason asked.

"You got it." Travis didn't have to wait in line. He gave

the girl his order and she took his money. It reminded him of filling a bucket with bottles of beer and hurriedly making change so he could move on to the next customer.

He carried the coffee and pies to the seats Mason had chosen and they ate and sipped coffee while they watched the people hurrying from one place to the other.

"So what does your Cathy look like?"

"Classy. Six feet tall. Blond. Pretty blue eyes. The color of steel and they can look right into my soul. She was kidnapped a couple of weeks ago," Travis said.

"Tell me about it. Old man like me likes to hear stories." Mason finished his pie and sipped his coffee.

Travis told him the story and Mason slapped his leg and guffawed at the part about putting the curse on Oscar and Duroc. "Then she marched into the place where her ex-boyfriend works and knocked the hell out of him and walked out just as classy as when she walked in."

Mason frowned. "And you let a woman with that much spunk get away from you? Man, you got empty space that should be filled up with brain cells. How'd you ever get to be a hotshot oilman anyway?"

A tall dark-haired woman touched Mason on the shoulder. "Daddy, I'm sorry I'm late."

"No you ain't. If you was, you'd be on time. Besides, if you'd a been on time I would've missed the best story I've heard in years. Travis, this is my daughter, Mary Lynn. This is my new friend who might be the dumbest man on earth, Travis."

Mary Lynn laughed nervously. "He's always picking up a new friend. Pardon him for calling you dumb."

"He's probably right." Travis's tone was filled with gloom.

"You don't have to keep that title. You can give it away if

you want. Thanks for the coffee, the story, and the pie...and enjoy Alaska," Mason said as Mary Lynn led him away.

Travis checked his watch every fifteen minutes and was ready to board at the right time only to hear an announcement that his flight had been delayed thirty minutes. Was it an omen? Another half hour for him to change his mind?

At five o'clock a lady in uniform appeared at the desk and the announcement was made for passengers with small children and those who were handicapped to board first. Travis waited until she called for the rest of the passengers. He shut his eyes and saw Cathy in those flannel pajamas in the hotel in Jefferson, Texas. He took a deep breath and caught a whiff of her perfume. He'd take the memories with him and hope they'd fade in a few years.

He boarded the plane. No one sat next to him so he wouldn't have to listen to another Mason telling him that he was making a big mistake. That was definitely an omen that he was doing the right thing. He buckled up and waited, then the captain's voice came over the speaker.

"I'm sorry but there has been a complication and we will be getting off this plane. In an hour we will board another jet. We are sorry for the inconvenience," he said.

Travis took his carry-on bag from the overhead and went back out to wait another hour. He bought another pie and cup of coffee at the McDonald's and sat in the corner away from anyone who might try to talk him out of going.

Cathy and Daisy worked behind the bar together that night. Jarod sat at the end on what had been his favorite barstool back when he was falling in love with Daisy. It was still hard for him to believe that Daisy had given up her precious beer joint and married him.

The first guitar licks from the jukebox caused several women to yell "hell yeah" as they jumped up and hurriedly lined up for a dance. Daisy yelled with the rest of the crowd when Gretchen asked for a big hell yeah from the redneck girls like her.

"You still got your Christmas lights on like Gretchen sings about in the song?" Cathy asked.

"You bet I do and I plug them in when I want to," Daisy said. "Remember what you said on my wedding day when I gave you the motorcycle?"

"I said 'hell yeah,'" Cathy said.

"You ever going to be that happy again?"

Cathy shook her head.

The dancers were thirsty after a couple more fast songs and hit the bar for buckets of beer and pitchers. Cathy noticed that they were down to their last tray.

"I'm going to gather up trays. Be back in a minute," she told Daisy.

She made it to the middle of the dance floor when Elvis started singing "I Can't Help Falling in Love." She shut her eyes and swayed to the music, remembering the night when Travis danced with her after hours.

When she opened them he was coming right at her. His eyes locked with hers. She blinked a dozen times but every time she opened them he was still there. If the fool didn't stop he was going to plow right into her. Maybe he was just an apparition like she'd seen so many times the past few days; just a hologram that would walk right through her and keep going.

He stopped inches from her. Every nerve ached to lean forward and feel her heart beat, touch her lips, push that strand of blond hair back from her cheek. He looked deeply into her eyes and saw his future all the way to the end of his life.

She was afraid to breathe for fear he would disappear but she had to know if he was real. She wrapped an arm around his neck and touched the curls on his neck. They felt real. She took a step forward and pulled his lips to hers for a long, hard, passionate kiss which left no doubt that Travis was not an apparition. When the kiss ended, he looped both hands around her waist and began to two-step to the music, singing the words softly in her ear as they danced.

Tinker made his way over to the jukebox and unplugged it the minute the song ended, then swiftly plugged it back in so that whatever songs had been bought were erased. He quickly fed money into the slot and replayed Elvis's song twice more.

Travis winked at him and kept dancing. Everyone in the place made a circle around the couple and Elvis's voice was the only one in the Honky Tonk that evening as two hearts melted together.

When the last words were sung and the last piano note faded, Travis Henry dropped down on one knee and looked up at Cathy. "Will you marry me, Cathy O'Dell? I don't want to live without you." He raised his hand and there was a diamond engagement ring sparkling on the first knuckle of his pinky finger.

"Hell yeah," she whispered.

CHAPTER 22

AMOS LEANED BACK IN HIS CHAIR IN HIS DALLAS OFFICE the next morning. "Well, it damn sure took you two long enough to figure things out. Sit down and let's talk. I thought for a while I was going to have to bring that engineer home from Alaska."

"Why'd you send me if you already had someone there?" Travis asked.

"To see if you'd really leave Cathy. If you did then you didn't deserve her. And to see if you came back if she'd leave the Honky Tonk. From the look on your faces and that ring on your finger, Cathy, I expect that you are?"

She smiled. "Yes, I am."

"Larissa buying it?"

"Can't sell it, Amos. That would be like taking money for my child. I'm giving it to her just like Daisy gave it to me."

Amos nodded seriously. "Not a very good business deal but I can understand. Ruby would like that. Now let's get down to business."

"I'll resign if it'll make it easier," Travis offered.

"Hell, son, I ain't lookin' to fire you. That'd be cuttin' off my right arm. What I'm thinkin' is this. I've got a little office in Shamrock, Texas. My office manager is retiring in a month. You ready to settle down?"

Travis nodded. "Is there a beer joint close by for sale or are we going to have to build one for Cathy to run?"

"Cathy?" Amos asked.

"That office got room for an accountant? I reckon I'd be satisfied for this cowboy to dance me around a honky tonk floor once in a while. I wouldn't have to own one."

Travis squeezed her hand. "You can own one if you want. I'm not a bit ashamed to say my wife is a bartender. Hell, I'll even help you run it after hours."

"I think I'd just as soon close up shop at five and have you all to myself after that," she said.

"Okay, then, here's the deal. You are both hired to run my Shamrock office. Get in there and get your feet good and wet and I'll sell it to you in one year if you like the area. If not, then I'll move you to another place until you find one you do like."

"Why would you do that?" Cathy asked.

"Ruby Lee should have married me. If she had, you and Daisy could have been my children. You both have her spirit. Travis is already like a son. You are just getting your inheritance while I'm alive instead of after I die," he said.

"Thank you, sir," Travis said.

Cathy jumped up and hugged Amos, tears running down her cheeks and wetting his shirt collar. "And you'll walk me down the aisle like you did Daisy?"

"Of course I will. In the Honky Tonk?"

"Hell yeah!"

They were married two weeks later with all the old crowd and the new, like the past and future blending together. Chigger and Jim Bob, along with the rest of the Walker clan and Chigger's mother, who declared that she'd had something to do with Cathy and Travis finding each other. The rig crew was there and Tessa, the office lady who was already a regular at the Honky Tonk. Daisy and Jarod flew down in the McElroy plane. Larissa insisted that she was officially taking over the bar that very day.

Daisy, Larissa, and Cathy waited in the apartment for Amos to come in and tell them that it was time to begin the ceremony. Larissa and Daisy both wore bright yellow satin gowns and carried a single calla lily tied with long yellow ribbons. They sat at the kitchen table while Cathy paced the floor.

"I can't believe I'm a bridesmaid," Larissa said.

Daisy smiled. "I can believe I am. Only thing that surprises me is that it happened so quick. Took me seven years. Cathy caught my bouquet and I knew I'd get to stand up with her someday."

Cathy stopped at the table. "I didn't catch the damn thing. You gave it to me."

"And it worked."

Larissa held up her hands. "Don't you dare throw yours at me. I've found my happiness right here in Mingus in this bar and I'm not leaving it for any man. Which reminds me, I've got something for you. It's in your suitcase in a big manila envelope."

"What is it?"

"You couldn't sell me the Honky Tonk because it was your baby. Well, your wedding present is this beautiful old restored two-story house in Shamrock not too far from the office. I didn't figure y'all would want a staff or grounds so big that you'd have to spend all your time mowing and weeding so I only bought two acres with the house. The keys and deed are in there."

"Holy shit!" Cathy said.

"I'm not sure if angels shit, but if they do, it's probably holy." Larissa laughed.

Cathy hugged her. "You've almost made me cry."

"If you do I'll take back my present. Daisy spent too long on that makeup for you to be messing it up. Fill up those five bedrooms with kids. All three of us know it's not any fun being an only child."

Amos poked his head through the door. "It's time. Now, ain't you all lovely. I swear y'all are all three just like daughters to me."

"Even me?" Larissa asked.

"Yes, you," Amos said and offered his arm to Cathy.

The bride wore an ivory brocade sheath with lace cowboy wedding boots and a circle of red roses in her hair. Her hands shook when Amos walked her through the door and across the dance floor to give her hand to Travis in front of an arch covered with ivy and red brocade bows in front of the pool tables.

Was she doing the right thing? Would she regret her hasty decision? Would she miss the Honky Tonk?

She looked into Travis's eyes and every single doubt disappeared. Her future was with him, not in an old weathered building with a bar and two jukeboxes.

"Dearly beloved, we are gathered here this fine afternoon to join Travis Henry and Cathy O'Dell in holy matrimony," the preacher began.

After vows were said and rings exchanged the preacher told Travis that he could kiss his bride. He led her to the very spot where he'd kissed her the first time and the long hard kiss he put on her lips had everyone in the place whooping and clapping.

"I love you," he said.

"I love you back."

"How long do we have to stay?"

"Until Chigger's momma and Jezzy say we can go. Don't worry, darlin'. We've got the rest of our lives together."

"That's just barely long enough," he whispered.

"But we'll make every minute count, won't we?"

"Hell yeah!" He grinned.

THE END

ABOUT THE AUTHOR

Carolyn Brown is a *New York Times, USA Today, Wall Street Journal, Publishers Weekly,* #1 Amazon and #1 *Washington Post* bestselling author with more than ninety books published! A RITA finalist, she's also received the prestigious Montlake Diamond Award and the Booksellers' Best Award, and is a three-time recipient of the National Reader's Choice Award. Carolyn was born in Texas but grew up in southern Oklahoma, where she and her husband, Charles, a retired English teacher, make their home. They have three grown children and enough grandchildren to keep them young. Carolyn credits her eclectic family for her humor and writing ideas.

BIG CHANCE COWBOY

At Big Chance Dog Rescue, even
humans get a second chance

After a disastrous mistake disbanded his army unit, Adam
Collins has returned home to Big Chance, Texas. He wants
nothing to do with other people, but when his old flame asks
him to help her train her scruffy dog, he can't say no. As his
reluctant heart opens up, the impossible seems possible: a
second chance with the woman he's always loved in a place he
can finally call home...

**"A real page-turner with a sexy cowboy, a sassy
heroine, and a dog that brings them together."**

—Carolyn Brown, *New York Times* bestseller

For more info about Sourcebooks's
books and authors, visit:

sourcebooks.com

IT STARTED WITH
A COWBOY

Will the Cowboys of Creedence risk all for love?

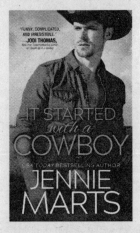

Colt James is back home on the family ranch, and he's done taking risks. A car accident ruined his shot at a professional hockey career and messed up his love life, and he's not taking a chance on anything that seems too good to be true. Especially not on Chloe Bishop, his nephew's irresistibly charming teacher and the one woman he can't stop thinking about...

"Funny, complicated, and irresistible."

—Jodi Thomas, *New York Times* bestselling author, for *Caught Up in a Cowboy*

For more info about Sourcebooks's
books and authors, visit:

sourcebooks.com

COWBOY SUMMER

Fall in love with Joanne Kennedy's sweet and sexy cowboys in her brand-new Blue Sky Cowboys series!

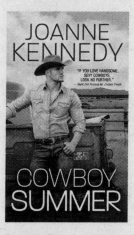

Jess Bailey left Cade Walker years ago, trading small-town simplicity for city sophistication—but she's still a cowgirl at heart. She heads home when her dad announces he's selling the ranch, and comes face to face with all she left behind. Cade is ready to win back the woman he loves—but can she abandon the career she worked so hard to build?

"Get set for the ride of your life."

—*Fresh Fiction* for *How to Wrangle a Cowboy*

For more info about Sourcebooks's books and authors, visit:

sourcebooks.com

Also by Carolyn Brown